EDINBURGH NIGHTS
Book Five

Secrets of the First School

T. L. HUCHU

TOR

TOR PUBLISHING GROUP
NEW YORK

SECRETS OF THE FIRST SCHOOL

Copyright © 2025 by Tendai Huchu

A Tor Book
Published by Tom Doherty Associates / Tor Publishing Group
120 Broadway
New York, NY 10271

www.torpublishinggroup.com

Tor® is a registered trademark of Macmillan Publishing Group, LLC.

EU Representative: Macmillan Publishers Ireland Ltd, 1st Floor, The Liffey Trust Centre, 117–126 Sheriff Street Upper, Dublin 1, DO1 YC43

The Library of Congress Cataloging-in-Publication data
is available upon request.

ISBN 978-1-250-44091-4 (trade paperback)
ISBN 978-1-250-44092-1 (ebook)

Our books may be purchased in bulk for specialty retail/wholesale, literacy, corporate/premium, educational, and subscription box use. Please contact MacmillanSpecialMarkets@macmillan.com.

First published in Great Britain by Tor, an imprint of Pan Macmillan

First U.S. Edition: 2025

Printed in the United States of America

10 9 8 7 6 5 4 3 2

For
Maximillian and Hildegard Musavaya

Principal Magical Institutions

Calton Hill Library, incorporating the former Library of the Dead: Destroyed by Sir Ian Callander after he was defeated by Henry Dundas, these were Scotland's premier magical libraries, both located under Calton Hill in Edinburgh's city centre. Together, they housed an impressive collection of magical texts and books. There was an entrance by the pillars of the National Monument of Scotland, on the summit of the hill. A second entrance was located at David Hume's mausoleum in the Old Calton Burial Ground.

League of Esoteric Philosophers: The original independent body of Glaswegian magicians that was later absorbed into the Society of Sceptical Enquirers during the nineteenth century at the insistence of Queen Victoria.

Our Lady of Mysterious Ailments: An exclusive holistic healing and therapy clinic on Colinton Road, Edinburgh. Clients include aristocrats, celebrities and the cream of Edinburgh society.

Royal Society of Sorcery and the Advancement of the Mystic Arts: England's foremost magical society claims to trace its origins to the mythical wizard Merlin, though contemporary scholars date its formal establishment to the late seventeenth century.

Society of Sceptical Enquirers: Scotland's premier magical professional body. It is headquartered in Dundas House on St Andrew Square in Edinburgh's New Town.

Principal Places

Camelot: A notorious tent city atop Arthur's Seat in Edinburgh, demolished in a clean-up operation for the king's visit. It was the home of one of the city's most powerful gangs, known as the Clan, and local residents hope to see a reduction in the levels of crime.

Dundas House: Designed by the architect Sir William Chambers and completed in 1774, this neoclassical building located at 36 St Andrew Square in the New Town was once the headquarters of the Royal Bank of Scotland. It remains the bank's corporate address and simultaneously serves as the headquarters of the Society of Sceptical Enquirers.

Melville Castle: This gothic castle located near the town of Dalkeith was designed for Henry Dundas, the First Viscount Melville, by James Playfair in the eighteenth century.

Dunvegan Castle: The ancestral home of the chiefs of the Clan MacLeod, built in the thirteenth century. Located on the Isle of Skye, it is the traditional venue of the biennial conference of the Society of Sceptical Enquirers.

The Isle of Iona: A sacred island in the Inner Hebrides off the west coast of Scotland. It is considered the birthplace of Scottish Christianity.

everyThere (The): This realm is a nonplace beyond the ordinary world. It is where deceased souls go before they can move on. Only a few among the living can reach and navigate it safely.

His Majesty's Slum Hermiston: This slum is located on farmland in the south-west of Edinburgh. It runs from the city bypass along the M8. The dwellings are a higgledy-piggledy assortment of trailers, caravans, shipping containers, garden sheds, etc.

Other Place (The): Little is known about this realm in the astral plane, but wayward spirits can be expelled there. It is believed there is no return for them.

Realms Beyond (The): Lying beyond the event horizon of the Astral Realms, these represent a higher dimension currently out of the reach of contemporary magical practice. Though much has been speculated about them, little empirical evidence exists to prove or disprove their existence.

Land of the Tall Grass (The): One of the Realms Beyond, normally inaccessible spaces in the astral plane. It is the paradise where the souls of the Shona people's ancestors reside. Theological debates as to whether it is open to other groups remain unresolved.

Royal Bank of Scotland: Established in 1727, the RBS is a major retail and commercial bank.

Principal Characters

Briggs: Coachman and servant to England's Sorcerer Royal.

Callander, Ian (Sir): Deceased Secretary of the Society of Sceptical Enquirers. Mentor to Ropa Moyo. Fell defending Calton Hill from the Dundas Cult.

Checkland, Morven (Dr): Consultant Psychomagician at Our Lady of Mysterious Ailments.

Cockburn, Frances: Director of Membership Services at the Society of Sceptical Enquirers.

Cruickshank: Ropa Moyo's magical scarf. A gift from her mentor, Sir Ian Callander.

Dundas, Henry: The First Viscount Melville and de facto head of the Society of Sceptical Enquirers.

Featherstone, Calista: Head teacher at the Aberdeen School of Magic and Esoterica.

Guthrie, Irene: Head groundskeeper at the Edinburgh Ordinary School for Boys.

Hutchinson, Hamish: Principal at St Andrews College, Scotland's second oldest school of magic.

Kapoor, Priyanka: Healer at the Our Lady of Mysterious Ailments clinic on Colinton Road. She studied healing and herbology at the Lord Kelvin Institute in Glasgow.

Kapoor, Ranjeeta: Priyanka Kapoor's mother.

Lebusa, Rethabile (Lady): Member of the Extraordinary Committee and the board of the Society of Sceptical Enquirers.

Lovell, Theodosia: Matriarch of the Travelling Folk and an old friend of Melsie Mhondoro.

MacDonald, Avery: Second son of Dalziel MacDonald and a student of theoretical magicology at St Andrews College.

MacKenzie, Bloody (Sir George): This seventeenth-century Lord Advocate was notorious for haunting Edinburgh's Greyfriars Kirkyard and meddling with mortal affairs until his ghost was exorcised to the Other Place by Ropa Moyo.

MacDonald, Dalziel: Clan chief of the MacDonalds of Sleat, one of the oldest and most powerful Scottish families.

MacLeod, Fenella: The only child of Clan chief Edmund MacLeod and a student of esoteric history at St Andrews College.

Maige, Jomo: Trainee librarian at Calton Hill Library and Ropa Moyo's ex-best friend. Member of the Dundas Cult.

Maige, Pythagoras (Dr): Head Librarian at the Calton Hill Library and Master of the Books for the Library of the Dead. He holds a doctorate in mathematics from the University of Edinburgh and is Jomo's father.

Mhondoro, Melsie: Ropa Moyo's deceased grandmother.

Moyo, Izwi: Ropa Moyo's precocious younger sister and a pupil at the Aberdeen School of Magic and Esoterica.

Moyo, Ropa: A teenage ghostalker from HMS Hermiston in the southwest of Edinburgh. Informally trained, she was, for a time, mentored by both Sir Ian Callander and Lord Samarasinghe but failed to gain a formal position in either Scottish or English magic.

Moyo, Makomborero: Ropa Moyo's deceased father.

River: Ropa Moyo's faithful vulpine companion.

Rooster Rob/Red Rob: Leader of the notorious street gang called the Clan. He governed Camelot atop Arthur's Seat in the centre of Edinburgh.

Samarasinghe, Lord Sashvindu: England's Sorcerer Royal.

Soltani, Esfandiar: Currently the Makar, the national poet laureate of Scotland, and an independent scholar best known for his biography of Robert Burns in verse. He is a non-practising magician and widower of Sir Ian Callander.

Walsh, Nathair: Deputy head boy and captain of the rugby team at the Edinburgh Ordinary School for Boys.

Wedderburn, Montgomery: Disgraced former rector of the Edinburgh Ordinary School for Boys.

Wharncliffe, Lewis: Student of sonicology at the Edinburgh Ordinary School for Boys.

The Somerville Equation

$$y = w(c+a-N)/t$$

y – yield

w – practitioner's potential

c – combustible material

a – agitative threshold

N – natural resistance

t – time

Discovered in 1797 by the polymath Mary Somerville, from Jedburgh, when she was only sixteen. This elegant equation was the first mathematical proof of the Promethean fire spell. Somerville's work is considered by most scholars to have been a key development in the shift towards magic becoming a true scientific discipline. Scotland's four schools of magic also use it to derive their pupils' potential by working out the 'w'.

The Four Magic Schools

These are the only accredited schools of magic in Scotland. They are highly selective and have very competitive admission standards. Qualification at one of these institutions is a requirement for professional registration with the Society of Sceptical Enquirers:

Aberdeen School of Magic and Esoterica, Aberdeen

Edinburgh Ordinary School for Boys, Edinburgh

Lord Kelvin Institute, Glasgow

St Andrews College, St Andrews

Oh well, I guess I'm dead now. This sucks. Like, I never got to vote or travel outwith Scotland, or try out the new atomic fizz-bomb at Decadent Delights in Morningside. I suppose it's my own fault since I went roughing and tumbling with the big boys. Let no one say I didn't take no responsibility for my own cockups. Still, death is the sort of thing that's supposed to happen to other people, you know? I thought I had main character vibes. Knapf.

Okay, chill, Ropa. Let's figure this thing out.

Bollocks to that. What am I supposed to do with my life now I got cast out into the Other Place? Ahura Mazda, cut me some slack right now. It's so fucking weird here. Back when I used to go astral projecting, I was entangled with my physical body so I felt like me, prancing about the everyThere, taking names and kicking . . . Now, I'm worse than numb. There's a cold deep inside me as if I'm in a meat locker. And I feel something like hunger in my belly. Not starving-starving, but that low-key emptiness that gnaws at you around teatime.

Come on, this is so unfair. I can't even form myself properly. My hands look like dehydrated husks and thank goodness there's no mirrors here 'cause I don't even want to see what my face looks like.

I don't like being deceased.

Used to be, I was a ghostalker, delivering messages between the living and the dead. I sure could use someone with them skills right now. I need to get word out to my little sister Izwi and my mate Priya.

But is this how I'm supposed to spend my afterlife? With my dad and this nutjob MacKenzie . . . Yeah, eternity's going to last a looong time.

'After everything I did to give you the gift of life, you wind up here of all places?' my father says with a snort.

'This lassie is the embodiment of foolishness,' Bloody MacKenzie replies, stoking the fire in the cave where we've been hiding out. 'I tried to warn her once.'

How long have I been in this bleak place? I've lost track of time. Everything feels like an eternal instant. This realm is unlike anywhere I've been in the astral plane. All black. Jagged rocks. An endless, formless desert of slag and mountain. Even the clouds in the sky take on a charcoal hue, and outside the cave a hailstorm of polished agate rains down. It sounds like a rattle, the ominous hiss of eternal damnation. There's no sunshine either, but a constant ultraviolet light permeates the atmosphere.

It was MacKenzie, looking like his former self, an old-school lawyer, complete with wig, who found me in the wilderness, after I dropped from the sky. One minute I was battling baddies, the next I was sucked into this almighty vortex which dumped me here like a bad ex. Talk about karmic justice. I never truly understood what I meant when I threatened the wayward souls of the deceased with banishment to the Other Place, back when

I was ghostalkering. Nothing can justify sending anyone here for eternity. Tentacled creatures, the likes of which I've never seen, lurk in the desolate plains of this world. They screech as though they're in everlasting pain and looking to take it out on anyone else. The voykor, the guardians of the everyThere, look like Shetland ponies compared to these Cthulhu sons of bitches. One of them spotted me as soon as I landed. Were it not for Bloody MacKenzie, I'd have been devoured. Soul death is the final end. There's no coming back from that. Your essence is absorbed and taken by another. You cease to be a part of the infinite.

Black lightning cracks in the sky above and thunder roars.

Oblivion might seem like a better option from where I'm standing, though.

MacKenzie was pleased to see me, no doubt a bit of Schadenfreude since I'm the one responsible for casting him out here, back when he was running a dodgy outfit called the Monks of the Misty Order on good old Earth. But why did he save me? Seems like in the time he's been out here, he's been working on some scheme with my dad. The two of them hidden out in this cave, cooking something up. Turns out my dad found MacKenzie when he dropped in and saved him from those ancient things, so maybe he was returning a favour. But everyone's got an angle, especially in a place like this.

My father can't take his eyes off me. It's strange being in his presence 'cause my memories of him are mainly from old photographs. The form he takes now seems professorial, a gloomy man, seven feet tall and clothed in darkness. An outfit that accentuates the bleakness of world we find ourselves in.

I take it as a sign of his arrogance to care so much about his appearance.

'How did you end up here?' Makomborero Moyo asks.

Bad luck. Glaikitness. A dash of hubris. All of the above. I don't know what to tell him.

'I always wondered what it would be like to see you again,' I say. 'My whole life, I wished you were there for me. It was hard not having my parents.' I have much more locked up inside me, but I can't find the right words.

My father turns and grimaces as though I've struck him. The man has not come near me since MacKenzie brought me here. It's as if he's disgusted or maybe even feart of me. Our reunion hasn't been warm, but maybe that's what this place does to you. The struggle to survive oblivion has taken its toll. On the way to the cave, MacKenzie told me new souls don't last long without help. Every so often we hear the heart-wrenching screams of someone new being devoured. It is so dreadful. Utterly.

'You have no idea the price I paid for giving you life,' my father says.

'What am I supposed to do – say thanks? It's been a crappy life, man.'

'Moyo, don't be sentimental now. Not when we've come so far. We can always come back for the girl later,' MacKenzie says.

'I am talking to my daughter,' my father replies. 'Leave us.'

MacKenzie opens his mouth, but a devious look comes over him. He steps back, bows slightly and walks through a narrow opening at the back of the cave. I'm left alone with my father and we spend some time sizing each other up. There's an air of inner turmoil about him. The way he purses his lips and tries not to give anything away. It's easy to tell he's not at all happy to see me here, and in this timeless place, the emotion might as well be tattooed onto my soul. The pebble rain outside intensifies and now sounds like a roar. A few stray rocks tumble into our cave.

We're on a mountain overlooking the peaks of the Other Place. It's kind of like being on the summit of Mount Everest, but without the snow – only the all-pervading blackness of this place.

I should have fought harder for my life. Been in a few scraps and all, and came out tops in most of them. But this time I was met by an opponent far superior to any I'd encountered before and I got my arse handed to me, with a tip added to my thrashing for good measure. Maybe my slice of eternity here is going to be spent ruminating on what could have been. Missing the still-living sister and the dead grandmother I'll never ever see again. If only . . . Nah. Maybe we deados have our own five stages of grief to go through. I'm still in the denial stage. But Makomborero Moyo's been here for yonkers now. This could be a blessing, he's not alone anymore. It's now him, me and the fine Scotsman that is Sir George MacKenzie.

He gestures to some rocks near the fire and we sit opposite one another. There is something grasped in his right hand. The flames burn off a fuel that resembles coal; there's not a tree to be seen anywhere. They are so weak I can barely feel a thing. I'm just so *cold*. I put my hands over them, still I can't feel any warmth. Then I pass my hands through. They don't even burn.

'It's just an illusion to fool your mind; the cold embrace of death never leaves you in this realm. Those flames remind me of a warm hearth back in Edinburgh. You don't know how long I spent trying to perfect that spell.'

'But how is magic even possible here?'

'It's everywhere, in every realm. Some places, it's harder than others. You just have to learn how to do it. As far as I know, I'm the first to manage it here. Even then, my powers are nowhere near what they were on Earth. It's all very taxing, but I've been studying this place. There are rules in every plane, physics reigns in the material world, eternal damnation here. No matter where you are, if you apply yourself, poke and prod, then you will find gaps in the fabric of the system. Then you can focus your will to bending and breaking the laws that govern the realm.'

'I wish Gran was here, she'd know what to do,' I say.

My father leaps up and rushes towards me. He grabs me and lifts me off the rock before shaking me. Something burning hot, the thing he's holding in his hand, sears me. I yell out and he drops me. Then he staggers back, shame on his face, the flash of anger melting away. His mouth twists into an agonized smile. There's pain in his eyes as if he's recalling something ghastly. I'm stunned, but I get up again and walk towards him. He shrinks from me.

'My own daughter. You really did a number on me, Melsie Mhondoro,' he whispers. 'Bravo.' He looks up and claps his hands.

'What's up between you and Gran?'

'She's the reason I'm here.'

'That's not true. Gran loved you and Mum. She always said you were the son she never had.'

'She's a fantastic liar.' He scoffs. 'Izwi too?'

The rain is easing off outside and the rocks patter down, much quieter. My father walks to the mouth of the cave. He stares out into the vast desolate waste. I've seen despair before, but nothing like what's in front of me now. Seems like my father didn't get on with his mother-in-law. Nothing too unusual about that, but his reaction was so visceral. Maybe he's spent too much time down here. But I need him to know Gran was a good person. That she did right by me and Izwi, and her love was generous like the summer rain, and with her wisdom she taught us what we know. We had a good life in our little caravan. And so I tell him all about it. Maybe I can help soothe whatever bitterness is in his heart. Sometimes ghosts get stuck and hung up about things that happened in the past. It could be big stuff or trivial things. That's why some of them refuse to move on. If my father had lingered in the everyThere – the realm of the dead attached to Earth – there's a chance I might have met him and helped out. Eased his passing to the Land of the Tall Grass, which would have been better than being here. Gran told me my father loved pancakes, and I let Dad know that on Sundays when I was little she would make some with me. And when the other kids in school were mean because my parents were dead, she told me they would always be alive through me and Izwi. I tell him she kept a few photos and had nothing bad to say about him.

'Gran once told me that you used to throw me up twenty feet high and catch me when I was little.'

'She lied – I never spent enough time with you. I was too busy working in my lab. If you didn't notice it's because you were too young,' he mutters. 'I thought we had more time. All my efforts were focused on creating the perfect family. I spent so long chasing things that I forgot to live. I have many regrets, but making you isn't one of them.'

'You sound like I was created in a factory.' I laugh, and he almost laughs with me. Then he gets all serious and tells me that he was taken from us by some cruel people before we could be the family he wanted us to be.

I've been told he could be a little 'odd'. Maybe that explains why he hasn't hugged me or anything. Ah well, we've got all eternity in this hellhole, so there'll be plenty of time for that. But I also sense his bitterness. There's something dark about him. The sort of vibe you get from a man with a score to settle.

'Do you remember the night I died?' he asks, almost whispering.

'You had a car crash on the A1 near Berwick. They said you were all alone. I used to have dreams of you flying off the cliffs into the North Sea. No one should be alone when they die.'

'That's the story they told you?'

'Don't you remember?'

Sometimes ghosts get confused about the circumstances of their passing. You have to help them with this. I guess I can keep on using some of my superduper ghostalker skills while I'm here. Even if the ghost is my own dad. I used to help folks like him find peace and move on. But there's nowhere else to go from here.

'I was working on a cure for the fundamental flaw with

humanity: our mortality. When Izwi was born there were complications. I was at Our Lady of Mysterious Ailments the night she was due. Your mother was in an awful lot of pain. She was bleeding heavily and the healer attending her – what was his name again? Ah, yes, Cornelius Lethington – was an incompetent imbecile. He botched the whole thing.'

'I know him.' I'm embarrassed to add that the consultant healer from Our Lady of Mysterious Ailments has saved my life more than once. How could I hate him now?

'It was not easy watching your sister born while my wife, the flower of my heart, lost her life. In one hand I held Izwi screaming and in the other I touched Cora's lifeless body and wept. I couldn't accept it. But I could bring her back. After all, I saved you, didn't I?'

'What are you on about?'

'I just needed her body. So I left Izwi at the clinic and took you and your mother back home to my lab. It was late at night as we rushed through the empty streets of Edinburgh. There was a way and only I knew how. Years of research . . .'

There's a bright burning rage mixed in with a dose of Victor Frankenstein's arrogance as he speaks. But it's impossible to reanimate a corpse . . . Except of course I was just killed by some mad magician who'd found a way to come back from the dead.

'You were a part of the Dundas Cult,' I say, retreating from him.

'The finest minds in Scottish science had been working on this task for hundreds of years. Some experimented with pre-scientific methods, blood rituals or the use of magical herbs, others tried to create mechanical artefacts, still more sought to invoke divine powers. They all failed, but I stepped on their shoulders. I devised a way. Do you honestly think I wouldn't use this knowledge to save your mother? We'd been told her body couldn't handle childbirth, but she wanted a family so badly that nothing could stop her. I pleaded that our love was enough, just the two of us, but she said that our love meant nothing if we couldn't make it manifest in flesh that was neither her nor me but both of us at once.'

There's pain written all over his spectral visage. These feelings have been bottled for so long that they fizz out of his mouth as though shaken. My father bows his head and closes his eyes. I'm stood there not quite knowing what to make of the knowledge that me and Izwi were never supposed to be alive in the first place. But we weren't an accident. They defied medical advice and brought us into the world all the same.

'Did your experiments involve working with children?'

'I could have saved her.' Makomborero Moyo avoids my question. 'I called Montgomery Wedderburn to assist me. I was in my lab in the basement when I heard the front door open. I was certain it was my dear friend and so I shouted for him to come downstairs.'

Turns out it wasn't Wedderburn after all. My grandmother Melsie Mhondoro and my future mentor Sir Ian Callander walked into the lab and told him to stop what he was doing immediately. They'd been informed by the folks at the clinic that my father had fled with Mum's body.

'I had one chance. They didn't want me to bring Cora back.

We could have been a family; we could have been happy.' His voice cracks and he slumps against the cave mouth.

I don't get it. Why would Gran do something like that? If I could bring Mum back, I would in a heartbeat. This doesn't make sense to me at all.

'How could Gran do that to her own daughter?'

'She fed you with lies. Your mother was half-Scottish, half-Zimbabwean, the child of the Kunakas, friends of Melsie Mhondoro. Munashe and Jessica Kunaka were what we wanted to be, a couple married forty years and still very much in love. Unlike Melsie who went through husbands like she was Elizabeth Taylor. She was a woman filled with envy and spite, and she stole you from your rightful family.'

'You're lying.'

'I wish I was.'

My head spins. I'm reeling from these words. How can Gran not be my real grandmother? This is impossible. Not my gran. I know she had secrets, we all do, but never in my wildest imagination could I believe she would do such a thing. She was a sweet, lovely old lady. That said, there's a whole 'nother side to her that I am only just beginning to uncover – a bit too late it seems. That thing about her being a tool for the bank that broke Britain, her work for the Royal Bank of Scotland that crashed the economy. Young Melsie Mhondoro must have been a nasty piece of work . . .

Everything I knew and believed was a lie. They say you find out the secrets of the universe after you die or some BS like that, but damn.

'I'm sorry I wasn't there to protect you,' my father says.

Turns out Gran and Callander weren't messing about. They told Makomborero Moyo they were shutting his lab down and that the results of his experiments would be handed over to the Society of Sceptical Enquirers. But he had everything written down in a code which they couldn't decipher. He was also not about to let them take his wife. 'And so they gave me an ultimatum. I refused, of course. Melsie and Callander are both formidable practitioners in their own right, but I held them off.'

The three had started fighting, trading spell for spell down in that basement.

'But as I gained the upper hand, I heard you coming down the stairs. The noise must have woken you up. I got distracted and that's when they got me.'

It hits me like a chainsaw, the memory of that day. I was in my pyjamas and carried a little stuffed fox. I stood there by the landing, frozen by fear. And I watched my father fall to the ground. I recall how he looked at me and said, 'It's okay. Daddy just had a tumble. It's o—' The blood pouring out of his mouth. And then Gran said, 'Oh, Ian, there's a baby in the house.' To which Callander replied, 'Damn, I thought he left them both at the hospital.' The next thing I remember was Gran scooping me up and rushing me back up the stairs. Then she sat on the leather Chesterfield armchair with me on her lap. 'Is my daddy okay?' I asked. And she rocked me before replying, 'Hush now, little girl. You are having a terrible dream and when you wake you won't remember a thing.'

It's all come back to me now, clear as day. As soon as she said those words, I passed out. The next thing I remember she was in my life, and I'd forgotten everything before that. All I had were the bits and scraps she fed me. My whole life from that day on has been a lie. There's a bright flash of white light against the dark sky, a new soul falling into this terrible world.

'I'd hoped if anything happened to me and your mother, then my friend Montgomery would help you. He is your god-father and was very fond of you.'

'I only met him later, when I was older.'

'Melsie must have prevented him. If he'd been there with me that night, things would have gone very differently.' My father weeps without tears falling down his face. There's nothing in his hungry soul with which to form them.

There's a loud screeching noise from the valley below. Suddenly my father jerks up all alert. Where there was sorrow, a grave concern now appears on his face. He extinguishes the flames and grabs my hand, throwing us into near darkness. The horrible screeching grows louder. That soul I saw streaking through the sky fell very near where MacKenzie picked me up. That must mean they chose this hiding spot for a reason, but I can't put my finger on it. Fair enough, it gave a vantage point from which they could see any new entrants coming into this world. But if that's true, then where is everyone else?

The screeching gets louder still.

'Ether demons,' my father says. 'If there is a God above, he really must hate me. But I make my own fate. Come, Ropa, we must go.'

He rushes me to the back of the cave and through the narrow opening MacKenzie took. It leads us down a passageway that twists and turns, winding like intestines. My father keeps looking behind, feart the ether demons are gaining on us, tentacles reaching out. It seems the one thing astral worlds have in common is guardians who lie in wait, ready to feast on lost souls. He starts running and I'm right behind him. I daren't look back.

'I wish we had more time,' he says.

'We'll make it,' I reply. It's the right thing to say, but truthfully, oblivion's more likely at this stage.

I'm still wondering how my father has managed to survive in a place like this. He pauses briefly, places his hand on the walls of the tunnel and incants, 'Beneath the fiery rage of Mount Etna, Hephaestus your hammer upon this rock, with the might of Poseidon quake and shake.' It's a coupled spell, which is more powerful than a standard one. There's a look of intense concentration on his face. A slight tremor. It's difficult to create a spell in a realm in which you have no Authority. I place my hand atop my father's and recite the spell too, and then we say it for a third time in unison, combining our wills. There's a groan and the rock splits, a boulder loosening and dropping down to cover the tunnel behind us. I feel strange, depleted even. I'm woozy.

'Careful, Ropa. You lose a bit of your soul when you do magic in this realm,' he says. Then he urges me forward. 'Hurry. That barrier won't hold them for long. The power of the ether demons is virtually limitless in this world.'

'I'd rather have gone to Disneyland,' I reply.

We crack on until we find ourselves in a large cavern where MacKenzie is stood waiting. He's looking anxious. Even from down here in the bowels of the mountain, he too heard those ether demons shrieking. There's a wrongness in the air. In front of him is a large grey vortex, like a tornado, but cylindrical instead of cone-shaped. There are faces swirling in there. Men and women, faces contorted in indescribable agony, spinning round and round. An evil power oozes out of the vortex. The desperation of the trapped souls is awful. I know it's usually bad people who get sent to the Other Place, but this seems like a violation.

Maybe if you don't want to risk your own soul doing magic here then there is a solution – other people's.

'I heard the ether demons. We must open the portal while we still can,' MacKenzie says. 'Hurry!'

'It's not yet ready,' my father replies.

'You said it only needs one more soul. Let's use the girl.'

'Out of the question.'

There's a bang, something powerful hitting the rock. The cavern we're in shakes. If the ether demons feed on souls then my father and MacKenzie have been depriving them of their food source. They'll be raging.

'I found the girl. Her soul's mine to do with as I please,' MacKenzie shouts. Then he softens his tone to something more lawyerly, more persuasive. 'Makomborero, sacrifices need to be made. Look at what we have already accomplished. You and me, we are survivors. We will be the first to return from the Realms Beyond. Imagine the power that awaits us. Think of the hard work we've done, the risks we've taken. It'll all be for nothing if we don't make it out of this godforsaken place.'

My father is frozen, deep in thought.

MacKenzie presses on: 'The girl must be sacrificed for our

sakes. Remember, we have an agreement and I've kept my end of the bargain, hunting souls for you.' He walks towards us, his eyes fixed on me. I look at my father, but his face is blank. He's frozen. Nope, I ain't falling for this. I step back but my father is quicker and he grabs my arm. MacKenzie smiles. I struggle but there's power in his grip.

'My word is my bond, Sir George. I'll cast her in the gateway. Begin the spell, just as I taught you.'

'Let go of me,' I yell, fighting to no avail.

MacKenzie turns and raises his hands. He begins to mumble something I can barely hear. From what I catch he's invoking Janus, the Roman god of doorways and passages.

'I'm sorry,' my father says, then he lets go of me and shoves MacKenzie into the vortex. MacKenzie twists and catches hold of him. The two men struggle, each battling to thrust the other into the vortex. MacKenzie manages to angle himself so my father's back is to the terrible swirling mass of souls.

'I knew you'd betray me,' MacKenzie shrieks.

'She's my daughter.'

'In that case, you will go to oblivion in her stead.'

MacKenzie shoves hard, and my father tumbles backwards, dragging MacKenzie with him. My father uses his legs to carry his opponent up and over and MacKenzie goes flying into the terrible vortex. The grey tornado bubbles, faces howling in agony, the old Lord Advocate in there with them. I turn away. It's all too gruesome.

There's a loud bang. Rock cracking.

'Come, Ropa,' my father shouts, beckoning me to join him near the vortex.

'This is evil,' I reply. 'What kind of person are you? Did you experiment on people when you were alive? Experiment on children?' Makomborero Moyo scares me. A man without limits.

'Here, take this. It's a key.'

He offers me a shining silver spiral triskele. I shake my head and he rushes over, grabs me and thrusts it into my chest, searing my soul.

'I lied to MacKenzie because I needed his help to build the doorway. He gathered souls for me so I could work this great piece of magic. Even if you hadn't wound up here, Ropa, only one of us was ever getting out. It took me years to formulate this spell. I will use the vital force of these souls to open a gateway out of this place. But there isn't enough power for two to pass through.'

'Have a great journey, Dad. At least now I know what you are.'

My father waves his hands and mouths the Janus spell. There's a large boom, the rock protecting us from the ether demons has cracked. We're screwed. I've resigned myself to fate. There's no point going on anymore. I'm done. But my father is intently concentrating on his work. There's an electric sound and the souls cry out in agony. They are being drained and the gateway slowly turns silver, getting brighter until it is unlike anything else in this world.

A gap appears in the vortex just as the ether demons enter the cavern, their faces full of fury. They come towards us, tentacles grasping forward, hungry mouths filled with shark's teeth.

'I do these things because I love you, Ropa. Go through the gateway now. The key is your pass back to the world you belong in. It will unravel into nothingness as it guides you.'

'I'd rather these creatures eat my soul than pass through your wicked gate.'

My father slaps me and shoves me through the gate anyway. I try to resist, I don't want to be part of this wickedness but his will is far superior to mine. As he pushes me in, the ether demons rush forward. 'I love you, my sweet child,' he says as a giant tentacle attaches itself to his face. There's a noise like thunder and I feel like I've been shredded into a million parts. Everything turns white and the Other Place disappears, my father with it.

I

I'm flailing like I'm drowning while fighting giant tentacles pulling me down, only I can't see shit and I'm swinging at everything. I don't feel like myself. It's like there's too many bits of me, a toe doing its own thing, my arms, nose, every part of me reacting to its own instinct. I'm falling in all dimensions, out of space and time. This is a bad trip. I feel so sick.

'It's okay, Ropa,' someone calls from a distance.

I know that voice. Trying to shout back but I have no voice. If only I can reach out and . . . I can't. The vortex drags me across realms I've never seen before, shooting me through narrow gaps in the astral plane, which spreads out before me like a cosmic spider's web. It churns and twists, dragging me with it. An echo of the anguished wailing of the souls who were used to create it follows me. A riot of intense colour giving way to bleakness.

'Ouch,' Priya yells. 'You poked me in the fucking eye!'

I'm gasping for breath, convulsing. I open my eyes and everything is a blur. I see fragments. There's grey walls around me. Broken clouds and a blue sky above me. I look around wildly, but my eyes don't see right. I'm only catching glimpses of things. Brief flickers of recognizable objects. It's as if my eyes are buffering. Weird. I pause. Okay. I'm naked in some kind of copper bathtub filled with ice and crystals and herbs. My ticker's pounding like . . . I have a heart.

I hold onto the sides of the tub.

My mind's all foggy. Feels like bits of me are still rushing in. I'm so weak, my body slumps backwards in the tub. I try to raise my head, but I can't move.

I have a body.

An anxious face cautiously peers at me. Raven-black hair and a silver fringe. It's my pal Priya, and I've never seen her look so spooked in my life. I try to say 'Hey', but I can't find my voice. Must be doing something funny because her eyes widen and she backs away a bit. Then she turns back and shouts:

'She's alive. Ropa's back!'

I try to answer, but I can't move. I mean, I can feel my body, my hands gripping the sides of this copper tub, but my limbs won't respond to my commands. Priya puts her hand on my forehead. She looks elated now, but there's dark rings around her eyes, like she hasn't slept in days. I think that's what I need, a good snooze.

Is this real, or is this what your soul sees as the ether demons devour it? Something soothing as you pass into oblivion.

I passed beyond the everyThere, into the Realms Beyond from which there's no return. I met my father and an old enemy. Didn't see my mother, though. There's no way I'm back on Earth. This has to be an illusion. Gran warned me you could get lost in pockets of the astral plane where you thought you were back in the real world. Everyone you know and love would be there. Perhaps the setting would be a time when you were happy and you'd be caught in a never-ending loop.

Someone's pulling my eyelids open. A bright torch shines right into my eye.

I wanna shout 'Cut it out', but I still ain't got no voice. Can't even keep my eyes open. Once again I'm back in darkness. Beyond the veil voices are speaking. I try to catch what they say, but can't keep up. It's as though they're talking in a foreign language. What is happening to me? I'm all numb – no pain – that's worrying. No more hunger or cold anymore. It's when you stop feeling that you have to start worrying. You feel, therefore you are. I keep trying to reach out in the darkness, to see if I can touch something or someone.

There's a calmness here that's so peaceful. It's bliss. Maybe that's what being devoured is. Oblivion. The gift of becoming nothing at all. I've been fighting for so long, I wouldn't mind this at all.

It's kind of nice.

Warm.

'Five more minutes,' I grumble. 'Just let me sleep.'

Someone's shaking me. It's so annoying.

'You have to get up, Ropa, or we'll lose you again. You're not yet properly tethered to this realm. Open your eyes. That's it.'

I half open my eyes and there're several faces hovering over me. Clearly there's no privacy in this bathroom. Where the hell am I? And what are Kebede, Lethington and Priya doing here? I'm hallucinating. Priya slaps me on the cheek again for good measure.

At the foot end of the tub, the Grand Debtera Qozmos and

Theodosia Lovell have their hands over me, incanting some strange spell in Amharic and Scottish Cant. The words tumble like a powerful stream washing over me, every syllable striking my soul like a whip.

I catch the word 'Sheba', and infer they are invoking magic from *The Book of the Shaded Mysteries of Solomon*. There was an almighty kerfuffle about that sacred Ethiopian scroll at Dunvegan Castle a while back. It contains the secret to bringing back souls from the Realms Beyond.

'Tiniša'ē.'

I try to rise, but my limbs are jelly.

Their words hurt. I want them to stop, but nothing comes out of my lips when I try.

A flash of red.

Moonfire.

The images refuse to settle in my sight, the Debtera and Theodosia splintering into multiple selves. Something heavy sits on my chest. I can't move. A bangled hand presses down atop the crown of my head.

No.

The head of Ethiopian magic is still on these isles and he's in cahoots with a wandering traveller? Their words lock together harmoniously, the spell shading an ultramarine and charcoal glow across the room. No, we're not in a room. This is a ruin of some sort. Empty arched windows. The triangular structure of the roofless wall. A horse neighs from somewhere nearby and a donkey brays.

There's something about this place. A lowered natural resistance to magic which enhances whatever spell Qozmos and

Theodosia Lovell are working. Lovell is a small woman wearing a traditional Romani dress, a red necklace and silver bangles, headscarf covering her hair and a colourful pleated skirt. She is short, gnarled like an old yew tree, where the Ethiopian magician is grand in his flowing white robes. A seagull soars across the sky. I try to speak, but gibberish comes out. I can form thoughts, but my mouth won't let me ask what the hell is going on. Priya wheels herself back from the tub so Kebede and Lethington can lift me out of it. My body's all floppy and I can't cover my bits properly. It's a bit undignified, but no one seems too bothered.

'Place her on the sleeping rug an' wrap her in sheepskin,' Theodosia commands, breaking her spell.

The colour seeps out of the atmosphere.

Priya looks like she's about to burst into tears or something. She stares at me, jaw sweeping the grass. This is definitely not a dream. I'm lowered back down and something soft, white and fluffier than a cumulus cloud is laid on top of me. At least I ain't starkers anymore.

'This is one piece of magic not covered in Scrymgeour's *Codex of Unfamiliar and Exotic Maladies*. I should write about it one day,' Lethington says.

I want to recoil from him, but I can't move. This is the man whose ineptitude caused my mother's death. He's inspecting me with interest, holding up my wrist to time my pulse. I can't even pull my arm from him.

'Hello again, my friend,' Kebede says in his gentle voice.

'Ggrrgl,' I reply.

'You're alive, you silly sausage.' Priya laughs hysterically.

Lethington turns my head to the left. I wonder what he's

doing here. I see grass and a broken low wall. The air's heavy with salt. Near the sea, perhaps.

'Ca—' I say.

'What?' Priya asks.

'Cal—'

'She's asking for Callander.'

No one says anything for a minute. The last thing I remember in this world is standing atop Calton Hill in Edinburgh. It was just me and my boss, Sir Ian Callander. No, I wasn't working for him anymore. What were we doing on the hill? It was at night. We must have been in the Library. That's not it. There were other people there. Lots of people, near naked, playing drums and juggling fire. The Beltane Fire Festival was on. Folks doing the pagan thing to welcome the winter or something like that. I try to shake my head, but I can't move. My head's all mixed up.

Remember.

It was me and Callander on the hill. He was on one knee, not proposing because he's already married. To who again? I remember his left hand was burnt to the bone. It smelled like barbeque. There was some kind of accident. A volcano. No, it was an explosion and Callander— The hill cracked and we tumbled into it. Someplace in the depths of the Library. Callander holds up his hand and a book appears before he offers it to me. He's just saved me from being hanged. I reach for the book but my hand passes right through it. I try to touch him instead, but he passes right through me like a ghost.

'She's hallucinating. Focus, Ropa. Listen to the sound of my voice.'

Callander whispers something, a magic word: 'Esfandiar.'

I blink and everyone's staring at me in this ruin of a building. I've got to go back. I need to get Callander. If I can just go back. Tears stream down my face. I left him there. I failed him. This is all wrong. I shouldn't be here. I should be on that hill with him.

'Everything's going to be okay,' Priya says. I've missed the sound of her voice.

'You are safe now,' Kebede adds.

Safe from what? There's no place in the universe that's safe. My father, those creatures got to him. I couldn't save him either. Life's meaningless if you can't protect the people you love. I don't want to be back here again.

'Tread cannyways. 'Tis early yet an' she's a wee bit drumly. Aye, she's been through Auld Nick's forge an' back. That's a right trek fer one so young,' Theodosia Lovell says. Her voice sounds like the roots of an old tree pulled up from the earth, shaking clumps loose.

'Our work here's done. Let's get her inside. She needs to eat and get her strength back up,' Lethington says.

Once again they lift me off the ground. This time I'm in my sheepskin covering. They make cautious steps on the uneven grass. It doesn't matter, though. I'm really not there with them.

I'm so far away.

II

The waves wash onto the white sand beach outside my window. From my view on the first floor, the turquoise water looks like we could be anywhere in paradise. My head's a little less scrambled. Not sunny side up; more hard-boiled than anything.

I'm in a pine bed with a memory foam mattress that feels like heaven. Two pillows under me, reclining and watching the sunset. It's so beautiful. If I could be lost in a moment . . . But I feel that subtle tick-tock. The movement of time that sweeps you along. The hot-water bottle on my back's doing the trick, though. Yep, this feels nice. I open and close my right hand. Not perfect, I can't get a tight grip, but it's working alright. Wiggle my toes under the sheepskin cover. That's nice, though my muscles feel mighty stiff. Knots everywhere.

A handprint on my chest, Dundas's mark, cracks me out of my reverie. I cover it up with the sheepskin and it burns and throbs like a wasp stung me.

I've dealt with ghosts for most of my life, but I've never given too much thought to becoming one myself. At last I understand why some hang on. Everything you know and love is in this world. Even if they offered you Heaven, nothing compares to being in this crazy rollercoaster realm.

The only problem is nothing lasts here.

Death felt cold, gnawing and desperate. There are no little pleasures like this hot-water bottle in the Realms Beyond. Nothing that can compare to this perfect view from my window.

A horse and a donkey that looks suspiciously like Mrs Guthrie's Benjamin walk together companionably along the beach.

I'm really here.

A gentle tap on the door. The person swings it open before I get a chance to respond. They bump against the doorway, back up and come in again.

'Tight angle,' Priya says, shimmying her wheelchair between the chest of drawers inconveniently placed near the door and the door frame behind her. The room we're in's pretty small. Must be a loft extension the way the ceiling slants in. Dated wallpaper, so last century, peels in places, revealing rotting wooden boards and damp crawling down the walls. Priya straightens herself out eventually before wheeling towards my bed. There she has to execute another awkward manoeuvre, angling between the blanket box and wardrobe before she can reach my side.

'Where's Izwi?' I manage to say. My voice is more of a squeak. Throat's dry.

Priya hands me a beaker on her lap. 'Steady on, hotlips. She's at school like she's supposed to be.'

Phew. I try to hold the beaker, but it slips out of my fingers. She catches it and brings it to my mouth. I take a sip, something hot and thick. Good ol' chicken soup for my soul.

'I suggested we start you off on garlic to see what happens, but the others objected,' Priya says with a laugh.

Some of the soup drips onto my chin. She dabs me with a napkin like I'm a bairn.

'Thanks.'

I go back to staring out the window, not quite knowing what to say. *Hey, I'm back from the dead, will you be my friend again?* What are you supposed to do at a time like this? And I just want to chill, take it all in, let everything settle.

Priya holds out her hand and I take it.

'You're like an ice block,' she says.

'I'm good.'

'Are you, though? Are you experiencing any sudden craving for brains?' She cackles.

'Not even funny.'

'Maybe a thirst for blood. Show us your canines,' she says in a fake Romanian accent.

I scoff. It's pretty funny, but I don't have the energy to laugh. My vitals are horizontal at the moment. Priya gives me a doe-eyed look and I squeeze her hand. My best friend. The girl I first met reading upside down in her wheelchair in the Library of the Dead. We've been through the trenches together.

'I still don't understand why I'm here. Dundas killed me, fair and square. I wasn't just passed out, Priya. My soul was disconnected from my body. And he left a right old mark on me too.'

I pull down the sheepskin covers and show her my chest.

'Some aloe vera might soothe that burn.'

'It's that bad, hey?'

'I wish I could humour you, Ropa, but it's not looking great.'

I remember the battle of Calton Hill now. A total disaster.

Callander pursued what Carl von Clausewitz would have termed *'one great decisive aim with force and determination'*, and was bested for it. Priya reaches out and touches the welts on my chest. She traces the lines and purses her lips. I place my hand on hers and bring it to my heart.

'Where are we?'

'The Isle of Iona. After our defeat, we had to leave the city. Some of us left the mainland entirely to regroup. The whole thing was a nightmare. We should never have gone up Calton Hill without knowing exactly what we were up against.'

'The others are alive?'

She nods.

'Doctor Maige, too?'

That means Calista Featherstone and Dalziel MacDonald made it off the hill. Story of my life. Not that I have anything against them, it's just that I would have preferred Callander to survive instead. But the Fates weave their patterns as they will. Or maybe we make poor decisions and pay the price for them. Cause and effect. Either way, this whole thing's ended pretty badly for us.

Outside, it's grown even darker. The sun sets pretty fast this time of the year. Must be barely after five if I know anything about it.

'The whole thing was fucked up, Ropa,' Priya says, a slight tremor in her voice. I've never seen her look so timid about anything.

'Catch me up.'

'We bailed on Callander. All of us. Left him up there with those jackals.'

'At least he took those bastards down with him. He sacrificed himself for us.' I remember how Callander invoked Poseidon, 'the Earth-Shaker', to bring Calton Hill down. And along with it Henry Dundas, Montgomery Wedderburn, Frances Cockburn, Octavius Diderot, Lady Rethabile Lebusa, Fenella MacLeod, the Edinburgh Boys, and my former best friend Jomo Maige. I shudder at the thought of Jomo buried under those rocks. He wanted to take the Library from his father. I guess he has it for eternity now.

Year by year my losses have piled up until they've become impossible to bear. Jomo was my pal. Lost his way, right enough, but you don't turn your back on friends. I should have known what was going on with him. Checked in. I was the one who protected him from bullies back when we were in school, and I should have protected him from himself. I can't keep losing people. I should be the one that's dead and stayed dead.

'Jomo's gone then,' I say, closing my eyes. This is more than I can take.

'I'm sorry, Ropa, but that's not how it went down. When Dundas knocked you down, I rushed to retrieve your body. Good thing I had the parachute your gran gifted me and I was able to paraglide out of there. Dodged a few thermospheres up in the air, but I got away.'

Priya explains that when she turned back to see what was happening, she saw the others scamper and Callander left alone with Dundas and his cult. Then there was a huge explosion on the mountain which threw rocks and scattered dust all over the city. Priya circled in the sky trying to see what was left, in between performing midair CPR on my body. She didn't yet know my soul had been ejected.

'When the dust began to settle, I saw something crazy. Dundas and all those with him were hovering above the collapsed hill. He'd managed to save them all. That was when I decided it was best to take flight with my tail between my legs. I couldn't be sure he wouldn't snatch us out of the sky.'

'They all survived and Callander went down alone?'

'It's worse than that, Ropa. There were a handful of librarians working there, unaware. The only silver lining is they were cleaning up and trying to get it back to a suitable state after Wedderburn and his crew trashed the place, so there weren't any magicians reading in there.'

'Mr Evelyn?'

'Him too.'

I pinch the bridge of my nose and take a deep breath. What a fucking disaster. When I open my eyes again I notice Priya's embraced her inner goth. Leather jacket over a black polo neck. The skin on her wrist is lighter where the bangles she used to wear have disappeared. She's always had colourful hair but now it's black. The only thing she's kept that reminds me of the old Priya is the silver fringe. The sparkle's gone from her eyes. Instead there's a burning rage, kind of like the waters of a fast-flowing burn are bubbling and boiling underneath.

'Thanks for picking me up, otherwise I'd be down there in the rubble with Callander.'

She shrugs. 'We shouldn't be talking about this. You need to get some rest.' Priya releases the brake on her wheelchair and makes to leave.

'Please stay. I don't want to be alone.'

Truth be told I'm scared. It's like the world's ended, the nukes have gone off, the apocalypse has come, and somehow I'm still here with the roaches and rats. It's not fair at all. I draw open my sheepskin cover, shift over and invite Priya into the bed with me. She moves her wheelchair parallel to the bed and locks her brakes again. There's a bit of space between her footplates and the bed, and so she uses her hands to place her feet on the floor. Then she slides forward on the chair a bit, places her left fist on the bed, lifts herself up and over into the bed with her back to me. Next she lifts one knee up, flops onto her side, and brings the other leg over into the bed. Then she pulls herself up until she's lying beside me.

I put my arm across her chest, hand on her shoulder and hug her. Reminds me of when we shared a bed in Dunvegan Castle. Fun times.

'It's nice and warm in here,' Priya says.

'We could stay forever.'

'That would be nice.'

Yep, this is the life. Priya kisses the crown of my head and I feel plenty safe. She rubs my arm and I feel a bit drowsy, but I can't sleep now in case my soul slips out of my body. Don't know where I'd wind up then. I might spend the rest of my life seeking the fountain of youth because I'm not keen on dying ever again.

'We should catch a boat to Shenzhen or Guangzhou. There's work to be had there. I once heard a geezer talking about it.'

'How's your Mandarin?' Priya asks.

'*Wǒmen zǒu ba*! I picked up a few phrases from an audiobook a while back. No doubt it's better than Scotland.'

'They wouldn't let me practise as a healer out there. Different qualifications for traditional Chinese medicine, though we've borrowed a lot from it.'

She goes quiet and it looks like she's deep in thought.

'I saw my dad in the Other Place, Priya. He's the one who got me out. But if I was dead, I shouldn't be in this body. That's not how it works.'

When I was working as a ghostalker I went to a few funerals and saw several ghosts try to lie back in their bodies, hoping to come back to life again. Used to take everything I had not to snicker because everyone's there in tears, the minister's giving his spiel, and these ghosts are trying to rouse a corpse. Good luck with that when your veins are filled with formaldehyde. Death is more than the heart stopping, it's when the soul loses its connection to the body. You can't reconnect it again. I know some people talk about out of body experiences and all that. Yeah, yeah, it's possible to project but that doesn't mean you're untethered. All the folks with near death experiences just had a wee untrained astral experience and they come back spooked by it, turn their lives around, get religion and preach to whomever will listen. But that's not what I did. I actually died.

Priya's about to say something when her phone rings. She shifts, removing me from her chest and gets it from her pocket. It's Lethington calling.

'Sorry, the boss is at me like I'm on call.'

'He botched up my sister's delivery. It set off this entire thing.'

Priya declines the call. 'You might want to talk to him about it.'

'Sounds to me like you know something I don't.'

'A lot's come out since you've been gone.'

'How long was I out for?'

The phone rings again and Priya groans. She puts it on silent and sighs. Outside the bedroom door, a cat meows. It comes in through the gap because Priya, tail on her arse, forgot to close it. The cat's a ginger skinny-looking fella with a triangular face and large ears. He struts in, rump in the air like he owns the place. He leaps onto the blanket box and from there slides through a gap in the footboard and onto the mattress. The cat slows down, never taking his eyes off me.

Then he stops and hisses, arching his back.

'Oy, piss off,' Priya says, launching a pillow at him. The cat leaps out of the way just in time, onto the floor, and darts out of the room.

'What the fuck did I do to piss him off?'

I take another pillow and throw it at the door, slamming it shut. Priya's avoiding looking me in the eye. I can tell she's got something she's holding onto. Nothing's going to shock me anymore, so I nudge her and tell her to get it out of her system.

'Did you know Lethington was also the healer who delivered you? It was always going to be complicated because your mum had hypertension and a few other problems.'

'Who told you this?'

'Lethington.'

'Why only now?'

Priya throws her hands up. 'That's why I think you should talk to him yourself.'

Somebody taps the door and calls Priya's name. It's the man himself. I tell him to come in and sit up properly. He pokes his head in, and then the rest of him follows rather reluctantly.

'You've caught me in bed with the patient, literally.' Priya laughs nervously.

'I've been trying to call you. You were to come down and report to me,' he says.

'Tell me what you told her,' I demand, glaring at him. Fuck his Jammie Dodgers, lies of omission are the worst 'cause they're craven in nature.

Lethington frowns and gives Priya a disapproving look, peering over his glasses.

'Confidentiality, Ms Kapoor, is such an important part of our vocation,' he says.

'She needs to know,' Priya replies weakly.

He puts his hands on his hips and uses his elbow to shut the door. He paces about, evidently in turmoil. The small room we're in feels even more cramped now. Lethington's head touches the slanted ceiling and he has to step back to the middle of the room.

'Cora Moyo was a complicated case and we did everything we could. It was hard getting any healing done with Makomborero Moyo constantly hovering, second-guessing any treatments we suggested. And no, I don't mean he was a concerned father – he wanted to know every single detail. There's a problem you have when you deal with a generalist like him, a man who's familiar with several branches of magic, enough to know certain things within your speciality, but not enough to know how much he doesn't know. It made him insufferable.'

'I already know what happened when Izwi was born – Mum died. Let's talk about me.'

'Oh, but I am talking about you, Ropa Moyo.' He waves his finger at me, then catches himself and balls his hand into a fist, covering it with the other.

The consultant healer pauses as if he's waiting for me to make up my mind. He's clearly vexed and wants nothing to do with this. I know that vibe, people have been hiding things from me my whole life. Family and outsiders like Lethington alike. He's just one more in a long line of deceivers. I'm boiling inside, proper ultra-radge, but I nod for him to continue, and he better tell the whole truth and nothing but the sauce.

'You were a fantastic example of everything that can go wrong during childbirth. We tried everything.' Lethington grits his teeth. 'I was there twenty-one years ago and I held you in my arms. You died during the procedure, Ropa.'

'Bollocks,' I shout. 'You're a liar.'

'I really wish that were the case.'

'Priya, tell him he's a fucking liar.'

She takes my hand and I snatch it back from her. Nah. I'm shaking. This doesn't make sense. Lethington must have me mixed up with someone else. If he's been delivering babies for all this time then it stands to reason he can't remember every single one. Memory plays tricks on us. It's not fixed but changes over time, becoming story. I know this because I used to go about investigating stuff for Sir Ian Callander. Some people lie, but others are just wrong. Let's see which category Lethington fits into.

'You said all this happened twenty-one years ago. That can't be right, you're five years off. I'm nearly sixteen.' Gotcha.

'Ropa, let's maybe take a pause. Okay?' Priya says.

'He's wrong and you know it. I don't know who he's got in mind but it ain't me.'

I'm breathing heavily and Lethington's still as a pole. His brow's furrowed and he looks again to Priya. She's shaking her head, trying to tell him to stop, and not being so subtle about it. This man botched my sister's delivery, killed my mum, and now he's trying to turn my life upside down. I'm not having none of it. There's no way I'm letting him get inside my head and make me out to be some kind of monster.

'My mistake. You are right about the timelines. My apologies. Kapoor, it seems I've disturbed the patient enough for one day. I'll be leaving now.' Lethington steps over to the door, grabs the knob, pauses for a second before opening it.

I'm proper radge. I want him gone, else I don't know what I'll do. Lethington turns and looks over his shoulder, something like pity written all over his face, then he steps out and shuts the door gently.

III

My body isn't quite my own as I make my way down the narrow, crooked stairs. It's like when you've put a jumper in the washing machine and it's shrunk a bit. Feels tight round the stomach, the sleeves only come halfway down your arms, *and* it's all wrinkly.

Nicked a pair of jobby catchers and a Napier University hoodie from the wardrobe in the bedroom. No idea whose they are, but I don't know where my gear is. I place one hand on the wall, the other on the handrail. I raise my right leg and hover it, trying to take the next step. Feels like the hamstrings of my left are going to give in, so I bring back the right and pause. I swear these steps are the steepest I've ever seen. Real trap to break your neck.

'Take your time,' Priya says from the landing above me.

'I don't know how you do this,' I reply.

'Magic.'

I would chuckle, but my legs are on fire. I'm cramping up and I sit back down on my arse.

'We can get some help for you,' says Priya.

'I'll do it myself. Piece of cake.'

I rub the backs of my thighs and then down my calves.

Reminds me of my old gran. Yeah, the same one who apparently wasn't really my gran. She'd take forever to do the simplest of things. Maybe I was in the Other Place for so long, I've returned a wee old hag. After a bit, the cramp passes and I get up using the handrail for support. I turn sideways and put both hands on the handrail, and then descend leading with my left leg, moving sideways like a crab. It's all pretty cumbersome and I keep having to pause for a breath.

There's dated pictures of saints and old popes lining the stairs. Might as well be the stations of the cross as I have to stop by every one of them. There's a pic of the Virgin Mary apparating for some reason in Carfin near Motherwell. And that must be the unlucky first John Paul who only poped for a month before popping his clogs.

I finally make my way right down to the bottom and reach the landing with all my gnashers intact. A feat on a par with scaling Ben Nevis the way I'm feeling. There're voices in the room to the left so I shuffle my way there, leaving handprints on the white wall. Behind me is the sound of Priya's chair clattering down the stairs.

The reception room I enter has a red Persian carpet and at least a dozen cats preening about or sat on the edge of the sofas. The one on the old-fashioned trunk in the middle of the room, a black-and-white moggy, spots me and hisses. This alerts the other cats who all turn towards me and hiss in chorus, showing me their fangs. I step back. My weak legs won't get me out in time.

'Choilleich, Cerin, Chrissa, the lot of you behave. This young lady is a guest here, same as me,' a regal-looking woman in a blue sari calls. The cats calm down immediately. 'Don't worry about them, Ropa. They're just surprised to see you, as am I, though I confess, I've rather been looking forward to it for a good few years now.'

'Who are you?'

The woman in the sari, sat on a Harris Tweed wing chair, motions for me to take the last free slot on a sofa. She's stroking a kitten that purrs loud enough for me to hear. I enter cautiously, making sure the cats don't try anything. Though I asked who she was, the woman's face gives it away. Age Priya by a couple of decades and that'll be her, grey hairs, bright red bindi on her forehead. She regards me with interest, a smile nearly formed on her face. Those lips, the elegant nose, that's Priya's mum. Has to be.

Theodosia Lovell's on the sofa across the room from me, perched in front of a cottage window. She has my mbira on her lap and studies it with interest. Beside her, in the middle of the three-seater, is the Grand Debtera, and Kebede, his translator, at the other end. Kebede gives me a not so subtle wave.

Mrs Guthrie, the head groundskeeper for the Edinburgh Ordinary School for Boys, is also here, occupying a wooden rocking chair the other side of the fireplace from Priya's mum. She wears an old straw hat that's nearly falling apart and has a pipe in her mouth. This goes well with the dungarees and wellies she's in, though I worry her footwear may melt given her proximity to the fire. She winks and clicks her heels together as if reading my thoughts.

There's a large crucifix on the wall above the fireplace.

Lethington is here too. Won't make eye contact with me, though. And there are two wizened nuns wearing black habits. It's hard to tell them apart, not because of the clothing, but they are exactly alike – identical twins. This must be their place given the excessive Catholic iconography on the walls.

Priya enters at last and takes her place beside me as her mum speaks.

'I hope you are somewhat recovered from your ordeal, Ropa. The Isle of Iona has healing powers. I take a retreat here at least once a year to recharge my batteries thanks to Sister Elspeth and Sister Edina . . . I forget myself. My name is Ranjeeta Kapoor, I am Priyanka's mum.'

'Hey, Mrs Kapoor,' I say.

If Priya's a bubbling brook, I feel like I'm staring at the Ganga river itself. Someone immense, with depths I can't even begin to fathom.

'Call me Ranjeeta, I've got the cool auntie thing going on. I know you're acquainted with everyone here, except me and the sisters. You have a knack for making friends with interesting people.' She chuckles.

'What's all this about then?'

'Straight to the point. No wonder my daughter loves you so.'

Theodosia Lovell twangs a note on my mbira. Gets on my nerves because that was my granddad's and no one else but me touches it. I bite my tongue, though. Theodosia gives off a vibe I don't want to mess with, and the Travelling Folk she leads strike fear even into the heart of the Clan, Edinburgh's most feared criminal gang. I'll hold my peace on that one.

'How are you feeling?'

'Irritable.'

'That's to be expected with any good resurrection.'

The nuns frown simultaneously and then smile before composing themselves. A young man with tousled auburn hair walks in carrying a large tray laden with cups and a kettle which he places on the trunk. 'We're out of the magnolia and the lemon balm tea, Sister Elspeth.'

'Mint then,' the two nuns croak simultaneously.

'Passionflower maybe?' he replies, wincing. 'It's getting more difficult to find supplies in the shops, even the basics.'

The two nuns tut and instruct him to serve the others first while they make up their minds. One of them's working what appears to be a black rosary but it has a pentagram and the triple moon on it. The beads must be obsidian, but there are a couple of amethyst ones thrown in too. I notice the Grand Debtera has taken an interest in it. He whispers something to Kebede.

No one in the room seems in much of a rush as they wait for the young man to serve tea. His wooden tea-bag organizer seems to have everyone else's preferred type of tea. Brodies black tea for Mrs Guthrie, ginger for Theodosia Lovell, green tea for Ranjeeta and Lethington. The Ethiopian wizards choose coffee but don't seem much impressed when they get an instant brew. Sisters Edina and Elspeth settle for the passionflower tea at last.

'Graeme, you forgot the biscuits again,' one of them says.

'Can't get the staff these days,' the other wheezes.

I'm still no nearer to telling them apart. Graeme offers me something too before he leaves, but I decline, fearing my stomach's not yet settled. The soup Priya gave me feels like it's turning.

The Grand Debtera says something in Amharic and Kebede responds without bothering to translate for us. The old man keeps an eye on me as he sips his Kenco. Feels like everyone's watching me. Even Mrs Guthrie's doing it on the sly underneath her straw hat.

This is an odd little gathering.

There are voices coming from where I assume the kitchen would be. Normally I'd be nosey, but I can't be arsed. I keep my powder dry and wait for Priya's mum to get on with it.

'I heard you conducted yourself with courage on Calton Hill,' Ranjeeta says.

'More like recklessness,' I reply. 'We got our arses kicked. It wasn't even a contest.'

She raises an eyebrow. That gesture alone has me bricking it. I'm not at the top of my game. I've made too many rash decisions in my time mucking about with the Society and it seems even death hasn't cured me of that.

'We don't blame the failure on you, Ropa Moyo. You're a child, a young woman, who was thrust into a situation that I'm not quite sure anyone could handle. No, the blame lies squarely with the magical practitioners of the Society of Sceptical Enquirers.'

'Aye,' Theodosia Lovell concurs.

'If it is true that their first secretary has returned and has designs on the mortal world, Edinburgh is lost to us. It's no longer safe there,' the one I think is Sister Elspeth says.

I sink back in my seat. One of the cats meows and yawns.

Everyone in the room is grim-faced; we might as well be at a funeral. The grandfather clock in the hallway chimes ten times. Its sound is chilling: time is on no one's side and shit's going to get worse.

Ranjeeta explains that after me and Callander were speedily dispatched, Henry Dundas led his cult from the rubble of the Library under Calton Hill and went to St Andrew Square to the headquarters of the Society. Frances Cockburn, the director of membership services, let him in via the transdimensional secret entrance and there, in the place most sacred to Scottish magic, Dundas declared himself secretary once more, by right of might.

'He was aided in this, every step of the way, by eager members of the Society who'd long sought his return,' says Ranjeeta.

'Shaness is all them gaffies and scalpions are aboot,' Theodosia adds.

The Grand Debtera Qozmos says something, trembling with emotion, which Kebede translates for our benefit.

'Would you expect anything different from a Society that's turned its back to the divine? I attended their conference at Dunvegan Castle and listened to them spew, with the pride of Lucifer himself, that their atheistic form of magic was superior to any. Is it a surprise that one from their ranks would rise up and install himself as a god, demanding all bow before him? This is an ancient folly.'

The two nuns exchange a look.

'And we thank you for your aid,' Ranjeeta says diplomatically.

'My old friend Melsie Mhondoro sent me a secret message

urging me not to proceed to Timbuktu in Mali. She said I was needed here to help with something important and so I waited in Scotland many months. I am happy to have helped bring her granddaughter back, but these matters you discuss have nothing to do with us in Ethiopia, and soon I shall set sail for West Africa where we have real friends,' Kebede translates.

'The strife for which Melsie Mhondoro asked your aid has only just started. We need your help still,' Ranjeeta replies firmly.

'And we owe you nothing. In fact, it is you who are in our debt, and you have refused to settle for centuries. I will no longer stay here where the weather is a true reflection of the character of the people on these islands,' Kebede translates, standing up with the old man. 'Your coffee is diabolical,' he adds.

Before they go, the Grand Debtera walks up to me and stands in my personal space. The strong whiff of oud hits me. He places both hands on my head and closes his eyes before opening them and stepping back. He says something which Kebede translates.

'It is a thorny path you've been set upon, but the sower has his reasons. I wish things could have been otherwise.' Then he turns to Theodosia Lovell: 'We've been delayed enough but our work here is done. We set sail tonight and let the stars lead us away from your petty conflicts.'

''Tis ne'er farewell fer the lig's a ring, round and round till eternity we go,' she replies with a subtle nod.

Ranjeeta manages to maintain her composure, sitting upright in the wing chair, her back straight, chin up. The rebuff must sting since she came as close to begging as a woman of her sophistication can. If she's trying to rally the troops then she's off to an atrocious start. I've learnt in my time that practitioners are wilful, fractious beings and you'd struggle to corral them for a piss-up, no matter how grand the brewery.

Kebede and the Grand Debtera sweep out of the room and leave a heavy silence in their wake.

''Tis fair though harsh as nettles on the tongue,' Theodosia Lovell comments after a short while, sipping her ginger tea.

'I'll have to see if he has a spot on his boat. Mali doesn't sound like a bad place to be right now if you ask me,' Lethington chimes in.

With calm, Ranjeeta Kapoor goes on explaining, most likely for my benefit, that once Dundas had taken over the Royal Bank of Scotland building on St Andrew Square, he moved quickly to gain the loyalty of Edinburgh's magicians.

'He has demanded blood oaths,' she says. 'No secretary has ever done such a thing.'

'Barming, nane of them has a puckle of sense,' Theodosia adds.

'A blood oath binds their wills to his.'

If I know anything, it's that will is super important in magic. That's why a computer can't do magic, even if you get it to recite a spell. This is all proven in the Somerville equation.

'What about the Extraordinary Committee? They exist to impose limits on the secretary's powers,' I say.

'Octavius Diderot and Lady Rethabile Lebusa were the first to swear their oaths to Henry Dundas,' Lethington says. 'I fled to Glasgow so I didn't have to. Can you imagine being so desperate you'd abandon your patients and relocate to *Glasgow?*

And now I hear they are chopping off the heads of the magicians who dare refuse. It's an outrage.'

'Says those ever keen to hang and burn at the stake. A cruel irony indeed,' the two nuns say in unison.

Lethington waves his arm, irritated.

Dundas is consolidating power, a move from a playbook as old as time. What for? That's the question. *Mind your own business, Ropa. It's this kind of thing that's got you in a pickle before.* Theodosia Lovell twangs my mbira again and I grit my teeth. It's off-key.

'Do you know who we are?' Ranjeeta asks, making a steeple of her fingers and resting it under her chin.

'Trick question?' I'm not in the mood.

She doesn't let my sarcasm get to her. 'I'm serious.'

'Whoever you think you might be, you're no match for what's come through from the other side. If you want my advice, leave it well alone. Think of Callander, Gran and Mr Sneddon before you waste your lives.'

Theodosia Lovell plays a note on my mbira again. This room is too hot. I'm sweating and it's dripping down my bald head. My dreadlocks . . . I remember now. The Rooster chopped them off. I move my thighs to stop them from going to sleep.

'Have you heard of the First School?' Priya's mum asks.

'Edinburgh Ordinary School for Boys.' That's the first school of magic in Scotland as far as I'm aware. Its former rector Montgomery Wedderburn kicked off this whole mess. I wouldn't trust any of its alumni as far as I could throw them.

The two nuns scoff at my words and Theodosia Lovell shakes her head pitifully.

'Older than that, Ropa,' Ranjeeta says, stringing things out.

'I'm sure you're dying to tell me.' I wish I hadn't said that, but I'm feeling all strange and irritable.

'There is a school whose history is older than the Edinburgh School. One whose exact date of establishment is now lost in the mists of time. This school takes no register. You don't apply to get in. It demands no fees. There's no curriculum, no home-work, no set exams. When you graduate you don't get a certificate—'

'What's the point of that?' Without the right qualifications you are nothing in Scottish magic. 'It sounds like a lame racket to me.'

'Let her finish explaining it, Ropa,' Priya says.

'It's okay. We always like to hear a recent graduate's feedback.'

I don't know what she means by that, but I recount that to progress in Scottish magic you have to be a graduate from one of the four schools, Aberdeen, St Andrews and Glasgow being the other three. If you're not from there then you don't get registered by the Society. I've worked as a ghostalker before, a profession ancillary to medicine, and I barely made a shilling. Then I weaselled my way into working for Sir Ian Callander.

'That's how it is in Scotland, formal education is a big thing here. There's a reason we were the first country in the world to provide universal education to both boys and girls as far back as the seventeenth century.'

Ranjeeta listens carefully until I exhaust myself, going in circles, making the same point via several different arguments. I run out of wind and end up schtum. At least I've given my jaw a thorough workout.

'Certificates and credentials. If that's all there was to it, none of us would be qualified to live this life,' Ranjeeta says, owlish. 'You learn to suckle at your mother's breast. I take it a certificate is needed for that too? With gentle encouragement you learn to talk and walk. The First School has always existed. It's not housed in any grand building. It could be in a hut in the Highlands, or a council flat in Inverness. Maybe even a small caravan in a slum in Hermiston. What official papers do you need to show that you were a student at Melsie Mhondoro's kitchen table?'

Gran used to try to teach me magic in our caravan, but I lost count of the number of times I brushed her off because she wasn't a qualified magician. I preferred book learning to the stuff she was trying to school me in. Face it, your old grandmother ain't nearly as cool as some guy with letters after his name in a thick, impressive-looking tome. But I was shocked when I heard Gran worked for the Royal Bank of Scotland and made serious mint. Must've meant she knew what she was doing.

It was there in front of me but I missed it. Old people are safe and boring. You forget they were young like you and probably did rad stuff too. They fought in wars and were once at the cutting edge of whatever was going on. I'd never have thought that what my grandmother was trying to teach me could be of as much value as what I learnt in school. Theodosia Lovell strikes my mbira again and I look at her. It's a different note this time but still off-key. Gran was the one who gave me that and told me it was my grandfather's. She's the one who taught me everything I know about being a ghostalker. I did it, but I took it for granted because I thought it was less than . . . My jaw drops to the floor, stunned.

'She kens at last,' Theodosia Lovell says.

Mrs Guthrie smiles with one corner of her mouth, sucking on her pipe and blowing a thick wad of smoke in the air. 'There've always been women, a good few men too, imparting things that were handed to them in rhymes and anecdotes. Echinacea to cure warts. On the first of May wash your face in the morning dew. Plant a rowan tree in your yard to ward off those nasty witches.' She makes a hand claw gesture. 'These things and more are taught to many. Some, a few clever children, master them and keep them close to their chest, ready to use them when the time comes. Most either forget them or dismiss them as old superstitions, signs of their grandmother's eccentricities. We had a rich tradition of witchcraft in Scotland once. Old hags who sold a charm or cure. Women who served their communities long before the advent of the scientific magic you're so enamoured by.'

In my time with Callander, he taught me this kind of folk-loric magic was primitive and lacked the rigour demanded by scientific magic. You could have two practitioners claim to cause the same effect with completely different spells. Nothing was standardized. Nothing was proven either. You had no idea who had real power and who was a charlatan. It was a chaotic mess. People got swindled or worse still drank strange potions that might have done more harm than good.

Magic is the second science. Through discipline and study, it can be mastered and analysed. And if Ranjeeta believed this bollocks, why did she have her daughter train as a qualified magician? They could do their quackery at home and see how far that took them.

'They came for the witches in the sixteenth and seventeenth centuries. Men who hid behind the coat-tails of Church and Kirk. How is it that the women who once cured maladies and delivered babies were replaced by men in white coats?' Lethington shifts uneasily in his seat. 'There was a whole profession that got wiped out and another replaced it.'

'The Society of Sceptical Enquirers is supposed to be a trade organization which protects the privilege of its members,' Lethington says.

'They tried to wipe the witches off the face of the Earth and so *we* had to adapt and bide our time.'

I sit up and pay closer attention. When I bailed from my gig working for Sir Ian Callander, Priya was drafted in to replace me. Callander was the Discoverer General in Scotland, the modern Witchfinder General, and now he's gone, I'd assume Priya is technically the remaining witchfinder. She should be torturing her mum right now, but maybe she ain't because she doesn't need to solicit a confession from her.

'We withdrew from the light, into the shadows,' says Ranjeeta.

'Some of us fell into the loving arms of the church,' Sister Elspeth and Edina echo simultaneously. 'There we continued to pray to our pagan deities and drew our symbols in their most sacred spaces. That's why the Celtic cross has the sun on it. We smeared our old ways onto their faith.'

'Some call us the Daughters of Scotia, named for the Egyptian princess who landed on our shores and founded the first kingdom in Scotland through her magic.' Ranjeeta spreads her arms wide. 'It was from her the women in this country learnt to wield great power. For a time, we were respected and, dare I say, feared. But our covens have been scattered – our knowledge was never in books and institutions, it was in blood and flesh. We carried on, more cautious than ever, knowing we had to wait for our moment. Some tried to claim we were the Fifth School, hiding away, but this was an insult. We are the *First* School of Magic. And though our structures are loose, our roots are deep, and many will tell you Theodosia Lovell is our school's head-mistress.'

'Stop with yer haver.'

'It's time for her to learn the truth. Ropa, Theodosia was good friends with your grandmother. Melsie Mhondoro may have thrown bones where Theodosia Lovell looked at tea leaves, but you'll find their magic wasn't so different and they both had the gift. These differences might matter to your friends in the Society, but among witches it was one and the same thing.'

I can't wrap my head around it. Priya's inscrutable. Surely she wouldn't throw away a perfectly good career to be part of this unscientific hogwash. And if these women are only telling me this now, it means they want something from me. Why else would they expend so much energy protecting my body? Nope. I can't be a part of any of this. I've done all I can for magic in these parts and I don't want nothing more to do with it. I don't know what Priya's thinking, but if these folks had seen half the things I have they wouldn't be playing around with this shit.

Daughters of Scotia, my arse.

'Word to the wise, you don't want to be dabbling with what's coming,' I say.

'I know you're scared, Ropa, but you're not alone. We've always been there for you, even though you might not have known it,' Ranjeeta says.

'You taking the mick? I've lived in a slum. I've lost people that I love. Then I learnt they weren't even who I thought they were. I've had to hustle. I've had my arse kicked more times than I can count. Now you want to sit there in your fancy chair and tell me you've been there for me? Bullshit.'

'I've been there with you,' Priya says quietly.

'This ain't a joke. Henry Dundas won't stop until he gets whatever the fuck it is he wants. I don't care if that's eternal life or all of Scotland, one way or the other, he's getting it and there ain't a goddamned thing any of you amateurs can do about it. I've been given a second chance and I'm not wasting it playing their stupid games – I'm going to get my little sister Izwi and then we're on the first boat off this country. I advise you all to get out of here while you can.'

IV

It's before dawn and I'm making my move. Nothing but darkness and a couple of stars outside my window. These witches
or whatever may have helped bring me back to life, but they
don't own me. I'm not getting mixed up in any business that's
got nothing to do with me anymore.

I turn on the lamp, throw off my covers, and slip into the
clothes I borrowed last night. Then I find a fluffy pair of mules
under the bed and put them on. They'll keep my trotters warm
on the road. I don't have nothing else with me, but I'll figure
it out on the road. I'm going my own way like my pals Fleetwood
Mac said I should. Reckon I can hitch to Aberdeen and make
it there in a day or two if I play it smart.

The floorboards creak loudly with my footsteps. Hell of a
time getting down those stairs too. I swear they're literally
squealing as I descend. It doesn't help that my legs are still
weak. It'll take a while before I can walk properly. More likely
than not I'll be crawling on all fours in half an hour. I make
it to the landing and am headed for the front door when a
croaking voice comes from the dark reception room.

'Ah take it yous off on a dander afore the screich.'

It's Theodosia Lovell sat in the darkness. I turn on the light and she doesn't even blink. She's still got my mbira in her hands. Despite her fearsome reputation, when she's on her own Theodosia Lovell looks tiny and fragile.

'I'll be on my way now.'

'Yer mind's set an' all then, even when yer mair drumly than settled?'

'Aye.'

'Then ye'll be wanting yer things.'

She offers me the mbira, which I hobble over and take, and then she points to the vintage steamer trunk in the middle of the room. I flip it open and see my clothes neatly washed, ironed and folded. And my boots which seem to have been repaired. Must have been done by a cobbler too since they've got new soles. I strip off in front of Theodosia Lovell – she's seen me starkers already. Then I put on my jeans and T-shirt. The boots are trickier because I'm so weak, and I finally settle on the sofa and put them on like an old person – I'm exhausted by the time I'm done. I get back to the trunk, turn my coat inside out so it looks black. At the bottom I find my katty and, to my relief, Cruickshank, my scarf. He coils like a snake and makes himself comfy on my shoulders. *I've missed you too, pal.* I pick up my dagger and sheath, and stick them on my belt.

Katty in my back pocket, I'm ready to go when I notice a chestnut-wood walking stick resting in the corner of the room. It's got a knob handle, and though it's been sanded and varnished there's knots and a few notches on it. The stick has a metal ferrule at the bottom, which means it won't wear away easily.

I pick it up and test it out. It's just right for my height.

'Anyone using this?' I ask. If Theodosia Lovell wasn't in here I'd have nicked it.

'It's yours.'

'Cheers. I'll be on my way now.'

'Fare yer well, Ropa Moyo. May the wheels of yer cart work their way back tae us.'

Fat fucking chance, I think, chucking my mbira into my backpack. I walk out a bit steadier given the support of my cane. Cruickshank shifts and I reckon he's a bit annoyed that the stick's getting all my attention. I open the door and step out into the dark. It's proper nippy and I find my old beanie in my jacket pocket and pop it on my bald noggin.

I take a few steps and see Priya waiting outside the gate at the front of the garden. When I open it she's staring ahead, pretending she's lost in thought.

'Which way, left or right?' I ask.

'You don't even know where you're going but here you are sneaking off again.'

'Left it is then.'

'You're doing it again, Ropa,' Priya says angrily. 'Every single time. After all we've been through, you'd set off without telling me. Death hasn't cured your bad habits and that's because you're a selfish prick. You haven't thought it through. You haven't planned anything and you probably don't have any money on you. I love you, Ropa, but I swear you can be the dumbest person I've ever met.'

'You coming or not?'

She turns her chair away from me and starts heading down the road the opposite way. I shrug – right it is then – and start to follow her. We go in silence for a bit, me keeping slightly behind her. My walking stick taps on the pavement. I like the sound it makes. Might give me character.

I'm being a knob. I'm focusing on me again without caring about what my friend's feelings are. From the first day we met, she's been there, loyal, looking out for me and never asking for anything more than my friendship. You don't get people like Priya walking into your life often. I keep pushing her away, though, 'cause I can't help myself. If I'm honest, part of me resents the fact that I had it hard for so long and when I look at Priya, I sometimes feel like she had it easier 'cause she's from the right side of the tracks – great family, good schools, the right networks, pearly gnashers. That's envy for you. Knapf.

'You're right. I'm sorry, Priya,' I say.

'Say it louder so the whole world can hear.'

'I APOLOGIZE UNRESERVEDLY.'

'That's better. Now we need to get to the ferry terminal and catch the boat to Mull. You only get one a day travelling across in winter, but from what I've been told, sometimes it doesn't bother turning up because fewer folks come out here. And the ferry's never on time, so who knows if we're going to catch it. So it might turn up, but we'll still have the whole morning to wait.'

We're on a narrow country road with a few cottages either side. I can just about make out hikers up the craggy hill beyond. There's carts and carriages in empty fields. The Travelling Folk are here too. An early riser has a fire going with a pot on the boil. He raises his hand to wave as we pass through.

My palm's already sore from the knob on my walking stick.

I must be leaning on it too hard. Thought I'd have to be a hundred to use one of these. But I definitely need it because there are times when I can't even feel my feet on the ground. The backpack ain't helping my balance either. Still, now I can say I've been to Skye and Iona both. Few folks from my old slum can claim that.

I'm longing to see my little sister again. It's just us left now. And River. Shit, I'd forgotten my fox.

'What happened to River?' I ask.

'I don't know. Things got chaotic.'

'You just left her there? That's bad. Really bad, she didn't deserve . . .'

'Foxes are survivors, Ropa. She'll be okay.'

'You don't survive a collapsing mountain.' My heart sinks. 'I got her killed.'

I raised her since she was a pup and she went to so many places with me. Helped me out of a few tough spots too. Now she's gone, just like that. I don't even know how I'll explain it to Izwi. Our little family's been ground to dust.

We continue down the narrow lane. River would have loved it here out in the countryside. No point thinking about it now, I guess. If I could swap my life for everyone I've lost, I'd do it without hesitation. I don't get why I have to carry on while they died.

'One moment, I need to catch a breather,' I say when we reach the old fire station. There's a disused engine rotting away in front of the building. It sits on its belly because someone nicked the wheels. That's life: if you burn you're on your own.

We start up again, past some dodgy old buildings and onto

a concrete jetty extending out into the sea. Some of the rusty metal railings on either side have fallen away. A leaflet on the ground has pictures of the old king and queen taken before they were murdered by the separatists in Edinburgh. There's no one else about and that doesn't fill me with much confidence. We might be a wee bit early then. There's an information board with ferry times a decade out of date. Priya goes up to read it.

'Check this out. They used to have one on the hour back in the day,' she says. 'And that price. Unbelievable.'

The world used to be better, so I've heard. It's like we missed the big party but somehow we're supposed to clean up the mess the revellers left behind. That's what it's like for kids like me. We're constantly wishing we'd been there when the cool stuff was happening. And we've seen the world as it was on old box sets and movie reruns. In Scotland, the best's been and gone. From now on things will only get worse. That's the one thing you can guarantee.

I can't believe I came back from the dead for this shit. I'm such an eejit.

'You look messed up,' says Priya. 'There. Why don't you sit on that rock before you take a tumble.'

Great idea, I sit my arse down and feel the wind sting my face. I check in my pockets for my mittens but no such luck.

'Your psychomagician Dr Checkland's on her way to see you. They got word to her out in Glasgow and she promised to come. We didn't figure you'd want to get moving so soon after—'

'There's nothing wrong with my head. I don't need a shrink,' I reply.

'We all do.'

'Maybe it's the world that's fucked up. Have you ever considered that? Like why would they ask Checkland to come over, so she can sort me out and tell me to cope with this bullshit? I'm not the problem.'

'Okay, Ropa.'

To be honest, I could use a chat with Checkland. She had a way of taking the bizarre shit that's happened in my life and making sense of it. I'd be her first zombie client. This ferry better get here soon. I'm proper shivering 'cause it's Baltic out.

I check out the houses nearby, a couple of them in disrepair. Life's always been tough out on the islands, and they bear the brunt of this broken world. Then I realize, just up the road is the ruin where they brought me back from. Then they carried me past the narrow lane which had a small newsagents on the corner. I'm getting my bearings at last.

'There it is. I think . . .' Priya murmurs.

There's a craft with lights on in the distance, sailing towards us. If it's coming our way, it'll be a good few minutes yet. I can't wait to see my little sister again. Get her out of school and out of this godforsaken country. That, I figure, is my only reason for being alive . . . again.

A few locals start turning up at the ferry terminal. They must have a good sense of when it's due. An old man remarks that he hasn't seen it arrive on time at six in the morning since before his divorce. The others agree. A woman has wares in a wooden barrow. There's a lad with two sheep on a leash who comes to join our waiting party.

'Strange goings-on at the ruins of the nunnery lately,' the divorced man says, adjusting his flat cap.

'It's the travellers doing unnatural rituals with their godless ways.' The woman crosses herself, eyeing us suspiciously. 'We'll be better off once they're gone.'

'I am partial to a little devil worship now and again,' the lad says, staring at us.

'Shut your mouth, Joe Curry, or I'll be telling your ma about what you do with them sheep in the hills when you think no one's about,' the divorced man replies. He gives us a lopsided smile, which I'm sure was meant to placate us.

Priya and me exchange looks, but decide it's best to leave them to it. I'm not one for dealing with country folk anyways. The ferry's gotten closer and it's a giant rust bucket that's seen better days. It docks cautiously and a massive mechanical ramp begins to descend onto the quay. The gears groan as the middle of the ramp lands, the front section still upright, failing to come down.

'How are we supposed to get up that?' Priya asks.

'This is a fine ferry, don't you worry, wee lassie. They'll get us on it.'

But first we have to wait for the people on the boat to come down. Part of the ferry's ramp is still in the water and a burly man in PVC fishing waders hops in. He holds out his hands and carries a bearded woman with a small travel suitcase off the boat and onto the dry concrete ramp. Then the man grabs hold of the next passenger's bicycle and deposits it.

It's Dr Morven Checkland and she waves, recognizing us. She huffs and puffs her way up the ramp, awkward in her wedges for the surface is a bit slippery. She's red-faced when she reaches us, but I don't know if it's the exertion or the cold that's nipped her face.

'I came as soon as I heard,' she says. 'But it seems you lot are going the other way. I've got my overnight bag packed.'

'Ropa's decided to leave,' Priya replies.

'So soon after the . . . eh, the procedure. How are you feeling, Ropa?'

'You lot get a move on or sod off,' the burly ferryman shouts. 'Lassie in the wheelchair, you're in first. Let's go, I ain't got all day.'

I start down the ramp and Priya follows with Dr Checkland in tow. The psychomagician must be wondering what's up but her thoughts don't seem to register on her face as normal people's do. It's like a blank slate you can project your shit onto.

'Lady, if you're making me carry your arse back on this ferry after I've just took you off it, it's gonna cost you extra,' the ferryman says.

'I have a return ticket,' Dr Checkland replies.

'And I've got the scabies on my willy – what's it to you?'

The foghorn goes off even though we're not in any fog. Must be the captain growing impatient already. The ferryman curses and walks over to Priya. He widens his stance, squats and bends over, taking hold of both wheels. 'Hands around me like I'm your long-lost Uncle Barney. Not round my waist, I'm not the paedo uncle, I'm the nice one. That's right, round my shoulders. Firm grip. Ready?' And with that he hoists Priya up, chair and all. Then he wades through the water and deposits her on the ramp of the boat.

'You with the fucking sheep, you carry them yourself. If they shit on my deck I'm chucking you in the sea,' he shouts, making his way back.

'Someone's not had their Weetabix this morning,' Joe replies, laughing. 'Barney, how's your wife?'

'How's your mother, you sheepshagger? Does she miss me yet?'

I'm not even ready when Barney scoops me up under the oxters like I was a little child. He smells of fish and onions and could do with a dip in the sea himself. 'This one's a tooth-pick,' he says, unceremoniously dumping me on the ramp. I say thanks, but he's already away to get the next person. These islanders are downright bizarre.

When Dr Checkland joins us back on the boat, we make our way up the metal stairs to the deck. This time Priya decides she doesn't want Barney's help and does it herself. I think some of his whiff has caught onto my clothes. We sit ourselves there in the open air, waiting for the other passengers to come on board.

'I was rather looking forward to seeing Iona again,' Dr Checkland says, stroking her beard. 'If we'd stayed longer maybe we could have arranged an excursion to Fingal's Cave on the island of Staffa. The sea makes the most beautiful music there.'

'Are you one of these witches too?' I ask her.

'I am. Fifth-generation Wiccan on my mother's side. I mean, I'm also a qualified psychomagician, but I see no reason to completely discard the ways of those that came before us. Things don't have to be either/or. Most people these days are absolutist in their thinking and it only causes grief. We can be many things at the same time. That's what it is to be human, I think. We carry all these contradictions and we don't fit into the narrow boxes they try to set us in. That's a residue of Victorian science still lingering in our thinking. How they catalogued plants, animals, rocks and people, foolishly expecting them to conform to what the scientists say they are. A very long answer to your short question, but I am rather proud of who I am. It's one of my many vices.'

'I thought you must have your shit together, since you spend all day dispensing advice to people,' I say.

Dr Checkland laughs heartily, her voice carrying into the wind as we set off.

V

We disembark in Fionnphort on the Isle of Mull fifteen minutes after we departed. The Isle of Iona's so close that we can still see it in the dimness of the blue hour before dawn. I'm gutted to learn the ferry to the mainland's at Tobermory, fifty miles away. I'm not going to be able to walk that. Not in my current state. The countryside sucks; if I was in Edinburgh I could walk or bike everywhere.

The odds of hitchhiking don't seem great either. Mull's pretty big, but the islands are poor. There's a ramshackle ferry office that's seen better days. Seems they used to sell snacks once upon a time when tourists came out this way. The road's potholed to the extent there are actual ditches in it. There's a powerline and lamp-posts but none of them are on. What a shithole. We stroll past the coastguard offices where a small electric car's parked. The only one there.

The car beeps and the lights flash twice.

Dr Checkland walks over to it and opens the door. She jerks her head, beckoning us to join her. The car's about the size of a field mouse and squeezing in me and Priya plus all our gear's a pain in every single orifice.

We drive off past the village where half the homes seem abandoned.

'How are you maintaining your charge?' Priya asks. 'We're a long way from Glasgow.'

'I use a Zeusean thunderbolt spell. It's very tricky getting the voltage right. I've blown two batteries since I got this car.'

It's a bumpy ride and we drive past empty fields without seeing a single cow or sheep. I'm squeezed in the back seat with my backpack on my lap. A hitchhiker on the side tries to flag a lift, but we don't have any room left in the car. These are lean times.

'How are you feeling, Ropa?' Dr Checkland asks, checking me out in her rearview mirror.

'Alive.'

'Do you want to talk about it?'

'I really don't fancy a therapy session right now.'

'That's fine. I just want you to know I'm here for you.'

I look out the window into the vacant wilderness. It's all bleak and grey, the only thing breaking the monotony being a church on the shores of a loch. The doors hanging off their hinges. Broken windows. The place would have been looted ages ago. I am not fine. Sad face.

Dr Checkland fiddles with her radio and plays something.

Okay, I'm not ever going to doubt the doc again because she plays a banger, Simple Minds' 'Don't You (Forget About Me)'.

Priya's singing along with the first riff. 'Come on, Ropa. I grew up on these oldies. My mum used to play this all the time. She said my dad would sing it to her back when they were young.'

'Sing it, Ropa,' shouts Checkland over the synths.

Not to be outdone, I'm belting away too. Makes it feel like we're zooming by but Checkland's a slow driver and the road's in a state so we're actually crawling along. The songs and blether pass the time and before we know it we're in Tobermory where we have to wait for the evening ferry to Kilchoan.

I remember the times in our little caravan when me and Izwi and Gran would kick back, watch a show or talk for hours. Simple days when all we had was each other and that was enough. But my father told me that Gran killed him. All families are screwed up but mine really takes the packet of biscuits. Still, knowing all the messed-up stuff they did doesn't make me miss them any less. The thing about losing people is it takes so much away from you. I would rather they were here so I could hate them all. When they're gone, what can you do? It's all on you.

There's others waiting for the ferry too in this depressing village. There's signs everywhere of a vibrancy that's long gone. A disused visitor centre. A museum teetering on the brink. I'm no different, holding on to all these pieces from the past. I get the feeling that everyone wants me to say I'm grateful to be alive but I'm really not. It's like despite all the madness they want me to smile and say some vapid stuff about what a blessing this whole thing is. I've got no fight left in me. This life is shit, but it's also scary knowing the other side's just as fucked up. Weren't we all supposed to wind up in the Land of the Tall Grass and be happy forever? Back in this reality I'm like that Greek guy doomed to roll the rock up the hill for all eternity.

I miss you, Melsie Mhondoro, you fucking murderer. I'd happily trade what I now know for the lies she raised me on. That's all our home in the slums was, an illusion cooked up by an old woman with a sick mind.

Checkland's eyeing me in her rearview, hoping I crack and start spewing my guts out. Priya's left the car because she needs the bathroom. I fiddle around with my walking stick, inspecting the workmanship of it. Anything to distract myself from these dark thoughts. Then I take a look at the metal ferrule at the bottom of it and notice a wee engraving: *MM.*

The ferry to Kilchoan's late and it's nearly eight at night by the time we leave. The sea's pitch black and frothing. I'm bummed I won't make it to the east coast to see my sister today. We make the journey inside of Dr Checkland's car, which she says is illegal – something about what might happen if the boat sinks. But the crew don't bother getting us out to the decks.

We eventually make it across to another dead village. As we drive away from the ferry port, Dr Checkland says, 'I can't come with you to Aberdeen. And there's no way you can hitchhike this time of night either.'

'Maybe we can find an open B&B,' says Priya.

'That's one option, but the benefits of the sisterhood include five-star accommodation in every shire. All we have to do is trek to Fort William.'

'How far away is that from here?' I ask.

'Two or three hours. It depends.'

I'm wondering if the roads are safe this time of the night. There can't be that much traffic passing through these parts.

In the Central Belt highwaymen prowl, but I stop worrying since I'm with two magicians.

The landscape outside my window is bleak and dark. It reminds me of the Other Place where I left my father's soul to be devoured. The hills here rise up either side of the road. I catch the outlines of fir and pine in the old plantations. Maybe this world is just another version of the Other Place. We spend half the time devouring each other. Who's to say this isn't Hell we're in? I rest my head against the steamy window.

This body still doesn't feel like it's mine.

I put my hand up my T-shirt and trace the outline of Dundas's mark on my chest. It's still there and it's very real. The crazy thing is that it might be the one thing about my physical form that feels like I own it. I haven't felt it burn since I left Iona. Sounds minor, but it's strange. And sometimes I have to remind myself to breathe. It's like I forget and then when my lungs start burning I mentally have to go through the motions of taking in air. I'm not all there. Bits and pieces of me are scattered about. Let me roll down the window – I need air. Fuck's sake, I'm cracking up.

'I'm not okay,' I blurt out. It's so sudden, spontaneous, but there's stuff inside of me I've gotta let out before I combust.

'Coming back from the dead is not something that's been covered in healing literature, Ropa,' Dr Checkland says, looking back in the rearview mirror. 'There's a lot you should process and you may never be quite the same again.'

'Feels like my life gets more bonkers with every choice I make,' I reply, jamming my eyes closed. 'Even when I do right, I'm hit with a cost I didn't anticipate.'

'The fact you are aware of that is good. Mindfulness. You need to be kind to yourself and lean on your friends, let them carry some of the weight.'

'I'm here for you, always,' says Priya, touching my forearm and squeezing gently. Then she rubs her thumb against my skin, drawing little circles.

'As am I. The path ahead will be a difficult one, no doubt.' Dr Checkland is stroking her beard with one hand like she does in our sessions at the clinic. 'Don't forget your breathing exercises if you get too overwhelmed. Let it out and talk when you have to. That's the best medicine. Don't hold on to things.'

'Everything I thought I knew was a lie. The grown-ups I thought were good turned out to be something else.'

'That's a powerful statement and it speaks to a level of disorientation. This can shake your sense of security and understanding of the world. What emotions come with that?'

'Fear. Hurt. Shame. Anger. A lot of anger.'

Priya slides her hand down to hold mine.

We continue my session with Dr Checkland until we wind up on a farm just outside of Fort William. The log cabin has lamps burning through the windows and we're greeted by two barking Border collies. Feels good to have my feet touch the ground again when I get out of the car. A woman holding a double-barrel shotgun aimed at us stands at the door. I raise my hands in the air.

'Go and try your luck elsewhere, you hear?' she shouts.

'But I heard this place has the finest cottage cheese,' Dr Checkland replies.

' . . . Morven, is that you?'

'Who else would be stupid enough to trespass on your property this late at night?'

'These kids are with you?' the farmer asks, still pointing her gun at us.

'Strays I picked up along the way.'

Checkland's walking to the farmhouse and we follow. I make sure I'm out of the firing line. If anyone's getting a slug in the face tonight, it won't be me. The woman breaks into a huge smile and throws her arms open, now holding the barrel of her gun in one hand. She embraces Dr Checkland, steps back and takes a good look.

'You're too busy in the capital to make time for us country bumpkins. Come on inside.'

There's a horseshoe above the door and a wood-burning stove warms the kitchen that we enter. It smells of herbs and roast tatties in here. I recall I haven't eaten all day, but I don't feel hungry. The log cabin's open plan on the ground floor and there's a red-haired woman in the living room sat reading *Ghosts I Have Seen*, the popular memoir by Violet Tweedale, the Edinburgh spiritualist. She looks up with the annoyance of someone interrupted mid-chapter.

'Well, pigs can fly if my little sister Morven can visit us out in the sticks, Seonaid.'

'Priya, Ropa, this is my sister Jeanie and her wife Seonaid,' Dr Checkland says. 'They are happy living off the grid and I don't visit as often as I should because I'm not partial to cold showers and compost toilets.'

'You make it sound like we grew up somewhere posh and

not Easterhouse in Glasgow,' Jeanie replies. 'Sit yourselves down anywhere. Don't stand on ceremony.'

There's candles on every windowsill and loads of jars everywhere, on tables, cabinets and on the bookshelves too. Drying herbs hang on the wall, and a frog is ensconced on a side table croaking away. In the furthest corner of the room is a space that looks like a dedicated shrine with some icons and idols, and, of course, even more candles.

Seonaid comes over with some homemade biscuits and milk, having left her shotgun in the kitchen. Priya dives in straight away, as does Dr Checkland. The biscuits smell nice, but they don't whet my appetite one bit.

'We need a place to sleep tonight,' Dr Checkland says.

'As though you need ever ask,' her sister replies. 'Did Morven tell you about when we were children, we went to the Gilberts for a birthday party and—'

'If you dare, I'll knock your teeth out, Jeanie,' Dr Checkland says sweetly.

Jeanie pushes out her top and bottom dentures and they all start cackling. I sense something about her, though – herbs and a mortar and pestle, a squirming chicken beheaded for a sacrifice. It's the whiff of unconventional magic.

'My friends need to go to Aberdeen tomorrow. Is anyone travelling out east so they can hitch a ride?' Dr Checkland asks.

'Lenny's off to Fraserburgh and for the right amount he could be convinced to make a detour. It won't be cheap and you'll be in with the sheep. They're not safe here with all them hungry people trying to steal a beast to feast on. Lenny's father-in-law has got an isolated, secure farm, so he's moving the flock there before it's taken off him.'

I'm one step closer to my sister. One more night and I'll be with her again. This time, I'm never letting her out of my sight, no matter what. I'll hold on to what I have left.

VI

Lenny is fed up and taking his family up north. Priya's getting a fantastic blow-dry and my bald noggin's freezing, arse sore, as we endure the slow trek through the highland country roads. We're in the trailer of his aged DAF transport lorry, sharing the privilege with several sheep, some packed suitcases, a few boxes, a three-seater sofa and feed. Priya's wheelchair's been chucked over some farm equipment at the back and she's sat next to me. The sharp smell of chips wafts in the air due to the fact that Lenny's using rapeseed oil for fuel. A bit wasteful that, considering folks are starving up and down the country.

We couldn't be up front in the cab where Lenny's wife Maude and their three children sit. The littlest sits on her mother's lap. The trailer doesn't have any windows and, being the driver, Lenny's wearing pilot goggles like he was flying a Spitfire, but the front's still better than being back here with no tarp or nothing to protect us from the elements. Priya and I huddle together in the back just behind the cab.

'Wouldn't be moving if it weren't for all the crime going on. Nasty business,' Lenny shouts above his engine and the wind. 'It's safer up north. Not as many starving people wanting to take your scran off you. I've got a twenty-two and I hope to

God I never have to use it. But I will if you try to mess about with my family. I'll put one right between your eyes. Why are you girls – sorry, you're a boy, ain't yer?' Priya gives me a look and rolls her eyes. 'Anyways, why are youse travelling about at a time like this? You should be home. Lock your doors and nail your windows shut.'

'We need to find our sister,' Priya says.

'I didn't think you two were related. Tell your brother to stay sharp and look after you. It's dangerous out here. He needs to get himself a gun if he can.'

Priya giggles looking right at me and replies, 'I'm sure he will.'

Ever since I went bald some folks think I'm a geezer. I guess I'm just that handsome.

'You heard the king's coming back to Scotland?' he asks, taking his eyes off the road and turning to us. 'The first time in decades. They say he's making a tour of the realm. I can't wait for him to arrive. That's a man who knows what he's doing, I'll give him that.'

'You think?' Priya says.

'Damn right. The last time we had chaos, all caused by the separatists, he put them down like the dogs they are. And he's going to do it again. Mark my words, when he sets foot in Scotland, there won't be no more of this rioting and looting. He'll bring back order and remind everyone of their place. Then he's going to go and pay homage to the place where they murdered his poor mum and dad. Bless their souls.'

'Lenny, they're too young for that kind of talk,' Maude says.

'If they can free range like this, then they can take it. Back in my day we used to sing "God save the Queen" at school. Now these kids think they can just thumb their noses at the monarchy and get away with it. No, sir, not this king. They'll all learn to bow and curtsey like they're supposed to.'

'And what do you know of it? You've never met no kings or queens,' his wife says.

'I've met plenty enough on my banknotes and I bow to those,' Lenny replies.

It's crazy to think the king's coming up here. Monarchs since James VI think they can rule Scotland with a pen, but this one seems more hands-on. It's pretty messed up that he wants to see where his parents were killed.

We make slow progress along the winding road that takes us through old plantations ruined by needle blight. Priya's yawning and getting all drowsy and she lies back on a sheep's rump. If I had my phone I'd take a photo but it wasn't in my gear when I got it back and I forgot to ask 'cause I'm a numpty.

'I had faith you'd come back to us when Theodosia Lovell said things would work out,' she says. 'I still can't believe it, though.'

'I was forced to.'

'Doesn't matter. You're here and that's all that matters, okay?'

Priya turns her head and snoozes. That would be the perfect picture, so I snap it in my mind and promise I'll always remember it. Lenny's still pontificating about one thing or the other while his wife parries his opinions. They seem comfortable in their bickering in that way people who truly love each other do. I reach for my backpack, which is squished by a sheep, so I have to shimmy it out.

Still feels strange to have my body again. It's like I have to be a kid, relearning what it is to be a corporeal being. It will take time, practice. In the meantime all I can do is more human-ing in order to remember what it is to be a person.

I place the bag on my lap, open the zipper and pull out my mbira. There's some chipping on the edges of the wooden board. I run my finger over just to feel them. Some of the metal keys are a bit bent. That's not good, but it's a hardy instrument so I might as well sort that out. My fingers are still frail and it takes an effort to straighten the keys. But I'm happy with the look of it after.

I'll have to do a bit of Nyamaropa tuning to sort out the sound, though. I sort of go with the Mixolydian mode in Western music but tweak that slightly because you don't follow the same half and whole steps when using this instrument. When I was learning to play, it was a bit confusing because some of the artists I listened to seemed to have their own idiosyncratic tunings. Like, it's not standardized, you kind of go with what works for you.

Grab a wee tabla hammer from my backpack. This is gonna be tricky given how juddery the lorry is and all the noise from the engine. But I'll give it a go. The simple principle when tuning the keys is that the longer a key is, the lower the pitch. I test the keys out. We gotta get those octave relationships DNA tested and verified. That's how you get harmony – they are a family. There are other tunings like Dambatsoko which is low-pitched, close to a major scale, but not precisely. Or you can do the Katsanzaira style, a lot juicier and high-pitched.

There's tons of ways to do it, but I'll do the style that's worked for me. I tap the key to lengthen a note and strike it.

Testing, testing. Hmm, this feels weird. It's not right at all. No mbira should sound like this.

It's good to have my body once again. To touch things. It's not the same as touching stuff with your soul. God, it's good to *feel* again. The mbira still doesn't sound right to my ear and I do a bit more tuning. Can't be that many people who've ever done this sat with sheep at the back of a moving lorry. Let me play a wee tune for them, see how that goes. I thumb out 'Tibayane', a song about a call to war by the Mazai Mbira Group.

'Right, young man, this is the Bridge of Dee. I've brought you as far as I can and it's cost me fuel that I wouldn't have burnt had your friend Dr Checkland not saved my marriage.'

'Too much information, Lenny,' Maude chides.

'I'm not afraid to admit my family's not perfect but I love them just as much as my sheep,' Lenny replies, laughing.

Maude baas in response.

'Thanks for the lift,' I say.

I nudge Priya to wake her up and pack up my stuff, making sure I leave nothing behind. I've not finished sorting my mbira, though. It's still sounding very weird, closer to pitch A, which is a Gandanga tuning, but even then it doesn't sound right. It's doing its own thing. That sound cuts right through you like a chainsaw, though. Never heard anything like it before. I must have bollocksed things up trying to tune it on a moving vehicle.

Lenny opens the trailer gate and I take Priya's chair and wade through livestock and furniture before passing it to him.

Then I go lift up Priya, otherwise there's no way she's passing through all this. It's a proper shift 'cause my body's just odd at the moment.

'You going to piggyback me all the way to the school?' she asks.

'In your wet dreams.'

Lenny helps her down from the lorry and into her chair, while I sit on the edge of the trailer and then slide down.

'We're late as it is. And the children are freezing. Let's get on with it,' Maude shouts from the cab.

'It'd have been nice if you'd let me have a piss on the side of the road,' Lenny grumbles, returning to the cab. 'Eyes open, ears peeled. Stay safe, and if you have to, go insane.'

And I thought I was the paranoid one. I give him a wave and figure we're going across the road and the opposite way since he's heading north, past Aberdeen and on to Fraserburgh. We better get a move on as you don't get much light in the north this time of the year.

The old bridge has several arches running above the River Dee. We're not going across, though. There's a couple of miles ahead of us, according to Priya who's checking her phone. Seems we have to track back a wee bit. The bonus is we're walking next to the east coast. We've gone from one side of Scotland to the other.

I'm soon drenched in my own sweat, relying more on my stick to move. My legs might as well be inflexible tree trunks at this rate. Good thing Priya's still sprightly.

'Nearly there,' says Priya, all excited. 'You know, if I hadn't gone to Lord Kelvin, I might just have wound up here in Aberdeen. It would have been amazing. They do excursions up to the disused oil rigs. I've always fancied checking one out.'

'They call this a city?'

'Okay, smart-arse, it's only the third largest city in Scotland. You think Edinburgh's any better?'

'I know it is.'

If Edinburgh took a pounding from the Catastrophe, Aberdeen got a real hammering. Feels like we're wandering through the set of a zombie flick. Doesn't help that the houses here are made of gloomy grey granite. Depressing, like the Other Place. The folks have stopped tending their gardens and some of the houses are dilapidated so nature's taking over in a big way. This area must have been nice once upon a time. A woman with a shopping cart ambles along the other bank. For a place this size there should be more folks about.

The only thing that's vaguely new or decent-looking is the bunting on lamp-posts. They have banners with the Union Jack and pictures of the old king and queen. None of their son, the current king, though. I remember the anniversary of their death is going to be soon. Maybe the king wishes to remind Scotland of its folly. Regardless, the banners don't much improve the state of the neighbourhood.

Aberdeen's thing was oil. They used to do fishing, and they even had a couple of industries: shipbuilding, textiles, the sort of industrial thing that used to go on when you could still get folks labouring in factories and stuff. But when oil in the North Sea became a thing, life was great here, so I've heard. There's signs wealth used to flow here in the architecture of the old houses, which, being made of stone, are still solid and only need a bit of TLC. Seems like they had shopping centres too.

Priya peers into the distance. 'Is that a park?'

'It's a jungle out here,' I reply.

A pack of stray dogs runs past us across the road. Their coats are dirty and shaggy, and all of them have ribs sticking out. If folks are starving, they might choose to let go of a few mouths to feed and the first to go's got to be the family pet for some. In Edinburgh it wasn't unknown for babies and toddlers to be left at churches. And that's before things got this bad. Maybe the king needs to come and see this shit with his own eyes.

I dodge a puddle of human excrement and get a bit ahead of Priya, who's checking her phone for directions.

'This way,' she says, taking us down a road with more pebbledashed houses. Darkness tinges the sky as the last rays of orange drain away. I can smell the sea from here.

Reckon the school used to be out in the sticks, but the city grew so much now these houses are nearby. I can't help being excited. I'm going to see Izwi again and hold her in my arms. Flutters. The last time I saw her it was all too brief. She's the only family I've got left in this whole wide world. I'm buzzing by the time we've left Cove Bay, proceeding on a dirt track next to the disused railway line.

'This is the first time I've seen you smile since you've been back,' Priya remarks.

'It's a nice night . . . And please stop reminding me I was dead. I get it. That's my Lazarus party trick.'

'That would make me Jesus. I like that.'

A little girl in a red-and-blue netball kit's running towards us. Can't be more than eight or nine, but she's moving at a fair clip as she zooms past us into the twilight. I've just turned to see her go past when another group of kids comes running from the same direction.

'Cross-country day?' Priya asks.

'In that gear and at this time of the day?' I reply.

Not all of them are wearing sportswear. Boys and girls in blue blazers come rushing down the trail. The boys are in grey trousers and the girls wear tights under their skirts. I step off the road for the group to go past. A portly man, red in the face and panting, shoos the kids along. He's wheezing, his academic gown all over the place, as he struggles to keep up with them.

He stops for a second, seeing us. And gasps for breath.

'Keep going, children. Get as far away as you can,' he shouts. Then he looks to us and says, 'You don't want to go that way,' before resuming his run.

'What's going on? Hey!' Priya shouts after him.

I pick up my pace 'cause something's definitely off. Spidey senses tingling and I'm gripping my walking stick hard. Where I'd normally be sprinting, I'm just hobbling and it's frustrating. A green firework explodes in the sky . . . Nah. That's a thermosphere.

There's a row of tall Douglas fir trees lined up with a small wrought-iron gate in the middle. And, in the far-off distance, a massive castle looms in the fading light. It's painted green by the thermosphere's fierce sparks. There's a massive sonic boom, louder than any thunder I've ever heard in this realm, and now I'm certain there's trouble up ahead.

Cruickshank, who was warming my neck nicely, uncoils until he's sat on my shoulders ready for action.

'This is not good, Ropa,' Priya says.

'No shit, Sherlock, my sister is in there.'

'Then get your undead arse moving,' she replies, picking up the pace as we go through the school gates, past the grove of fir trees. A window in one of the castle turrets shatters and someone in a fluttering academic gown falls down three storeys onto the lawn with a sickening thump. Erm . . .

'Go check on whoever that is,' I tell Priya. 'They might need your help.'

'Be careful, Ropa.'

Lights in all the colours of the rainbow flash through windows on every floor. There's an acrid chemical smell pervading the air, ammonia and sulphur. Smoke's pouring out everywhere. I go up a set of steps leading to a grand entrance, the wooden door bust open. Gotta keep to the left and stick to the walls. You don't want to be an obvious target and I have no idea where I'm going.

There's no one in the grand hallway beyond, unless you count statues of serious old dead guys standing about. Up ahead is a courtyard, or I could go left or right, through some corridors. There's a pair of magicians duelling in the courtyard. The two trade spell for spell, neither yielding, but they're fighting hard, fancy signatures infused into their thermospheres forming a phoenix against a fist. They step in vigorous choreography, almost like they're dancing a paso doble. One's in academic dress and she seems to be leading; I figure I can tell the teachers from the intruders that way. The other one is a posh-looking lady in designer togs. She has her back to me, but I know that body structure and sleeked hair. That's Lady Rethabile Lebusa. Who else makes a habit of attacking magical institutions in Scotland?

Gotta be careful and make sure she doesn't spot me. Element of surprise.

If you were turning a castle into a school, where would you put the classrooms? Ground floor, I reckon. At least that's how I'd do it. That means the offices or dorms are on the top floor? Or it could be a different wing. I've always believed that taking action is better than lounging, so I make a decision to go right and up the stairs. I'll figure it out from there.

Can't use my katty 'cause I have a bloody walking stick in one hand and I need it to walk, otherwise I'd lead with that. There's a crack like lightning and a man cries out from upstairs. I speed up as best I can.

'Izwi!' I shout.

I need to get her safely out of here. I go past some bathrooms and spot a kid in his school blazer darting into an arched corridor on the right, so I follow and call out. He turns around, muttering.

'I'm not here to hurt you. I'm Izwi's—' I say, too late, 'cause the kid's sent a soliton down the corridor. I incant an anemoic spell to counter it. Maybe I don't do it in time, 'cause this little shit's spell hits me and staggers me back a few steps before I plant my stick behind me. Thankfully, it's not too bad, just like

I've been shoulder-barged. The kid dashes off before I can do anything to retaliate. *Good for you.*

I turn up a set of stairs with a sign forbidding running indoors. There're voices that seem to be coming right from the top floor. I stop at the landing, proper knackered by all this climbing, when I hear whispering at the door opposite. It has a sign that says 'Therapets'. I stand at the side in case someone fires something out.

'I'm here looking for my little sister. Please don't do anything crazy, okay? I'm opening this door.'

I try the handle and whatever idiots hid out in here must not know how to use the key, because it opens. Here goes. Poke my head in a fraction just to check and there's two little girls, a redhead and a blonde, about Izwi's age, who look petrified. They stand there like deer in headlights. The short one's weed herself judging by the puddle at her feet. I hold up my palms, go in slowly and shut the door, making sure I lock it.

'I'm not one of those people. You can trust me, I'm Izwi Moyo's sister. Do you know her?'

'*Know her, know her, know her,*' a parakeet in a cage to my left mocks.

'Shh.'

'*Shh, shh, shh.*'

There's a good few animals in cages here. A hedgehog. Tortoise. The furry one with big eyes appears to be a flying lemur. We did not have this kind of thing at my old school. I walk closer to the girls, keeping my hands visible.

'Have you seen my sister? Please, I don't want her to get hurt.'

The smaller girl who peed her pants opens her mouth and the redhead stomps on her foot. I like these kids already. Best to speak to the person in charge then, so I turn my attention to the redhead.

'How do we know you're her sister?' Fair point, kiddo.

'Her favourite flavour of ice cream is hazelnut and she likes Marmite.' The kid blanks me. I'm getting pissed off but I channel my Mandela aura 'cause she's in the right. 'Come on, how do you want me to prove it?'

'What breed of dog does she have?' little redhead asks.

'Izwi doesn't have a dog, but we did have a fox called River.'

'So it *is* true,' she says, turning to her friend. 'And you said she was fibbing all this time.'

'Guys, I don't have time here.'

'Go to the drama room, she'd have been rehearsing for *Matilda the Musical* before we got attacked by the bad people.'

That doesn't sound like the Izwi I know, but who knows what fancy boarding school will make you do.

'And where is the drama room?'

The girls give me directions and I tell them to lock the door and shut the damned parakeet up otherwise someone might hear them. The drama room's in the basement, which used to be the old dungeon. This flight of stairs doesn't get you there. I have to go across the whole bloody castle to the north wing and make my way down from there.

I hasten my way past noticeboards with posters and pictures. I go by a window overlooking the courtyard and see Lady Rethabile walking across the pristine white pavement looking rather satisfied with herself. The woman who was valiantly fighting her lies defeated, fertilizing the lawn with her blood. Her gown's over her head and her legs are twitching.

I have to get Izwi.

A loud boom and slates fall from the roof, crashing down and breaking like pottery. I can't help but notice how antique and expensive everything here looks. No idea how they keep this wool carpet clean. There's the occasional bench to sit on at the side of the corridor. I pass by a stacked trophy cabinet and a board with the names of old headteachers. Rows of hunting trophies; a stag, a lion, buffalo and moose.

No time for that.

I head down the stairs. A couple of boys in maroon rugby jerseys are coming up but turn tail when they spot me. But why would Lady Rethabile Lebusa come here of all places? If she's with the Dundas Cult then they obviously want something. Another magical artefact? Nope, not this time. I'm minding my own business. That's what got me into deep manure the last time. I went around poking my nose into things that didn't concern me and I paid the price. If you'd asked me a few months ago what I'd do when I saw any one of those bastards, I'd have said I'd make them pay. Now, I'm cutting my losses from this rigged casino. I'm not having nothing to do with Scottish magic ever again. They can keep their scheming and have their nasty feuds. Leave me out of it. All I want is to get my sister and fuck off on the first boat out.

There's a big old sign with 'DRAMA STUDIO' pointing to the left. The hallway's lined with mannequins. A drumset sits to the right with a saxophone leaning against the bass drum. At the far end's an open double door which I hobble towards.

My stick's making too much noise tapping on the stone flooring, but I can't help it.

I walk into a room's got eleven students lying face down on the floor. A couple more are similarly prone on the stage up front, which has been set up with boxes marked with letters, like wooden alphabet blocks. The lights overhead are bright and brilliant. The curtains are drawn open and I spy a pair of feet in men's loafers, someone hidden behind them. I check out the kids lying down. None of them's my sister, so I go over to the stage and no one's there.

'I'm not one of them,' I say. 'Can you tell me where my sister Izwi Moyo is? Please.'

A few heads rise up on the floor. The man behind the curtain peeks out, eyes wide open and scanning to see if the coast is clear. He's in his thirties and has spectacular eyebrows.

'Is it over?' he whispers.

'I was told she's here,' I say.

'Anyone see where Izwi went?' the drama teacher squeaks, finally stepping out from his hiding place, revealing orange and green baggy harem pants. 'Perhaps she's gone to use the bathroom. She'll be back anytime now.'

'They took her, sir, Mr Loughty,' a boy on the floor says.

'Dear God, I thought this was a safe school. The best in all of the north and one of the four schools of magic in Scotland,' he says theatrically.

'Where is my sister? It's your job to protect her.' If he were nearer, I'd poke him in the chest with my stick.

'Who, me? I'm, uhm, it's not really my . . . You must understand, I've only been in this job since the term started.

I don't do any of that magic stuff, I'm here to teach drama, that's all. Okay, I qualified at St Andrews, but what I really wanted was to get into theatre. This is my fallback. I don't get paid enough to—'

Mr Loughty's a blubbering wreck and he's craven. Wouldn't last a week by my ends the way he's carrying on. I turn to the boy on the floor with a moptop haircut. He spoke earlier and seems braver than his teacher to me.

'Stand up and tell me exactly what you saw.'

'A girl and two boys. They threatened to kill us and stuff. And then they made us lie on the floor. Izwi was right beside me.' He points to the empty floor. 'Then one of them told her to get up. And it's like she knew who he was because he was telling her not to be frightened. He told her that she was in danger at this school and he'd come with his friends to protect her. They were going to take her to Edinburgh where she's safe.'

'What was his name?'

'It was a girl's name. I think she called him Juno. And Izwi was refusing to go with him, but he told her that you were in Edinburgh waiting for her. He said it was you who sent him to get her. That's when she believed him and went with him.'

My heart sinks. 'Juno' has to be Jomo Maige so he was here with them too. My ex-best friend is now in deep with this cult and there's no way back for him. Thick as thieves we used to be. But if he so much as lays a finger on Izwi's head, those years we were besties won't count for nothin'.

'You let this happen.' I point my walking stick at Mr Loughty, who hunches his shoulders. *Focus, Ropa.* Jomo's taken Izwi, but what possible use could she be to them? They already have what they want: Henry Dundas is back from the dead. I don't see how Izwi can help them with anything at this stage. I'm already walking out of the drama room. This cult is on a mission and they wouldn't make such a move unless they thought it necessary. Why would they risk coming here?

The cult is made up mostly of folks from the Edinburgh School and St Andrews. That means they haven't secured the support of Aberdeen and Glasgow, so this maybe serves as some kind of warning. The Doric School is the smallest of the four. Trashing it sends a signal they mean business. Maybe they are hoping this attack will get Glasgow to yield. I'm speculating, but none of that gets me nearer to finding Izwi. I rush out the doors, making my way onto the school grounds. There's a calm in the air now, though it's still filled with smoke and acrid scents. Magic is at work.

There's a purple glow and my shadow's long in front of me. I turn round and see the top floor of the castle's burning with flames so brilliant they shoot out of the windows.

A group of people is walking towards the sea. And with them is Jomo, holding my little sister's hand. I'm about to call her name but my voice catches when I notice one of them wearing a greatcoat like Napoleon reincarnate. Henry Dundas, the Viscount Melville, is here personally. The motherfucker who ended me. Beside him is a large Maine Coon, the resident cat at the Society headquarters on St Andrew Square in Edinburgh. It brushes against his legs. I have to be super stealthy. No point rushing into a situation that could see me in the Other Place a second time, and I don't fancy that no-frills holiday.

I'm proper bricking it now. Part of me wants to flee, but for

Izwi, I'd go all the way to hell and back a thousand times over. I steel myself and throw the dice.

'Hey,' I yell.

Dundas stops and slowly pivots round. He wears a horsehair wig, which does little to enhance his look. That would be his natural ugliness, 'cause the flesh on his body is brighter and more vigorous than the leather bag he was in our last encounter. Around his neck is half of the Fairy Flag stolen from Dunvegan Castle. This magical artefact from the Fae on the Isle of Skye has the power over interdimensional movement. I suspect he is using it to stop his soul from being sucked back into the everyThere. The other half was taken away by Esfandiar, Sir Ian Callander's husband.

Dundas smiles. It seems painful for the flesh on his face to pull back. The cat beside him hisses menacingly. Now I understand why Callander didn't like it.

'Remarkable. You came back to this world, I see. It didn't even take centuries like it did for the rest of us. You must have been in a *rush*. Now you know what it's like to be in the eternal cold, dear girl. Surely you must understand why I had to return? Nothing out there can compare to life here. My first life only lasted a fleeting five and a half decades. Hardly any time at all.' Dundas's voice has the brittle quality of the pages of an ancient book turning. There's something authoritative about it. I fight the urge to nod my head.

'You're not supposed to be here,' I reply.

'And what are you going to do about it – exorcize me? You've already tried that once.' He chuckles.

'Come on then, let's go for round two.' I'm bluffing, 'cause inside I'm shuddering and weak at the knees. The scar on my chest where Dundas struck me on Calton Hill burns like I've bathed it in acid. It takes everything I have to stand firm, planting my walking stick into the lawn, gripping it tightly. I take a deep breath to calm myself. I don't much fancy dying again, been there, done that, the T-shirt sucks.

Don't show any signs of fear.

Montgomery Wedderburn steps forward and asks Dundas's permission to speak. This is insane. The former head of Edinburgh's school of magic has to ask permission like a mere schoolboy. I guess some people just love to have a tyrant take control and tell them what to do. Wedderburn's outfitted in a Harris Tweed suit, which offends me because it reminds me of Callander, the friend he betrayed. But he'll never be half the man Callander was.

'Show some respect, young lady. You should kneel when you address a god,' Wedderburn says.

'If you like bending over, that's your kink,' I reply, and he turns red with rage.

'There are many things you don't know, Ropa Moyo, for you are young. Your father's work was instrumental in bringing about this moment. I know you've been on the other side of the parapet, as it were, but you are undoing everything your father worked hard to make real.'

'My father was a douche. I met him.'

Wedderburn was his pal, best man at his wedding and all the rest of that jazz. Not that Wedderburn was ever there for me in the past. But if he's trying to pull the legacy card, he should know my dad and me are two different beasts.

'Thanks to your father, our dream of making Edinburgh the Athens of the North is once again revived. We shall rebuild the Parthenon with Henry Dundas, our *Zeus*, guiding us. This is important work.'

No use wasting my time with a zealot who believes a ghoul is a god. I've been to many other realms and there are all sorts of wondrous things out there, but I'm yet to meet a god. Men who've tried to be one, well, that's a grift as old as time. Instead, I attack a weak point.

'Jomo, what the actual fuck?' I say. 'Let her go.'

'He told me you were in Edinburgh,' Izwi says, realizing she has been lied to.

She tries to let go of his hand but Jomo holds firm. He looks embarrassed to be doing this, but like a coward he does so anyways. I'm still seething. A smile flickers on Dundas's dry lips. He's got to be used to this, people picking his side.

'Why don't you make it easy on yourself and join our cause? That way the two of you can be together,' Dundas says. He was a shrewd and cunning politician in his day. The most powerful Scot in Westminster after the Union. Such was his influence, some called him King Harry. I guess he knows how to make offers folks can't refuse.

'Izwi, I've come to get you,' I say, remembering Gran's advice on dealing with ghosts. 'I'm not here to bargain.'

Dundas laughs, a dry cackle full of amusement.

If there's anything I learned from the Rooster in his many wars against rival gangs in Edinburgh, the old British Empire tactic of divide and conquer pays dividends. Find any group of people and you'll have differing interests. I've hit Jomo, now's the time to switch tack and keep hacking away.

'And you, Frances Cockburn, is this why you abandoned Sir Ian Callander, so you could go about kidnapping innocent lassies?' She's in her drab, grey suit hovering in the background. 'All your bullshit about the Society's rules, but you're just a coward. Same as you, Montgomery Wedderburn. Callander cared for you both, but you stabbed him in the back. And for what? So you can go around burning schools down. Is that what you meant by restoring Scottish magic?'

Cockburn takes a deep breath but doesn't respond. I'm trying to drive a wedge. Wedderburn takes off his golden monocle and cleans it nonchalantly.

'This is a touching reunion, but we have matters of import and time is precious,' Dundas says, turning his back to me.

'Shall we take her too?' Wedderburn asks.

'We only need one, and she'll be too much trouble. Fenella, this one shouldn't tax you too much. After all, you were the one who performed the brilliant task of murdering Melsie Mhondoro in her sleep. You might as well take this scalp too. You've earned it. The rest, with me,' says Dundas, walking away.

I'm reeling. Fenella again. She's vicious, a real viper, and while the order might have been his, she's the one who went out to our slum and— She wears a derisive scowl, sizing me up. Slight thing, fair and anaemic-looking, but far from inno-cent. She's taken so much from me. No chance I'm letting them get away with Izwi.

This cult exists because of Henry Dundas. If I drive him back to hell, they'll have no reason to be here. And so I focus my rage and try to find a nexus point – channelling everything I have, I incant the most powerful lightning bolt I can.

'Chief of the gods, wielder of the gifts of Arges, Brontes and Steropes, shake the Earth with your wrath.'

There's a crackle, and the hairs on my arms stand, as though a drastic entropic shift might occur. I channel my will into the spell, holding its form in my mind, and cast my hand towards Dundas. There's a white spark and a puff of smoke, but the spell does not take. Fenella's walking towards me, pale as snow, skin matching her white dress. Her eyes are fixed on me, murderous in intent.

Why did my spell not take?

There are places with heightened resistance to magic. Nah, not at a magic school. Somerville taught that natural resistance was eroded in places where magic was frequently practised, so the inverse is more likely. Could be I overcooked it, tried to get a big bang beyond the limits of my practice. I try again with a more familiar Promethean fire spell, which fails to elicit even a single spark.

No, no.

Izwi's looking back and crying. She's got her eyes on me, reaching out with her free hand. But Jomo's dragging her and he doesn't even turn back. Why's my magic not happening? Is it because I crossed over and no longer have Authority here? It could be I'm too stressed out and frazzled. But there's more than one way to skin a cat. I grab my dagger and advance to meet Fenella MacLeod, whose cold and hungry eyes remain fixed upon me. I'm already worn out and if I'd been my old self I'd rush her, but all I can do is shuffle.

'You're not a real magician and you'll never be one,' she says, playing the superiority card.

'Go fuck yourself.'

'I stood outside the caravan and listened to your grandmother and her boyfriend talking about you. It's a pity, because soon they fell asleep inhaling carbon monoxide.' The corner of her mouth turns up with some sort of sick self-satisfaction. 'Do you want to know what she had to say?'

She's so close to me, I lunge but she sidesteps me and I slice thin air instead. Nearly makes me fall, but I use the walking stick to support myself. This makes her laugh. I turn to face her and walk towards her. I swing the stick and she leaps out of the way.

'Murderer,' I yell, furious at my impotence. I want her head on a pike.

'I've seen old women who move better than you,' she taunts.

'I'm going to kill you, Fenella.'

'I can trace my family back seven hundred years, while you sprang up like a weed and all I have to do is pluck you up.' She holds her index finger and thumb together and flicks her wrist.

There's an explosion from the school and I bloody hope the kids I left locked in the therapet room got out of there.

My sister's nearly down to the shore. They're taking her on a boat and this snake's stopping me from getting to her. I lunge again and Fenella steps away smartly, clearly toying with me. That's the psycho-game of someone who's developed a taste for taking lives. She betrayed her father because of this fucked-up issue she's got about being the little girl who grew up in a castle on the Isle of Skye with everything she could ever want or need.

'I stood outside the caravan for a while before Melsie Mhondoro slept and she kept asking her lover if she'd said the wrong things to you. She was afraid you'd abandon her. In a way you did, because if you'd been there maybe you could have saved her . . . Or I'd have killed you already.'

'You're a murderer.' I grit my teeth.

'My family's been doing it for a long, long time. I've heard things about your father and his barbaric experiments with children. Unlike you, I own it. I'm proud of who I am.'

I time my next lunge – aiming for her torso – spot my moment and rush in. This time Fenella comes in to meet me and cold water from a Poseidon spell splashes my eyes. She grabs my right hand, twists, and shoves my dagger towards my shoulder. Good thing my jacket's impenetrable. I'm blinking, trying to get the water out of my eyes when Cruickshank rises up and grabs Fenella's hand.

'That's cheating,' she says. 'Vulcan's forge!'

There's a flash of purple and a sizzling grey flame erupts on the tassels of my scarf. Cruickshank lets go and swirls around in the air helplessly. I stab Fenella in the bicep and she yelps, jumping back. But I've left my dagger in her. I hold Cruickshank's burning tassels and extinguish the flame in my fist. He calms down, but falls limp to the ground.

'You stabbed me, you bitch.' Fenella casts a soliton and it hits me like a sledgehammer, throwing me into the air and then back onto the ground.

I've dropped my stick.

As I'm reaching for it, Fenella hovers over me with my dagger in her hands. It's dripping blood. Her blood. The clouds have broken and I'm looking up at the stars. 'I was going to use magic, but I think this will be more personal.' I try to scarper, but my limbs are useless. Fenella bends down to stab—

All I see's a flash of green light and the wheel of Priya's chair flying into Fenella's head. The sound of bone snapping. Fenella falls to the ground next to me. She's not moving but her eyes are open, staring at the twinkling stars. She's facing the infinite void. Blood ruins her pretty hair.

Priya wheels her chair next to me, parks and offers me a hand up.

'You move like a little old lady,' she says.

'Thanks for the save.'

'I wasn't about to let you go a second time.'

I stand up and am a bit woozy. My dagger's in the ground, on the spot next to where my head was. I pick up my walking stick but leave the dagger behind. It's of no use to me. Fenella can have it. Maybe it'll help her in whatever hell her soul's off to. I'm more worried about poor Cruickshank. He's my guy and he's taken a few big hits saving my arse. Don't know if he's going to be okay this time. I give him a wee rub and he curls up.

I'm hobbling next to Priya and we make it to the shore. Dundas has cast off on an inflatable raft already. They reach a catamaran in the distance. Too far to swim. All we can do is stand on the beach and watch the bastards sail away. They've taken my sister and I have to go after them.

VII

I'm proper seething as I watch the last of the purple flames in the castle being put out. The staff are rushing about the massive grounds like headless chickens, trying to find missing pupils. The ones that are there glare at me and Priya with suspicion. There's cages of their therapets on the lawns. I go up to them, open every single one and let the animals out.

'What are you doing?' Mr Loughty shrieks.

'I wouldn't start with her if I were you,' Priya replies.

I watch the parakeet fly away and the hedgehog potter along the grass. The tortoise is going nowhere, though.

It was a mistake sending Izwi to this bloody school. I can't believe I pushed for it. At first she didn't want to be here, but I thought it would be great for her. A chance to be a real magician and she could be in a 'safe' place where she had warmth and food. I didn't know how sick this profession was at the time. Did I do it for her or was I trying to get Izwi to fulfil my own desires? Either way, it's a disaster. She is the only thing I have left in this world and I let her slip out of my fingers with barely a fight.

'We'll get her back,' Priya says, reading my thoughts.

'I've never been good at magic, Priya, but since I've come

back, I haven't worked a single spell. Fenella had me easy. If it hadn't been for you, I'd be toast. I was pathetic.'

'We'll work on that. Together, right? We're a team, Ropa.'

I nod, but I'm not so sure. It seems I've made a series of bad moves, one after the other. The principle of compound interest applies to my errors and the price I've paid is too high. Fenella's blood isn't worth a toenail on Izwi.

I guess this is war then, and I have to turn to Carl von Clausewitz who wrote the book on it. 'Although our intellect always feels itself urged towards clearness and certainty, still our mind often feels itself attracted by uncertainty.' He also said: 'War is a conflict of great interests which is settled by bloodshed, and only in that is it different from others.'

Do I even understand what he was trying to say? I go about spouting all these strategy books I've devoured and crammed, but I've still made bad moves despite their advice. I know well enough to avoid indecision, one would rather be resolute, but how? Come on, von Clausewitz, give me something.

'We need Ms Featherstone,' says Priya.

'See the state of this place? She's not even here.'

'Trust me. We'll need her help,' she says, and the penny drops.

'You're right. One of two things are going to happen tonight. The Doric magicians will show their bellies and submit, or we can get them riled up. We can't beat Dundas alone. We need to raise an army.'

Priya gives me that disturbing grin she saves for when shit hits the fan.

*

Teachers wander about the school anxious in their fancy gowns even though the danger's passed. There's a lot of grumbling and complaining, and I remember a fair few faces from the conference at Dunvegan Castle a while back. These aren't fighters, they're tutors doing long hours, exhausted from dealing with potty-mouthed brats. I know, I was one. Still, I wish more of them had turned up instead of hiding in their supply cupboards.

This is why the few will always rule the many. Dundas and his lot were outnumbered and these guys know their magic, but few of them took a stand. The ones that did were overwhelmed and killed because they didn't have support. The whole thing's tragic.

It's after midnight by the time we get to see Calista Featherstone in the staff room in the south wing of the castle. The room is surprisingly bright and airy, more colourful than the drab castle the school's housed in. There's a U-shaped pink sofa and a large photocopier near the kitchen unit where the headteacher is stood making three cups of tea. Ms Featherstone is formidable, but I really wish I could count on my old patron Lord Samarasinghe just now. He's ruthless and has all of English magic behind him. But he's also a right wanker, and he betrayed Sir Ian Callander at the crucial moment. He can't be trusted unless he has something to gain, and right now I have nothing to give him.

'Milk and sugar?' Ms Featherstone asks. I guess this is the best time for a cuppa. 'I saw Priya snatch away your body on Calton Hill, but I never figured resurrection was possible.'

'It seems there are some things your so-called magical science doesn't know about,' I reply.

'I have my suspicions about who might have brought you back. It's the *method* I'd love to know.'

'Perhaps another time,' Priya replies uneasily.

Ms Featherstone raises her eyebrows briefly. She's in red, a double-breasted suit, and Clarks high heels.

'I've had to field calls from angry parents. They all want speak to the head. Problem is, there's only one of me,' she says. 'I have a few who are coming to pick up their children *tonight*. I was in the city for a fundraiser when all this happened. They're already calling for my resignation.'

'What're you supposed to do about a ghoul invading your school?' I say, trying my best to be sympathetic, although it grates me a bit she wasn't here to look after the kids.

'What I won't do now is get flustered,' she says. '*If you can keep your head when all about you are losing theirs and blaming it on you. Kipling.*'

Calista hands me a cup of tea and I thank her for it. I have to admire her preternatural composure.

'As far as we know, only your sister was taken,' she says. 'I'm so sorry.'

'But why her? You've got tons of pupils here. Some of them are from connected families. They'd be more suitable as bargaining chips,' Priya says.

'That lot aren't after money,' I reply. 'I wonder what we're missing. Dundas said something strange about how they didn't need to take me since they had Izwi. It must be something to do with my father. But that's speculative. We need something more substantive. Do you keep any magical artefacts at the school? Maybe something to do with transdimensional travel since we took half the Fairy Flag off them. Could be they thought it was here.'

'I have people checking our inventory. It's difficult to say with the fire, but nothing stands out yet,' Ms Featherstone replies. 'Izwi is an extremely gifted pupil, but we have a few of those. She shares your interest in necromancy, though we've been diverting her to more scientific aspects of magic which will guarantee her a solid future in the Society. But she's not of the age at which her practical magic can be of use to anyone. It'll be a good while before that happens.'

Her red lipstick leaves an imprint on her white cup. She maintains her composure, but I can tell she's just about holding it together. Moisture on her top lip, and that's not steam from the coffee. It can't be easy being the person everyone's demanding answers from. But that's what it is to be a leader, holding your shit together when everyone else is going ape.

'Henry Dundas is the Secretary of the Society of Sceptical Enquirers now. He's won it. There's nothing anyone can do about that, so why is he resorting to this kind of thing?' I ask.

'Not all practitioners in the Society are happy with that arrangement,' Ms Featherstone replies. 'There are a number that believed in Sir Ian Callander. Some wanted him gone, but I assure you none wanted him dead. He was a good man and killing him has caused a lot of anger. I don't know what Wedderburn and Hutchinson think about all this but it's time for us to put a stop to it.'

I wonder if Ms Featherstone's aware of the whole witch situation, which seems to be a big secret. These magicians have sticks up their arses and can be snooty. She was there on Calton Hill with Callander. She saved Jomo's father, Dr Maige, from certain death by getting him away from there. She's been fine with me in the past, but would she just as easily work with people like Theodosia Lovell?

'We need you to get the practitioners up north riled. Capture that Highland fury that had them march into Edinburgh back in the day,' I say. 'We need fighters, not these professionals and businesspeople you have all over the place. I mean people with sharp teeth that are willing to go all the way.'

'It's a different era, Ropa. I don't know how many we can take with us.'

'As many as you can.'

'They may come if they know Glasgow's going to resist too. Alone, as you've seen tonight, we couldn't possibly risk going against Edinburgh and St Andrews,' Ms Featherstone says. 'Glasgow has to be on board.'

This was always the fault line in Scottish magic. Aberdeen and Glasgow on one side, Edinburgh and St Andrews together; and now things have come to a head, I bloody hope that fact holds. Ms Featherstone's mobile rings and she groans, taking the call. Priya goes on her phone and sends out a text message.

I go to stand by the window and watch the people moving to and fro in the grounds of the school below. Two electric vehicles come in. I suspect it's more parents here to get their bairns.

My sister's out there. I can't go to Glasgow to rile up magicians. I have to go straight to Edinburgh and get her. All I need's a plan.

'Priya, you need to go to Glasgow and see if you can get us help from the practitioners there. I'll be off to Edinburgh where I have some knackies and rubiators from the Clan who can help.'

'The only thing you'll find waiting for you there is another grave. One that you can't crawl out of this time,' Ms Featherstone says. 'You need all the help you can get. Now, unless you're telling me you've become a more powerful magician than Ian Callander, then I suggest you stop this foolishness.'

'We already discussed this. No more doing stuff on your own,' Priya says.

'Old habits.' I back down – this time.

It grates on me, but they're right. I need to stick with what we agreed to. As von Clausewitz taught, 'firmness cannot show itself, of course, if a man keeps changing his mind.' Now I might not be a man, but I've made up my mind to try a different course of action. No more diving in without getting the team in on it. I'll kick this old habit easier than a jakey off his drink.

'That's settled then. You can use our school bus. I'll get the driver to take you all the way to Glasgow where you're to seek out Professor Cattermole at the university. Now, if you'll excuse me, ladies. I have panicked pupils, hysterical parents, and on top of that I have to call Edmund MacLeod and tell him his only daughter lies dead on the grounds of my school.'

She's stony-faced when she gets up and leaves the staff room. There'll be plenty more people dead by the time all this is done. I just have to make sure my little sister isn't one of them.

VIII

We wanted to leave straight away, but the bus had to delay till the morning because some parents in Glasgow wanted their kids returned to them. I'm on edge because every moment counts. Day's breaking and I'm standing on the drive, waiting for the driver to turn up.

It's one of those sunny winter mornings. Birds are singing in the bushes, along with a parakeet that's swearing like a trooper. In the light, the school's castle – the bits of it that haven't burnt down – looks grand. Those round turrets with triangular pennant flags flying. Priya's checking out the rising sun sending its broken rays our way through the treeline.

'How're you feeling, Ropa?' she asks.

'I'm not quite myself. Don't know how to describe it.' I stop. Can't be feeling sorry for myself when there's so much at stake.

'You're not the only one. There's things happening which I thought I'd never see. It should be anyone else but us dealing with this stuff.'

'Like who?'

'*Anyone else.* Absolutely. You've been through the most, pal.'

No idea if it's the cold or my worn-out body, but I have tremors in my hands. Didn't sleep much last night despite being put up in a nice bedroom in Ms Featherstone's house on the grounds of the school. I take my katty from my back pocket.

'What're you doing with that?'

'Practice,' I reply.

I pick up a rock from the side of the drive and choose a target, the trunk of a silver birch. My hands are trembling so much, it's hard to aim. I finally pick my moment and fire. What a miss. Not even close. I don't bother trying a second time. Something's very wrong with me if I can't do the simple things I used to take for granted. Used to be a time I hunted squirrels and rabbits with that katty. Now I can't even hit a goddamn tree.

'Come sit on my lap,' says Priya, opening up her arms. 'Now, you silly sausage.'

I relent and plonk myself down on her legs. What I'd give to go back to the way things were once upon a . . .

'I had a little sister called Aditi,' Priya says, after a pause.

'You've never mentioned her,' I reply, noting Priya used the past tense.

'She died a few months before you and I met. The big crab in the zodiac got her with its pincers. She was a fighter. I was lost when I met you. Carrying so much with me, but you filled a void that was in my heart.'

'Why didn't you ask me to find her in the everyThere?'

'She'll be reincarnated when it's time for her to come back. Maybe she'll be a bird, a fish or even a mouse. She liked mice. There's no way of knowing. That's what mum believes anyway. But I watched her in so much pain, going through treatments that wore her little body out. I was relieved when she passed. I loved her enough to know that when her time came, she should go someplace else that might be happier than here.'

I take Priya's hand in mine and say nothing at all. You get caught up in your own shit so much that you don't realize the person carrying you is also dealing with their own shit. I lean back and rest my side against her body.

'You're squishing my chebs,' she protests.

I lean back harder and we laugh so much tears stream down our faces. Okay, I've lost a lot and that's been on my mind. But I've also gained an awful lot along the way.

'You're my sister,' I say to Priya. She squeezes my hand. From now on it's going to be her, me and Izwi, all the way.

The Aberdeen School's given us an electric minibus to travel with. It's an old but well-maintained Ford, painted in the blue colour of their uniform. The school crest of a silver kelpie in its half-fish, half-horse form rising from white ocean foam is displayed on the sliding door. The seats are lusher than our last transport, so we have that to be grateful for.

'It's a real shame what happened last night,' says Dougal, our driver. 'Forty years I've been driving buses for this school. I've seen all sorts of queer things but never anything quite like that. When the fire was blazing last night . . . all I could think of was the children.'

We've got four of them travelling in the minibus with us. One of them is the redhead from last night and she moves from the back to come sit beside me. She wears a ribbon in her hair and has fine freckles all over her face and arms.

'Did you find your sister?' she asks.

'I'm working on it.'

She scrunches her face then offers me her hand.

'I'm Leana. It means Helen if you didn't know. Leana Maisie Kirkpatrick-Powrie. I'm in your sister's class.'

'Does she have friends at the school?' I want to know if Izwi's happy there or if we put her into a place where she's a fish out of water.

'Everyone except Lisa Brown, because they're both bossy and want to be right all the time.'

That sounds like the Izwi I know. A little menace. She can be a pain in every single orifice, but she loves just as fierce too. The driver puts on the radio and we have to listen to stuff about horse racing. Priya's back on her mobile bashing out messages and I decide I need to get a new phone.

'Why's your scarf like that? Can I see it?' asks Leana, pulling at Cruickshank.

I unwrap him from my neck and hand him over. The scarf's mostly intact, but the tassels have been burnt through. Cruickshank hasn't stirred since the fight. I wonder if he's recuperating or whether this is him signed out? I should have acted quicker to put out the fire. Everything I do is so slow. I need to practise my spellcraft again. Get back in the game.

As we're driving along the coast, I can't help but look out to sea in case there might be a catamaran hanging about. It's silly, I know, but I can't stop hoping they had engine failure or something. Nothing to see except a few small fishing boats. Every so often we pass by a young man or two walking together on the hard shoulder. They're all so famished, shuffling along to where they've heard there's work or food. If this was my bus, I'd let them on and drop them off in Glasgow.

The other three kids are younger than Leana. One of them's a blonde boy with brilliant blue eyes, levitating a marble above his palm. He nearly drops it every time we hit a pothole or make a turn. The other two are girls and one of them reads a picture book, while her friend is playing games on a hand-held console. Leana's brought out a wee case filled with pens, scraps of cloth, wool, string, some needles, the sort of ma-terial Gran used to keep for her knitting. She's fiddling about with Cruickshank and I want to stop her, but she's got this intentness that stops me.

A rainbow-coloured holographic butterfly floats through the bus.

'No magic on the bus. You know the rules!' Dougal shouts.

'Sorry!'

I start to nod off, feeling well zonked, but I can't bear to. Way too much on my mind still.

'You children see the William Wallace Monument yonder?' says Dougal.

It's a massive tower that looks like it could hold Rapunzel and her fancy hair. I've heard the story a thousand times about how Wallace led his men to victory at the Battle of Stirling Bridge.

'They have his sword in there. I've been to see it,' Dougal says. 'It's longer than most of yous are tall. I bet he chopped off a fair few heads with it. If he came back, no one would mess with us.'

'You're sure about that?' I ask.

'It'll be the best thing for us. He was a great leader.'

The idea of yet another person from the history books popping up fills me with dread. They did things differently back then. Most of the guys who got monuments got them because they were effective killers. They get more kudos than nurses and binmen, but we could do with less warriors and more people making sure stuff ain't falling apart.

What would William Wallace do in my pickle?

I recall he met with a gruesome end.

'Spark of Prometheus from the eternal flame of Mount Olympus, I call upon thee to light this forge of mine,' I whisper, hoping to see a white crackling spark of light.

Nothing.

I bow my head, frustrated, and close my eyes. According to the Somerville equation, you have to put your will into a spell. And that's what I tried to do with the whole finding my nexus point thing. It's like I've slid back to the very beginning. Fenella's taunts are ringing in my ears. She said that I wasn't a real magician, all because I don't have no fancy certificates or nothing like that.

'Are you trying to do a fire spell? It's easy, let me show you how,' Leana says, still fixated on Cruickshank.

'What did I say about magic on the bus? It's right there on the sign and you can all read,' Dougal says. 'I'll be telling Ms Featherstone about this.'

'I was only trying to show her.'

'He's a boy, you call him *him*,' the driver says.

'I'm a girl,' I sigh.

Must be taxing shepherding these kids around everywhere.

The driver's checking me through his mirror. It's like a rearview, but because we're in a bus, it doesn't see out the back. It allows the driver to monitor his passengers. He takes his eyes off the road several times before he's satisfied. I figure I might as well play a few tunes and try to get my mbira working properly.

A tune doesn't come to me immediately but I place the instrument on my lap and keep my hands on it. What's wrong with me? I know a hundred songs. I try to pluck the keys but my fingers are shaking. It's all too much. I close my eyes and do the centring breathing exercises Dr Checkland taught me to help with panic attacks. In these moments it feels like I'm one of those people who wake up and discover they're in a coffin and they start banging away screaming and shouting, but no one can hear them.

Breathe.

You're safe.

My fingers begin to move, almost of their own volition. It doesn't feel like I'm controlling them, but they very deliberately move across the metal keys of my mbira. Softly. A tune so low and quiet, it's barely audible to me under the sound of the engine and the horse racing commentary. The keys are yielding and pliant under my thumbs. It takes me a few seconds to catch the tune I'm jamming because it's automatic. I play the kutsinhira, concentrating on the top notes on the left side of my keyboard, before briefly straying into the base notes. The mbira's still off-key and the sound is strange to my ear, unlike anything I've ever heard before. There's a force to it, like it's pushing back against my body. The vibrations in the air are harder, and if I were to play louder I'd be blown away, so I keep it down. I wonder, is it my choice of music? I'm playing Mbuya Dyoko. Her first name was Beaular, Mbuya just means grandmother, and she was Zimbabwe's first female mbira recording artist. Gran introduced me to her beats. Her style never appealed to me at the time because it felt so dated and I was more into contemporary mbira players. But now I play her song 'Makuwerere' and begin to understand the hints of sadness behind what sounds like a celebratory tune. Maybe that's why I didn't like it, 'cause it was hiding something. And now I sink into the rhythm, tracing the patterns of Mbuya Dyoko's composition with my own fingers. I lose myself in her. I'm no longer really me, but an echo of someone else. A person I never met. It's as though the music overwhelms me and I become a different person, a conduit of their style, their artistry, and with it aspects of Mbuya Dyoko's own creative personality.

The minibus swerves, wheels screeching on the tar. 'Bloody hell.'

The children cry out and Priya, who was drifting off, wakes with a start.

'Jesus Christ!' she yells down the bus.

'Don't you see them?' Dougal says, accelerating, which pushes us all back in our seats.

'I've never seen birds like that,' Priya shouts, staring out the window. 'This is not good. What on Earth is going on?'

'You're supposed to be the magician!'

'Drive faster. Go, go, go.'

'*Ropa!*'

I'm still playing, lost. I don't care about the dodgy driving or speeding. It's bliss being connected to someplace else in some other time. In the corner of my eye, I see dark things rushing beside the minibus. They fly like a murmuration of starlings seeking to overwhelm our transport. I hear a sound like rain hitting metal as the swarm strikes the roof of the minibus.

But I'm zen, playing my song without a care in the world.

The murmuration darkens the light inside the minibus until only pinpricks reach through.

'An umbrella or armour, strong and sturdy, around this craft Soteria wield your protection,' Priya incants, placing her hand against the glass. There's a strong entropic shift and the darkened interior of the bus glows green.

She's winging it, since instead of addressing the threat, it's a broad-spectrum spell invoking the goddess of protection. Magic is the product of will, and you get less out of it if you don't quite know what you're dealing with.

The dark bird-like swarm outside squawks and makes a dreadful noise. They look like murderous corvids diving at us, only to be repelled by an invisible barrier. But more of them swoop in, a few of them get through, and they keep attacking until soon the shield Priya conjured has holes all over it. The kids are panicking, yelling and screaming. Most of them have their phones out, filming. Fuck, I need to—

'Ropa, snap out of it. I can't hold this spell together. We need to choir up.'

'Hurry up with whatever you're doing because something big's coming our way— Oh dear God,' Dougal yells, before muttering that psalm about the valley of the shadow of death.

The kids are proper bawling, and finally I snap out of the zone, lifting up my head in time to see through the windscreen a rushing swarm of black bird-like creatures heading straight for us. It's like some shit from Alfred Hitchcock's *The Birds* and they're coming at us in a temper. I drop my mbira and try to think of a spell from the books I read which could protect us.

'They're closing in,' Priya shouts. 'Ropa, recite with me, you pupils too, I need you all with me on this one: Periphas and Acanthis of beak and wing, into this dreadful storm we beseech your—'

Before the spell is even done, the dark, flying things vanish quicker than a puff of smoke. There's nothing but tar and bush around us. I'm thrown forward and hit the seat in front of me with my head as Dougal slams on the brakes. Leana luckily bumps into me and the vehicle skids for a bit before halting in the middle of the empty motorway.

'What was that, even?' Dougal asks, his hands on his head.

'Something the Black Lord sent our way,' Priya replies. 'Luckily, we found the right spell in time to dispel it.'

'Those were not birds,' Dougal says.

Statement of the bleeding obvious. I touch the bump on my head and check on the kids. A bit of shock and some bruises, but nothing broken. If this is what we're up against, our odds have slipped from minuscule to zero.

IX

This is my first time out here, like ever, but Glasgow's a real city where Edinburgh's a town that's had too much processed sugar. All my life, I've been taught to thumb my nose at Weegies, but I have to admit, where we have style they have size. The way the city sprawls into the distance makes me kinda wish I'd been born and raised here. Looks like a place with nooks and crannies one could explore forever. Priya did uni here and she seems comfy with it all.

Everything here's bigger and better. We have Hearts and Hibs, they have Celtic and Rangers. We had finance, they had industry. I press my head on the window of the minibus as we drive through the centre.

'I'll drop you two off at Buchanan Bus Station. What you do from there's up to you, but gauging from what I've seen coming after yous, I'd recommend you keep your heads down,' Dougal says. He's been sombre the rest of the journey. 'In all my years driving a bus . . . Get out.'

'Thanks for the ride,' Priya says.

'Just go. Please.'

I'm about to get off when Leana hands me back Cruickshank, who now has some silver tassels that she must have taken off her own school scarf. Oh my God, I could weep with joy. The scarf has been stitched up and he looks uglier for it. 'A warrior needs a few battle scars,' I say, before rolling him up and putting him in my pocket instead of round my neck as I usually do. I want him to have a rest. He deserves it. 'Thank you.'

Then Leana holds out her hand like a little grown-up person. 'Good luck finding your sister,' she says.

'Yeah, I appreciate that.' I shake her hand and get out of the minibus.

Unlike Edinburgh, which I know like the back of my hand, I'm not quite sure where we are. But I know rough-looking types when I see them and so I tell Priya we need to get a move on. In Edinburgh my former gang the Clan runs things in the city, but I've heard Glasgow's on another level, having bred guys like Paul Ferris and Arthur Thompson and the legendary Tartan Pimpernel, Walter Douglas. These were serious bampots and our lot in Edinburgh are tame by comparison.

Takes me a second to realize I'm bricking it.

Priya on the other hand's a real cucumber and waves to some lad who shouts something random at her. We cross the road and I feel a wee bit less nervous. I might as well be a country bumpkin, though. Litter blows along the pavements like tumbleweed in an old western. The place is livened only by the banners of the old king and queen that hang across the streets.

'We have to meet Esfandiar at the Tea Rooms,' Priya says.

I freeze on the spot. 'No.'

'I've been messaging him and he wants to see you. He needs closure.'

'You should have told me beforehand, Priyanka. I can't deal with that right now.'

'There'll be a meeting of Glasgow's most powerful magicians tonight and he'll be speaking there. We need his help too.'

I tap my walking stick onto the ground a couple of times, but I don't see any way out of it. We're here now. So many thoughts are turning in my head. It's so overwhelming. There's so many ghosts in the centre of Glasgow. Could be because it's a larger city. More people means more ghouls, though I'd been taught Edinburgh was the ghost capital of the world. They blink in and out of view. Ghosts struggle to tether in our world, so they usually get sucked back into the everyThere for a fraction of a second after they get back into our realm. Reckon there's good pickings here for folk in the ghostalkering trade.

To distract myself from the ghosts, I ask Priya about the place we're going and she tells me about Glasgow's long history of tearooms, which started a couple of centuries back to help get the Weegies off the bevvy. There was a time Glasgow had over three hundred of them. That's a lot of cuppas going down gullets and we're talking before the humble teabag was ever a thing. The one where we're to meet Esfandiar is run-down, same as all the shops around it. Most of them are already shuttered.

Apparently some guy called Mackintosh who was rejected by the Lord Kelvin Institute, Glasgow's school of magic, for being 'distracted, absent-minded, and unlikely to amount to anything much', turned his hand to something more suitable for his temperament. He became a rather decent architect and artist in his day.

'Nowadays, the Lord Kelvin Institute likes to claim him as one of ours. They point to the school's emphasis on rigour as being the reason why his buildings were modern and restrained, following simple patterns, compared to the more elaborate works of his contemporaries,' she says, as I hold the door open for her.

'Sounds like a load of bollocks to me,' I reply.

That's kind of how these places go. They kick you out, and then when you make it, they suddenly fall in love with you, open their arms and try to make you out to be some sort of symbol of how progressive they are. Mackintosh was lucky to get out of Scottish magic with his soul intact. His decaying tea rooms are a remnant of the old grandeur of Scotland in the Empire and they haven't stood the test of time in this modern age. Everything about them is dated and retro. It's not deliberate, and in the winter gloom the decor seems a sad reminder of better days. There are stains on the peeling wallpaper. Bits of the ceiling plaster are cracked.

I take one look at the menu: 'Who leaves their house to drink tea at these prices?'

'You can't put a price on a good cup of tea,' Priya replies.

'Yes, you can.'

Given the fact that half the country is starving, that can only mean they have a certain clientele. The kind with very deep pockets. There's hardly anyone in here except for Esfandiar Soltani, who's on the four-seater table near the entrance. He has his back to us, shoulders hunched, facing the wall. The poet seems diminished in his high-backed chair and the emptiness of the tea rooms only enhances the effect. I approach and notice there's a full cup of tea on the table, no longer steaming. It's as though he poured it and forgot all about it.

I approach on his side, but he's lost, staring at the wall; he doesn't even notice me. His mouth is slightly open, eyes glazed. Priya moves the chair beside him and Esfandiar startles, looking as if he doesn't recognize her, and then quickly apologizes.

'I, erm, I forgot to move the chair. How silly of me,' he says.

'It's not a problem, seriously,' replies Priya.

'Oh, but it is,' he says, banging the table with his fist, and then he bursts into tears.

I go over and hug him as he weeps. Priya strokes his arm gently and it's a good few minutes before he regains composure, sniffling and dabbing his eyes with a linen napkin.

'I'm making a fool of myself,' he says. 'Is that really you, Ropa Moyo?'

'Mostly me, but not a hundred percent,' I reply.

Esfandiar looks up at me, a film of tears in his eyes. His make-up is smudged, mascara round his eyes, streaks on his cheeks. The napkin's come away stained with colours. Esfandiar is a man of deep and intense feelings which he wears on both his sleeves.

'When you part from your friend, you grieve not;

For that which you love most in him may be clearer in his absence, as the mountain to the climber is clearer from the plain.

And let there be no purpose in friendship save the deepening of the spirit.

For love that seeks aught but the disclosure of its own mystery is not love but a net cast forth: and only the unprofitable is caught.'

When he is lost, Esfandiar often bursts into verse. He's one of those old people who's crammed full of this stuff. Much like how I memorize strategy, only more beautiful.

'That's a little one from Kahlil Gibran. I've been turning to *The Prophet* these days. Its verse soothes my suffering a little. But, uplifting and eternal as it may be, seeing your face has given me greater joy. If only you knew how my darlings Ian and Melsie, both of whom are lost, loved you so dearly and so truly, then you would understand why it moves me so. But I am an old man, and you are young, and my words are laced with sentimentality. Forgive me.'

'It's good to see you again. I—' My voice breaks.

He pats my hand and directs me to sit on the chair next to him. His eyes are bright and a smile is on his face, though the furrows on his brow remain. This is why I didn't want to see him. I can't take away the pain he's in. He is a widower, his husband lost on Calton Hill. I recall Callander holding his good arm in the air, whispering Esfandiar's name, and then bringing down the hill atop himself in the ultimate act of sacrifice. But what is sacrifice without love?

'Did he suffer?' Esfandiar asks.

The image of Callander's burnt arm fills my mind. I recall the smell of it. Like an overcooked Sunday roast. How bone showed under burnt flesh and Scotland's foremost magician seemed lost to a greater power he could not comprehend.

'It was quick,' I lie.

'Small mercies. A good death is rarer than gold.' Esfandiar folds his napkin. 'We must be thankful for those at least.'

I know what it's like to be in this place of loss. How it overwhelms you, shrouding everything in darkness. It used to be kind of abstract for me, but now it's real, it resides in my battered body. I rest my stick against the table. I am so tired.

A waiter appears and places menus in front of us, which I ignore. He says something about a house special, but I'm really not listening.

'I'm not waiting about,' Priya says. 'She'll have your soup of the day, and I'll try the wartime special.'

'I'm not that hungry,' Esfandiar says.

'Give him a muffin,' Priya says firmly. 'You both will eat something.'

'Perhaps you might want to try the scones?' the waiter asks.

'Yes, and some of your vintage port,' Esfandiar adds. 'I might as well.'

'A small glass,' Priya says, peering at Esfandiar.

When I first met Esfandiar Soltani at Dunvegan Castle, he dressed flamboyantly in bright, sometimes garish colours. Now he's in a drab black Nehru suit. The nail polish on his fingers is flaked and needs redoing. It looks like he's been chewing on his nails too, the state they're in.

'They didn't even have a body for me to hold and kiss one last time,' Esfandiar says. 'I would give *everything* for one brief moment.'

I take his hand and squeeze.

'Seeing you here gives me the vain and foolish hope that maybe Ian will pop up too, you know. I've even considered going to a medium – half of them are charlatans, I am aware, but still.'

Callander's not coming back anytime soon. The everyThere, the realm next to ours, is where the newly departed hang out like in an airport lounge. It was closed off to my grandmother Melsie Mhondoro, and I am certain they shut Callander out too. If you cross the everyThere, it's impossible to come back . . . I did, but I doubt anyone else is using my father's questionable methods.

'When we were on the way to Calton Hill, your husband told me that you were the best thing in his life,' I say.

'You're lying to me and I thank you for it,' Esfandiar replies, detecting my bullshit. 'Here's my port; it too shall tell me sweet nothings.'

My stomach sinks. I was just trying to help and now I seem to have succeeded in making him feel awful. Sometimes I don't know what to say. We've been amputated and we're both still bleeding. And Esfandiar should have a good moan 'cause it sucks; that it happens to everyone doesn't make it any less sucky. Only when it happens to *you* can you even begin to wrap your head around how big it is.

'We grieve and we limp on,' Esfandiar says, raising his glass and turning round to toast the empty restaurant.

'Aye,' Priya responds, raising her glass of water.

There've been riots in the city, starving folks gone past griping on the internet, taking their grievances onto the street. And here we are cosy, waiting to be served. This world, man.

'The king is coming to Scotland,' Esfandiar says. 'I don't know why on Earth he'd visit at a time like this. I can't imagine his horse and carriage going through George Street without having excrement lobbed at it.'

'They wouldn't dare,' Priya replies.

'The separatists are at it again. Painting their symbols in

alleyways. Holding secret meetings in the Govanhill Inn and getting up to all sorts. Those with country estates or second homes by the coast are packing up and leaving.'

'That's the least of our worries,' I say.

I'll let the bigwigs and those types worry about matters of state. I've got my own fish to fry and my charcoal's all wet. When our tea and scones arrive, I don't much feel like eating. Priya insists and we have no choice. Esfandiar's nibbling. Seems like a right effort with each mouthful, but he tries for her sake.

He's all fragile, but we do need him to get things moving with the magicians in Glasgow. Esfandiar always described himself as a third-rate magician, but his presence should remind Glasgow's magicians of their loyalty to Sir Ian Callander. Let's just hope that will be enough to sway them, because if Glasgow tumbles Aberdeen's got no chance against Henry Dundas and his lot. No amount of scone's about to change that equation.

'I keep thinking I should have gone with Ian,' Esfandiar says. 'But that's just my vanity. Instead he sent me away with this.'

He fishes into his jacket pocket and brings out a neatly folded, yellowish section of the Fairy Flag. He unfolds it and holds it up. You can see the section where I tore it playing tug of war with Jomo at Arniston House in Gorebridge. In this empty restaurant, it looks like a discarded rag.

'They asked me to bring this, so the Glaswegian magicians can keep it safe from the Viscount Melville. I am happy to be rid of it.'

'Let me hold on to it for you,' I volunteer, eager to have it in my possession. We've gone to a lot of trouble over this artefact and I want to make sure it's in safe hands and I trust my own over anyone else's.

Priya gives me the subtlest of nods. No need to burden this poor poet. He's been through enough as it is.

X

Wellington on a horse with a traffic cone on his head's an image that sticks in the mind. I've become wary of dead guys with statues on Scotland's streets, seeing how they seem to fancy coming back, but the Duke of Wellington was Irish and they have better sense than that. At least I hope so. We're standing by the statue, in front of the great big columns of the Gallery of Modern Art on the Royal Exchange Square, and I get the feeling we ain't about to be tourists. The place looks like a big temple. Dedicated to the worship of what exactly, I wonder.

A pair of coppers on horseback trot past and I look ahead, resisting the urge to turn aside. You don't want to act suspicious, these guys can nab you for any reason.

The gallery apparently is home to the vestigial League of Esoteric Philosophers, who are for all intents and purposes the local branch of the Society of Sceptical Enquirers. Esfandiar explains that for nearly a century Glaswegian and Edinburgher magic developed separately and it took until the nineteenth century before they were rolled into one institution. Something about Queen Victoria getting involved and settling the matter.

The Weegies didn't fancy giving up their perks and privileges in order to be run by toffs in Edinburgh.

It seems their motivation to finally join up may also have had something to do with the Royal Bank of Scotland, because the building they use for their headquarters used to be a bank branch.

'Do we get in via a crack in one of the columns?' I ask.

'Glaswegians are too practical for that sort of thing. Someone will open the door and let us in when they are ready,' Esfandiar replies. 'No secret entrances and hidden dimensions here.'

'Glasgow's magic was always more grounded, more interested in solving problems in industry and trade than lofty theory. That's why Lord Kelvin produces more sensible magicians than the Edinburgh School,' says Priya, who's clearly biased.

The grand building was built by William Cunninghame, a tobacco lord who made good mint from the slavery triangle thing. It was enough to plonk this neoclassical monument in the heart of Scotland's largest city. But his money and good taste in architecture wasn't enough to stop Cunninghame popping his clogs as we all must one day. And at some point the Royal Bank of Scotland bought the building, and succeeded in getting the League of Esoteric Philosophers to make use of the facility, just as they did with the Society of Sceptical Enquirers at St Andrew Square.

'When the bank moved out to Buchanan Street, they expected the magicians to come along, but the Glasgow practitioners were rather fond of their location, so they refused to go,' says Esfandiar. 'In their spendthrift fashion, they thought it wasteful to buy the building outright, but they insisted on holding on to their little section and having that included in the deed. So, no one can ever own the whole building since they refuse to leave. This has put off a lot of big corporations over the years, and that's why it's a gallery instead.'

The doors swing open and we go up the steps to find Euan Cleghorn, the head of Glasgow's Library, waiting to meet us. Cleghorn raises his eyebrows when he sees me, but if he has any gripes he keeps those to himself. It's the briefest of slips, 'cause soon enough he's got both hands on Esfandiar's shoulders and pulls him in for a warm embrace before shutting the doors and following us inside.

I walk into the art gallery where I spot Dr Pythagoras Maige standing in front of a large painting that looks like a spreadsheet with stuffed animals in the rows and columns. Jomo's father is no longer in his red robes. Attired in a patch-pocket blazer and black chinos, he may as well be a middle-management type out pretending to enjoy art they know nothing about. Though he does make a good show of concentrating on the piece.

I go up to him, and he tilts his head.

'I don't understand any of this. Why not just draw something beautiful?' he says.

'There's different kinds of beauty,' I reply.

'I'm sor—' Almost, but he's not the type of person to apologize and so he interrupts himself. 'These are incredible times we find ourselves in. My wife and I had to flee to Glasgow. Edinburgh's not safe for us anymore.'

'This city's hardly better,' Cleghorn says, but I'm certain he knows it's not the rioters Dr Maige is getting away from. It's his own son, Jomo.

'We are grateful for your hospitality.'

Once Dr Maige was in charge of Scotland's most important magical library. Now he's in Glasgow sponging off the very institution whose books Calton Hill Library stole in order to enhance their place in the snooty practitioner pecking order. It must sting asking for the help of people you knowingly shafted. But if Cleghorn's bitter, he's not showing it.

Maige looks somewhat contrite. He doesn't carry himself the way he did in those flowing red robes of his. There was a time when he was a stickler for the rules, but when Dundas put his neck on the chopping block, it was amazing how quickly Dr Maige dispensed with all that. Jomo's a coward, and that's a trait he inherited from his father. I want to tell him something to this effect, but kicking a beaten dog's got no thrills for me right now.

I scan around the gallery. There's an exhibition on. A large banner with writing about Mongolian graffiti artist Khosbayar who's on a world tour with his Eternal Winter collection.

'Let's not keep them waiting, Esfandiar,' Cleghorn says, and he proceeds to lead us deeper into the gallery. 'Why are these two here?'

'We have a message from Aberdeen. You'll have heard of what happened there?'

'My phone was ringing off the hook last night.'

'Yet no one came.'

'I am a librarian, not a magician. Let's see if you can find someone more suitable to raise their head above the parapet.'

Dr Maige follows our group, sheepish in a way I've never seen before. A head librarian who lost his library. I sense his insecurity, the way he keeps looking around, pretending to have some interest in the art.

He eventually ambles over to me. 'Could you maybe try to talk to Jomo and convince him to leave that dreadful cult? They brainwashed him,' Dr Maige says.

'And whose fault is that?' I snap. 'Your son kidnapped my little sister, so I don't exactly owe you any favours.'

Dr Maige lowers his head and shuts his eyes for a brief while. He was hard on Jomo until the wee fella snapped and crossed over to the dark side. Now he wants me to fix this for him? Where do I even start? For a mathematician, Pythagoras Maige seems to have very little understanding of cause and effect. Even less, the ironclad law of unintended consequences. I feel angry that his ill-treatment of my best friend caused a chunk of this mess. Maybe I should have been the one standing up for Jomo. I don't know anymore.

'Have you heard of Walter Stirling, Ropa Moyo?' Cleghorn asks, turning back to face us.

'Should I have?' I reply.

'Few in the east of Scotland have, but out here we remember his brilliance. He was an avid collector of magical texts, alongside other books of the more general sort. Unlike your contemporary magical libraries, Stirling's collection was open to the public. But Glasgow City Council complained that lending books to housewives was leading to them casting spells on enemies and making a nuisance of themselves, and so he was banned from loaning out grimoires and the like.'

'I could never allow such a thing,' Dr Maige says in alarm. 'And look where it got you.'

It's a bit harsh, but given their history, it's understandable.

'There was a brief and glorious period when the library and League cohabited in this very building,' Cleghorn proudly declares. 'Now, this way, if you will.' We pass under a massive cupola, which must be dope when there's sunlight pouring in during the summer. The Society headquarters in Edinburgh has a cupola too, so this seems to be another competition between the two.

Euan Cleghorn takes us into Stirling's Library, which is housed within the Gallery of Modern Art. Back when I was a rookie, I'd have been impressed by the folks waiting in the room; now grand old buildings with stuffy folk don't have that effect on me. You come to realize something dark lurks behind the pageantry and elegance.

A ghost shuffles across the room and goes through a painting of a toilet hanging on the wall.

Professor Fergus Cattermole's at the head of a table with five people sitting around it. He opens his mouth briefly in surprise when he sees me, then collects himself. Three men on the left, two women on the right, leaving two empty chairs at the table. He's droning on about something important-sounding, but I've been around magicians long enough to know it's likely hot air. We're in a small and rather unimpressive room with bright tapestries hanging on the walls. Apart from that, we might as well be in a linen cupboard.

Cleghorn directs Esfandiar to sit opposite Cattermole, while he takes the last remaining seat.

I'm content standing, but I can tell Dr Maige's sullenly accepting his new station. It seems that the honours of his former office don't transfer to his person. A head librarian without a library is a butt-naked beggar. Chickens roosting and all that jazz.

When Professor Cattermole's finally done talking he stops and smiles at Esfandiar Soltani. Though his lips are drawn back, there's something lacking in this expression. This is not the genial Glaswegian academic of times past, but a wolf, an alpha baring teeth and asserting dominance. I've grown to learn that beside the outward politeness and shows of civility, Scottish magic is a dog-eat-dog world governed by the pursuit of power above all else.

'We are honoured tonight by our guests from Edinburgh. These are difficult circumstances, but we are always happy when they grace us with their presence,' Cattermole says.

'On the rare occasions they deign to come our way, since they always expect us to come to them,' says a man with white hair and eyebrows.

'Now is not the time for old hurts, Mr Laidlaw. When the Society calls, it is our honour to assist as best we can.'

The other magicians are very tense and I notice none of them face Esfandiar directly. It's as if his grief is too repulsive for them to bear. The wrinkles on his face are etched with sorrow. Sometimes folks don't want to have to deal with that. Esfandiar gathers himself and tries to sit up straight to demonstrate strength, but he's too broken and it shows. Where his dead husband had a way of bending the room towards himself, the poet seems to want to hide away in his garret.

'And you, Ms Moyo, have more lives than my house cat,' Professor Cattermole says. 'We heard you'd fallen on Calton Hill.'

'You heard wrong,' I reply. 'Your friend Calista Featherstone sends her greetings. The Doric School was attacked and you lot didn't come to help.'

'Distance prevented us from doing so.' Cattermole shifts uneasy in his chair despite his composed response.

Something's felt off since we walked in and I'm wary. Has the allegiance of Scottish magic held or is it about to snap? Cleghorn prompts Esfandiar to begin.

'You were all good friends of my husband,' he says. 'And you know he was a man of honour and courage. While he is no longer with us . . .' The poet falters, his chin trembling. 'We need your help to right this wrong and free Edinburgh from the Dundas despotism.'

'But he is now the rightful Secretary of the Society of Sceptical Enquirers,' an older woman sat diagonal from Cleghorn says in a clipped accent.

'That's not true,' Priya says.

'New information has come to us,' says Cattermole and he sweeps his arm across the table. In its wake a mist forms in the air and from within the fog grey figures materialize. There's no landscape, and the figures have ill-defined faces, but they have an uncanny resemblance to the folks who were there the day Callander died. One particular figure stands out, starkly resolved in the foggy image. It is Dr Maige, a slight red glow marking his garments.

'*No, wait.*' His image is quivering and uneven in the fog. '*The rules are archaic, and they were not designed to factor in a former secretary being brought back from the dead. Technically this is an interesting position to be in, and so the rules must be reinterpreted to cater for this unexpected event.*'

This was the moment Jomo's father sold Callander down the river to save his own hide. There's shame on his face now as his exact words are replayed to us. It was he who sanctioned the duel; otherwise Henry Dundas could not legitimately claim to be head of Scottish magic, even if he harmed Sir Ian Callander. Dr Maige made that possible. Esfandiar shoots him a look of alarm and disappointment. We are already divided when we should be moving closer towards working against a common enemy.

'They kidnapped my sister,' I say, trying to shift things away from the events on Calton Hill.

'She is a student at a school of magic and so the secretary is well within his rights to press her into his service if he sees fit. There is precedent,' Cleghorn says, dismissive. 'Listen, we have established that the Viscount Melville has no desire to do us harm.'

'You've got to be fucking kidding me.' I bristle.

'We intend to preserve harmony with Edinburgh.'

As von Clausewitz warned, 'The conqueror is always a lover of peace; he would prefer to take over our country unopposed.' They make up the rules as they go along and we get them shoved up our bumholes.

We are too late. Dundas was a shrewd political operator who rose to the top of the Westminster machine back when no other Scotsman could even come close. He was deft at playing people off, knowing what they desired and using that against them. And he would have realized that our only chance against him was roping in Glasgow. Glasgow and Aberdeen needed to stand together and reject his leadership. I figure he's given Glasgow the carrot and, to emphasize his point, Aberdeen's got the stick. The old divide and rule tactic from the days of the Empire. How easy it is to draw a wedge between two groups with common cause against you, getting them to turn on each other for crumbs instead.

'What did Henry Dundas promise you?' I ask.

'Young lady, how dare you?' Mr Laidlaw protests.

'Priya, we need to go,' I say, opening the door.

Esfandiar looks surprised, but he was never given to getting involved in the messy politics of Scottish magic. It takes a while for him to realize what is happening.

'We have reverted back to our status as an independent entity. The League of Esoteric Philosophers will henceforth no longer be affiliated with the Society of Sceptical Enquirers. Glasgow will chart her own course and keep her wealth instead of submitting to Edinburgh,' Professor Cattermole declares boldly. 'But, Esfandiar, dear friend, you are now in possession of half of the Fairy Flag. I sense its power radiating from within this room. If you would be so kind as to hand it over, we could then fulfil our end of the bargain with the Secretary.'

There it is then, the stab in the back. The Glaswegians have been given the illusion of freedom under a new order. It all seems so neat and clever and clean. Cattermole and his fellows appear satisfied with themselves. Maybe they'll enjoy the cream off membership subscriptions and the like for a bit, but I know these things won't last. They're a bunch of melts, the lot of them. I touch Priya's arm and we hurry out the door before they learn I'm the one with the Fairy Flag.

XI

Me and Priya burst out the art gallery and back onto the streets of Glasgow. I let her lead 'cause she knows what's what and where's where in this city. We go round the back of the building and under an archway with a white sign for Royal Exchange Square and find ourselves on a pedestrianized thoroughfare. There's a blue police telephone box that briefly makes me hope a travelling Time Lord could bail us out. We'd make the perfect companions, but only if it was one of the Scotsmen.

'We shouldn't have left Esfandiar there,' Priya says.

'He'll be safe. They can't touch Scotland's Makar without creating an outrage. And I don't think he's cut out for all this running about.'

I say this with the handle of the walking stick chafing the palm of my hand. We bust a gut, making a couple of turns in order to throw off anyone who may have come after us. No idea where she's taking me, but I don't think it matters right now. We're some place on Mitchell Street, according to the sign, near a disused multistorey car park. All along the way are sandstone buildings and old office blocks. There're a few shops that don't look too healthy in this narrow lane.

'Let's head over to Argyle Street. We can shake off anyone in the Central Station,' Priya says. 'I would never have thought in a million years the head of Lord Kelvin was a rat.'

'We'll figure something out,' I gasp as we near the bottom of the road.

Three mountain bikes skid from Argyle Street into our little lane, blocking our way.

'Ropa, hop onto my lap right now,' Priya says.

It's Nathair Walsh, the deputy head boy of the Edinburgh School, along with Lewis Wharncliffe, also a student there, and the only one wearing a helmet. Lewis was someone I once thought of as a friend. Can't trust no one among this lot. The last rider, looking furious, eyes red, is Avery MacDonald, a St Andrews student who also happened to be Fenella MacLeod's boyfriend. He clenches his jaw and there's daggers in his glare.

Dundas roped in some little henchmen to help with his nefarious schemes. Young men looking to be a part of something great.

'Look who it is, boys, Priyanka Kapoor and her pathetic girlfriend,' Nathair says. He's clearly the leader and likes to flaunt it. There's red scars on his face like he walked into a thorny bush some time ago. 'Everywhere the two of you go there's trouble for us. Well, the gloves are off this time.'

'You killed Fenella,' Avery growls. He appears to be suffering. Seems like even the worst people have folks who love them enough to grieve. That trick we do of glossing over the bad when it comes to people close to us and exaggerating it for the ones we hate.

'Boohoo, cry me a river,' I reply. 'Maybe you can get your boss to bring her back. Isn't that what you lot are up to?'

'Dundas will only bring back people who've distinguished themselves in science, art, business or war, so they can be gods to guide us into a glorious new age,' Avery says.

'You're all eejits.'

Priyanka snickers and I can't help but join her. These kids with a half-decent education are so easily swayed by fancy-sounding, recycled phrases. 'Glorious new ages' have been a schtick since the dawn of time. They consume this crap and it turns their brain to mush, so they can be used as cannon fodder. I almost feel sorry for them. Where Avery's face is contorted in anger and pain, Lewis is far more casual. He's the picture of someone who's in too deep with nothing personal at stake, but he can't back out now, so he tries to appear invested to his peers. But he's doing just about as much as required and nothing more.

That means it's only Avery and Nathair we really have to worry about.

'Give us the Fairy Flag and we'll let you go. We know you have it,' Nathair says. I guess it's back to business.

'Fenella's family won that,' Avery says. It's all about his dead gf.

'Yes, yes, Avery. That too,' Nathair says without the enthusiasm. No real sympathy for his pal. Boarding school produces more than its fair share of psychopaths.

'Onto my lap *now*,' Priya says.

Before I even land a bright green light explodes in front of the riders, causing them to shield their eyes. I'm crossways in Priya's lap, grabbing my katty, and we're already moving. Ballsy stunt by Priya – she charges head-on through the bikes and knocks Lewis down as we clatter onto Argyle Street, swerving past a horse-drawn carriage, and making the driver wave his fist and shout rather inappropriate comments about our genitalia.

Couldn't give a toss 'cause we're on this rocket, Priya's wheelchair powered by Helios's own horses. We're not dragging the sun along, we're getting our arses out of here. I take aim with my katty, since I can't do no magic, and fire one off, only grazing Avery's quiff. Not that it stops him pedalling hard, and Nathair replies with a sepia thermosphere that rushes over us and singes the shutters of a fast-food outlet.

Glasgow Central Station is directly ahead. It sits atop a bridge above us as we burrow into a dark, dank tunnel filled with jakeys and junkies, reeking of piss and despair.

'What kind of fucking wheelchair is that?' a homeless man in a sleeping bag says.

'Electric,' someone replies as we zoom past.

'Hold on tight,' says Priya.

Priya leans to the right, causing her left wheel to come off the ground and neatly swerving us into the station entrance. She has a mad grin on her face and I figure she must know something I don't. Takes a fraction of a second for me to realize that the folks on the streets might not care too much for a wheelchair beyond making a casual remark, but bikes are worth something, and she's gotten them three into the thick of it.

'You came here on purpose,' I say as we roll onto the concourse of the old station where even more homeless people are sleeping or milling about.

'I did outreach work here when I was at uni. I know some of these people, but if they don't know you, there's trouble.'

A loud commotion ensues behind us. There's a fair bit of shouting, threats and cursing. A bike clatters onto the ground.

'Get away from me, you creep,' Nathair yells.

Then an almighty scream follows. We didn't think this through. The folks at Glasgow Central can handle your ordinary thugs, no problem. But these three are trainee magicians and not averse to hurting people.

Priya looks over her shoulder and I know she's thinking the same. But we can't turn back because Avery vaults through the air and onto the concourse, headed straight for us. I aim my katty and fire my last rock, catching him on the chest, but he's so angry he rides on regardless. That's likely to hurt in the morning.

Priya's on the move and we find ourselves out of the station in front of a modern building with loads of glass.

'They're gaining on us,' I say.

'I don't know what spell they're using on those wheels, but it's impressive,' she replies.

We zoom into a junction, and I can see Avery incanting something. I try an anemoic wind spell to put him off, but I might as well be blowing out birthday candles. There's a bright blue soliton signatured into an armoured fist, which punches the right side of our wheelchair. It's like being hit by a hurricane and we're thrown into the air, Priya going one way, my stick the other, and my feet are above my head, gear pouring out of my backpack.

I'm crying out when I hit the tarmac hard and bounce a

couple of times. Priya slams into the glass front of an office block, just as Avery skids to a halt, already dismounting. My side hurts and I try to get up, lurching onto my knees, just as my mbira drops onto the pavement on the other side of the road with an almighty twang, all the keys striking the ground at once.

Priya's just lifted herself up onto her side. She can't rise further and her wheelchair is out of reach.

Lewis and Nathair stop behind Avery, who has his fists clenched. Avery is a scion of the Clan MacDonald and has that old-school Celt vengeance thing about him. Fuck me.

'Good job,' Nathair says. 'You should have seen how I burnt that guy's face back there. We'll do the same to these cows.'

Lewis takes off his helmet and runs his hand through his hair.

The sky above us darkens. There's a subtle change in the air, not quite an entropic shift, but a different kind of energy. It's as if the fabric of space is splitting. This makes me even more feart than I am of these boys, 'cause there's a wrongness about that darkening void opening up like a hungry mouth. I crawl over to Priya, every bone in my body hurting like hell.

'Ain't this a right old nip,' Priya remarks dryly.

I reach her, spent but desperately looking for a way out. A manhole. Anything.

'Finish them off, Avery. Get your revenge,' Nathair Walsh urges him on.

Avery steps forward and incants, the air around him crackling the sparks of lightning, and I know well enough we're going to get smitten the old-school way. Priya's countering, threading a negative charge that makes the hairs on my arms rise, static on my clothes. The mouth in the sky flips and dark things fall out of the void, rushing towards us. It's those corvid-like creatures that attacked us on the motorway. Avery MacDonald's stitching two spells together at the same time.

'Stop what you're doing, Priya. Right now,' I hiss.

Nathair Walsh looks up.

'What the—'

'Is that Avery?' Lewis asks, panicked with what he's seeing. The awful terror of it.

The creatures from the void descend and I feel their hunger for life. So swift do they come, a swirling swarm, drawn to the electric charge built up around Avery, they surround him and start to feast on his power. He casts a lightning bolt, which passes over us and the window above explodes, scattering glass. The bird-like things don't relent, circling him, pecking, sucking, feeding upon his immortal soul; I see pieces of it being dragged out of him and devoured. His screams are unlike anything I've ever heard.

When I was a child Gran told me stories of dark creatures of Zimbabwean lore, which they called zvishiri. An unholy swarm of birds that fed on travellers on rural footpaths at night. Villagers lived in fear for no one who encountered these terrible things ever lived to tell the tale. Then she'd laugh and say, of course, nothing like that was possible.

Nathair Walsh and Lewis jump on their bikes and pedal furiously down Wellington Street. The swarm is done with Avery, and a mess of bones and flesh fall upon the tar in a heap. Unsatiated, it takes off after the two boys.

'Now's our chance,' I say, half-rising and dragging Priya to her chair. I pick up my stick from the road, and then hobble to get my mbira. It's scratched, but intact. Tough instrument, you'd need a sledgehammer to break it. I stick the mbira in my backpack and zip it up properly this time. I look up to the still open mouth in the sky which seems to be smiling with malice. Nope. Not tonight, Lucifer. I'm not hanging about for this shit. I hop onto Priya's lap and we get the hell out of there.

XII

Priya's mum lives in a massive flat on Crown Circus in the West End of Glasgow. The area is green and pleasant with loads of lime, lawn and shrubbery. Exhausted, pumped up with adrenaline, we spill into her place, and I'm paranoid checking out through the windows in case those things are coming after us. All I see is rooftops and church spires.

Strange, but at last I really feel alive again. Like I've just woken up from a dreadful nightmare.

We were kind of blabbering, but Ranjeeta tells us to calm down and goes off to the kitchen. Priya retreats to her old room to freshen up, and I'm stuck in the living room with her dad Shashi Kapoor, who's reading the *Financial Times*, feet up on a pouffe, paying me little attention. There's tons of electric cars below. The folks round here don't seem to have any problems when it comes to cash. He's a skinny man with a severe moustache and a combover that doesn't mask his baldness. It looks rather like a barcode. He sips occasionally from a cup of chai, wetting his moustache.

'Where did you say you were from again?' he asks absent-mindedly.

'Edinburgh.'

'And your parents?'

'Zimbabwe,' I say.

'It's a pity about the cricket team,' he replies.

'I don't watch cricket.'

'That's tragic. Well, I failed to get Priyanka interested in it too. She can't tell an LBW from a wide, despite my best efforts. Young people today, all you want to do is play on your phones. It takes patience to sit through a test match.'

I get the feeling that if I'd known a bit more about the sport he would take an interest in me. Don't mind, though, 'cause I'm not up for chit-chat.

When I finally calm down, I randomly realize I've never been in a flat that's got two floors before. Mad that. Were this not my bestie's parents' place, I'd be scanning for stuff to steal. Bad habits, I know. The feature wall in the living room's a dark blue emulsion. Loads of plants shade the room with green foliage. There are pictures of the family on the walls, but it seems the only ones allowed are graduation photos, which hang alongside degree certificates. I go up to read them. Shashi's Doctor of Philosophy in economics from the LSE. Priya's healing degree from the University of Glasgow, which the Lord Kelvin Institute is a part of. Her mum's got an MBA from the Open University. It breaks my heart to see one final qualification on the wall. This one has a big rainbow and some confetti drawn in, and it says 'Certificate of Nursery School'. It was awarded to Aditi Kapoor. The young girl's got a big smile on her face, dressed up in a graduate's gown with a cap. There's a mole on her left cheek.

'I've got you both a lovely chamomile and valerian blend,

which should calm you down. Shashi, why didn't you light the sandalwood candles like I asked you to?' Ranjeeta says, walking back in with a tray which she places on the table. 'Sit down, Ropa. Where's Priyanka gone off to?'

I tell her she went to freshen up.

Paper rustles as Shashi turns the page.

Ranjeeta hands me a bone china cup and I'm dreading I might break it. 'I am happy you decided to come back to us,' she says.

I decide I'm going to be honest. 'It wasn't by choice.'

'There are times in our lives when our kismet drags us down a path we'd rather not be on. Swimming against the river will only exhaust you, maybe even drown you. But if you tread water and let it carry you, who knows where you might find yourself. Fate plays a strange role in this world.'

'You really believe in all that?'

'Okay, since there won't be any peace and quiet in here, I'll be in the study if anyone needs me,' Shashi says.

'I think we'll manage fine without you,' Ranjeeta says teasingly. She still gets a kiss on the crown of her head despite all this.

It has me wondering what my life would have been like if Mum and Dad hadn't drop-kicked the bucket. Priya's got it good. Ranjeeta gives off a vibe of being firm with a kind heart. Her intelligent eyes seem to always be searching, looking through your soul or something. I'm trying not to wilt under her gaze. Instead I turn to check out the areca palm that's growing out of control in the corner. They have so many pot plants in the house. Amongst them I spot ruffled fan palms, spider plants, a handful of succulents on the window sill, and a hanging pot with devil's ivy.

'I'm worried about Izwi,' I tell Ranjeeta. 'We asked the Glasgow practitioners to help, but they refused. They've cut a deal with Henry Dundas. Without them coming on board, the Doric magicians won't dare either.'

'You were scared too, were you not?' she asks.

'Terrified.'

'But you found a reason to fight. It's never easy to ask someone to put their life on the line. You have to discover that for which they may be willing to lose it. And if ever you find that thing in yourself, then you are more fortunate than most people who've ever lived.'

'—'

'Your sister is safe for now,' Ranjeeta says.

'How do you know?'

'We have a spy on the inside relaying information to us. They are still trying to figure out why Izwi was taken. But Dundas is not telling them anything.'

'Who?'

'I couldn't tell you.'

Gets me thinking of all the folks I know working in the Dundas Cult. Which one could be a spy? It's hard to say from the outside. But if the witches, the Daughters of Scotia, have someone, then why haven't they done something about this already? My guard goes up. I'm tired of being lied to and if Ranjeeta's saying this to keep me here, I'll be miffed.

I take a sip of my hot drink. It tastes earthy and nasty, not the nice herbal blend I was expecting. It'd be rude to leave it, though, so I keep drinking.

'You know it's funny how in every culture witches like us have been hated,' she says.

'I'm not a witch,' I reply.

'I apologize. You are an accredited ghostalker, am I right?'

I don't respond and she holds my silence. This drags on for a bit and Ranjeeta's more comfortable with it than I am, this being her house and all.

'We saw some weird shit today,' I say. She gives me a gentle nod, closing her eyes briefly and opening them with it. And so I lay the whole night down on her, including the awful creatures that gobbled up Avery. 'I think he tried to do some kind of forbidden magic and it backfired on him.'

'That could be the case, as you suggest. But what kind of magic? Did you feel any heat, an entropic shift, as they say?'

Come to think of it, there was little heat, nor was there any smell, which is strange for a spell that powerful. Avery did study theoretical magicology at St Andrews College, so it's in the realm of possibility this was a thing he cooked up himself. If it was, then he knocked his own stumps. See, I know some cricket – if Shashi was in the room I'd have used it.

Ranjeeta tells me that in India there's myths about witches there that ate men. There were many different kinds, some that dug out people's livers and cooked them, spirit-witches that ate nothing but human flesh, some like the churel that married men and lived with them as wives until they became emaciated and died.

'My husband thinks I'm one of those,' she jokes.

Then she tells me of witches that were said to kill people with a gaze, and others that caused wasting disease by drinking people's blood. These Indian witches consorted with ghouls and demons. Ranjeeta flashes a mischievous grin which makes her appear younger, almost as though we were age-mates. It's gone in a blink when she reverts to her serious self.

'It wasn't witches who killed Avery MacDonald,' I say.

'I never suggested it was. Though you have to wonder why the myths are so similar across different cultures. Your grand-mother told me about Zimbabwean witches too. She said it was claimed they wander about naked and would dig up recently buried dead bodies and eat the flesh. Or they killed little chil-dren and turned their bones into charms.'

'How did you know Gran?'

'I did a brief stint at the bank. She was my mentor and a dear friend. Shashi was in finance too – he still is, but we don't like him much because he was with the Bank of Scotland, rivals of ours.'

There's the Royal Bank of Scotland and the Bank of Scotland, which can be quite confusing for anyone. The Bank of Scotland is the older of the two, dating back to the seven-teenth century, but for some reason they didn't bother sticking a 'Royal' in their name. Snooze, you lose is the name of the game. Still, if it were up to me, bankers would be lined up and shot. They're the ones who set off the Catastrophe and everything went to shit after that. All we have left is box sets of a better world and reruns on telly.

So Gran was pally with Ranjeeta 'cause the both of them were into witchcraft and banking. Makes me wonder.

Outside the window, on the road leading to the city, I see an old-fashioned bowtop wagon trundling towards our end of the street. The kind that looks like someone's cut up a large whisky barrel and stuck it on the flatbed of a carriage. It's driven by Artchival Fleckie, a big man with an eyepatch. Met him once in Leith and that was a shitshow. He's smoking what appears to be a cigar as he scans the neighbourhood. I know a kindred spirit sussing out a good mark when I see one.

The carriage is driven right up to the stairs where that street meets Crown Circus. I move to the window in time to see Artchival help Theodosia Lovell out of the carriage and down onto the ground. He does it with the finesse of a footman aiding his mistress.

'You invited the Travelling Folk?' I ask.

'No, I didn't. You don't *invite* Theodosia Lovell, she comes and goes when it suits her,' replies Ranjeeta.

'A friendly house call then?'

'Mind-reading was never one of my talents,' she says.

It's still pretty useless for them to come here. Without the aid of the best magicians from Glasgow and Aberdeen, the Viscount Melville has us by the balls. I don't see what good any of this will do us. The doorbell rings. Must be nice to have one of those. Let's see what the Travelling Folk have come here for.

Theodosia Lovell enters the room with Priya, and Artchival follows, boots thudding on the floor. There's something regal in Theodosia's bearing despite the poverty of her dress. In many ways she resembles Gran.

'Yer've dealt with the lassie and prepared her brew as I telt yer tae?' Theodosia says.

'Yes,' Ranjeeta replies.

I look at the dregs in the bottom of my cup. It'd gotten more fragrant with musty tones as I almost finished it. 'What did you give me? What is this stuff?' My stomach feels weird. That was no chamomile blend. Reckon I've been poisoned. I want to throw up but nothing's coming up the pipes.

'Mum, what's going on?' Priya asks, rushing over to me, concern written on her face. She quickly takes my hand and places her fingers on my wrist to check my pulse. 'Slow pulse, pupils dilated – what did you give her?'

'A dreaming potion. Ropa needs it to face what's going to happen.'

'There are serious consent issues with this. Ropa, how're you feeling?' Priya asks. She's giving her mum the daggers. 'Seriously, Mum, how could you do this?'

'Don't worry – she'll be fine. It is for the best,' Ranjeeta replies.

I'm all woozy. We've been played again? The voices in the room are muffled. The cup drops from my hand and crashes to the floor. My thoughts are . . . fragmented. I can't . . . join up things. I take a swing and my arm splits into fractals . . . Those colou—

The sun's blazing hot like we're in the middle of a heatwave. Brilliant blue skies above and the scent of cattle dung sits heavy in the air. I'm on a narrow footpath and walking out of the long savannah grass, yellow as gold. Up ahead are four round huts with a straw thatch, and beside them a mud granary whose walls are cracking in the heat. The air has a certain shimmer, tinged with light aquamarine.

So, not Glasgow then.

What am I doing here?

There's a constant pounding noise, a group of four women with pestles working a single wooden mortar. Their age ranges from really old, middle-aged, twenties, to a teenager. The mortar is a large wooden cylinder which resembles an African drum. Hollow, without the skin covering over the top. It reaches the women's thighs. They each have their own pestle, at least four feet long, and rhythmically work, pounding whatever's inside. The sound they make is like a metronome in its precision. This takes skill and coordination like synchronizing a double Dutch skipping competition or something. If one of them goes at the wrong time, their pestles might hit each other, causing the mortar to fall to the ground.

The women wear kanga cloths of black and white tied around their waists, but they are topless, save for their necklaces. They all have their hair covered in doeks. Their feet are bare and they are intensely focused on the task at hand.

The compound they're in seems to be in the middle of nowhere. There are some fields with millet and sorghum, dried up and ready for harvest beyond the huts. A few trees with good shade are dotted about the land, but they work in the sun. There's a familiarity to this scene which I can't put my finger on.

'Hello,' I say.

The women ignore me and continue about their business.

A hen crosses the bare earth followed by five chicks. It stops to peck the ground for a worm and quickly moves on.

'What's going on?' I say.

'Munhu wako auya, nhai muzukuru. Wakutoshanyirwa usati wagara munyikadzimu kana masvondo maviri,' the eldest of the women says.

'Akasiya kusina kunatswa. Ngaagadzirise nhorondo yake; kokuno tinongoswera wani zvedu,' the middle-aged woman says.

I get hints of the Shona language spoken, but not all of it. I was never fluent. Bits and pieces I picked up from Gran. A few fragments from my dad. It's like I have a jigsaw puzzle map, but all the pieces are scattered. I picked up the first lady was saying something like: Munhu – *person*, wako – *yours*, muzukuru – *grandchild*, mu-nyika-dzimu – *the-land-spirit*: Shona goes back to front sometimes so it should be *the-spirit-land*, and maviri – *two*. This means your person, or your grandchild in this land, there are two. I'm probably wrong on this, but that's all I've got. I picked up even less from the middle-aged woman: kusina – *without*, ngaagadzirise – *fix*, nhorondo – *story*. So, I don't quite know what story has to be fixed with someone's person.

The youngest girl stops working and rests her pestle on the dirt, like it's a shepherd's staff. In an instant, the rhythm of the women's pounding changes, like a song switching over. It becomes something else, still complete, but different. The girl uses her left hand to shield her eyes from the sun as she checks me out.

'Usangotituzu nhai mwana wekwaMhondoro?' the middle-aged woman says, and they burst out laughing at the girl. It's the kind of good-natured banter that happens between people who love one another. No one's feelings are hurt. At least that's what it looks like to me.

The girl, very shyly, walks over to me, guiding her steps with the pestle. She doesn't leave prints on the bare earth, and I notice she doesn't have a shadow. Nothing in this place has one, except for me. I shrink back, afraid.

The girl reaches towards me with her free hand. She's still a distance away, but suddenly she's right in front of me, her hand inches from mine. There's joy in her eyes and she looks like she might weep.

Wait a minute, she has flawless skin, but those liver spots, their pattern across her face and chest and arms.

'I have missed you so much, Ropa,' she says, smiling, a film of tears in her eyes.

'Gran?'

'I forget, you remember me like . . .' She ages six decades in an instant and becomes the Melsie Mhondoro that I knew. '. . . this. Funny, I never quite saw myself as old. It helps that I'm the youngest here, those women are ancient, so they treat me like the baby of the clan. Fancy that. Welcome to the Land of the Tall Grass, my dear child.'

A cow moos in the distance. Gran told me her people were obsessed with cattle, so it figures after you die you might go to some place and receive a big herd, so you can drink beer and watch your cattle graze day and night.

'Will you not embrace me?' Gran says.

You murdered my father.

I'm torn and I pull back from her. I want to touch her. With all my heart, I do. But since she's passed I've heard so much about her – she's not the woman I thought I knew. The first part of her life was consumed with the pursuit of money, selling her soul to the Royal Bank of Scotland and crashing the economy in the process, causing untold misery to millions. She's a phoney, and it's dizzying.

'You're not my real grandmother. I've been to the Other Place, and saw my father suffering there while you kick back in paradise. You condemned him to hell.'

'I *am* your grandmother, but what you say is true about your father.'

The work at the mortar and pestle has sped up. 'Stop lying. You've been doing it my whole life,' I shout above the pounding.

'My own blood, Ropa. I lied to you so that you could know the truth,' she says, with a wistful look. 'And now look, you have grown.'

This woman and Izwi used to be my entire world. Outwith our little caravan in the slum in Hermiston, there was nothing. I feared if ever I left, I would be like those ancient sailors who travelled too far and fell off the face of the Earth. It was a hard life, but one I'd have happily gone back to if things were not as they are now. My entire life was a series of steps she laid out for me, nudging in certain directions. All my closest friends are because of her. The jobs I've had were because of her. And dare I say, more than a fair few of my problems are because of her.

Gran made me.

My upbringing has messed me up big time. I can't trust her now she's dead any more than when she was alive.

All the stuff they tell us about being yourself is bollocks.

You are who you are because of other people. She used to call this the principle of Ubuntu. I am because of her, and she is because of . . . these women pounding grain under the scorching sun in the savannah? How far back does it all go?

Gran walks past me to the edge of the compound. There's a steep drop there, a cliff made of granite. It evens out in a plain that stretches away until it meets a river where the cattle are drinking. The horizon never meets the ground as it does on our Earth. It just keeps going forever. If you look, your gaze follows it as the land turns into miombo woodlands, mountain ranges bordered by rainforests, to small villages where they dance to the beat of the drum, to cities with massive stone walls surrounding them, into more bush, and on and on it goes, into infinity, for your eye can never find the point at which it ends.

I go over and stand next to her, trying to take it all in.

'The world we are from is a strange place, the jewel in all reality. Look at this paradise where we are right now. Everything is perfect, it has always been and will always continue to be. But the world you've left behind is a rollercoaster. There's nothing else like being alive there,' says Gran.

'I know that now.'

'It's a complex and frightening world, no matter what stage you are in life. There's so many layers, contradictions and complexities there. When you're a child, you are told stories so you make sense of the world. Your mind couldn't grasp the things you are being taught otherwise,' says Gran. 'Yes, I did tell you lies, fables, tall tales too. That world is a stage, and we were all actors, our lives passing as story. I lied because I didn't know how else to break the script to you. Ropa, have you ever wondered why it is you took to ghostalking like a duck to water? Your mastery of travelling the astral plane by instinct, which takes others years to learn? Most never even succeed.'

I scrunch my face up and think. I recall the first time I saw a ghost in a barn. Then there was the time I was eight years old, when I woke up looking down at my sleeping body and wondered what was going on. It became a game for me. Late at night when I was bored and didn't want to sleep I'd slip out and wander cosmic realms while my body was safely tucked in. Until Gran caught me. We met hovering about the house in Forrester where we lived then and she ordered me back into my body, like you'd tell a toddler to stop stomping in puddles.

Got a right rollicking from Gran that night. But I never considered it to be anything special until I started mingling with magicking folk. And they looked down on it. It was just a thing I did, no different from imagining stuff at play.

'Some people are just talented, I guess,' I finally reply.

'Is that what it is? Wouldn't life be simple if that's how it worked for everyone?' Gran replies. She bends down to touch a blade of grass, but she doesn't pluck it.

I want to say it's an innate thing, the same way some people are good at drawing or singing without really trying. My talent's a little more esoteric . . . but I get the feeling I'm way off.

'The night Cora gave birth to you, I was helping Ian Callander out in his new job as secretary at the Society when he got a panicked call from Cornelius Lethington. He said he'd done an emergency delivery, but things hadn't gone well for the baby.'

My instinct is to call bullshit, but this lines up with what Lethington told me. He wasn't lying, then.

'Cornelius broke the news to your father who was in the delivery suite. He said your father screamed like a man possessed. Then he declared: "My daughter did not die. She will live." They could not console him as he began weaving a spell. This wasn't allowed in the clinic. Makomborero was not a registered healer and had no right to work magic there, but he was a powerful man and Cornelius was too afraid to interfere. No one can doubt your father's formidable talents, but he was keen on breaking rules and not averse to the practice of dark magic. And so he bound your soul to this world without a vessel instead of letting you cross over as nature intended. It should never have been allowed to happen; your body was buried but your spirit remained trapped in this realm. We knew of it, but Callander decided we could turn a blind eye. Scottish magic had a lot of problems in those days.

'It's also true that we didn't pay attention when babies started to go missing from the Royal Infirmary. The local newspapers wrote about it and the Edinburgh baby snatcher became infamous. No matter what security they had at the hospital, every couple of months a baby, sometimes two, would go missing. This happened for five years and left behind a trail of misery. Those families never got closure.

'Then, years later, Makomborero proudly announced he and Cora had a new baby and invited us to his house. We were happy because we knew Cora and he had been trying for years. But I knew you were a bit queer the moment I laid eyes on you. The way you moved your body in the pram was too coordinated. You seemed to understand the adults when they chatted. You didn't like people making baby noises at you. Cornelius didn't attend the party, but he did call Callander afterwards and say that he'd not delivered this new baby and there was no evidence of Cora having been back at the clinic. He'd rung up his colleagues at the Royal Infirmary and they confirmed that your parents hadn't been there either. Ian and I confronted Makomborero about this and he feigned offence at this invasion of his family's privacy. Then he spun some line about having engaged a surrogate mother who'd taken the money and caught a ship to Ghana. There was nothing we could do. Everything seemed above board and he had the paperwork, though we couldn't track the woman to verify his claims. We had other pressing matters amidst the chaos and violence of the time.'

I'm in shock trying to keep up. Sure, some folks get told they were adopted, or there's some weird DNA revelation to contend with, but my background is super fucked-up. It doesn't even begin to make sense. This is some wild shit. I now understand why Lethington didn't finish telling me this stuff. It was an act of kindness.

On that fateful winter's night, I was dead on arrival, according to Gran. But my father held my soul hostage and didn't let me pass like I should have. He spent the next five years doing all sorts of insane experiments until he was able to swap me into someone else's kid's body. My body ain't my own. Oh, my days. That means I'm not even myself. I'm just a parasite living someone else's life.

'What happened to the little girl whose body my father stole?'

'Soul-death. His experiments extracted the ultimate price. We don't fully understand how Makomborero did it, but we know he was receiving financial backing from an anonymous group. Ian and I destroyed most of his research, the material we could get our hands on. It was too dangerous. We believe he would have destroyed her soul and used its vital energy to cloak your being so the body would believe you were her.'

I could weep from the shame of it all. 'Did she have a name? What about her parents? It's horrible.' How they would have suffered because my father killed their child so I could live. 'I didn't want any of this.'

'It's not your fault, Ropa. There's no use blaming yourself.'

'I wish I'd never been born.'

'Don't say that, child. It's our fault for not having stopped Makomborero in time. His dark magic led us here.'

There's no difference between dark magic and normal magic. Most people think that the dark stuff must be diabolical, blood rituals and that kind of thing, but magic is created by people's will. Rituals, spells, those are just ways of focusing the will into an actionable magical event. What separates dark magic from normal magic is the practitioner's intent. A Promethean fire spell can be used to warm the home on a cold night, or it can be used for arson. It's the same magic, but with a different use. My father could have used his will and power for good, but he chose to serve his own selfish desires. This has become my heritage.

I don't even want to know what my mother thought of it all. Did she go along with it or was she in the dark? I'm too feart to ask Gran these questions. No. I must know everything.

I close my eyes and wait for a moment before damning myself again.

'Why did my mother let this happen?' I ask. 'Surely she must have known right from wrong.'

'Cora was not a magician, Ropa. She was as much a victim in all this as everyone else involved. That your father loved her was never in any doubt, but he could be domineering too. He had an intense, obsessive love that suffocated everything around it. Before Cora, your father was a studious man, more interested in things than in people, so I've heard. He was destined for a brilliant career as a researgician in one of Scotland's academies. He was good-looking, and the ladies swooned at his feet, men too, but he had no interest in any of them. They say he loved Cora at first sight when he went to her shop to get a pair of trousers adjusted. Soon they became inseparable. The one thing Cora wanted above all else was a family.'

I don't understand how a person capable of love could ever do the things my father's said to have done. Still, he risked his soul for me in the Other Place, sacrificing himself so that I could live. But he'd also casually destroyed Sir George MacKenzie. And all those souls that he'd trapped in that dreadful creation. How can all this be the same man?

I feel so sorry for the girl whose place I took. I am sorry for the pain her family suffered. How can I even begin to make amends? This is not my fault, but it is my curse.

Gran takes my hand and I allow her to hold it. She rubs her thumb against the back of my hand. This poor woman, just as flawed as my father, loves me too. Maybe we could stay here in this paradise and leave the Earth to itself. It can't be any worse off without us. But that'd mean abandoning Izwi. I can't do that. But what if my love for her is just as toxic as my father's?

XIII

The grass in the plain below ripples like under a gentle breeze. It's like a golden wave. The Land of the Tall Grass is where you go to meet your ancestors. There's supposed to be lots of chilling and drinking mupeta. I have a decision to make. Should I go back out into a dangerous world, roped into a fight I can't possibly win, or can I stay here?

My soul's taken a different form. I can't picture myself as the girl whose body my father stole, so I am something else, the vague outline of a teenage girl. The only thing that reminds me of who I was is the outline of a handprint upon my chest. It stings my soul just as much as it did my – her – body.

The women near the huts continue pounding their millet. They are singing together now.

'*Tinoshandira nhimbe yemambo,*
agotipa nzimbe
Zadzai matura mudye mutakura
Tichatambira pachanaya mvura.'

It's a simple verse which they repeat in unison, though one of them is a bit slower than the others. Their pestles work in time as the percussion accompanying their fine voices. Maybe there's room for a fifth in their band.

'Cora waited a good few years before she got pregnant with Izwi. Your parents' marriage was no longer the bed of roses it had once been. Your father had an intense emotional relationship with an actress-magician called Siobhan Kavanagh. You remember her from the game show we used to watch together, don't you? It simmered, but never went beyond that as far as anyone knows, but it was unsettling for your mother. Maybe she thought a new baby would see off her rival. By now Ian and I were sufficiently concerned about what Makomborero was up to. He was protected by wealthy, connected people, but there are limits and Makomborero was constantly flirting with his own ruination.

'Cornelius contacted us the night that Cora died giving birth to your sister. Izwi was a bouncing, healthy baby, but the pregnancy had taken its toll on your mother. Despite his expertise, Cornelius was unable to save her, and he was alarmed enough to call Ian when Makomborero took his wife's body. We rushed to your home. It was our intention to talk some sense into your father.'

I've heard this part of the story from Lethington and I know how it ends. Still I find myself wishing that Lethington got it wrong, or there was some kind of mistake. Gran squeezes my hand and I lean towards her before resting my head on her shoulder.

'When we got there we were horrified by what we saw. There was another woman strapped down on a gurney, her wrists bleeding where the cord your father tied her with had cut into her skin. Her mouth was gagged and she was in terrible agony.

165

Makomborero stood above her with Gray's intromissioner in his hands, transferring her life force into your mother.'

The Gray's intromissioner was a flask-like device that Sir Ian Callander had taught me was used during the Great War to try to save injured soldiers. Unfortunately, the side effects on the donors were deemed too catastrophic and the recipients didn't get much benefit from it either, so the practice was banned. I'd seen this equipment used by a celebrity called Siobhan Kavanagh who was experimenting on children. My father's mistress.

What an almighty mess.

'Remember, none of this is your fault, Ropa. We don't get to choose our origins,' Gran says, nudging my head with her own. 'Callander ordered Makomborero to stop, but he was hell-bent on bringing his wife back. We had no choice but to use force to save that poor woman's life. He was powerful, able to withstand us both. We traded blows, but Makomborero was always a step ahead. I was a seer and should have been able to read his movements, yet somehow he bested us. But when a toddler came down into the basement, and Makomborero was distracted for barely a second, I took my chance and brought him down.'

She makes it sound like she took out something feral, a man-eating lion.

'That child who came down the stairs was me,' I say.

'Yes, it was you. After all we'd seen, I decided to banish Makomborero Moyo's soul to the Other Place. We couldn't risk the chance he might reanimate himself. The magic he had created was a danger to the world,' Gran says. 'Alas, your mother's soul died too that day, caught up between two worlds. I've grieved for her every day, since I was unable to help her pass on.'

And so with both my parents dead, and a heavy conscience weighing her down, Gran decided she would not leave the children of the man she'd slain to the whims of the system. She took us in. And then she wove a story to keep us safe from knowing the truth about ourselves.

'You became my world. I really was your Gran, if not by blood, but there are higher bonds than that. Time was not kind to us, but the moments I spent with you and Izwi were the best in my life. And I know you loved me with an innocence and purity which I was unworthy of. I hope you can still love me even now.'

There's fear in Gran's voice. Even with paradise at her feet, this formidable woman is afraid that we could stop loving her.

This is all too heavy for me.

The pounding and singing from the women at the compound continues.

'They've been working on that millet for two hundred years and they aren't sure when it'll be ready,' Gran says, shifting the subject in the way she used to do when she was alive. 'A few hundred more's the blink of an eye here. When they are done, they'll brew beer and invite their friends from the next village. It should only take a millennium or so for that to happen.'

'Must be boring out here.'

'Don't let them hear you say that. The art of kudyura requires a certain degree of finesse and determination. They've perfected it and they say I should be happy I've joined them. Someone should have told me my mother, grandmother and great-grandmother were all a little bit mad.'

The world below us shimmers. A slight tremor passes through it. I hear voices talking.

'You're waking up and we don't have much time,' says Gran, staring up at the darkening sky. 'You have my heirlooms and I wish to fight alongside you, my child. I believe you were always destined to be a svikiro, a great medium, and I'd like you to choose my spirit for your guide.'

I know about Shona mediums. Gran wants me to bring her soul back to the world. To do something similar to the shit that caused all this in the first place.

I shake my head. *No, Gran, you have to stay here in paradise.*

'Ropa, let me help you make things right,' she begs. 'Together we can—'

'I think you've done quite enough already.'

Groggy as anything when I open my eyes. The room's spinning. Makes me want to puke. I lean over the side of the bed and dry heave. This is different to returning from a wander in the astral realms. Everything that happened was a dream, one all too real, and I'm pretty confused right now. I lean back in the bed.

The room I'm in's filled up with burning candles in glass jars. They're all over the floor, leaving a narrow path to the doorway. There's a bunch of herbs on the covers, lavender, sage and some dried-up hops. The walls might have been white and pristine before, but someone's drawn an open door in charcoal on the one opposite me. They've squiggled symbols arching around that doorway too.

I turn to the side with the window. There's a small bedside table with a mirror set atop it. Pains me to look at my face. Not mine. It's someone else's face that was stolen from them by my messed-up father. I raise my hand. Not mine. And touch my cheek. Not mine.

Who was this poor little girl?

Tears stream down my face. Why did it have to be her? I've stolen many things in my life, but never something as wrong as this. Maybe it was all just a dream. That witch drugged me up with powerful herbs. I must have been tripping . . . But I also know dreams speak truths to us. I wish I could return to the lie that was my life before today.

How do I live with myself?

Theodosia Lovell enters the room with Ranjeeta tailing her. From the looks of things, they've been riffling through my stuff again, because Theodosia's carrying my jacket, mbira, scarf and Gran's walking stick in her arms. She looks ancient in the flickering candlelight and her shadow is cast on every wall and on the ceiling too.

'I saw Gran,' I say.

'Aye, ah ken. The two of yous bargain an' reach common ground?' Theodosia Lovell asks, placing the objects at the foot of my bed.

I'm wary of these women. They are no different from Gran. Everyone who dabbles in magic's got an angle, the practitioners of the Society use raw power and influence, while the witches prefer guile and subtlety. Must be something this craft does to our personalities. I sit up, uncomfortable in my own not-body. My skin feels like Poison Ivy's vine's crawling over it.

'We gave you a dreaming potion prepared by a friend of ours, a shaman from Mexico,' Ranjeeta says. She claps her hands, stomps her foot once like a flamenco dancer and the candles extinguish and the light turns on, making me squint. 'They use it to open up their consciousness and access higher dimensions to speak to their ancestors and gods.'

'You could have warned me.'

'I know, but intention sometimes misdirects the dreaming. When you drank it without knowing, the potion took you to where you needed to be.'

'Don't ever do it again,' I say.

Ranjeeta lifts up both arms in surrender. I understand why that dream felt so real now. I wonder if Priya knew they were up to this. No, I heard her say something about consent. She's a pro, unlike these two amateurs. But if there's one thing the drug didn't help with, it's my coordination. My feet spasm in the bed involuntarily and I wish they'd stop so I don't embarrass myself. What's more worrying for me just now is the fact that I'm being used again. Like, my life with Gran was a set-up for this looming confrontation. The witches have their own interests, which align with some of mine, but I can't help but be wary, still.

'Here be yer heirlooms. Love lies in that which was left behind. Through these we touch those that are long past,' Theodosia Lovell says.

The first was my mbira, passed to me by Gran as a gift from my grandfather, her first husband who I never got to meet. She said he was an expert mbira player and craftsman who'd built the instrument from the wood of a mubvamaropa tree with his own hands. It enabled me to communicate better with the spirit world.

The second was my scarf Cruickshank, gifted to me by Sir Ian Callander in the Library of the Dead not long after I'd met him. The woman who knitted the scarf for her friend was my seer gran Melsie Mhondoro. It's entirely plausible she gave it to Callander with the full knowledge that he would pass it on to me.

The third was my jacket, given to me by Esfandiar Soltani at the Society conference at Dunvegan Castle on the Isle of Skye to keep me warm in the autumn weather. Esfandiar told me that it had been left by my grandmother at a party at his house many years ago. I wore it because it was stylish and I was cold. It turned out that the jacket was impenetrable and it became my armour.

The fourth was my walking stick, virtually presented to me by Theodosia Lovell herself to help me move, for my body is fragile and my soul doesn't quite fit anymore. The walking stick in Shona culture's a symbol of authority handed down from the ancestors who gifted us life.

Theodosia Lovell called these 'heirlooms' and I understand what's happening from the stories Gran passed down to me. Shona mediums would be given the articles of the spirit that possessed them. It is said when a person became a medium, they would be taken to a room with many objects, and if they picked something that belonged to the ancestor they were working with, then the community would know they were the real deal. These are all tied to my Gran.

I shake my head and reject them. I don't want to be used

to fight someone else's battles. These people have their own history with Scottish magic and I've been caught in the middle of it all. Best I stick to my own mission.

'These be lean times upon each and all, Ropa. The price yer've paid's mair than all lowry in this warld. It isnae a fair lig we trudge upon, but I've read me tea leaves an' soon I too shall lose a piece of my own heart. Dinna be hasty, stead be ged of the choice yer make fae we are as the quilt yer Grannie's woven. Oor strands cannae be unplucked,' Theodosia Lovell says softly, imploringly.

'I don't owe you spit.'

'Fare cannywise upon yer agley if this ganche cannae turn yer. I ken yous ettling tae trod even if it be moich.'

I won't be under Gran's shadow, these women's or anyone else's. I'm going to find my own way to get my little sister back. That's the most important thing for me. It's a good thing I know some nifty burglars in Edinburgh who might be able to help me out.

XIV

There's no chance in hell I'm wearing Gran's cast-offs ever again. Instead, I go to Priya's bedroom to have a rummage. She's got the only bedroom downstairs, which is right next to the lounge. In a building this old, I figure it might have been a dining room back in the day.

Childhood bedrooms are a mishmash of dated relics and clutter. They lose their function when the little one flies the nest and Priya's is no different. It seems frozen in her formal schooling days before she decamped to Edinburgh to work at Our Lady's. There's a single bed, which gives her a lot more room to move around in her chair. A desk with some old study material and make-up kits and perfumes on it. It's very neat and tidy. I kinda wish I still had my old berth, but even our old caravan's out of bounds for me now. Priya doesn't know how lucky she is to have all this.

She's lying in bed, watching me raid her gear.

'So you turned down their plan,' Priya says.

'We have to find our own way,' I say. 'We've done it before, you and me.'

Priya nods, but I can tell she's not convinced. It would have been better to go to Edinburgh in strength, but without the

Glaswegian and Doric magicians we have to do what von Clausewitz called a 'small war'. We're going guerrilla style, baby.

I rummage through her wardrobe where I find a pair of black Levi's. Like, these aren't the fakes from the market. They're the real, actual deal. Then I have a hard time choosing from her T-shirt collection. A girl after my own tastes.

'Help me pick one,' I say, holding up a white Dog Faced Hermans T-shirt and a faded black Strawberry Switchblade one which has Jill Bryson and Rose McDowall on it.

'You can't even compare the two, but with those jeans, I'd go with Switchblade,' she laughs.

'That's as Glasgow as I'm ever gonna get,' I reply. 'Please cover the mirror for me.'

Priya does so without questioning me. I don't want to see myself. I mean, to see her, the girl whose body I'm in. When I was showering, after I ended my conversation with Priya's mum and Theodosia Lovell, I could hardly bear to touch my body.

Priya gives me a spiked metal bracelet and I put it on my left wrist.

She inspects her handiwork and says I look great.

Last but not least, I have to pick out a new coat. It's Baltic out and I don't want to freeze these chebs off. All her jackets are on a freestanding clothing rack in the corner of the room. I settle on the Gothicana coat, black of course, with red lining inside. It looks like the sort of thing a vampire would wear, and since I'm technically undead, I might as well.

Priya groans and flops back on the bed.

'I knew you were going to pick that one,' she says. 'That's what I bought with my first proper wage because I wanted to impress a boy I liked. He didn't even notice me. Come here, let me do your lipstick.'

I take the make-up bag on the desk and give it to her.

'Shadow and liner?' I nod. 'Let me guess, you want it in black.'

Priya starts to do my eyes, singing 'Paint it Black' by the Stones 'cause she wants to piss me off. And when she says I have lips like Mick Jagger, I punch her in the arm. Then I get up and do a strut for her. It's easy enough 'cause I'm so unco-ordinated right now. I need a new walking stick. Like I can go for a bit without support, but I tire easily.

'Get back here and let me finish,' she says, laughing.

Priya applies the lipstick carefully, working away like an artist. And when she's done, she says I look 'badass'. Normally I'd have the urge to check it myself, but I'm good right now. Maybe putting on this make-up makes me feel a little more like me and a little less like that little girl.

I realize that I'm never going to be the same, knowing what I know now. Whatever shred of innocence I once had is now gone. I'm complicit in the bullshit that's happening in this world.

'Here, take this,' Priya says, leaning over to reach under her bed. She rummages for a bit and then pulls out a litter-picker. 'This is my old grabber. It's pretty tough and you can use it as a stick. Bonus points because you can reach stuff on the top shelf in supermarkets, if you're a hobbit like me.'

'You're the best friend a lass could have,' I say.

'Stop, you might just make me blush.'

We're giggling like we don't have a care in the world. It's

almost like we're stretching the moment, drawing it out for as long as we can. Here, in Priya's mum's house, we can be, for a time, two boring, ordinary lassies who don't have to care about the rioting and looting and scheming and murdering in the world outside. Moments like this are the diamonds in the muck of my life. They shine bright, hardened by the pressure we're under.

I get up off the bed and test the grabber. It's got a solid grip and feels sturdy when I touch it to the ground. Reckon it can support my weight no problem.

I wait by the door as Priya gets in her chair and gathers her gear before we set off. I hold it open for her, and when we get into the corridor, Shashi and Ranjeeta have set up a roadblock. Shashi's looking all embarrassed, like he's been dragged out to stand with his wife against his better judgement. Then he knits his eyebrows, face morphing to try and look stern.

'Ropa, you cannot hope to win this fight without us. But if you're hell-bent on throwing everything away, then you can't leave with my daughter,' Ranjeeta says.

'Mum,' Priya says.

'Go back to your room, Priyanka,' Ranjeeta commands. Talk about forceful, I'm actually impressed.

'*Mum*,' Priya says.

'I won't hear anymore. This is reckless and dangerous. We witches are good at keeping our heads down and letting the storm pass without being seen. Lord knows, we learnt that when they were burning and drowning women like us. Melsie Mhondoro was a leader and my mentor. She invested everything in preparing you, Ropa, for what was to come. What's your plan now? Getting your sister and running off into the rising sun? You've already seen what Henry Dundas is capable of.'

'Hey, I didn't sign up for any of this, so don't go laying your expectations on me,' I reply angrily. 'You have no right drugging people in your house and expecting them to follow your little whims. I'm not that person.'

'Then go,' Ranjeeta says, pointing at the way out.

'You're coming, Priya?'

My best friend's quiet, rooted to the spot. I realize that I've just asked her to pick between her parents and me. I might be a dick, but I'm not an arsehole.

'Fine, suit yourself,' I say, heading out.

'Ropa, just wait. Let's all talk about this,' Priya implores.

'The only thing I'd like to know is where that spy of yours says my sister is being kept.' I look Ranjeeta in the eye.

She holds my stare for the longest time and then sighs, shaking her head.

'Melville Castle in Dalkeith.'

'He's gone home then.'

'Ropa, don't—'

I walk out the door and slam it shut behind me. My legs are shaking as I reach the stairs and I pause for a second. This is the exact scenario Priya had tried to warn me about. My thing of going off on my own.

I guess I am who I am.

The worst thing I can do right now is to start doubting myself. I blow air out of my mouth hard, and begin my descent. I'm resolved, but part of me wishes I'd hear the door open and for Priya to follow me. This holds until I'm on the ground floor, out the main door, and onto the wide open streets of Glasgow.

I have no money and no phone.

I shove one hand in my pocket and walk out, the cold air freezing my bald head. From here, I need to get back to the capital, back to the city where it's all happening. There's a couple of shilly-shillys that run between Glasgow and Edinburgh, but being private vehicles I don't stand a chance of catching a free ride. Option B, walking. Not with these trotters.

I should have asked for Esfandiar's address the other day. He'd have bailed me out. I have a long walk through Dowanhill to figure things out. This takes me via the University of Glasgow complex. Grand old buildings, but hardly anyone's about. The rioting's put people off. I stroll through a homeless encampment in Kelvingrove Park. I might not know the city well, but I know if I keep going east, I'll wind up in the centre.

It's a snail's pace. A woman in the park offers a pair of herrings for an exorbitant price. She whispers like she was selling something illicit. The fish are in poor condition and absolutely howling, so I crinkle my nose. No one'll be having those, certainly not me, so I walk on by.

At least I have plenty of time to think. Dundas is back from beyond the grave. He griped about only living to fifty-five the first time round and he's done awful things to have another go. It's strange to me that someone so accomplished wouldn't simply count up their chips at the close of business and call it a day.

Think, Ropa . . . There's something I'm missing.

History is littered with men who think they are better than

others, smarter, good genes, more money and so forth. This breeds the worst kind of entitlement. They want all the fine things in life, but they also wonder why they should have their time allotted by Atropos's shears much as every other person. They think they're above all that.

How does Izwi fit in with this?

It's bugging me by the time I get to Queen Street Station. I've not even needed to stop and ask for directions. Unlike the hodge-podge of Edinburgh, Glasgow's a neat grid-style city. It's very modern in this outlook. It should be dull but there's a range of different architectural styles to make it interesting, even as you follow the relentless straight lines.

The steel-and-glass facade of Queen Street Station's seen better days. There's a queue stretching outside and onto the pavement. Others are pushing and shoving to get inside the heaving building. Only two trains travel to Edinburgh every day. The morning and afternoon service. You miss those and you have to wait till the next day to try your luck. Reckon I'm already late.

There's young kids peddling cigarette lighters, toothpicks and sweets on the concourse. A girl selling plastic packets of water passes by. They're cheaper than plastic bottles, although you can't be sure where exactly the water's come from. A man's complaining about someone stomping his foot. I decide to take a chance and jump the queue, slipping in between the heaving crowds. Good thing I'm skinny as a stork. I get caught in the press and drift in the wrong direction for a bit before I manage to squeeze myself out of it. An electric cable dangles danger-ously from the roof, swaying overhead.

The train's filling up as I get near the front of the queue. The pushers, professional men employed by ScotRail, do the work of shoving people into the train to pack it out. Sardines have a far better experience. A lad in a bowler hat sat atop the train reaches down and offers me his hand.

'You're better off coming Delhi style with us if you want to go, wee man,' he says.

I take his hand, and put my foot against the train so I can climb up. I slip and nearly fall, but his grip is strong and he helps me. A fair few folks are already comfortably ensconced on the roof of the train.

'Three carriages, that's all they've got for us today,' a woman with a saffron tartan scarf grumbles atop the train. 'I paid for first class.'

Everyone within earshot laughs.

The Central Belt looks forlorn in the gloomy weather as we chug past desolate towns and villages wrecked by our current circumstances. Proud working-class areas fallen into disrepair. But there's a beauty in the broken landscape, the occasional loch and green hills in the distance. At each stop people hop off the top of the train and others climb up. Bunting and banners in the colours of the Union Jack commemorating our deceased regents are on proud display.

The memory of the dead. They refuse to be swept away into the dustbin of history.

Up ahead, the city is cloaked in an almighty haar which reminds me uncannily of the everyThere.

At Edinburgh Park, so close to my old home of Hermiston Slum, I see a wispy ghost inspecting a picture of the old queen.

It gets me thinking about Gran and how we were happy before all this. The three of us, and River, in our little caravan huddled together through the cold winters. I miss the laughter. The image is striking in my mind, and I think of the one thing our current king might want above all else. The same thing anyone who's unfairly lost family and for whom grief weighs heavy might want.

King or commoner, we pay the same dues on this account. Is there anything we wouldn't give to have it all back?

I mull on this, chew the cud, unsettled.

'You're looking awfully troubled for one so young,' the woman in the tartan scarf says to me. 'When I was your age I had not a care in the world. My parents were rich once.' She falls silent, lost in remembrance.

'Aye' is all I can say.

The miasma of the haar, scents of decomposing mulch, digs into my pores. A bitter cold bites my toes and fingers. I am glad when I'm helped off the roof of the train at Haymarket Station, the furthest we can go because Waverley remains drowned under the new loch. The only hint of the journey ahead lies further along – a dark tunnel up ahead where the tracks disappear.

On platform 2, I'm surrounded by a sea of bodies and ghosts. Above us, hung up on every truss are tiny Union Jacks.

I clamber up Arthur's Seat, the big hill in the centre of town and home of the Clan. Strange, there're no sentries posted to protect Camelot from rival gangs. Either there's been a truce, or the Rooster's getting a smidge too cocky.

This doesn't feel like our realm anymore. There's a white orb somewhere in the sky, a weak sun whose rays carry little heat through the fog. A flock of seagulls are overhead, but they don't seem to be soaring. It's more like they're fixed in position given how slow they move through this treacle in our atmosphere. Every so often, a ghost flickers into view and disappears again. They are everywhere. Coming up from under the ground. Some are in the air. They wander, dazed and confused. I think whatever Dundas is doing with his half of the Fairy Flag's causing an imbalance between our world and its conjoined twin, the everyThere. Where we have light and colour, the everyThere has grey and gloom. We have life and it has death. Things happen in our world; there, everything remains the same for all eternity. Or at least that's how it's supposed to work out, generally.

I check out the flickering ghosts popping in and out of our world. Or maybe it's us who are popping into their world. A voykor soars across the sky with giant tattered wings, its horse head prominent against the darkness. Fuck me. This is worse than I thought. That's a non-human creature in our realm. Every place has its own guardians and the voykor ensure that only dead souls are permitted in the everyThere. They exist with a great hunger. One of these loose in a city the size of Edinburgh would be catastrophic. The voykor vanishes, dragged back into its own world.

The fabric of our dimension is unstitching. Lord knows what else may come through. I can't believe, in the face of this overwhelming evidence, the Edinburgh magicians still choose to side with Henry Dundas. The city's become the first spot of a rot that will spread out, infecting the world we know. It'll be the end of everything. Dundas may have come hoping for eternal life and to establish himself as a god, the One Above All, but Earth is a place of cause and effect. It's a finely balanced world. A bit of CO_2, an alien compound here and there, a tiny bump from a wayward asteroid, the slightest, silliest things and it spins off-kilter. When something goes wrong, Mother Nature's answer is usually to wipe away everything and start again, but nothing can prepare this world for merging with the everyThere. Dundas will reign over nothing but ash. I make my way up the incline, observing the extranatural activity infecting Edinburgh as I go. This is what they call the new Athens of the North?

The Palace of Holyroodhouse below has a menacing air. It is surrounded by destruction, as though there was an earthquake and it alone was miraculously preserved. And further in that direction are dark, jagged rocks and rubble. The city's skyline has changed irrevocably since Calton Hill was destroyed. It's hard to make out in the dense grey atmosphere, but gone are the pillars of the Parthenon, no more Nelson Monument pricking the sky. Everything that was built on the hill is gone. St Andrew's House and the grand old Royal High School buildings. The devastation of the hill's collapse took out the Old Calton Burial Ground and the New one too. Virtually everything on the north side of the Royal Mile has been ground to dust.

All those people in the tenements.

My heart sinks and an overwhelming sorrow hits me in the gut. They had nothing to do with any of this, but they paid the price. Did Callander know that his heroic sacrifice cost so many lives?

It was my failure to stop the resurrection ritual that led to this.

The world blurs around the edges of my vision and my chest tightens. I lean into my grabber and battle the hydraulic press crushing me. It's like I'm in a cage. The instinct is to flail around and fight, but I take the slow, deep breaths Dr Checkland taught me. Pins and needles in my face – I know I'm having a panic attack. The awareness of what's happening helps a bit, though it doesn't make it any less shitty. Knapf. I have to let it wash over me.

It takes its time, and I'm rooted to the spot. But after a while, the attack eases off. I wipe away my tears with the sleeve of Priya's jacket and compose myself.

Okay, here we go, Ropa.

I continue slowly up the hill. Nothing that gets the pulse racing. I try to push all those people who lived near Calton Hill from my mind.

As I get to the top of Arthur's Seat, my heart sinks again. Where there used to be a thriving tent city, now there's hardly anyone. The place is filled with litter upon grass and gorse, spread out as far as the eye can see. There's upturned broken bits of furniture, a table and some chairs. A barbeque grill lies on its side beside a pink toy unicorn. Gone are the sheep and the tents that used to sprawl out here. Only a handful remain. Strewn clothes. Old firepits where folks here used to cook their meals. It's as though a hurricane swept through and carried everything off. I can't believe it. Even Rooster

Rob's magnificent circus tent that used to dominate the hill is gone.

A large rat scurries across the road, disappearing under a cardboard box.

I survey the debris and sink deeper into despair.

This was Camelot, Edinburgh's biggest and brightest tent city. These people were my people.

There's tragedy behind me and tragedy ahead of me. Everywhere I turn's filled with desolation. Makes me feel helpless in the face of it all.

Would von Clausewitz flinch at this too, or would he stare at the calamity with equanimity?

He'd make a plan if his sister was kidnapped.

I walk through the debris strewn over the hill and step over an old wedding photograph. I'm still here. I'll walk over skulls if I have to.

The military-green teepee I'm heading to is right by the shores of Dunsapie Loch. The waters of the loch are murky and filled with litter too. The scent of rot is overpowering, and I notice a dead bloated animal, possibly a pig, floating on its back with its legs up.

'Anyone in there?' I yell at the teepee. Best to announce yourself. The last thing you wanna do is piss off an already scared and irate person. That's how it hits the fan.

There's no response, so I poke at the tent with my grabber.

'Sod off,' a man shouts from inside.

Something else stirs, all excited like, prancing about in the small teepee. He must have a dog with him. I don't want to get bitten so I back off a few feet.

'I only need to talk,' I say.

'Calm yersel. *Fuck*,' he says, and I don't think he means me. But I know that voice and it makes me smile for the first time since I set foot in Edinburgh.

Fiddly, fiddly, and the zipper of the teepee is opened. A red vixen bolts out, coming straight for me. Takes half a heartbeat for me to realize it's River! I go down on one knee and she flies into me, knocking me onto my back and licking my face. I'm giggling, delighted she made it off Calton Hill alive and well. Full winter fur, not a scratch on her either.

'Did you miss me, girl? I missed you loads,' I say, grabbing on and giving River a big hug. 'How did you get off that mountain?'

She replies in Gaelic or Foxish, I'm not sure which. Foxes are the ultimate survivors. Maybe she took off after Priya when she rescued my body. It's the first good thing that's happened to me since I got back. River was part of our little family in our wee caravan. I could weep.

A head pops out of the tent with a groan.

'I'd heard the polis snatched you,' Rooster Rob says.

'I'm the Artful Dodger, innit? Hail to thee, king of the hill.' I get up and give Rob a theatrical bow which earns me a V-sign. 'You coming out of that tent or what?'

The Rooster shakes his head. He's still got the red mohawk that earned him the moniker, but the sides have grown out a bit. It's not like him to leave it so tardy. The spikes aren't really even there anymore and his hair's flopped to the left – the king's crown frozen in the act of falling off. I run my hand over my own bald head. There's stubble on Rob's face and he appears run-down and depressed.

'That fox's gobbled me oot of hoose and hame.'

'What happened here? Where's everyone?'

'The king's coming tae Edinburgh,' he replies, squeezing his eyes shut.

'What's that got to do with anything? Did you lose a war with one of the other gangs? That's impossible. No one was strong enough to challenge you.'

He pops his head back in the tent and I hear him flop back on whatever he's lying on. Camelot was a living, breathing place. Now it's in ruins and Rob's not a king anymore, but a bum. This city brings its mighty low. I go over to the teepee and stand in front of the open entrance. The reek of cheap cider and stale fags hits me. Good thing Rob's not burnt this tent down. He's lying back on a sleeping bag with his eyes closed.

'The council's decided to clean up.'

Turns out with the monarch visiting, the Edinburgh City Council's targeted the homeless, streetwalkers, and any riff-raff that may give the city a bad look. Keeping up appearances. It's incredible, since the king will be surrounded by rubble and ruin in his palace. I guess if he can't have Calton Hill then at least Arthur's Seat could be spruced up for him. God forbid his delicate constitution's disturbed by the sight of his subjects sleeping rough. It's proper messed up.

'They treat this king like he's a god, Ropa.'

Rob tells me that the council and police conducted an un-announced dawn raid. Despite having spies in the filth, he was caught out. They weren't even given a chance to gather their belongings. All they got was truncheons and boots up the arse. It was proper ultraviolence. But it's one thing to beat up poor folk, it's another altogether to take their stuff. The police said everything on the hill was considered 'proceeds of crime' and confiscated. Fair enough, there were criminals here, Rob was one of them. But there were loads of civilians too, people who'd wound up here due to circumstances. Those people had so little, if you took something from them, you virtually destroyed their lives.

I've never seen the Rooster seem so helpless.

The law stayed away from Arthur's Seat due to some fear of the Clan, but also, and more importantly, 'cause Rob greased a few palms, paid them to look the other way. That's how it's done. This was his kingdom after all. Without the Clan he's just a middle-aged dude that might be holding onto his youth at the peak of punk rock. It's not a good look.

Rob's got a flat, a grow house in Bonnington, but he's chosen to remain on his beloved hill where he once told me he felt free. Before this round of forced evictions, Camelot had been razed to the ground thrice, and like a phoenix, thrice he'd brought it back to life. But this time the destruction looks complete.

Tread lightly, Ropa.

'How're you doing for food?' I ask.

'Not had a bit of scran in yonks. They seized my stash, every last morsel.'

The last time I was up on this hill, Rob, through some uncanny insight, had gone from stealing high-end electronics to building up a stash of cans to eat. The grey plague bollocksed up the harvest this year. Then there's the massive rat infestation that's been eating up supplies too. It's the perfect recipe for disaster, one we ain't seen since the Highland Potato Famine in the nineteenth century. I guess it's true what they say: history's just a series of circles and we keep coming back to the same place over and over.

'You look rough, pal,' I say.

'Get tae . . . Look, just take the fox and piss off.'

River paces around and pokes her nose into the tent. Rob doesn't stir. He just remains in situ giving corpse-level vibes. I don't think I've ever seen the Rooster in a funk like this before. Dare I say, he's actually moping. I guess that's what happens when your entire life's work is torn to the ground.

I still need him, but will he even be in his element? The Rooster, at his best, is a cold, calculating businessman, orchestrating a web of underworld operations with dozens of souls tied to him. It's not easy being the man responsible for half the crimes in Edinburgh, and, crucially, getting away with it. I used to wonder why he wouldn't just take off with his stash. It's because it was his job, and this was his city.

But I need to get Izwi back and that's going to take muscle.

'I wanna make you an offer you can't refuse,' I say.

Rob sits up, then slowly zips his teepee shut, and I hear him slump to the ground again. Okay. He can be a big kid, I guess, but I need him and I can't give up now. I look up at the sun, trying to gauge what the time might be. I have to make a move tonight. As von Clausewitz taught, 'The backbone of surprise is fusing speed with secrecy,' and I want the cake with the stripper up front and centre in the synagogue of this new religion tonight.

I rub River behind the ear and wait.

'You'll need to get up and pee at some point, and I'll still be here,' I say. 'I've got no place else to go.'

Gramps used to make me watch old kung fu flicks back in the day. In them, a novice would get his arse kicked and his father killed or some shit like that. Then he'd go off into the mountains to find some funky master of the stork and the floating lotus or some secret martial art. The master, sat around a roasting duck or chicken, would refuse to teach the student and then the hungry student would try to eat the chicken and the master would, without ever getting up from his spot, prevent him with slick kung fu moves. Of course, the student had to be patient and eventually the master would get sick of it and promise to teach the student this super-duper style that would help eliminate his enemies. It was the same formula every flick.

Wait a minute, does this make Rob the Shaolin master on this hill? He does have that down-and-out look about him now, and he's all alone.

'Sensei,' I say.

'Dinnae be an annoying, wee c—' Rob unzips the tent, pulls out a Pall Mall from a packet and lights up.

'There he is,' I say.

'This better be good,' replies Rob, taking a drag.

'Can I have one?'

Rob gives me the death stare, and I say, 'I'm just kidding, geez. It's bad for your health, you know?' When I first knew

Rob, he had a pack-a-day habit. Then when I returned to the Clan after a wee sabbatical, he'd stopped. Looks like the gremlins have him hooked again.

At last he gets the strength and he steps out of the tent and onto the shores of the loch with me. Rob's in a onesie with a hoodie, which must keep him warm, though he braves the cold in bare feet. He smokes, scanning his destroyed kingdom. With the gig I'm going to offer, perhaps he might have the means to rebuild what he's lost after that other king returns to England. Monarchs don't stay in Scotland long.

'Out with it, Ropa Moyo. This better be worth my time,' he says.

'I know a big old castle with lots of cool stuff that we can nick. They'll have food, artworks, silverware, jewellery, antiques. You can move this stuff, I'm sure. This will get you and Camelot back on your feet. How about it?'

'Robbing a castle, hmm? What's in it fer yous?'

'While we're there, we need to rescue my little sister who's being held against her will. Kill two birds with one stone. Save my sister and make a bit of change on the side.' I know Rob might dabble in lots of things, but he reserves a special disdain for folks who peddle human flesh.

'When?'

'Tonight. It's got to be tonight,' I say.

'Wow, wow, wow. You cannae just waltz intae a castle like it's yer ma's fanny. We need a plan. That and some prep work. Setting up a team. The works,' he replies, ever the consummate professional.

'I've got a great plan.'

'We need a *perfect* plan . . . I'll sort it.'

'The enemy of a good plan is the dream of a perfect plan,' I quote from von Clausewitz. 'We have a narrow window of opportunity and if we miss it then the whole thing's off. There's rich pickings if you come with me on this one. Think about it, Rob, you've done jobs all over Edinburgh. More than anyone cares to count. But the ultimate test of what you can do will be if you can take a castle. That makes you Ronnie Biggs and me Bruce Reynolds. We can get this thing done before the morning.'

The Rooster scratches his chin and lets out a plume of smoke through his nostrils. Then he flicks his cigarette into the loch. I know he's desperate, but he's still considering his odds. I like that. The fact he's not jumping in feet first. I need level heads with me tonight.

'Which castle?' he asks.

'Melville Castle in Dalkeith. You know the one?'

'Aye. But I've got a bad feeling aboot all this.'

'Think of the dosh. And I need you to do me a favour. You've got Priya's number, right?' He nods hesitantly. 'Send her a message to ask which room my sister's being kept in.'

This is brilliant. Me and Rob need to assemble our team in the next couple of hours. The Viscount Melville won't know what's hit him.

XV

It's great to be back with the old squad. Best of the fucking best, the A-Team, I'm talking Premier League, not SPL here. We've got the skinny, ginger guy, Squid McLaughlin, who used to work for a security company setting up home alarms, CCTV, that kind of thing. He knows all about response times, and used to get the Clan juicy pickings in the suburbs before his boss found out and sacked him. They couldn't get him arrested because it would've messed up their reputation. We're in the back of an old Transit and Squid's checking out the gadgets in his black bag.

Adrian Gibson used to work at Timpson's over in Corstorphine. Great wee business known for rehabilitating ex-cons, which is sweet. He's all morose, giving off the vibe he'd rather be anywhere else but here in our vibrant company. Adrian had been on the straight and narrow for a good few years until his brother got in debt with the Clan. The brother would have had his knees capped if Adrian hadn't volunteered his expertise as a locksmith to the Rooster. Somehow it turns out that debt's never fully repaid. Interest is a bitch.

It's tense out in the back of the Transit. No seats, so our arses are on the floor. There's a spare tyre, some blankets, ratchets and straps. Smells of oil too. The thing that worries me's the crate of Molotov cocktails, bottles tinking against each with each bump in the road. Our getaway driver Kieran's in his early twenties and has tattoos all over his body, up to his neck. He says he wanted to be an F1 driver, but good luck with that, laddie from Niddrie. Drives like a demon, so his talent's not entirely wasted.

The lads at the back appear a wee bit apprehensive. The only ones who're cool are River, who's sat between my legs lounging like she's Fantastic Ms Fox, and the unflappable Rooster. Not the other lads, though. That's understandable, 'cause we're breaking a cardinal rule tonight. See, it's easier burgling the middle class and the poor. They can't afford good security and live in easily accessible neighbourhoods. The rich, on the other hand, and we're talking the aristocracy here, have a lot more to lose and they'll make you sweat for it. The other problem is that the police tend to take a real interest when the rich get robbed. All of a sudden they become professional and willing to go above and beyond. You don't get that burgling the plebs, all they do is fill in a report and that's the end of that. I don't think any of these lads have been inside of a castle, let alone robbed one.

'Think of it, boys, we're tourists tonight,' I say, trying to liven up the mood. Von Clausewitz thought morale and the will to fight was important, so your troops have to have an incentive. 'We're going to make serious money tonight.'

'And you'll be helping with that granny stick of yours, right?' Lennox says.

'I'll shove it up your arse if it helps,' I reply.

The lads laugh and it breaks the tension a bit. There's many skills needed for the perfect burglary, like stealth and finesse, but when shit hits the fan, you absolutely, one hundred per cent have to default to old-school, I'm talking Viking, Highlander, Pict levels of, violence. Lennox and Logan, buff, monstrous twin brothers, are the muscle for hire, which is why they've got Adrian sandwiched between them. These lads are Rob's go-to debt collectors. They also handle the extortion side of his business too. Brains need not apply. You can tell them apart because Logan's lost most of his gnashers so his cheeks are sunk in.

'The wee lassie's got bigger balls than all of yous,' Angus Anderson says.

He's sat next to me and I appreciate his sentiment, 'cause the last time we met I challenged him to a boxing match and had my arse handed to me. Like, it was no contest. He goes by the name of 'Big Beef', the fourteen-year-old who's a hot prospect and can take out much older competitors. It kinda sucks he has to do this with us, since he really should concentrate on his boxing which may give him a way out of this crushing poverty. But he works part-time with the Clan as muscle to make the rent. His dad's also here with us, looking out for his son. The dad, Duncan Anderson, checks the converted replica handgun he'll be using tonight if needed. Both him and Rooster Rob have shooters; Rob, being the big man, carries a shotgun.

Angus is sat next to me. He's a huge lad and his shoulder brushes against me unintentionally. I shift to my left a bit. I feel soiled and don't want to be in physical contact with anyone just now.

The Rooster doesn't normally like carrying pieces to jobs, but I had to warn him there were serious people at the castle. I figure even if there's dodgy magicians, none of them can stop shells. I certainly hope not. The guns even out the score.

We've also got a spotter with us. Name's Kai – youngish, probably twelve or thirteen, with his whole future ahead of him, on the streets or inside of a cell at this rate. You always need a spotter on these jobs. Rob swears by them since they can get you out of sticky situations by giving you info in time. It could be a returning householder, the neighbourhood watch or the fuzz. Their job's to hang back and watch to see if anyone's coming back to whatever house you're nicking from. There's no job too small for having one, according to Rob.

Kai pulls out a Mars Bar from his pocket, opens the wrapper and takes a small bite. You can tell he's saving and savouring.

'You're gonna share that or not?' Lennox says.

'I'm sorry, who are you again?' Kai asks.

'Wow. Talk about being a little shit through and through,' Logan says, reaching out and snatching the chocolate from the kid. He breaks a chunk off and gives it to his brother, then throws the remainder my way.

I haven't had chocolate in ages. The scent of it gets me salivating. It's a tiny chunk the size of my thumb left in the packet, but I break it in half and pass the rest to the Big Beef. I hold my cube in my fingers, savouring the moment, and then pop it in my mouth. Mother of God, that is divine. The way the sweetness bursts on my tongue. I swallow and lick my fingers, waste not and all that.

'Give me your phone, Kai? I need to look something up.' I hold my hand out.

'You don't have one?'

'Hand it over,' Rob snaps.

I take the phone and go online to look up information on Dundas. Everything I know's from historical accounts I listened to on history podcasts, but there's stuff I need to be certain of before we get there. Now that the Library has been destroyed, the cloud's the next best thing.

'You hear about the woman who got groped by a ghost? Sorry, Ropa,' Duncan Anderson asks. 'I heard it on the radio. Somewhere on Bell's Wynd, she was minding her own business when she felt someone reach out and touch her holies. There was no one else about.'

'Utter bollocks,' says Lennox.

'I'm telling you, there's all sorts of strange things going on in the city,' Duncan replies.

'I saw a ghost just the other day down in Leith by the shore,' says Kai, proper animated like. 'I'd been to get a controller from my pal Freddie, he's got a squat in the Ocean Terminal, that old shopping mall. Nice place, it used to be a restaurant and he's got views of the sea from his window. Anyways, I'm plodding along, minding my own business, when out of nowhere – straight up, and I swear on my mother's life I'm not lying – it was there right in front of me, just as you are. This woman, right? Only she was dressed all funny like them Victorian people with big dresses. She was wearing a hat and had an umbrella—'

'Wind your neck in, Kai,' Logan says.

'Let him finish,' Duncan says.

'That was it,' Kai continues unabashed. 'I legged it out of there, as fast as I could. What did you expect me to do? Ropa, you see them too, don't you?'

'It's a grift. Look at her all smug like a pug. The kid preys on the weak and soft upstairs,' Lennox answers on my behalf.

Increased spectral activity is one thing, but normal people seeing them is pretty worrying. I mean, it happens from time to time, but it seems there's more of it going about. And then there's me, back from the dead, technically a ghoul too, albeit one with meat and bones. Melville Castle also has a resident ghost, but I might just keep that one to myself. Won't help my cause to spook this lot.

The one person I'm missing right now is Priya. I left her behind yet again, even though she'd asked me not to. Maybe I should have waited to see if she found a way out. She's a good egg and all, but if my mum was alive, I wouldn't leave her to go prancing about with this nonsense. I did the right thing, but I get the feeling we may need a magician.

I whisper a Promethean fire spell, hoping to cause a spark in the air, but nothing happens. Knapf. It was worth trying, though might not have been wise with the Molotov cocktails in the van. Screw it. I fiddle around with the walkie-talkie I've been given. It's got earphones. We've all got one. Rob figured mobile reception might be a problem in the castle – I don't have a mobile anyway. But with the walkies, we should be able to communicate.

The van stops abruptly and the engine's switched off. It's mighty cramped in here and without windows the air's gone proper stuffy, filled with farts. Savages. The door opening and slamming shut. Footsteps and then someone fiddles with the door handle which seems stuck.

There's more clanking until, finally, the back doors are both flung open. It's dark outside and we're in a country lane. I don't know why I expected us to be bang in the middle of Dalkeith, kinda like how Edinburgh Castle is in the city centre, but right now we're in the sticks.

Kieran stands by the open doors and the Rooster's the first one out, back bent, his mohawk brushing against the roof of the van. He takes a good stretch once he's out and beckons the rest of us.

'We've not prepped this through,' Squid complains. 'We should have scouted ahead for a week, figured out the layout, and got specifics on the human and electronic security. There's too many unknowns on this one. Adrian, you've got to tell them. Who knows what kind of security they've got here?'

'Fancy a tub of lube?' Lennox answers menacingly and Squid looks puzzled.

'The problem with a good plan is you think of another one and another till nothing gets done. Ain't that right, Ropa?'

'That's not quite how I— Never mind, Rob.' I let it go 'cause I'm not going to get anywhere debating the merits of von Clausewitz with the Rooster.

'I prefer daytime gigs,' Adrian grumbles.

'Same difference.'

But Adrian does have a point. See, night-time burglary is riskier than during the day. The best option is to target a house where people go off to work in the day – I know that's a wee bit tricky in the age of mass unemployment, but there are a fair few folks still working. You just have to find them. And so you break in during the daytime and have your pick of their stuff. It can be so easy. Night-time burgling requires a different set of skills: you need muscle in case of a scuffle. There's pros and cons to everything. What I hate is dogs, though. They'll bark, howl and whine, or even give you a gnarly hickey in the process. Insane business.

'Alright, masks on and out you come,' Rob says.

It's just gotten real and I step onto the dirt road. I fiddle about with my ski mask. It was clearly made for someone with a larger noggin and keeps getting in my eyes. There's unkempt hedging on either side of us. Some fields give way into woodland, fine country living right next to the city. We're somewhere in the hinterland between Dalkeith on one side and the village of Lasswade further along. Both sleepy places with fuck all to do as far as I'm aware.

'Every one of yer bastards kens what they're meant tae dae. Let's make some money,' Rob says. I swear I could picture William Wallace giving this rousing speech at the Battle of Stirling Bridge before he defeated the English. That's the kind of thing that makes your spirit soar.

I check my side for my dagger and remember I left it with Fenella's body in Aberdeen. Make sure I don't appear perturbed 'cause the lads know this mission was my idea. I have to project confidence like I'm a Prussian major-general. Squid McLaughlin brings out a tablet that shines like a beacon in the darkness, he scans it and says, 'This way,' climbing over the wooden fence where the hedge is broken.

'An hour tops or I'm off,' Kieran says.

'I'll break your fucking legs if you leave here without me,' Logan replies, and he sounds like he means it. I wouldn't mess with him and his brother 'cause they're the ones lugging the Molotov cocktails.

'Stealth,' Duncan whispers.

We're on. I wonder if this is how it was back in the medieval days when you went to attack the neighbouring tribe's land. Nothing new under the sun. We keep doing the same things over and over. Sometimes I'm not even sure we choose this. Like, we all have a part to play, and we get dragged through the script as we go along. I'm confident, though. Not so long ago, me and Priya raided Arniston House, and we came up tops with a bit of help from Mrs Guthrie. There's an art to breaking and entering and I'm with real experts today. This'll work.

It's a quick trek through the soggy open field and my boots squelch as I go. I'm used to trench foot, but I pity Big Beef and Kai in their fake designer trainers. Those'll be ruined by the end of this. The husk of an old, long-abandoned tractor sits silently rusting away in the field. It's an extravagant waste of scrap metal.

We go through the conifers and I sidle next to Rob who's leading from the front. He's got a grim look on his face, but he's moving with the barrel of his shotgun nestled in the crook of his arm like a gentleman farmer out hunting pheasant. I know it's hunger driving him on. That promise of one last job that'll get him back where he was before the filth took everything away. I know what it's like to be robbed by the cops too. The night they stole my rent sent me down this roller-coaster which has become my life.

River stays up close to me. She's scanning the darkness and can see better than the rest of us. I wish she could talk and tell us what's up ahead.

'What's the word from Priya?' I ask.

'She said she's still trying to get an answer from her mum,' Rob replies.

'Tell her to hurry.'

Bastard. This is a huge place we're going to and it won't make much sense to try every room to find Izwi. That'd be too risky. We need the right intel. If Priya doesn't come through, then the Clan'll still get their pickings whereas I'll come out empty-handed, and who knows if we'll get another bite of the cherry. This has to work.

I scan the treeline ahead. Nothing there. An owl hoots in the darkness. Duncan crosses himself. Even thieves have to believe in something. He seems like a good man who's out to look after his family. When there's no honest work to be had, it's either you starve or you do something about it. Messed-up choices but the rules weren't written for the rest of us. They were made to protect the rich who've been robbing us blind since the dawn of time. That's how I see it. Breaking the law's a middle finger to the powerful.

Kai peels away as soon as we reach the treeline. He's headed right, which should give him a cushy vantage of the west of the castle. Rob's taking the east. They'll both be spotting. The boss doesn't go inside anymore. Perks of being at the top of the food chain. But he will come if there's any trouble, you can bet on it. Like this one time we did a house in Portobello that turned out to have some hardcore Polish geezers who took exception to being liberated of their possessions. It went to shit until the Rooster came in and kicked ass.

We enter the woodland of giant elm, lime, sweet chestnuts and some sycamore. It's deathly quiet here. The fog clings to you like a blanket, almost as though it's trying to absorb your form. I'm glad 'cause that means no one will see us coming. We tread carefully, taking care not to make noise until we make it to the entrance of the open car park.

There it is: Melville Castle hunkering in the fog like a goliath in all its gothic glory.

I thought burning down Arniston House would have Henry Dundas join our wee homeless community for a bit. He was always welcome to our old caravan in Hermiston Slum, but he chose his second gaff instead. I was reading up on it on Kai's phone when we were making our way here. There's something unnatural about its structure that I can't quite put my finger on. It's beautiful, yes, but it gives off a sense of unease. Almost as if there's some dark energy radiating from within. The architect James Playfair was the father of William Henry Playfair who designed a lot of the New Town in Edinburgh, including the now destroyed Library of the Dead at Calton Hill. It seems both men had done business with Dundas.

We wait in the dark, taking our time as we watch for signs of life through the windows. Rob and Kai have gone to guard our flanks. The car park lies between me, Squid, Adrian and the castle. I'm at the edge. We avoid walking on the gravel surface 'cause it has that crunch noise. There's a pile of firewood in the middle of the car park. The logs are stacked together and a long one's upright, planted in the ground.

Waiting's the worst. Can't help feeling unsettled but I remind myself that this is for Izwi. There's no lights or any funny business in the castle. It's just after one in the morning and we're hoping everyone's tucked up nice and warm. Not a mouse stirring would do just fine, but you can't be sure on a job like this. Patience is the name of the game. Waiting, watching, waiting.

My earpiece crackles.

'Squid, Adrian, you're up,' Rob whispers.

Well, shit, here we go. I was hoping we had a bit longer but the Rooster also knows if you hold back too long cold feet's what you end up getting and no one gets any bread off that.

Squid and Adrian skirt around the car park. Going in direct would set off any motion sensor lights or alarms the building may have. The sensors are usually high up, so getting as close to the walls as you can helps avoid tripping them. Squid used to help set this sort of stuff up so he knows what to do.

I swear this ski mask's going to drive me insane. It's making my bald head itch and I scratch to make it stop.

My heart's in my mouth as I watch Squid and Adrian scurry along. The two lads make it to the castle wall and nothing's gone off yet. I'm super nervous right now. It takes the slightest error, a cough, a twig breaking, some middle-aged guy with a weak bladder getting up to pee, an act of God, sheer bad luck, and a gig's blown. That's the risk we're taking.

It's too gloomy to see exactly what they're doing. But they make it to the door and it's time for Adrian to work his magic.

Locksmithery is its own branch of the second science. I rate him up there with pickpockets in terms of the sheer artistry of what he does. Breaking in through a window is the noisy secondary option. But there's also the risk of them being alarmed.

I watch Adrian, knelt in front of the door, picking at the lock. Henry Dundas married into this prime piece of real estate. A shrewd move wedding Elizabeth Rainne, though she did fuck him over later on, so I've read. Turns out she was screwing some captain and she took off with him, leaving Dundas with four kids. I wonder if she was the baddie in all that or if Dundas was such a dick she had to bail and find love elsewhere. She got her divorce and married the other guy. Dundas got his own back, though, ruthless even then – she never saw her four kids again and died penniless. Pretty wild. Maybe the Viscount Melville's incapable of loving anything other than power.

Come on, Adrian. Get it done already.

Dundas must have had great affinity for this place, though. He raised his kids here for a time after his first wife had left. It's impressive enough, despite the spook factor that's got my spidey senses tingling. I find ghosts like to return to places they frequented when they were still alive. The old buildings in Scotland hold an essence of the past within them. Times might have moved on, but solid stone, well preserved, carries within it echoes of the distant past. For a ghoul this might give them strength and ground them since they aren't in the timeline when their shit was relevant. Old ghosts can get a bit cuckoo without something anchoring them to this world. Normally that should be family or other people they knew, but absent that then buildings and familiar spaces will do. Once I get Izwi out, Lennox and Logan will fire off their Molotov cocktails and we might be able to take this touchstone away from Dundas. I'll burn it down just like how they took my home from me.

'Ropa, Angus, Duncan, showtime,' the Rooster says on the radio.

Adrian's done it. Him and Squid showed us the way in. It's like walking through a cleared minefield, we have to follow their exact route. If we don't we might set something off. Duncan's got the shooter in case things go south.

'Now's the time for Priya to come good, Rob,' I say through the walkie-talkie.

'Top floor, room with a view, third door to the right,' he replies. 'She's well miffed with you, I'll have you know.'

We can handle that later. Priya's solid like usual. I still wish she was here beside me like the talisman she is. I give River a reassuring pat with my free hand.

Melville Castle used to be a luxury hotel. That's generally what happens when aristocrats get broke and sell up. I mean, it's more of a large country house, so back when Scotland had tons of tourists folks must have been queuing up to spend a few nights in a castle. Been there, done that at Dunvegan Castle last autumn. Overrated, in my opinion.

They've obviously thought to put Izwi in the place she's least likely to be able to escape. Ground floor, it's a short hop out the window to terra firma. Ditto first floor, so right up top it is.

This bloody mask keeps covering my eyes. I take it off at last and throw it onto the ground. Duncan turns back, furious.

'Put your mask back on,' he whispers.

'Don't care if they know it's me.'

'Amateur,' he says.

He's too cool to start an argument during a job. I've already caused him to make noise and I'm sure he'll rip me a new one, come the morning. We make it past the lion statues at the entrance to where Adrian and Squid are frozen in place. They look like statues too.

'I'm done and out,' Adrian whispers.

'You're fucking not, you little shit,' Duncan says, sticking the handgun in his ribs. 'I swear you'll get lead up your arsehole.'

'I have a bad feeling about this. I want to go home.'

'The only way you're going home is snug in a hearse if you think you can leave the Clan, arsewipe.' Duncan's blunt but he of all people knows the score.

We need Adrian in case of any more locked doors inside – I can't imagine anyone holding Izwi in an open room. The kid may be going to a posh boarding school, but she's from the slums through and through. If there's a digital safe then we have Squid. Him and Big Beef are going to prowl the place, getting what they can while me, River, Duncan and Adrian go upstairs to get my sister. We have ten minutes tops to get in, get what we want and flee.

It's my party so I'm the first one. Stone floor, I'm light with my makeshift cane so as not to make noise. River has no such problems with her soft paws. The portrait of some old laird in a red robe sits above a fireplace. It's pretty dark in here, and though our eyes have adjusted, stuff is still hard to make out. You can see bits of the wallpaper, the edges of furniture, that sort of thing.

It smells of dank and rotting things. The scents you get from hospices and end-of-life care facilities. Like death lingers over every surface. These grand old castles cost a mint for maintenance. Without business, the place must have fallen into disrepair and so we have to watch our steps.

I take the left, past some columns, and towards a staircase leading up, moving very slowly, making sure my ears are pricked. Squid and his crew go right, already hunting for loot.

I hold onto the banister and give it a wee shimmy. Nice and firm. I hope that's an indication the stairs are solid. Duncan's breathing loud through his nose behind me. I check back and he points up with the muzzle of his gun. Here goes. I take the first step up, foot landing lightly on the carpeting, and then I shift my weight onto it. The slightest creak, and my heart sinks. I was hoping for flagstone stairs. But the sound means that we have to go up one by one. All three of us will cause a racket. These old places suck like that. Still, the staircase is intact. It'd be more of a problem if it wasn't.

River goes up confidently without making a sound. I figure she's just showing off. My next step isn't as bad, and I try to speed up without compromising stealth. There's no avoiding making these creaking sounds, and in the stillness of night, the sound is exaggerated. However, this place is large, so I can only hope that means anyone who might hear is too far away to notice. And so I carry on, under the chandelier. There's portraits on the wall, vague faces I can't quite make out.

Shit, there's someone at the first landing. I nearly jump out of my skin and off the stairs before realizing it's just a statue.

Clasp my chest and take a breath. These weird rich people and their art.

I'm nearly at the landing when a ghost glides across. It's looking straight ahead and doesn't see me. Close call. If I'd made it up a minute sooner it'd have spotted me. I don't know if this one's connected to the cult or if it's just the resident ghost. I feel like reaching for my mbira and then remember I gave it up.

Bigger fish.

I make it up onto the first floor and scan the corridors in the darkness. There's no one about.

'Kai, you there?' Rob says, voice coming through my earpiece.

'Someone's out here . . . My bad, that's just a branch swaying. All clear,' Kai replies over the airwaves.

'Lennox, go cover Kai.' Rob doesn't take chances like that.

'Copy,' Lennox replies, like he's in a movie.

Adrian's already making his way up the stairs. I'm not liking the sound of them squeaking. It's too loud. I can hear it from way up here. Duncan must decide this is taking too long and he follows. Right decision, 'cause the stairs sound the same with both of them on. I begin to make my way up to the next floor. Might as well, though I go slow. You don't want to get cut off from the others.

My nerves are on the edge now we're deep inside the belly of the beast. This is what von Clausewitz meant when he said 'everything takes a different shape when we pass from abstractions to reality'. Making battle plans is one thing, but once shit hits the fan and all the pieces are in motion, you don't know how it'll play out. I guess this is the reality so we have to see how it will go.

A crackling, wet rattle comes over the airwaves.

'Kai, Lennox, you there?' Rob urgently whispers.

Nothing but crickets at the other end.

'Answer me, goddamn it,' he says.

'Boss, we have a—'

There's something like a grunt that comes through my earpiece, and I realize we've been made. 'Logan, now,' says Rob urgently. 'The rest of yous get oot.'

'No. I've got to get my sister,' I say.

'Duncan, get her oot of there noo,' Rob says.

Fuck. I make a dash up the stairs, not caring about the noise anymore. There's no way I'm leaving Izwi here. As I'm climbing up, frantic footsteps pound on the floor below – that'll be Adrian getting out of here. So much for having a locksmith's services then. Duncan's rushing up after me, swearing under his breath, but I'm already up that flight of stairs, dashing right and going to the third door. But which one is it, the one on my left or the one on my right?

I open the one on my right, facing the back of the building, and stumble into an empty room. I switch on the light. There's an antique four-poster bed, a wardrobe and some basic furnishings. But no one's here.

Duncan takes hold of my shoulder.

'Cinderella, the ball's over.' He points the way out with his gun. Typical enforcer, does what he's told, no question.

'Give me a sec,' I say. 'One more room.'

I turn round and cross the hallway to try the other door. He's still got his hand on my shoulder, looking around anxiously. The door refuses to open. I try it again. Fucking

210

Adrian, I could use you right now. This has to be it. I press my head to the door and say, 'Izwi, open up. It's me.'

Duncan cocks his gun.

'Kieran, get that engine warmed up,' Rob says over the walkie-talkie. 'Logan, what's taking you—'

A gunshot shatters the night. It's loud even though we're inside the castle. I hear doors opening beneath us. 'Fuck,' Duncan says. 'Angus, get as far away from here as you can, son.' Even with all this chaos he thinks of his boy. There's mayhem on the radio. Everyone cursing and jabbering at the same time. I can't hear myself think.

Duncan shoves me to one side, aims at the door and fires. He kicks it open, still pointing his gun.

'Where is she?' he says.

I step up and look into the room, standing under his outstretched right arm. Octavius Diderot's sat in the room, reading a thick book. He's one of the higher-ups in the Society of Sceptical Enquirers who betrayed Callander.

'Give me my sister or get a bullet in the head,' I say.

Diderot looks up from his reading and smiles. He holds up the book and says, 'The Papers of Tony Veitch, have you read it? I love William McIlvanney – so gritty and raw.'

There's a crack and a squelch, some liquid sprays onto my head. Duncan buckles and falls, his gun hand hitting my right shoulder and sliding onto the ground. He lands with a thud. Octavius Diderot goes back to reading his novel. I look down and see Duncan Anderson lying lifeless on the floor. The blood's pouring out from the gap at the back of his head where half his skull used to be. What remains of his brains looks like a cold clump of porridge spilt onto the floor. River's near it, sniffing away at the mess.

Oh, Izwi.

I retch. I'm swaying on my feet, holding onto my grabber. It's all gone to shit. A blood-curdling scream comes from downstairs. I don't even know who that might be. I look up the corridor and see Henry Dundas calmly watching me. He has a self-satisfied grin on his face. And at his feet is a Maine Coon, the massive cat from the Society offices at St Andrew Square. It licks its lips and there's blood coating its fur. Did it attack one of my guys? It's a vicious-looking bastard. Montgomery Wedderburn and Lady Rethabile Lebusa stand behind, flanking him.

I turn in the opposite direction and there's Wilson, Jomo and a bunch of other magicians blocking the corridor. Another dumb move.

XVI

Between a rock and a hard place is that sweet spot where you are well and truly juiced. 'In war, the advantages and disadvantages of a single action could only be determined by the final balance,' according to von Clausewitz, and my side of the ledger's empty. I had a bad hand and I dug in and it cost me and the Clan. I can only hope some of the lads got away, but the silence in my earpiece indicates otherwise.

Standing over Duncan Anderson's corpse, I face my enemies. I've experienced violent death a couple of times now, often as a spectator and once as a participant, either way I haven't yet quite gotten used to it. Staring out the window, beyond Diderot's shoulder, I see a figure in flames running and flailing as he burns. There go our Molotov cocktails.

I'm so sorry, Rob. I shouldn't have brought you here.

I shake my head, half hoping to incant a fire spell that'll take us all down. But I don't feel the magic in my veins. The Somerville equation tells us magic results from will, but every time I've clashed with Henry Dundas, I've been bested. Those with the strongest wills win every single time.

River growls and Dundas's cat hisses at her. I hold River

back, keeping her close to me. I don't want anything to happen to her. She deserves better.

'Welcome to my home, Ropa Moyo. Though it's not quite as grand as I remember it. Time is the enemy of everything,' Henry Dundas says. 'You are quite persistent. A remarkable quality in one so young. It's a rare spirit, and one I think we both share.'

'We're nothing alike,' I reply.

'I can see why you'd feel that way. But you and I have both returned from beyond that dreadful veil. Were you pliant, I'd name you Athena, sprung forth from her father's head, in my new pantheon. But Athena was the goddess of wisdom, an attribute you sorely lack. I think Artemis might suit you better – the hunter, wild and impulsive.'

'You're no god, you're just a ghoul.'

'How dare you,' Wedderburn says, stretching out his hand, a golden thermosphere lighting and hovering in the space between us.

'Ropa, don't make this any worse than it has to be,' Jomo says. 'I'm begging you. You could join us. There's a lot you don't yet understand. I've learnt so much in my time here.'

The mark on my chest burns.

I smile sadly; even when he's doing evil, he still wants you to think he's a good guy. My ex-best friend. What a plonker. At least I go out with my honour intact. I don't even want to give Jomo the satisfaction of a response. He's too far gone for me to pull him back. He's dead to me.

Henry Dundas gently lowers Wedderburn's arm and the thermosphere extinguishes. In the light I see that Dundas seems to have grown. He towers over his followers like a colossus. This is his natural height, his family renowned for that back in the day. His complexion seems to have improved greatly since I last saw him. There's a healthy colour to his skin, ruddy red cheeks and an impressive nose. He looks like a man stepped out of a classical painting. I fear he's well tethered to this world now.

'This one is too feral, but I'll hold up my end of the bargain. Perhaps her father can make her see reason,' he says. 'Take her away and lock her up. If this was a different era, I'd have her shipped off to Australia. We can decide what to do with her later.'

My father? Impossible. His soul was devoured by the guardians of the Other Place. Is the Viscount Melville playing mind games? Nah. I should be finding a way out of here, but I'm surrounded. Checkmate?

'Come on, sunshine. Let's put you where you belong with your little spy,' Wilson says, as he takes me by the arm.

Like an attentive butler, Wilson politely leads me back down the stairs. I'm not even surprised when I see Abdul, Carrie, Sin and Aurora from the Hamster Squad. I try to look them in the eye, but they turn away from me. Sin mouths, 'Sorry,' and confirms most folks are jellyfish. Spines are rarer than the clap in our age. These guys worked with Callander and now they'll happily do Dundas's dirty work. Scottish magic is well and truly buggered.

The lights are on now and I properly see that the castle's in a right state. Rotting tartan carpets. Peeling wallpaper. Some fixtures have been stripped off, leaving holes in the wall. A few hotel signs remain nailed in place.

'I tried to warn you, sunshine, but you didn't listen,' Wilson says, not without glee. 'I only wanted to help you. We could have been friends, you and I.'

Kill me now.

'The likes of us can't afford to get all uppity. We know our place. We were born to serve great men like the viscount. No point getting notions we can join them at the high table. But if we're faithful, then when their history is recorded, they'll say we were good servants. Our names will be in there too. Small footnotes, but they'll be there.'

'Shut your pus.'

He shoves me hard and I nearly fall down the last bit of stairs. My litter-picker keeps me upright, thankfully. He thinks having his name next to Dundas will give him some sort of immortality.

'Through there,' Wilson says, dropping the honeyed tone.

We're in the basement now, in front of a white door. He takes out a key, unlocks the door, and orders me inside. I take some deep breaths. Confined spaces bring back horrific memories of Arthur Lodge, the last place Wilson had me imprisoned. I came out on top then, but now we've come full circle. The universe has a mean sense of humour.

'In you get. We don't have all day,' Wilson says.

I go inside and see Frances Cockburn's sat on the floor in the corner. The room's tiny, maybe twelve by twelve. Must have been some kind of cellar back in the day. The walls are bare, cement and stone showing. None of the fine trimmings in the ruins we saw upstairs. There's a solitary light, an old-fashioned filament bulb that must have been left over from the dark ages.

The room's dusty, a fine coating on the walls and on the floor too. There's cobwebs in the corners. Whatever shelving was here's been stripped out, but there are lines and a couple of nails through the stone walls showing where it might have been.

Wilson slams the door shut and locks it.

Cockburn's had it in for me since I first tried to join the Society of Sceptical Enquirers. It's a deep, mutual dislike. Who better to torture me, or whatever the fuck they want to do to me down in this basement?

I stay in my corner of the room.

River paces about, not quite sure what to do with herself. Let her – I reckon I might need her hyped up in case of whatever Frances Cockburn's cooked up for me.

I'm sure Wilson's waiting outside ready to jerk off when the show starts. I take off my backpack, put it on the floor and wait. And wait. Cockburn's dragging this out. The sadistic psycho probably wants to savour every morsel of my discomfort. But I won't give her the satisfaction.

If I could still do the magicking thing, I'd have burnt off her face by now. Struck first like von Clausewitz advised. I suspect Cockburn might want to catch me off guard, lure me into a false sense of security before she nails me.

I hate her so much, that narrow goat-like face. The way her bones jut out of her flesh. Everything about Cockburn fills me with revulsion. Maybe the cavalry's going to show up any time. I'd rather be with anyone else than having to deal with Cockburn.

I snap my fingers twice.

'Hey, Frances, can we get on with this already? I've got places I want to be,' I say.

She just blanks me. What a douche.

My feet are sore so I lean against the wall. I hope some of the Clan made it out. Failed them, failed Izwi, and now I'm failing to wind up Cockburn one last time. That's about the only thing that I'd say would be a positive outcome, if nothing else, given the way things have gone tonight.

This was a bad, bad move. I shouldn't have dragged the Clan into a job for magicians, but I was desperate and thought it might work. The memory of Duncan lying in a pool of his own blood flashes in my head. Try as I may, I can't get it to leave. It's not my life but his flashing before my eyes.

'Frances, hey. Let's get this over and done with,' I say.

Cockburn starts, shakes her head and blinks like she's only now seeing me for the first time.

'You stupid, stupid, child,' she says, burying her face in her hands.

I'm about to pop off, but I hold my gob.

Hang on.

Nah. No freaking way.

Cockburn betrayed Callander up on Calton Hill. The gaffer was proper gutted 'cause he had so much faith in her. She was like his super-efficient employee and Director of Membership Services at the Society. But when push came to shove, she left him and joined the Dundas Cult. I saw it with my own eyes.

Ranjeeta Kapoor told me that they've got a spy on the inside and that Izwi's fine. Yay, we've got someone on the inside. I start laughing, 'cause you have to, and I hope von Clausewitz is laughing with me because he tried to warn me that 'The deceiver by stratagem leaves it to the person himself whom he is deceiving to commit the errors of understanding which at last, flowing into one result, suddenly change the nature of things in his eyes.'

Ropa, you dumb fuck.

I got the Melville Castle address off Ranjeeta. I decide to go ahead, and then I get the exact location for where Izwi's being held from Priya. Information from the rat in Dundas's camp. And so I wind up here with the Clan, ready to mash up the place and get my sister. It'd have been so slick had I not been dealing with the guy who was hardcore in a war against France and a key mover in expanding the Empire in India. Dundas ain't no muck. You don't get to rule without intelligence, pun fully bloody intended.

'You were the spy feeding the witches information, weren't you?' I say.

Cockburn sighs. Her eyes are red, with dark circles – she's going through the wringer. Betrayal is always treated harshly in war and spies get it worst of all. There's the slightest of tremors in her hands. I'd almost pity her if I didn't have a visceral dislike for her. Have to admit, despite the fact we're both in a pickle, I might cut off my nose here and say I'm happy she's getting it too.

It'd be poetic justice to go down with my nemesis. Ha.

'I didn't think you had it in you, Frances,' I say.

She takes it and doesn't give anything back. Well, this makes for a change from our old encounters. She is really in the deepest of shit, like in those old movies with quicksand everywhere. I try my radio, which Wilson's not been savvy enough to take away from me.

'Rob, you there?'

Crickets.

'Beefie, Squid, Kieran? Is anyone out there?'

'Don't waste your time; your friends are all dead,' Cockburn says. 'You've got us all killed. Well done.'

'I've never been good enough for you, have I?'

Cockburn turns to the wall next to her, averting her gaze from me. Her cheek bulges as she runs her tongue inside it. She's sweating and looks like a wreck. But there's no way she just happened to decide to spy for the Daughters of Scotia on a whim. She must have been doing this since way back. That's how it's done, right? You plant a mole and then wait. That means Cockburn was spying on the Society where she rose up high enough to get close to Callander.

'I don't like you, Frances, but we have to set our differences aside and bust our way out of here,' I suggest. 'How about it? You and me as a team for a change.' If my father could use Sir George MacKenzie, I can bloody well use Frances Cockburn. 'I need you to fire off a soliton strong enough to break that door down. Then we make a break for it.'

Cockburn says nothing.

'It's better than waiting to get our arses fried,' I say, trying to sell this to her. If my magic was magicking, I'd do it myself, but I'm a bit limp at the moment. Sometimes in a bad situation, you've got to rally some people. They freeze up, and I dare say Cockburn might be one of those. Stripped of her authority in the Society, she's . . .

I missed it.

'What did they do to you?'

She doesn't respond. It's like she's withdrawn to some other place where she can't get hurt. To me right now, she looks young and vulnerable. Knees up, she clasps her hands around her legs and rocks back and forth. I saw this happen to Torquil, one of the quadruplets who guarded the Library of the Dead. Frances Cockburn's been neutered. Magic results from will. You can stop a magician from doing magic by breaking their will so they can no longer perform spells. It's a violation.

Without her magic, Cockburn's as useless as I am.

I cross the room to her, place my back on the wall and slide down, so I'm sat right next to her. My nemesis. Dundas and his folks have crossed so many lines. Cockburn and me are floaters in the same shit creek now, we might as well paddle together. I put my hand on her arm, and am surprised she doesn't pull back from me.

Cockburn slumps over and puts her weight on me before dropping her head onto my shoulder. Her hair's soft against my neck. I prefer mean Cockburn to pitiful Cockburn. If I could, I'd swap this moment for one in which we're sparring each other. She just seems so completely defeated. The spark inside her's gone.

She sobs once, then stops herself from crying.

I can't help blaming myself for this. If I had stopped Dundas when I was supposed to, Callander would still be here and Cockburn would still be a twally. This wave of disaster spreads out from my every move. Every direction I turn, I'm damned.

'I really believed you betrayed Callander that night. Doesn't matter, even with your help the result would have been the same. Dundas is too powerful,' I say.

'I know,' she replies.

I point to the metal bucket with a roll of toilet paper next to it. 'Do they really expect us to use that?'

'The viscount is used to much older methods. That's why there's no bedding in here either. That's how it was done in the eighteenth century.'

'I guess that's alright then.'

We laugh. Doesn't last long cause the melancholy sets in real quick. I'd never have pictured Cockburn for a spy, though. Always so prim, proper and officious. I suppose that's how you fool folks if you do it long enough.

'I never hated you, Ropa,' she says.

'You damn well did a good job showing it,' I reply, still sore about how she treated me before.

'There was a debate before you joined the Society of Sceptical Enquirers. Your grandmother sent word to Ranjeeta Kapoor that your heart was bent in that direction, and fate had conspired you fall under the wing of her old friend, Sir—' Her voice chokes, and I see she truly did care for him. Can't even bring herself to say his name. 'I would have saved him if it was in my power, but my part was decided for me a long time ago. He was a good man.'

Callander, irritable, gruff, but underneath that exterior was a legend. Anyone who can get Esfandiar Soltani to fall in love with them could only possess a pure heart. That's the very thing that gets you killed in this world.

'Ranjeeta was against you joining the Society and she asked

me to make sure you'd not fall into this path. I did my best, but you kept pushing against me. I was impressed, but infuriated.'

'Why, though?'

'Melsie had a lot she wanted to teach you. There are other ways of doing magic – there always have been.'

I found it easier to learn from books than I did listening to Gran. My fault really. I mean, she was my gran, and I could never quite see her having a life before I popped up. In my eyes she was old and had always been old. Safely boring. I could never imagine she was a witch. Feels weird even calling her that.

'Are you a . . . ?'

Cockburn nods. 'From my mother who got it from her mother, down to me. Same as your friend Priya and her mum.'

'Was my mum a witch too?' I ask.

'She was a fine seamstress. That's its own form of magic, but she was no witch,' Cockburn replies. 'It doesn't always run in the family. You can get adopted by one too, the very thing Melsie tried to do for you. She also meant to do the same for your little sister, but Callander had other ideas. He'd learnt of her potential.'

'But Priya went to uni and everything.'

'It's possible to be both. I went to St Andrews. That doesn't mean I forgot the things my mother taught me. Witchcraft must be passed down from woman to woman. Men too, far fewer though – it's hard work being a witch and it's long been feared their little brains would explode or their testicles would fall off.'

Cockburn makes me laugh, and I'm surprised I didn't realize she always had a wicked sense of humour.

'Regardless, there are a few men who've risen above their gender to become decent witches: Cornelius Lethington whom you are acquainted with and also Mr Sneddon at the Library of the Dead. Rest his soul,' says Cockburn. She sits up and looks at me as if I'm the first kind face she's seen in ages. I must know more.

'This means Calista Featherstone is one of you, right?' I ask.

'She's not a witch, but she knows of us and is the most sympathetic head of the four schools we've had in centuries. It took a while for us to come to trust her but she's a good woman. There's no set route to becoming a witch, a lot of women are and they just don't know it yet.'

'How many witches are there?'

'In Scotland, far fewer than we need. We've been hunted and slaughtered by magicians for over four hundred years until they became the face of magic. With it they amassed fabulous fortunes. Before the magicians, the Kirk and the state, witches used to aid people. Healed ailments, gave charms, birthed children, helped farmers and traders; people came to us with their problems and we solved them. Now tell me, can you get any of that for free from the Society or do you have to pay through the nose for it?'

Cockburn explains how the rise of scientific magic guided by witchfinders was hastened through the persecution of witches. Over the sixteenth and seventeenth centuries more than two thousand five hundred witches were executed in

Scotland. Those were the ones given trials and recorded. Many more were simply erased without any due process, just hearsay. The minds of the people were poisoned. These women who helped so many were seen as something to be loathed and feared. Crude depictions of warty witches flying on broomsticks emerged. The Kirk and Church both were keen to portray them as consorting with the Devil and blamed natural disasters on them. There came a time when the slightest misfortune could be tied to a witch.

'It's so easy to turn people against each other,' Cockburn says. 'There was great profit for the men who engaged in such practices. They became your magicians, priests, doctors and so forth, changing our way of life, our beliefs and customs forever.'

'And then they got big old statues for it,' I say.

'We may hide in nooks and crannies, always in the shadows, one misstep from discovery, but we are still here,' Cockburn says.

I thought I had her sussed out, but there's the far side of the moon I've not seen before. I've been fighting battles and losing 'cause I didn't spot the four-hundred-year-old war that's been raging on. If you don't know your history, you're flailing in the dark. War is an act to compel the enemy to your will, and the Society's been fucking over the witches for centuries. The thing about power is it metastasizes and wants more and more. It has a ravenous energy that won't stop consuming. First the witches, now everything, it seems. But they've not won it yet.

'Hardy like bindweed,' I say.

'If only,' Cockburn replies. 'It takes a long time to make a witch. There are no formal institutions, but we've taken to calling it the First School. The knowledge must be passed down from mother to daughter, incrementally. There were women who tried in the past. Sarah Siddons Mair, you've heard of her?'

I shake my head.

'A remarkable woman from the eighteen hundreds who lived at Abercrombie Place in Edinburgh's New Town. She felt that the best chance for us was to do the same thing as the magicians. Initially she fought to have women accepted in men's schools. The Edinburgh Ordinary School for Boys was off-limits, as was the University of Edinburgh. She fought for the vote too, but that's another matter. She was instrumental in founding St George's School for Girls in 1888, right in the heart of Edinburgh. It would have been the school for witches if she'd succeeded.'

'What happened?' I'm liking the idea of a girls' school I might have gone to.

'The other side of the argument. The Society tried to standardize magic with a Victorian tenacity. They prefer neat lines and *rigour*. It creates conformity and turns them into mindless beings devoted to acquiring money above all else. Even the best of them, like Sir . . .' She trails off. It must be taxing to have been in the centre of an institution that stands against everything you believe. 'But with witches, though we may be sisters, our practice varies radically. There's room for improvisation. Knowledge transmitted orally shifts and changes depending on the listener and morphs again with each retelling. We've never believed in sitting small children down for hours on end, cramming them with facts to regurgitate on a piece of paper. A school would have changed all that.'

Cockburn tells me how the Daughters of Scotia rejected Sarah Siddons Mair's embrace of what the magicians were doing. And she in turn renounced her coven and turned St George's School for Girls into a normal institution covering the same curriculum the boys got in education. This rift with her sisters caused her a lot of pain and bitterness, but she thrust her energies into other things and became president of the Edinburgh National Society for Women's Suffrage.

'To this day, there are some witches who believe this was a mistake. The Mair debate is far from settled and flares up from time to time,' Cockburn says.

'Which side are you on?' I ask.

She smiles and says nothing. Not that she has to. I already know where she stands. I reflect on the fact that Edinburgh's been at the centre of the most seismic events in the last couple of years. It seems the Auld Reekie wants to shake the world one more time.

River comes over to us and squeezes in between our legs. She makes herself comfortable and lays her head on Cockburn's lap. I can't believe Cockburn's delight, stroking River's fur. Her face lights up when she smiles, and to think I knew her as a woman of ice. In another life we might have been cool.

'I've noticed Edinburgh's changing. It's becoming the world of the dead. Did you see it too while you were there?' I ask, hoping to learn something of Dundas's plans.

'It's dreadful, isn't it?' Cockburn replies. 'I'm afraid I wasn't such a good spy, since it seems they were only feeding me

227

scraps of information that they wanted me to know. It takes time to build up trust, so you learn the deepest secrets. I can't say anything with the certainty I once thought I had.'

'I'll take whatever you've got.'

'All I've discovered is something very big will happen in the next few days. What or why, I honestly have no idea, but Wedderburn said something about wiping the chessboard.'

A chessboard, hey? Gets me wondering. There's a wee chessboard on Bruntsfield Links out in the city. Maybe that could be some kind of secret magical location? I also know out in Leith Links they hold games of chess sometimes. Chess in Scotland's been played since the medieval days. There's got to be something I can figure out. I wish I could use the Library of the Dead right now.

Me and Frances chat through the night. I think she's really amazing. Like, she knows all this random stuff and it feels like I'm chatting with the big sister I never had.

XVII

Me and Frances are mighty drowsy when we hear the key clunk into the door. River's asleep in the spot between us. The door swings open and a bright light burns my eyes. I squint and make out Wilson's silhouette in the doorway. Ever the butler, he's immaculate in his tailcoat, and wears white gloves hiding his deformed hands.

'Morning, ladies, come with me, we'll make sure you have a decent breakfast today,' Wilson says, flashing a diabolical smile. 'This was a fabulous hotel back in the day and I won't be the one to let standards slip.'

He takes a dark pleasure in this sort of business, and I'm kinda impressed he's true to his nature like that. I get up, as does Cockburn. My tailbone hurts from sitting on the hard floor all night, and my glutes aren't thanking me either. The stiffness's set in and I feel the blood rushing back down my legs.

We hobble out the door and are met with two young Edinburgh magicians who step alongside us. One of them is Abdul from the Hamster Squad. He's lanky and moves awkwardly in his cheap navy-blue polyester suit. This isn't the admin gig he signed up for with the Society. The other geezer's a short, blonde guy I've not met before. If I was still magicking, I'd take my chances against them. Cockburn would certainly have been able to handle things. But as it stands they might as well be pit bulls guarding us.

Wilson leads us to a room with a sign on the door that says 'Brasserie'. There's some square tables in the middle and booths lining the walls. The furniture's seen better days and rats have had a fair go at the upholstery. This must have been the hotel restaurant back when it was operational. One of the tables is set and so I place my grabber against it and take a seat and Cockburn goes opposite me.

'This morning we will provide you with a full Scottish breakfast,' says Wilson. 'Would you like a hot drink with that? We also have fruit juice and water.' In his aged butler's suit Wilson looks like the perfect host. He seems attentive, almost eager to please. When we don't answer, he says, 'Very well, tea for you, sunshine, and a black Americano for Ms Cockburn.'

Wilson leaves, but we stay under the guard of Abdul and the blonde pug. Minutes later Wilson returns with a tray balanced on one hand, and retrieves two plates laden with food for me and Cockburn. We have forks but no knives. Like, what are we supposed to do with blunt cutlery? Then again, I am thinking of sticking this fork in his neck. It's tempting. The plates are covered by cloches which Wilson removes with a flourish.

'Enjoy your breakfast, ladies,' he says over his shoulder, walking away and leaving Abdul and the other magician to guard us.

I pick up my fork and am about to dig in when I think,

What if this stuff is poisoned? That would be a horrible way to go. But I am hungry. Cockburn picks up her fork.

'Dundas wouldn't kill you with poison, Ropa. He's a *gentleman*,' she says, delicately breaking a corner off her Lorne sausage.

It's messed up how this lot has good food while half of Scotland's starving to death. Waste not on my part; I gobble down a tattie scone, dipping it into the baked beans for a bit of flavour. While I'm blitzing through, I notice Cockburn's nibbling away but her hand's shaking. She's putting on a show of eating for me, but it seems she's really not hungry. Her loss, cause this is the best brekkie I've had in yonks.

'Eat up. It's really good,' I say.

I give River my Lorne sausage and black pudding and she wolfs them down pronto. Frances Cockburn takes her share and puts it on my plate. Though her hands are shaking, there's a kind of serenity to her this morning. Reckon if she's this great spy-witch then there's a good chance she might yet find a plan to break us out of here. For now we might as well comply and make out we're not a threat.

In no time I've destroyed my plate, and half of Cockburn's. My belly is full and, despite the circumstances, I feel a lot better. I might have to sign up with Dundas if the food's so great. God damn.

Wilson returns with our hot drinks and sets them down. This time Cockburn takes her coffee and drinks it quickly. My tea's hot and I figure hers is too, so the pace at which she gulps her drink means she must have iron lips and a throat to match.

'My only vice,' Cockburn says, raising her cup.

'Not the worst I've seen,' I reply.

'This is nice. Thank you, Ropa.'

'What you thanking me for?'

'The company. I've been deep behind enemy lines for so long, I've forgotten what it is to enjoy the simple pleasures with someone I can trust.'

'I'm not too sure this qualifies.'

'Oh, but one day when you're grey and old, you might think of me sitting opposite you at this table. I want you to remember me happy,' she says.

There's a finality in her tone. I have to unlearn everything I used to think of her. She holds out her hand across the table, reaching for mine, and I take it. Feels a bit awkward being all intimate with my nemesis.

'If you can, please tell my mother I love her very much,' she squeaks, her voice becoming so small and childlike.

'We'll find a way out of this,' I say.

Cockburn tries to smile, but I see fear in her eyes. She purses her lips and sniffles. It's like she's been carrying tension all these years and now the dam's about to burst. The moment is interrupted by Abdul swooping in, noisily clearing away the plates. Wilson hovers around with an air of enthusiasm. The mask he wears of the servile butler doesn't fool me; beneath his demeanour's an air of menace.

'Did you enjoy your last meal?' he asks.

'It was lovely,' Cockburn replies.

'Good, that pleases us. Shall we?' Wilson extends his hand, gesturing towards the door.

What's all this pish about a last meal? Cockburn's been

acting all weird, understandable given where we are, but there's been more to it and I've completely missed the cues. She's been under pressure for a reason. They're going to kill us. No, *her*, otherwise why would she be asking me to pass on a message to her mother.

'Where are you taking us?' I ask, refusing to stand. I keep a tight hold of Frances's hand.

'It's time,' Wilson replies, as if that answers anything.

'Where—'

'It's okay, Ropa. Just don't forget to tell Mam,' Cockburn says, getting up.

I'm panicking. So, I'm the enemy, no doubt about that for the members of this fucked-up cult. But Frances Cockburn is worse than an enemy, she's a traitor. The gravity of the situation hits me. I keep hold of Frances's hand. They're not taking her.

Think of something fast, Ropa.

'Prometheus,' I call out.

Nothing happens. The Greek gods have abandoned us. 'Anemoi!' Nothing. 'Poseidon.' I call out every spell I can think of, but there's no entropic shift, no magic. Just my voice echoing against the stone walls of this castle.

'She's not going anywhere,' I say, frustrated.

'You're coming along too. The Viscount Melville demands you bear witness,' Wilson says.

In the midst of all this, Cockburn's regained her composure. She stands proud, with that officious look I hated so much when she wore it in the halls of the Society. She comes round the table, pulls me up onto my feet and hands me my grabber.

'I feel stronger holding your hand,' she says.

'Frances, no,' I reply.

It's her who's giving me strength. We just need a plan. A little more time and I'll think of something. There might be a weakness in the architecture, a secret tunnel. Maybe one of the Hamster Squad might be able to help. With a bit of time we can turn it around. I look around the room, trying to find something, anything at all, but there's nothing.

'We mustn't keep him waiting,' Wilson says.

'Lead the way,' Cockburn replies.

I bloody hate this fake politeness. How these prim and proper people do vile things while hiding behind delicate language. It's so messed up. Where I grew up, if someone didn't like you, you knew about it. If they were going to rob you, they told you in no uncertain terms. But these Society people, fake butlers and all, they do wicked things and try to appear like paragons of virtue. They value seeming proper over doing the right thing. I don't know why I ever wanted to be part of this bullshit.

'Ms Cockburn,' says Abdul.

'Shut up and make yourself useful elsewhere,' Wilson says.

'You worked with her, Abdul. Do something,' I say.

'I can't, Ropa. The secretary's word is law.'

I hock and spit on his shoe.

'Coward.'

Abdul shrinks back from me. He has a wide-eyed look, but very quickly he turns back to his work. It's as if he wants to clear us from his own memory.

'Let's go now,' says Wilson, sweeping his arm, urging us along.

We follow him through the dilapidated building. In the daytime its state of disrepair is stark. The smell of damp hangs in the atmosphere. Every carpet is rotting, the plaster's cracked and sections have collapsed off the ceiling.

As we go out, we're met by many gawking magicians. The ones who've embraced Henry Dundas's return. This lot worked with Frances Cockburn for years. There's not a single practitioner who'd have been a member of the Society who wouldn't know who she is, yet none will lift a finger and come to her aid. I can sense they're nervous. You get that when people know they're doing the wrong thing but would rather turn off their consciences than stand up and do the right thing.

How could I have wanted to be one of these people?

We wind up outside the castle in the car park leading to the front gate. A body lies facing upward. That red, messed-up mohawk. Rob's lifeless eyes stare into nothingness. Even from this distance I can make out the claw marks on his face and hands where he was protecting himself. There's bite marks puncturing his throat. It seems the cat went for the jugular and Rob bled to death.

There's another body in the treeline. I can only see the soles of their shoes, but it looks like Big Beef was running away towards the fields before they got him with a thermosphere in the back. The kid didn't stand a chance. He should never have been with us in the first place.

They've rearranged the firewood I saw last night. Now the logs are deposited around the tall pole staked in the gravel car park. These damned practitioners stand in a semi-circle around it as we approach. At the centre of it all is their Black Lord,

Henry Dundas. Beside him is my little sister. His evil cat rubs against her leg on the other side, guarding her.

'Izwi!' I rush towards her, but Wilson blocks me.

'You try that and it's back in the hole for you,' he says.

Izwi's looking furious as she stands beside Dundas. I've seen that face in many a tantrum back in our little caravan. 'Touch my sister and I'll kill you,' she says. This makes the magicians laugh.

'I wouldn't dare, young lady,' Dundas replies. I notice how soothing his voice becomes. 'Your father asked me to protect you and I'll honour my word. Tonight, your sister's voice will be that of a queen.'

I don't know what deal my father struck working for this cult, but if Dundas sent me to the Other Place before, then I'm pretty certain he's not holding his end of the bargain. Other people's lives mean nothing to these so-called great men.

Frances Cockburn lets go of my hand as Dundas turns his attention fully to her.

'What's your mother's name?' I ask as she steps away.

'Theodosia Lovell,' she replies, eyes fixed on the firewood at the centre of the semi-circle.

With that she walks over to the waiting ghoul, leaving me speechless. They're related? In Glasgow, Theodosia said something about losing a piece of her heart and now I know what she meant. This is her sacrifice. To me, Cockburn was a cold toff while her mother was earthy and grounded. Nothing in her accent or dress gave away the fact Cockburn was one of the Travelling Folk. Seems she was putting on those posh airs. My ticker's pounding and I'm scanning the surroundings.

There has to be a way out of this for us. Me and Cockburn should make a break for it. But every conceivable avenue of escape's blocked.

'It is time for us to return to the old ways,' Henry Dundas says in a booming voice. 'We've watched you from the beyond as you lost your way and squandered the inheritance we gave you. Everything we built was wasted by a generation born with silver spoons. But have no fear, for in our acts we turn the clock back to how it should be.'

'Hear, hear,' cheers Montgomery Wedderburn.

'Frances Cockburn, did you not learn the adage "Repay your benefactor frequently with gentle favours in return"? We embraced you, took you in and showed you the wisdom of our ways. And you burrowed deep into our core to spread corruption, but we were always a step ahead. We see deep into your weaselling soul and nothing is hidden from us. There are severe consequences for defying the gods. Prometheus was tied to the rock and his liver eaten in eternity for crossing Zeus. Marsyas challenged Apollo to a contest and was flayed alive when he lost. Athena caused Arachne to hang herself. By your own actions you have sentenced yourself to death, and now, Frances Cockburn, you must burn at this stake as Ixion too was punished for his betrayal. I take no joy in this, but heavy is the head that wears the crown.'

Most of the practitioners watch with disturbing glee, but there's alarm on Sin's and Carrie's faces. Before this they were paper pushers in the Society. They know Frances Cockburn – they used to work for her. Aurora covers her mouth. They are not the only ones who seem utterly distressed. This has gone too far. There's no way they can allow this to happen.

'This is madness,' I protest. 'Are you all going to stand here while this ghoul makes you do evil deeds against one of your own?'

'Silence,' Wedderburn shouts. He points a finger at me and then slowly raises it to his lips.

'No, you don't get to shut me up.' I stride forward, pointing an accusing finger at the Hamster Squad. 'You worked with Frances Cockburn for years and this is what you want to do to her? All of you know her. If the words of this ghoul hold more weight than your honour and decency then your humanity is lost.'

A heavy silence descends. I try to catch as many people's eyes as I can. To sway them, to make them see reason. Many avoid looking at me. Others, like Mary Hanley, stare at their own shoes, unwilling to speak up. Jomo's hiding away behind some people. I have to keep pushing. I open my mouth, but a hand covers it from behind and smothers my speech. They leave my nose free, but I can hardly breathe. I try to break free. They are too strong and all I can make are muffled noises. The man holding me pulls me to him and wraps his other hand over my chest so I can't move my arms. I try to bite but he's wearing leather gloves.

Hamish Hutchinson, Principal of St Andrews College, ushers Cockburn onto the pile of firewood. He stands her by the stake, takes a bundle of rope from his suit pocket and proceeds to tie her hands, and then her legs. I want Cockburn to resist, but she stands there, gentle as a lamb, as Hutchinson binds her. How can he do this?

Frances has to fight.

She's just looking into the distance at the sun hidden behind the grey fog.

Frances Cockburn atop the pyre has a beatific look about her. Did she know this would happen? In this century? The Viscount Melville is dragging us back to a savage past. I want to say these words, but it's as if everyone in the crowd is somehow transfixed. No one wants to put their head over the parapet. It's as if they expect someone else, anyone else but them to do something. This is how things go too far in a cult. All it would take for one person to break the spell is to say 'Stop, this is wrong'.

Why won't they act?

Someone. *Anyone.*

Hamish Hutchinson finishes securing Cockburn to the stake. He gives the ropes a good tug to make sure they're secure, and then he clambers off the pyre and onto the ground before taking his place beside Montgomery Wedderburn.

There's an ominous stillness.

Maybe this is a test. Dundas is playing mind games with his followers. He's testing their loyalty and driving home a point. They used to unnerve people with mock executions in the old days. Henry Dundas suspends the moment, holding every one of us locked in. I get what he wants from all this. He wants Frances Cockburn to beg forgiveness, the great ritual of a show of mercy. We'll all breathe a collective sigh of relief when he stays his hand.

Cockburn remains impassive.

She's got to submit.

'Do you have any last words?' Dundas asks.

There! That's the moment. He's given Frances Cockburn the briefest of off-ramps. And she knows it, I can tell by how she takes a deep, weighty breath, her decision held up in that simple act. Take it, Frances. We'll live to fight another day. There's no shame in it at all. We can go back to our cell and plan. This is more of a chance than Rob and the Clan were ever given. Tap out, Frances. She swallows hard and we hang by a thread, waiting to hear her speak.

'Ye began with witches so shall ye end with witches,' Cockburn says boldly and loudly.

Fuck's sake, Frances. My heart sinks. She's done it now. Anyone who's been to the Old Town knows the story of Agnes Finnie, the woman who first uttered those words. Agnes Finnie was a successful shopkeeper in Edinburgh in the 1600s. She was a short-tempered, no-nonsense woman, and I can relate having run my own business – if you're soft people take the piss just 'cause you're a woman. You have to be tough and not take shit from no one. She also ran a moneylending gig, which may not have endeared her to her neighbours, but she was doing alright. This was balanced off by the fact she healed sick kids in the poor tenements where doctors didn't bother to go. Eventually her neighbours got pissed off with her. They blamed her for their sicknesses and misfortunes. Soon, the Kirk took it seriously and they tried her for being a witch. Agnes wasn't a sweet little old lady, and neither is Cockburn.

Henry Dundas places his hand over Izwi's eyes.

'Put your fingers in your ears, little one, and don't take them out until I tell you,' he commands. Then he gives a nod to Hamish Hutchinson.

The head of St Andrews College is frozen for a fraction of a second, as though he too can't quite believe it has come to this. He's wide-eyed for just a moment, and then just as quickly, he regains himself. He whispers, 'Breath of the Colchian dragon,' and the logs at the fringes of the pyre burst into a lilac flame like potassium burning. The fire colours the air around us and it seems almost strangely beautiful.

The logs begin to crack.

Frances Cockburn faces the far-off sun with a determined visage.

The magicians watch with fear as the flames continue to grow. Aurora quietly weeps, but her tears don't douse the fire. Neither does Carrie's impassivity, nor Sin's stoic look. And as the fire touches Frances Cockburn's feet at last, she flinches, throwing her head back against the stake.

Dundas's cat purrs loudly and contentedly. It's the only one making a sound apart from the fire.

With a roar the flames grow, crawling up the fabric of her suit. At last, Frances Cockburn shatters the air with a hideous scream as fire envelops her from head to toe.

It's too much and my body falls limp and I would fall were it not for the tight grip of the man restraining me.

XVIII

When I come to, I'm on the floor of my cell in the basement of Melville Castle. The scent of burning flesh is firmly lodged in my nostrils. My ears are ringing, ringing with the sound of Frances Cockburn's blood-curdling screams. They burnt her alive like the witches of old.

I feel sick. They stood by and did nothing as this woman they knew was burnt alive. The same thing Agnes Finnie's neighbours did when she was executed. People simply watch. River's lying on the floor not far from me. She seems sad and exhausted. There's more compassion in this fox than in all the magicians I've encountered.

The floor is cold, but I don't care. I'm numbed out.

Even if I were to see Theodosia Lovell, what could I tell her? That I stood by while her daughter was murdered. That's what it was, cold-blooded murder. They better kill me too, 'cause the way I feel, if I got a chance, I'd slaughter every one of them. God help me, I'd make no distinction.

A grey ghost walks through the walls of my cell. The bare outlines of a man with unruly hair holding his hands behind his back. My father Makomborero Moyo.

'How?' I say, sitting up from the floor.

'My little girl,' he says, tilting his head to the side and admiring me. I normally need music in order to be able to hear ghosts, but it seems I don't need that anymore. It's like I'm still one of the dead.

'You said the portal was a one-person ticket out of the Other Place.' Part of me is happy to see him, but knowing about his deal with Dundas makes me anxious.

'That was true. I got you out and the guardians reached me, meaning to devour my soul. But we Moyos never give up. As the gateway collapsed, I used its exhaust energy emission to slaughter them, and then I realized I could use their essence to power my own way out in the wake of the disturbance your vortex left in the Other Place. I hastily cobbled together a spell that thrust me back into the astral plane. And so here I am, back in the world of the living, but it cost me dearly.' He sounds cocky and arrogant, the genius who defies the laws of the universe.

'A woman was burnt alive in front of my eyes,' I say.

'Omelettes and eggs,' he replies with a shrug.

'She had a family and she was loved.' If he had a body I'd punch that gob of his.

'That's fairly common,' my father replies. 'There's a lot you have to learn. What makes this realm special and its inhabitants distinct from any others out there is that we are in a place where cause and effect reign. Actions have meaningful consequences here. It's a devilish, chaotic construct because no matter how smart you are, you cannot figure out every possible permutation. The only thing that's inescapable is that you have to play the game.'

There it is. He's no different from the other magicians in the Society of Sceptical Enquirers. Life is one big game for them and other people are pawns to be used and cast aside.

'Once this great work is done, I am going to be Hades and shall have dominion over the dead. That's our family's great gift. Can you imagine the power we will wield then?' he says. Unbridled ambition burns in his eyes. 'I need your body. Allow me to possess you so we can complete this task together.'

He floats forward and tries to control my body, but something ancient around me rebuffs him. It feels timeless and smells of earth after the first rains. It's a moat around me, impregnable. Makomborero Moyo looks stunned. He tries again and is knocked three feet back. He yells in pain but quickly composes himself. That flash of rage made him demonic.

'What have you done, Ropafadzo? What is this sorcery?'

My father floats around the room agitated. He's scheming, I can tell. This is a man who's come so far only to see his plans thwarted.

'I am your family,' he says, voice buttery.

The strange thing inside of me remains silent. There's a haughtiness about it as though my father is beneath it. But I feel a surge of confidence. I am certain that this man cannot own me.

'What makes you think you can trust Henry Dundas?' I ask. 'He's responsible for the misery of millions. He used his influence to delay the abolition of slavery by fifteen years. How many people were trafficked and died because of your Zeus's actions? He cares nothing for humanity. That's the man you want to lead your pantheon?'

My father takes a few more steps into the dingy cell and stands in the centre, under the light. It makes his form more ethereal.

'Young people think they know everything. I was like you once – lacking perspective.' I'm sick of being patronized by fossils. 'Joseph Knight was a slave born in Guinea. He was trafficked and sold to a master in Jamaica who had him serve in his household. And then he brought him home to Scotland. Here Knight sued for his freedom and the case was brought before the courts. Hazard a guess as to who his counsel was.'

He smugly begins to walk around in a tight circle, but he is still studying me, trying to find a way in. I have a flashback, a memory of him walking around deep in thought in his lab.

'You guessed it, one Henry Dundas,' my father continues like there was no pause. 'It was Dundas, then the Lord Advocate, alongside others who stood up for the principle "no man is by nature the property of another". Tell me, is that the mark of an evil person in your eyes?'

'He only did that because the English weren't averse to taking Irish slaves and the Scots might be next if they opened that door.'

'It doesn't matter. I think you should be thanking him instead. Look, Ropa, you have to trust me. What is fifteen years in the grand arc of history? Dundas was in a different position and power requires balancing interests – even those you do not agree with. You don't rise to the top by being a good person. If that were the case, the world would be ruled by namby-pambies. Instead, it is governed by those who have the *will to power.*'

'Go fuck yourself, Dad,' I say. 'Henry Dundas said Izwi will be the voice of a queen. Is she is just another pawn to be used in your games?'

He smiles condescendingly in that patient way of someone who's already won the argument in his head. I'm thankful I didn't have to grow up under him. It would have messed me up.

'Power is the only thing that matters. Amass as much of it as you can and only then will you be safe from the buffeting waves of this chaotic cause-and-effect world. This is what I want for my family. An eternity for you and me and your sister. You need never fear death or harm again, for I will have tamed the eternal darkness for you. This is my gift.'

I shake my head.

'I can bring your mother back,' he says and I jerk up straight. 'Once we are done, I can turn my attention to the problem of time. It's much knottier than this, but once I have the power over millions of souls I can untangle it and undo her death. There'll be no limit to what we can do.'

A yearning for her hits me. The possibility of . . . It's been hard growing up without my parents. My dad's fucked up but with my mother back, maybe . . . It'd be good for Izwi.

No.

'You're a psychopath. I've dealt with people like you all my life and you can jog on, pal.'

'There's much we must do yet. A king must be played and an English sorcerer and his court brought to heel. Then eternity is ours. I'll leave you here to think things through. You'll be well taken care of, my darling, and when all this is done you will see how I did everything for you. I can't waste any more time with your wilfulness. We are going to the New Town; the king is arriving tonight from Berwick-Upon-Tweed and he will receive a grand welcome.'

My father's ghost vanishes like a puff of smoke, leaving me and River in that dank, grey cell. We're not family to him, we're abstractions, pieces of a jigsaw he's trying to complete.

There was a time I'd have given anything to have my parents back in my life. Death took them away from us. The stories I was told about them were all lies. But I see now how undoing any of that would cost other people their lives and families. It's not a price I'm willing to pay, under any circumstances.

I stand up and go over to the walls of my cell.

'Come on, River, help me find a way out.'

I'll check these stones one by one for any gaps or cracks. No matter what, I'll find a way to stop Henry Dundas and my father. Time's not on our side. I have to roll the dice one more time. Maybe that's the one good thing I inherited from Makomborero Moyo: when the chips are down, I take another swing.

XIX

I'm soaked in sweat by the time I'm done searching every inch of the wall for a gap or way out. In movies, castles usually have secret tunnels hidden away somewhere. But if there's one in Melville Castle then I'm stumped.

Still, what can I do without magic?

I need to access the power inside of me that protected me from my father.

I bang on the door with my grabber. Solid oak, opens outwards. Reckon with a well-powered soliton blast it could be blown away.

Come on, Ropa, find your nexus point and let's do some magicking.

I incant an anemoic spell invoking the gods of the wind and flick my hand out. Knapf. Right, really focus and get into it. I didn't read all those magic books for nothing. I psych myself up, bouncing on the balls of my feet. All I need is will. Let's go hardcore with this next incantation: 'The giant of storm-winds and tornadoes Typhoeus lay waste to trunk and branch!' I bellow, throwing both hands with fingers spread out towards the door to channel the spell . . . But the only thing that gets going is the breath out of my lips.

I yell out and kick the door so hard my foot hurts. 'Bastard,' I say, and limp back, seething.

Plan B. I take my backpack and empty the contents onto the floor, hoping to find something I can use. Some clothes, lip balm, sanitary pads, tissues, mobile phone charger, sticky mints that must have been in there since before World War Two, my sunglasses – I've been wondering where those went. I should have kept my dagger. Or even Cruickshank. He'd have helped.

But I was too pissed off with Gran. The bag feels empty but I give it one last shake and out tumbles my mbira. It lands on the block with a wooden thud. That shouldn't be in there. I'd refused it when I left Glasgow. The iron keys shine bright under the harsh light of the filament bulb. It's been altered. A perfect circle's been cut out of the wooden keyboard and the Fairy Flag's been threaded through it.

Theodosia Lovell must have put it in there against my wishes. Sneaky old bat, she's probably messed up the tuning even more. What I need right now's an axe not a musical instrument. But there's never been a time I've seen Theodosia Lovell say or do anything without intention. My mbira is a magical artefact and so is the Fairy Flag. Both of them have the power to affect worlds beyond this one. It never occurred to me that the two could be combined like that, but it seems this is what Theodosia has done.

I'm going to have to eat humble pie.

I've spent all this time learning scientific magic. Now I have to face it, whenever shit hit the fan I always defaulted to the stuff Melsie Mhondoro taught me or gave me. That stuff is in my soul and not just my head.

'What do you think, River?'

She twitches her ears.

'What does that even mean?'

River yawns.

My stuff's scattered all over the floor and I've tossed my backpack to one side. I stand over this gear, thinking. The king is coming tonight. Izwi will 'have the voice of a queen'. My kettle's whistling 'cause something's brewing. They're not going to try to marry her off or something crazy like that, surely? This ain't the dark ages, but I mean it was only in 1929 when they changed the law in Scotland, before then girls could marry at twelve and boys at fourteen. It's all gone pear-shaped: executions, violence, so is forced marriage a possibility, I wonder? I'm way off here, the king's a despot but he's no sicko, though the royal family's had a fair few of those in the past.

I can't allow my pride or pigheadedness to get in the way. The moves I've been making haven't paid off. I need help. I have to turn to Lord Samarasinghe now. If I can get to him, I can show him that our interests in this brief sliver of time are aligned. In fact, I can do him a solid even after he shafted me. The Sorcerer Royal's slippery and capricious, that's his nature, but I know him now and if folks can tame tigers and charm snakes then I'll have to see what I can do to get English magic on my side of the ledger.

'There's no other way, girl,' I say to River. 'We have to try something.'

Here goes. I pick up my mbira, then go over to the far wall

before I slide down and cross my legs once my butt's on the floor. There's a buzzing sound in my head and I feel a panic attack brewing. Funny how you become better at telling when they're coming. Only one thing for it, I close my eyes and do the centring exercises Dr Checkland taught me. It takes a minute or two before my mind empties, calmness descending. Used to take ages, but if you can get in before the peak, you can ward off the attack.

I cradle my mbira in my hands and place my thumbs on the cold iron keys.

Wait.

Back when I used to talk to ghosts, I knew playing the right tune tied in to their harmonics and I could ground them like that. I've never tried summoning before. Gran taught me it was a violation. But even when summoning was done, you could only work it on the ghosts in the everyThere, the cold dead realm next to ours. There was no way to access ghosts that have passed beyond its walls.

Focus and find your nexus point.

I won't play any song. Let the melody come to me when it's ready. I am just a vessel.

My heartbeat slows. I can feel the blood sluggish in my veins. Stray thoughts fly here and there. But as I calm myself some more, I reach a space of emptiness. I'm there somewhere, but my being's dissolved into nothingness. The only thing that remains is an intangible essence.

My left thumb strains against the key. The iron pulses under me, pliant, almost like I had my finger atop the pulse of something living. It's a strange sensation. I'm filled with something like euphoria. The music consumes me and my heart vibrates to the notes I am playing. I've never felt unity or flow like this, everything moving as it should in the perfection of the notes.

River whines.

And then the melody pours out from deep within me. It starts slowly at first, like light rain falling atop the fibreglass roof of our old caravan. And then it builds up and up into a rushing torrent. I'm rocking back and forth to the tune until I lose all sense of direction. My body's lighter than air and still I play. Only the three-quarter signature matters. It has volume, mass, length, density, filling every measurable space in my being.

River barks. I can hear her pacing in front of me and then she ducks under my armpit, hiding.

I should stop, but it doesn't feel as if I'm playing the music, rather something deep inside of me that I don't recognize has taken control. It may be a piece of the little girl whose body my father stole, or of myself, or us both. I don't know, for knowing is less important than being. Here. In this song. I keep on strumming my mbira, the cold keys warm up, but it doesn't feel like an entropic shift. This is different. No work has been done.

Mhondoro dzinomwa muna Save-eh

Mhondoro dzinomwa muna Save

My grandmother used to sing me this song. She said when she was a little girl, they would sing it to make the rain fall from the sky and quench the parched earth. It's an ageless song passed down from generation to generation among the

Shona people. Gran would hum it in our caravan when it rained. In those days she seemed truly happy, especially when I joined with her, mangling up the words. But I knew the song like a nursery rhyme. Gran liked it because it used her surname, Mhondoro. Where my grandmother is from, names carry meaning. Hers is the name of the lion, the king of the jungle. It's the name of the major ancestral spirits. And they drink in the great river Save. It feels like this mbira and I have become one. It's alive and the notes are filled with power beyond anything I've ever felt and it shatters the fabric of the room I'm in. Space, time, every dimension is ripped open.

I open my eyes and my grandmother stands in front of me. She has become her young self again, around my age, and she glows fierce like the midday sun and it hurts to look at her. Behind her is a long line of women that stretches beyond history. They are all there watching me. Surrounding the portal are the dark bird-like creatures from beyond. The same ones that attacked the school bus and killed Avery MacDonald. Their movement is unnatural, menacing. You can't read their intention and at any moment they might pounce.

I become very afeart. This is outwith any experience I've ever had. These fearsome, hungry things hold at the fringes of the portal, their focus on me.

'It's taken you long enough,' Melsie Mhondoro says with a smile. But this isn't her voice as I remember it. It sounds like a choir speaking to me, her voice has a part of all the women before her. 'I knew you'd get there, child. I placed all my faith in you. Choose your question wisely.'

I have a question. It sounds like I'll only get one. This is like a test from the fairytales. If you had only one question, what would you want to know? I ponder this for a second then take my punt.

'How?' I ask.

Gran laughs and it's terrifying.

'Not why? Clever child, a question that asks everything in a single word. Okay then, let me show you,' Melsie Mhondoro says, stepping out of the portal.

Were there not a wall behind me, I would bail. Gran's spirit hovers above me and then she falls into my body, taking control. There's a burst of astonishing white light which banishes the darkness away. My body jerks around. I can't even control it.

River's going bonkers barking and then she lets out a high-pitched howl.

There are things we failed to learn when Gran was alive, but now we are filled with a new understanding. I'm hit by a splitting headache as though my skull will cleave into two, and I flop to the floor, writhing in agony. So many voices and sights and sensations overlapping. There's memories not my own, some of Gran's, others of women whose names would burn the tongue to pronounce, and those are within us now, not learnt any more than one learns to breathe, they are etched in our nerves and in our cells.

XX

When I come to, I'm lying on the floor and the world has become calm again, shrinking down to its normal dimensions. Colourful dots dance in my vision. The ceiling above me is plastered and painted grey. I no longer feel infirm, as I did when I returned from the Other Place. This body feels a little more like my own, comforting my soul like a well-used, familiar blanket. The world seems serene, time no longer rushing, but flowing gentle like a small burn in spring.

I have invited the ancestors into myself.

Eew, I clean up the drool on my cheek using my sleeve.

Back in the day, my grandmother's people, the Shona, had mediums who connected them to their ancestors. They put their faith in them and were rewarded with empires and wealth. But that came to an end when a new way of being was forced onto them. They discarded the old ways and embraced Christianity, much as the Picts and pagans in Scotland were converted too. The same circle of history playing out in a different place, in a different era.

But the old ways cannot ever be entirely extinguished. They are of earth and nature. You may plant your garden, but the old ways pop up now and again like weeds. They have strong roots hidden and unseen. They lie and wait for the season to re-emerge.

Among my grandmother's people, a child might fall sick with an unexplained ailment that defies all forms of treatment. But the old and wise consult the traditional healers, and they discover that their child has been called. I remember Gran as a little girl in a mud hut in the savannah. It's not my own memory, it's hers, and like all good memories, it has layers and has been confabulated and altered over time. There's a vagueness to it. A gecko running on the walls. Yellow thatch blackened by smoke and supported by timbers.

Young Melsie lies on a reed mat next to the fireplace, a hole in the ground. She remembers the feeling of the mat against her back. A warm blanket thrown over her despite the oppressive heat. She's feverish, sweat soaking her jujet dress, as they called the georgette in her village. It's been weeks she's been burning. In this time her parents have withdrawn her from primary school. They've tried the mission clinic nearby where the nuns and nurses first blamed malaria. When their treatments failed to work, a Cuban doctor from Harare said it was schistosomiasis, an infection caused by parasites in the gut. He spoke authoritatively and prescribed medicines Gran's father had to walk half a day to purchase. They called the Catholic priest who sprinkled holy water on Gran and made them perform a novena to St Roch. None of these interventions worked.

The elders in the village consulted and it was decided Gran should be taken to a healer, else they would lose her. Her father refused at first, but faced with the prospect of his daughter dying, they took her to the svikiro of their clan. And it is in this hut, with hung animal skins and calabashes filled with potions and herbs, that the svikiro cast bones and divined Melsie was being chosen by her ancestors. He ordered beer be brewed to appease them since they were angry her parents had first taken her to the clinic.

'Do you think we who know every herb cannot look after our own daughter?' the spirits demanded.

But they softened when their throats were quenched with beer and struck a more conciliatory tone. Melsie's father had refused their call when he was young: even with death knocking at his door, he stuck to his guns until the spirits reluctantly released him from obligation.

'I would rather let my daughter die than become this,' he railed. 'She is intelligent and destined to devour books that will lead her into a nice office job one day. Now you tell me she is to wear animal skins and cast lots like a heathen.' His Christian faith was strong.

'It is not your choice to make,' the svikiro responded. 'The ancestors are through with you.'

While her father forced them to Catholic mass every morning, by night, when no one was watching, Melsie's mother would take her aside and teach her the old ways, swearing her to secrecy. Her mother, a respected married woman who participated in the church, also dabbled in the old ways. She encouraged her daughter in secret to accept the gift of her ancestors.

To her father's horror, Melsie Mhondoro became a svikiro too and a custodian of her clan's heritage. But her father forced her to continue with her schooling, hoping it would strip this culture from her. When that did not work, he contacted an old friend abroad, who facilitated her move to a university in the cold and wet capital of Scotland, thinking it would cut her off from traditional practice. And so Melsie left and got her degree, but this did not dampen her vocation like he'd hoped. Instead, she met sisters who in secret dabbled in other kinds of magic. There she could play with her talent of seeing into the future.

In time an opportunity arose to use her gift to enrich herself, Melsie grabbed it with both hands and began work for the Royal Bank of Scotland. There she did well and made a small fortune.

And like my grandmother, I am now invited to become a vessel of the spirits and to learn their magic. It is a lot more than my mind can contain. It's stretched me, bent me, turned my brain inside out. I once wanted with all my heart to become a scientific magician. But that was never my path. I've at last accepted where I am to be and what I am to become. Now I understand what her plan for me was all along. Even her falsehoods were the sugar that coated the bitter pill of wisdom.

We teach children with fables.

Those stories are nothing but lies.

Until they are old enough.

But before they can comprehend, first they reject all we have taught.

Until understanding comes to them and they discover deeper meanings within those lies.

And that is how truth is woven into this world.

This is the way.

I let the spirits flow into me.

It's scary 'cause for the time I was a ghostalker, I had two aims: getting the departed to move on or casting them out. Now it's to work with them and be their vessel. That's going to take some getting used to. It's really strange 'cause I can access their memories and knowledge, but it works both ways and they can see into my stuff too. Cringe. When the spirits are upon me they can see my weird, embarrassing little secrets.

Note to self: think clean thoughts only.

'Shall we give this thing a spin?' I ask River. She eyes me suspiciously. 'I don't blame you, girl.'

There is a difference between svikiroing and possession. This ain't forced or nothing like that. Ultimately I have control over what's happening. Gran and them spirits are there to guide me . . . At least that's what round one felt like . . . Between bouts of spasms and drooling.

The world around me feels richer, somehow. These grey stone walls pulse with life. The air has a light shimmer. Even the ground vibrates with some kind of vital animation. Reckon this is what it's like getting a new pair of specs and the world comes at you in glorious detail for the first time. It's the same world, but now it feels so different, like I'd not seen it properly at all.

Our lives are hard, but this realm is a jewel and that's why folks like my dad and the Viscount Melville want to be here forever and ever, amen. I check out the back of my hand, how my skin touches the cold air, energy passing from one to the other, cause and effect wrapped up in infinite overlapping loops.

Dust to dust. Ashes to ashes. Everything growing and dying, recycled time and again.

I reach out and touch my mbira again.

This instrument blazes with a newfound energy more brilliant than anything else. Almost feels like I've put my hand out and touched the heart of a reactor. The energy of the room seems to flow around my mbira. I suspect it's got something to do with the Fairy Flag tied to it. It makes me question this world we're in. A unity and unintelligibility that baffles the mind. They say you can't step in the same river twice. There's a source and a mouth, meanders and distinct points, yet all are different facets of the same thing. That's what this world we're in happens to be: a dazzling collection of elementary particles vibrating with energy in differing configurations.

Energy dancing like the vibrating keys of my mbira.

I understand it now.

There are different ways of doing magic.

I twang a bass note and watch it disturb the air around me, a wave rippling out, crashing into the walls and breaking with a pfft. Was that a soliton? I do it again and observe the effect on the atmosphere.

Interesting.

I play the x key in the middle of the keyboard and a shower of white-hot sparks explode into the air. They fizz for ten or more seconds, then quietly burn out. I sniff. No acrid chemical scent. This is weird. Let's try that very gently – a solitary spark pops into existence as though the fabric of space has been perturbed.

The treble slices the air open and one those corvid-like monsters pops out. I watch it fly around the room before it returns to the void. My ticker's absolutely thumping.

I've got to be careful.

The twenty-two keys on my mbira must correspond with some aspect of the universe. I don't know what will happen when next I decide to play a tune. I wish I was back in the underHume at the Library of the Dead having a blast with Priya. But it's just me now.

I play my mbira slowly and carefully, observing the different effects. Now I understand why Dr Maige insisted on his mathematical universe as the theory that explains magic. By playing my instrument I can create magical effects. Music is an expression of mathematics too. There's a strong relationship to geometry, trigonometry, number theory, differential calculus. And many phenomena in the universe mirror mathematical theorems. This is how Pythagoras gave us his scale. It all seems separate but it's cosmically connected. Music is soundwaves, patterns, frequencies, beats and counts. You can use fractions to divide notes into parts. This must be why we're moved by vibrations – music affects our will. It makes us feel a certain way and it can create profound effects, memories which last a lifetime.

The mathematical universe is how Doctor Maige theorizes the Society's mastery of magic. They use their will through language to change and affect the fundamental equations that govern the physical world. But music is a step closer to the purity of maths and dispenses with clunky invocations to the Greek gods. You cut out the middleman and go straight to the source.

At least, that's what the voices of the grandmothers in my noggin said.

They did magic another way and I ought to try it.

I get up and walk to the door. Have a good feel of the oaken door for the second time. Then I place my mbira against it, mubvamaropa wood against a distant dead cousin. The two repel one another. It's so slight you could miss it, but it's there, an enmity between the mbira that's for my freedom and the door that seeks to keep me imprisoned. Everything has a consciousness as the panpsychists believe.

The door sets itself against me.

I take four steps back, and decide that's not enough, so I take a couple more.

'River, you might want to get behind me,' I say.

I lightly thumb a bass key and feel the vibration from my mbira reach out and touch the door. It's a sonic pulse and I use that to test out the oak. Just a little handshake. The door resonates and, in a sense, talks back to me. Now I give it a firm grip with my next note and the wood creaks, straining to hold on to its hinges. It's resisting, true to its function, but it feels the pressure I exert regardless. I'm getting excited and it takes everything I have to restrain myself from getting all giddy.

Fuck that, let's rock 'n' roll. I strike the keys as hard as I can, pulling off a quick riff. The wooden door strains on multiple points, creaking against the force. It bulges unnaturally, but still it holds until I go Van Halen on the mbira and there's a loud explosion, the wood bursting into a thousand splinters that fly out. They smash into the walls and the air's filled with dust.

'Check that out, River,' I say. 'I've got my mojo back.'

There's a boom and the castle trembles. Uh-oh. I must have messed it up. Nah, that can't have been me, surely? I pop out into the corridor, afeart this place might tumble onto my noggin. A man screams and then falls silent. I prick my ears, but there's nothing else. So I make my way to the stairs, my fingers on the mbira, ready to jam it out of here.

XXI

The castle thrums with an invisible vibration. It feels like everything is alive, the walls, the floor underneath my feet, the air tingles against my skin. It's like I'm connected with the world in a way I wasn't before. I'm wary of the commotion coming from above until I hear a wheelchair clattering about. I know that sound from anywhere, but I shouldn't be hearing it all from down here. Yay, superpower activated – take that, Banshee. And so, very cautiously, I make my way back up the stairs where I spot Priya roaming the corridor.

She pivots quickly in her chair, a green thermosphere already ignited and aimed at me when I call out, 'Chill. It's only me.'

'Bloody hell. I could have fried you to a crisp,' she says angrily.

'What are you doing here?' I reply.

'It was obvious you'd try something stupid so we were forced to come here,' she says, barely holding back her annoyance. 'This is a mess, Ropa. And what the hell is going on? I saw a burnt body outside.'

My cavalry's here and it's crabbit like I'm the one who's trying to take over the world or something. I open up my arms for a hug, and walk towards her. The thermosphere extinguishes just before I make the Sunday roast and I get to Priya and embrace her sulky arse. Don't quite know how to break the news about Frances to her, though. Makes me feel sick just thinking about it.

'Better?' I say.

'Wanker,' she replies, face in my belly.

Priya shoves me back and takes a good look at me. I can tell she's still a bit miffed, but I'm not going to have a back and forth about how she's the one who was grounded by her mum. That wasn't my fault. I know I'm right but sometimes you've got to bite your tongue, especially when folks have come to rescue you from being taken like you were David Balfour.

'What's with your aura?' She squints, inspecting me. 'It's not off, but strange, so many layers that weren't there before. Is someone else in that body with you?'

'Being locked up in a castle does that to you,' I reply.

Your granddaughter's a liar, Melsie.

She learnt from the best.

'Hmm. There's more to it. Anyway, where's Frances Cockburn? She didn't make contact with mum last night, and with you coming out here, we put two and two together and made five,' Priya says.

My stomach sinks.

'Did they take her with them? We had to wait until the majority of the Edinburgh magicians were in town for the king's visit before we could come here for you. She's not been picking up her phone. I know you don't like Frances, but Mum will explain everything later.'

'She's in the car park,' I say.

'Where? I came through that way and . . .' Priya slows, the news dawning on her. She's in disbelief and her eyes seem to be begging that I tell her it's not so. 'Car park,' she repeats.

'It's her,' I say.

Priya freezes. I know she's trying to take it all in, but it's huge. Their coven's become smaller. The only thing I can think of is how I have the horrible responsibility to tell Theodosia Lovell about what happened to her daughter. If she asks me for a play by play, I won't be able to do it. I can't go over this morning again.

Back when I was a ghostalker, I used to deliver messages from ghosts. In the main, the recipients already knew their person had passed. Very rarely did it come as a shock. But to deliver the last words of someone who was breathing what seems like just moments ago is much more difficult.

'Is Theodosia here with you?' I ask.

'This is not happening,' Priya says. 'Did Dundas light the flames personally or did one of them do it? I need to know, Ropa.'

'Please don't.'

'You're going to tell me right now or god help us all,' Priya says. Her tone is flat and cold.

'Hamish Hutchinson,' I reply.

There's something utterly chilling about seeing Priya like this. We've been in a fair few scraps and she's always been jolly, but now all she radiates is raw rage. Even for me, a friend, I find it disturbing to see her in this state.

Smoke hangs in the air, and from the scent of it, I can tell some serious magic's been at work. A man, one of the cultists, lies bleeding on the carpet in the reception area. He has a hole through his chest. I stand next to his body and see the wisp of his soul leaving with his final breath. I cast it out to the Other Place, giving him no chance to linger in the everyThere. It's a cruel thing for me to do, but they deserve it.

'Let's go,' Priya says.

'How do you go back to Our Lady of Mysterious Ailments after all this is done?' I ask.

'Probably with lots of counselling and heavy meds,' she replies wryly.

'This life's changed me, Priya, and I'm not talking about the walking stick situation. I don't feel like I'm really myself anymore. I'd happily go back to being the lavvy heid from Hermiston Slum whose only worry was delivering messages accurately.'

'I'll be friends with whichever version of you pops up,' she says.

But every step we've taken since I met Priya has led me much further than I could have imagined. Away from being the person I used to be. Perhaps some of it's for good, I don't know. With each death I've been restored as something new. Version 3.0 in the house. I'm tired of everything, but I have to rally one more time and poke my middle finger into people's eyes.

Priya leads the way, stiff, wheeling her chair mechanically. I can see she's carrying a hell of a weight right now. The bubbly daredevil who was my best friend's still in there somewhere, but right now those healing hands want to end people's lives permanently.

I stop her by the main door of the castle, placing my hand on her right shoulder. She uses her left to touch my hand and massages it with her thumb.

'Is China still an option?' Priya says. 'I'm asking for a friend.'

'That boat sailed a few days ago,' I reply.

'Pity, we could have done the Great Wall.'

I let go of Priya's shoulder before my hands start shaking. They should have come sooner.

And when we exit Melville Castle, into the gravel car park, there's a small group of women standing in front of the burnt-out stake. The smouldering remains of this morning's fire. Its scent hangs in the muggy air.

'I see we've got Ropa, but where is Frances?' Ranjeeta asks.

Priya squeezes her eyes shut. She hesitates, slowly shaking her head, and Ranjeeta looks first to the remains in the ash and then to her daughter, the realization dawning on her.

'That's her.' Priya's voice cracks.

Theodosia Lovell falls to her knees and weeps, her dress flowing over the ground. Ranjeeta Kapoor stands over her with a hand on her shoulder, the horror stencilled on her face. I turn away, unable to look at Frances's remains.

Jomo is also on his knees blubbering with Mrs Guthrie keeping a close eye on him. His black robes puff up, making him look small, a kid playing dress up. Gone is the cool confidence he displayed when he was running about with Dundas's crew. His eyes are filled with terror, now he's on his own with the folks he's wronged.

'I swear I had nothing to do with any of this. It's not my

fault. I tried to tell them it's against the law. I swear I did but they wouldn't listen to me. Tell them, Ropa.'

Jomo swears on his parents and siblings and everything holy that he was never sure of what was going on and is not connected to any of this. He turns to me, imploring with his face, reeking of desperation. He knows what he's done, what he's become part of.

'Please don't kill me. I'm on your side.' Jomo sounds convincing, like he's fooled himself into believing that he did nothing wrong. Flips the switch and he's rewriting his story to save his hide. 'They wouldn't let me leave.'

'Shut it, you snivelling waghorn. Get Theodosia inside; no mother should have to see this,' Mrs Guthrie says, doffing her straw hat. 'We'll take care of this, won't we, Artchival?'

'Priya, help me,' Jomo pleads.

With one word, I could make this so much worse for him.

'There'll be more blood 'ere the night's done. Mark my words,' Artchival replies. 'The Rooster we respected; Frances we loved.'

There's a rage smouldering out of him as he stands next to Theodosia Lovell's horse and carriage. The Travelling Folk are a hardy and honourable people. Causing trouble with them is just asking for it. Rooster Rob recognized this and though he ran the racket in Edinburgh, he made sure there was peace with the Travelling Folk when they were about. The Clan may have had wars with the other gangs in Edinburgh, but never with Artchival's people. It speaks to his honour that though he grieves for Frances Cockburn, he does not entirely forget Rob too. And they are not alone. They've turned up with a dozen or so witches, which is great, but we could have used them this morning.

Artchival strides over to Jomo and drags him back up to his feet using one hand. He makes a show of dusting the eejit's robes off, patting him down with his free hand, but each strike is hard and painful. The traveller's seething and I wouldn't fancy anyone would cross him now.

'How aboot we take a nice stroll intae the woods? Just you and me, laddie. Dinnae stress, a wee blether's all I'm after.'

The big man's got a firm grip on Jomo and my ex-bestie flinches, goes limp and nearly flops to the ground, but Artchival holds him upright. He starts dragging him away from the rest of us. This isn't who we are, though. We are different from the magicians. We are better than that. I'm beyond done with the arsewipe, but for the friendship we once had, I can't let him go into the woods with Artchival when I know he's not coming back.

'We're going to need information on what Henry Dundas is up to, and that's the only witness left behind. I think he'll be useful,' I say.

'I dinnae care,' Artchival replies.

'Ropa is right,' Ranjeeta interrupts. 'We need information from the boy. But mark my words, if he tells a single untruth, that'll be it for him.'

Artchival grunts irritably, but obeys all the same. He can't mask the bloodlust on his face, though. I'd hate to be in Jomo's shoes.

Dr Checkland and Ranjeeta help Theodosia Lovell to her feet. She's so weak and dazed they have to hold her up by the oxters. I fight back my own tears. Cockburn's mother is unsteady on her legs and they support her as they take her back to her carriage. The grief she's in hits us all, such pain and turmoil. Her eyes are red, tears streaking down the grooves and wrinkles of her face. There's so much love contained in that pain, I understand why Frances asked me to pass a message on to her. She knew her mother's heart would be shredded to bits. Her last words were an act of love. I should tell Theodosia, but now's not the time.

Calista Featherstone, standing a little distance away but still distinct in her red hooded dress, now strides towards us. She is prim and flawless, displaying no emotion. She stops beside me, but doesn't take her eyes off Melville Castle.

'I heard about what happened in Glasgow. I suspected as much but hoped they'd be decent. The Doric School stands for what's right. There's always been a difference between us up north and you lowland Scots.'

Only one of the four schools of magic in Scotland stands on our side. St Andrews and Edinburgh are corrupt, Glasgow's only in it for what she can gain. But I've seen the mass of magicians Henry Dundas has with him. We are no match for them as things stand, but they've now lit a Frances-shaped match that can't go unanswered.

I watch as Mrs Guthrie and Artchival reverently gather Frances's remains. Artchival has laid out a fleece blanket onto the ground and pokes through the ashes for bits of her.

The mbira thrums by my side. If only I'd known this morning what I now know. Now I carry with me memories of the women before me. Even remembering Frances Cockburn feels like the memory of déjà vu. I carry in my spirit the recollections of a woman chased and killed with an axe in rural Zimbabwe a mere five years ago. A more distant memory of a grandmother who'd lived to nearly a hundred, but her life ended when she was beaten with a log and her clothes set on fire. That happened twenty-one years ago, the year my first body was born. Among my grandmother's people witches are hunted and persecuted. Mostly women, just as here in Scotland.

There's nowhere in the world for women like us to hide.

Artchival's rage rolls into my gut. He is sobbing out loud as he does his work.

Ranjeeta Kapoor comes back from the caravan. She is dressed in a black sari with sequins embroidered like silver stars, the aanchal draped over her left arm, while her right is free. Her authority oozes and it's almost as if she takes our pain and our collective anger and fear, purifies them and reflects them back with a firm intention.

'You bore witness?' she asks.

'I did,' I reply.

'And you all see what's been done here to one of our own, sisters?' she says.

'Aye.'

'Had we more time, our coven would gather in the grounds of St Andrews Kirk in North Berwick as we have for centuries, so we might decide. But we must make haste. Tell the others we will meet by Louisa Stevenson's grave in Dean Cemetery at sunset and there we'll chart our course,' Ranjeeta says. 'Ropa Moyo, I see you've embraced your grandmother's gifts at last. We brought your stick and scarf and your jacket should you wish to have them back. You're under no obligation, but we wish you would join us.'

'I'll tell you all I know, and thanks for my stuff, but there's someplace else I'll need to be before I can join your coven,' I reply. I'm kinda glad to have my things back now. Using the grabber was a pain in the arse . . . *And sorry I abandoned you, Cruickshank. I have issues, man.*

'Have it your way,' Ranjeeta replies. Then she turns to Calista Featherstone. 'Burn it to the ground.'

Ms Featherstone almost smiles, the corners of her lips rising up, and she incants the fury of the Minoan Eruption upon Melville Castle. With the extension of her hands, a dazzling red flame erupts in every window. The flames must be devouring the carpets and rising up the upholstery, moving with speed and intent. It's as if there's a riot within.

The windows of the castle break and the flames spill out, spreading over the bare stone walls and melting them like they were plastic. The heat's so intense it's as if we are standing at the mouth of a furnace. As Melville Castle crumbles to the ground, I decide I must talk to Jomo before I make my way back to Edinburgh. The things he knows may well help when I deal with the Sorcerer Royal.

XXII

Being back inside of a wagon feels like home. I sense the bit of Gran's soul inside of me sigh and am hit by a flash of memory from the dark ages, when Gran and Theodosia Lovell were young women. Gran had visited Theodosia and they were drinking loose leaf tea, handy for tasseography, and discussing potions. When they were done, Gran noticed Theodosia Lovell divine her future in the tea leaves, but Theodosia never told her what she saw in that reading on that day.

'What did you see?' Gran had asked.

'If I telt yer, the thread mightnae go through the eye of the needle,' Theodosia replied.

'When I look far ahead, all I see is dark clouds.'

'Aye, behind those lies the silver lining an' if fortune favours us, oor coven shall rise fae the shadows intae daylight. We all have oor part tae play.'

The Burton wagon we're in's traditional. It looks like something you'd see in an old film. Yes, it's tiny, but it's a home with a bed at the back. It has a woodfire stove near the front so it's nice and warm inside. Above our heads is a narrow hatch that opens up to the driver outside. The interior is made of a wood so light it's nearly yellow: it could be pine or even cedar. Intricate craftsmanship, which is surprisingly durable given how rattly the wagon is, hitched to two chestnut mares whose shoes clip-clop against the tar. It smells of pine, though that might be from the air freshener hanging off a hook in the ceiling. There's some long, narrow mirrors on the wall, and it has windows on three sides letting in what little light's filtered through the fog. Melville Castle's blazing behind us casting a thick plume of smoke into the air. This wagon also has a bench with a mat on the left side. No space is wasted, there are wee cupboards and drawers under the bench and bed.

I see now how Theodosia Lovell must have been the reason Gran chose the caravan after we'd lost our house in Forrester due to my grandfather's gambling debts. Gran yearned for some of her friend's freedom. It's the life of an explorer. Camping out in the forgotten villages in Ayrshire, seeing the mountains and lochs in the Highlands, breezing through our broken-down cities. It must be plenty fun being the master of your own destiny. At least that was the case when Gran's car still worked, before we settled permanently in the south of Edinburgh.

Cruickshank's round my neck, but he's not giving me any love. I think he's a wee bit miffed I left him behind. I stroke him gently 'cause that's the only way I know to say sorry, pal.

Jomo's sat on the bench while I'm on the bed. He's stonewalling me, but if he doesn't get to chatting I'll have to let Artchival have a go and that would be a bit wild. We've also got Priya in her chair, blocking the only exit. She's looking well peeved, and if I had a phone I'd take a photo. The wagon in front of us is carrying Theodosia Lovell and what remains of Frances Cockburn, with Artchival driving.

'I'm sorry, guys,' says Jomo.

'You're only sorry you got caught,' Priya replies.

'You've never liked me anyway, Priya. The only reason you hung out with me was because of Ropa. You came to the library and stole my best friend from me. Ropa and I were tight like this before you turned up.' He crosses two fingers.

'Really, dude?' Priya replies.

'You went off on adventures, doing stuff together without even asking me along. What was I left with? That stinking library and my dad?' Jomo says bitterly.

I look at him and he averts his gaze. He's pitiful, pathetic even. Eyes bloodshot and afro unruly, there's a feral being that's burst up from his craven insides. There's a couple of whiskers here and there under his chin where he's started to grow a beard. It's still him, though. But I tried to be a good pal to him and see where it got us? I wonder if there's anything I could have done to stop him from taking this path.

I didn't bring Jomo with me on missions 'cause he's more brains than brawn. The places I've been ain't the sort a nerd with spots on his face can handle. Priya's solid whereas I had to keep the bullies off Jomo and fight his fights for him at school. Carl von Clausewitz said, 'War is the realm of danger; therefore courage is the soldier's first requirement.' Courage is one thing Jomo's got very little of, so I was trying to protect him. He must've seen it some other way.

Sometimes you've got to let your friends fall, say the spirits inside of my head. It's weird now. All these thoughts and memories and ideas that aren't my own. The voice in my head sounds like me, I've been used to it since forever, but now there's another that sounds old, a woman's but with a lower pitch, somewhat hoarse too. It's pretty fucking weird and if I didn't know it was Gran, I'd have to take something for it. But if I'd let Jomo get roughed up, how would that have prevented anything that's happened since?

The voices say nothing on this.

The wagon hits a pothole and we judder.

'So, you'd burn down the world 'cause you're jealous?' I ask.

'I thought we were cool,' Priya says. I know she was fond of Jomo too, and she sounds hurt.

'You wouldn't understand,' he says.

'Make us, then.'

'It's not like you care anyway.'

He turns away and looks out the window. The trees are dark shadows in the fog. There's an embankment where the old Borders railway runs into the city, coming all the way from Tweedbank. Jomo had it rough from his dad and he seems to think the world's against him. Including me and Priya. If he was telling us something real then maybe we could try to fix it, but all this stuff is from inside his own head. I remember when I was growing up—

Yes, I taught you that.

—Shut up and let me think, I say to the voices in my head. Geez.

Sorry . . . But I did warn you about that and I'm glad you remember.

'Shut it.'

'You said something?' Priya asks, looking concerned.

'Not . . . Erm, I was thinking how it is that sometimes we make stuff up in our heads and instead of talking about it, we hold it in and think it's true. And so we behave like our misconceptions are real. Then we cling on to them, let them fester into this big old boil we refuse to lance. We begin to identify with those ideas and they make us feel like the victim – make us feel like we can blame everyone else for being shitty ourselves. That's all.'

Not quite how I'd have said it, but close enough.

Shut. Up.

She is a feisty one.

'Why are you blinking like that? It's weird,' Priya says.

'Yeah, I'm with her on that one,' says Jomo.

'You don't get to be, pal,' Priya replies.

'Sorry.'

Always apologizing, always shrinking, except the one time he dared stretch, it wasn't towards the sun but up his own arse. I miss the dork, but we've gone too far now. You don't abduct my little sister and get away with it. Fuck that.

Do you have to swear so much?

You're the ones in my head, not the other way round.

Fair point.

Don't say that. It'll just encourage her.

Leave then, the girl's not holding you hostage. Ropa, here's a few new cuss words you should try: mhata, beche, mboro.

The girl hardly knows the language, and you're just being disgusting.

'Will you just shut up?' I say out loud again, shutting my eyes tight and opening them again. Restore factory settings.

Jomo holds his hands up. He's proper weirded out and I'm losing my shit 'cause I'm having a dozen conversations all at the same time. It's ridiculous. Priya raises an eyebrow, eyeing me suspiciously.

'My dad hates me,' says Jomo, all pathetic. 'I wanted to show him I could be better than him.'

'He is a psycho,' I say.

'A dick.' Priya adds the proper medical term.

'You guys don't know what it's like when you're told every day you're not good enough. Lazy. Useless. Everything you do's a mistake. There's times I wish I wasn't even born. I never asked for any of this.'

Jomo bursts into tears and the floodgates open again. He sobs so loud and it's heart-wrenching. Tears and mucus out his nose, all of it pours out of him. Even Priya's face softens a bit. Let him have a good cry if that's what he needs. That's the problem with holding stuff in, lord knows I used to until I started seeing Dr Checkland and talking about my shit. These things fester until they come out the wrong way if you don't address them.

'You should have talked to us, Jomo,' Priya says. 'We're your mates.'

'I just wanted to man up.'

'By joining a cult and doing whatever some ghoul tells you to do?'

Why not join a gang like normal kids do? Okay, maybe that's not the best suggestion, but anything's better than what Jomo's done. I think of Mr Sneddon, the librarian who died at Dunvegan Castle, and Jomo runs off with the team that did that? It makes no sense to me. He's going to have to come clean.

Ropa, be gentle.

'I don't give a toss about your little problems, man,' I say. 'You kidnapped my sister and gave her to Dundas. That was totally fucked up.'

'I'm sorry.' He looks down at his hands.

'That's not good enough. Look at me. I said, *look at me.* There're people here that would very much like to see you dead. Blood for blood. The only way you're getting out of this is if you come clean and tell us everything Henry Dundas is planning. And I mean *everything.*'

'I wanted to be a part of something big. Don't you want to make a difference too? Think of what life was like in those old TV shows you like so much, Ropa. That's what I was told this is all about. Great men like Henry Dundas changed the world once and they can do it again.'

'Spare me the propaganda,' says Priya with some exasperation.

Jomo finally looks me in the eye. 'Please forgive me. I made sure Izwi didn't get hurt. We took good care of her, I swear. She's like a little sister to me.'

'We don't have time for this. Call Artchival in,' I say.

'No, no, no, don't do that.'

The hatch up front opens and the traveller driving us pokes her head in, giving Jomo a glare that would freeze the Devil on a sunny day in hell. She's got the reins in one hand and a cigar in the other. Smoke bellows into the wagon. 'Just say the word if you're really serious about doing that and I'll get Artchival to pull over,' she says, then she turns back and shuts the hatch.

'All I know is that Izwi shares your talent. Your family has a way of dealing with dead people. It comes to you naturally. I don't know the specifics, but there's someone important who's beyond the everyThere that Dundas wants to channel tonight. It's not within his power to do so 'cause he only has half the Fairy Flag, but he believes Izwi can help.'

'What do you mean, channel? Who? Why tonight?' I ask.

'I honestly don't know. It was mentioned in passing when he was speaking with Montgomery Wedderburn about the great work. I'm not sure but I think it's a royal they want to summon.'

'Which one?' asks Priya.

'I don't know, but once they take over Edinburgh and all the magicians in Scotland, there won't be any limit to what they can do,' says Jomo.

This is worrying. At last, I see the pattern that's been woven: saving my sister means stopping Henry Dundas and that means saving Scotland too. The dozens of voices in my head argue about the meaning of this and what could be done, but even in that cacophony, I'm able to piece out what I need in order to butter up England's Sorcerer Royal. It'll be a huge challenge, but our side of the ledger needs a bit of a hand from the auld enemy.

XXIII

I get dropped off in Slateford 'cause the witches and Travelling Folk are avoiding town for now. Instead, they'll follow the Water of Leith. Priya's got to stay with Jomo until he's handed over to friends of the Daughters of Scotia. I had to make them promise he wouldn't be harmed, 'cause no one's in a good mood right now.

'We're not like those magicians,' Ranjeeta said to me, meaning Jomo's going to be okay. 'But we will slit his throat if what he told you is untrue,' she added.

I guess it's up to Jomo then.

The city's half deserted and that suits me and River just fine. The old girl's in her element, darting ahead, disappearing into side streets and then randomly popping back out of hedge-rows. The air smells rotten tonight. This is an old place with layers of history composted underneath it. If you start bringing the old layers to the surface, it'll kick up a stink.

All the rioting's maybe put off some folks from coming out. I pass by a corner shop and am shocked at the prices of the few things they've got on their bare shelves. A can of chicken soup costs an arm and a leg.

I'm feeling much stronger now; the legs aren't as shaky as

they've been since I got back, but I've still got my walking stick to reassure me. I also feel better with Cruickshank around my neck. The scarf strokes me gently. Still feels a bit weak, but the wee surgeon's done a good job and he'll be right as rain in no time. I like the clothes I'm wearing now, all black, ninjaing into the city.

'God save the king,' a middle-aged man in a duffle coat says.

'Long may—' Nah, I'm not doing that shit anymore.

I follow the road through Fountain Park where some teenagers are hanging around the old complex. Banners hang from lamp-post to lamp-post, advertising how proud Edinburgh is to receive the monarch again. It's been decades since the Scots offed the old king and queen, and their son doesn't have much reason to love the city. There are periods when the monarchy's pissed off or just loses interest in Scotland. Like when George IV visited in 1822 for a couple of days. Back then it had been two hundred years since the monarchy had come this way. That's when the whole tartan thing took off, 'cause they had to play dress up for the king and we've been stuck with it ever since.

There's mounted police ahead with their backs to me. I'd imagine they won't be fucking around tonight since the man himself's going to be around and so they'll make sure riff-raff like yours truly aren't anywhere near there. I pop my hand in my jacket pocket and feel for the mbira, just in case. The windows are broken in all the shops, restaurants and most of the other businesses. It's like walking through a war zone. I was wrong in thinking the protests had only gone as far as the centre of town. Maybe that's the case, but looters, on the other hand, don't seem to have too many qualms about hitting the small businesses here. I wish they went for the bigger chains 'cause the little guys are trying to earn a living and will struggle to recover from this.

I continue all the way to Lothian Road where I take a left, then the first right which leads me down towards the Grassmarket. Up in the sky, a pair of voykor soar as though this were an ordinary day in the everyThere. The line between our world and the land of the dead is blurring and if it continues, soon we'll be swept up in something truly awful. For now they stick to the upper atmosphere, testing out the old barrier. If it's not fixed then we'll have a whole different magnitude of problems to deal with. There's plenty of souls in Edinburgh to feed on. The same balances in ecosystems on our small planet extend out and apply to the worlds beyond. That's why the guardians of other realms don't want us on their turf: we're messy, leaving bubblegum and chippie wrappers on pavements. Doesn't matter whether you mean well or not. The voykor in our world would be a disaster.

The few people who are out and about have no idea how much danger we're all in now. They spend too much time looking down and very little looking up. It's as though the city's in a deep depression. Folks are hungry and scared, and there seems to be no end in sight. A newspaper page floats by with something about grain shipments from South Africa. Can't be enough to feed us all, can it?

On any ordinary day, the Grassmarket should be packed. Normally the police wisely choose to stay away, but right now they're here in force. The street sellers and folks who'd normally fill up the Fleshmarket beyond are all absent. All that remains is heaps of litter. The binmen daren't go where cops fear to tread either. There's maybe a dozen cops standing off Candlemaker Row, so I cross the street to the other side and decide I'm best turning off onto Victoria Street instead.

'Is that her?' one of the cops says.

'Nope. Dreadlocked lass with a fox is who the sarge is after, not some old baldy with a cane.'

'You put in for overtime from last week?'

'It's the day rate, even with the royal visit.'

'I thought we got TOIL?'

I pick up the pace, though Victoria Street is *so* steep. I wrap Cruickshank around my mouth and nose so I'm a little less conspicuous. There's banners everywhere of the old king and queen. Today's the anniversary of their regicide. Who's making the cake for that? It's been decades and their son is finally coming to Scotland. There's been no news of his elder brother, the true heir, in New Zealand for years and no one speaks of him. It's not like they wrote a law against it, but we all have to behave like we forgot about him. We're stuck with the spare and he don't take no prisoners.

No way I'm taking the Royal Mile today, so I head down the bridge and over onto Chambers Street. The city seems bleaker still. I put my right hand into my pocket and feel the mbira thrumming. It resonates with the city, vibrating to its frequency. I resist the temptation to play, knowing the power beneath my fingers is building up and waiting to be unleashed.

One of the old podcasts I listened to back when I was delivering messages spoke of the universe as being made up of a series of vibrating strings; not dots or point particles, but one-dimensional strings, and everything resulted from them. It was pretty strange and awesome because it made you think of everything as a sort of cosmic orchestra. The woman doing the podcast said that the stuff that makes up matter was constantly vibrating at different frequencies. Each one had its own kind of resonant frequency marking it as different from the others. So an electron was a string that was going through a certain vibration and a strange quark would undergo a different one. She described it as a kind of violin – it creates different notes depending on how you vibrate the string. Reckon my mbira is perturbing matter at the fundamental level and the effects show up at the classical scale where we experience the reality.

There are mysterious forces, child.

Ancestors with powers.

What was she trying to say?

Shut it. I still prefer some of the stuff I got from scientific magic. It makes it easier to understand certain things when they happen.

A world without wonder?

Just because there's an explanation doesn't make it any less wondrous. Is a rainbow any less beautiful whether you think of it as God's bow after the flood or light refracted through moisture in the sky? Are the stars any less beautiful if you think of them as massive nuclear macthingys?

The girl has a point.

I still don't get what she's trying to say. There were no schools when I was alive. We didn't even have books.

I swear these ancestors suck. No wonder they used to demand beer from people before they helped out. It's a grift. They were just trying to get hammered. I make it back onto the Cowgate and head down towards the old parliament's arse. It's a gentle slope down from here.

Up in the sky, lost souls wander about in confusion. They fill up the sky and it seems as if they might rain back down to the ground. The everyThere has no direction, so they might be upside down, or sideways, shuffling in every possible orientation. We are well and truly screwed if that realm merges with ours. You sense their desperation growing. They want to be alive again. To experience this maddening rollercoaster world to which nothing else compares.

But there's an order to things and I have to set it right, I think, watching a voykor flap its gigantic wings. I stop and have a good look, and I can almost swear it sees me. Like our eyes make contact. It shouldn't be possible.

When inexperienced astral travellers fall into the everyThere, they are usually gobbled up. The voykor hunger for fresh, living souls, as opposed to the dead, which they seem content to leave in peace. Our world must seem like a buffet to them. For now, it's just out of reach and we have to keep it that way.

I carry on, feeling worried. This thing has to stop. Dundas and my father are risking this entire realm with their foolishness.

'We've got our work cut out for us tonight, River,' I say.

Arthur's Seat appears to my right as I near the parliament. The memory of Rooster Rob mauled to death sticks in my head. What's Camelot without its king and his court? As soon as the other gangs in the city get a whiff Rob's dead, there'll be a war for the centre of Edinburgh. What remains of the Clan won't hold without him. It's sure to splinter into different factions all vying for the spoils and the city will never be the same. With Camelot gone, maybe they'll turn it into a lifeless genteel park again.

I'll make this up to you, Rob. These bastards will pay.

My blood's boiling but von Clausewitz says that it's essential to have 'the ability to keep one's head at times of exceptional stress and violent emotion'. Something about how that's a marker of strength of character. No use flapping about like a headless chicken. I have to focus on the job at hand. We can always mourn our losses later, or at least dine together in the Elysian Fields, which is the closest thing the Greeks had to Valhalla. Yeah, there'll be time for that later.

I pass through the narrow corridor between the ruined Parliament and what used to be Dynamic Earth. The Parliament is a dreary grey concrete thing which blends well with the smothering fog. But things are still a bit too visible for my liking. There's plenty of pigs around Holyroodhouse today and if I can see them, that means they can see me too. If the men with Heckler & Koch carbines and Glock 17s aren't enough of a deterrent, the palace sits behind tall walls and wrought-iron bars.

Here goes.

Standing in the shadow of the ruined Parliament, I place the walking stick under my left armpit and reach into my pocket to retrieve my mbira, but before I play, I form an intention inside my own mind. It's a clear expression of everything I wish to do going forward. I reach into the everyThere and sync my instrument to its dreadful fog. The voices in my head echo my thoughts and so unto myself I've become a choir. There's a harmony and unity that feels like ecstasy, me and Gran and the ancestor babes all locked in, like a band.

Shadow and darkness.

I play the keys lightly, you don't rush a spell like this, and I have to hold all the strands inside my noggin. It strains every neuron and it's building, slowly, slowly.

It starts like a light gust. No, a gust is too strong – something gentler, the wind that licks the sweat off your skin on a hot summer's day. The fog begins to churn here and there. Through my mbira, I can sense the currents within swirling around.

Bing Wu would be proud of your skills as an effectician, Gran says in my head, subtly boasting about a fellow magician who riffed off her work. And that's what I have inside me, brewing from this connection with these mothers present under my skin, deep inside my veins.

It begins to take shape gradually, and then the souls hovering in the sky begin to march downwards.

'Oh shit, that's not supposed to happen.' I panic.

Lean into it. This has always been the gift you avoided.

The souls of the everyThere converge around the Holyroodhouse Palace. There's confusion on their faces, like they've been lured in by the Pied Piper. Downward they descend, others rising from beneath, for the everyThere is glued to all places in our world. Ever there.

They drag with them the essence of their grey, desolate realm and the fog thickens until it becomes impenetrable and you can't see more than a foot or so in front of your face.

'Come on, girl,' I say to River, and make my way across to

the gates of Holyroodhouse. I move cautiously, planting my feet softly so I don't make too much noise. River stays close, sniffing me out, she doesn't need to see me to know where I am.

'What's that strange sound?' a policeman in the fog says.

'Sounds like music,' comes the reply.

'Music? Nothing makes noises like that.'

'You're the one who asked.'

I touch the black iron gates and incant *zarura gonhi*, softly under my breath so my words blend into the notes I'm playing, there's a click and they open. I'd have rather put the cops to sleep, but human beings are vessels of will, so it's bloody difficult to do magic to the body. Of course, you can by coercion or consent, but short of doing stuff to kill them, I have to try this instead.

'Someone's out there.'

'Where?'

'How are we supposed to see in this bloody haar?'

I slip past in the confusion and walk among the ghosts I inadvertently summoned. I slide between the dead and the living. A light goes on, one of the guards near the castle doors has turned on a torch or lamp, but the fog grows animated, pushing hard and smothering the light. The policeman wheezes.

'Can't breathe. I can't. I can't.'

'Turn off that bloody light.'

The light clicks off and he gasps for air, but I've gone past the main doors and into the palace. The fog rushes inside, casting the rooms in the same bleak monotone grey. I use my mbira to lock the fog in place, almost the same way a fisherman would set up a line.

Hurry, this won't hold forever, says Melsie Mhondoro.

I head up to the library where I know the Sorcerer Royal does his work. We used to come here together, back when I was working for him. I had hopes then that I'd go to England and train to be a magician there. Like most things in my life, it didn't go according to plan, almost as though fate had other plans. But I don't believe in any of that 'cause you can't leave stuff to chance like that. Makes you feel like you're a passenger in your own life.

Everything inside the palace is bathed in fog. Ghosts wander around like they own the place. Someone bumps into me.

'Sorry,' she says. 'I can't see a bloody thing at all. I'm having to hold on to the walls. Which way's outside?'

'That way,' I reply, confident like I'm supposed to be here, and slip away.

'You're not much help. Hello? Are you still here? Don't leave me by myself in this.'

I open the library door as quietly as I can and step inside the one room which the fog seems to have neglected. It's got bookshelves from floor to ceiling packed with leatherbound editions. There's an antique desk and a chair in which the Sorcerer Royal's sat with his back to me, writing on parchment with a feathered quill. He dips his pen into the ink pot and scribbles something as I tiptoe nearer.

'Take one more step and I'll have your insides for haggis,' Lord Sashvindu Samarasinghe says, voice full of confidence. 'This fog of yours is an interesting diversion, a petty trick more suited to dilettantes.'

'Yet it's got me in here, past your security, to see you,' I reply, putting the mbira back in my jacket pocket and retrieving my walking stick from under my armpit, planting it on the solid wood floor.

Lord Samarasinghe pauses and then sets his quill aside. He pushes back from the desk and the chair drags across the floor making a din. Then he stands up and clasps his hands behind his back. He swivels round and takes a good long look at me. The Sorcerer Royal is in a black parade jacket with golden buttons. It has raven's feathers for epaulettes. He looks ridiculous.

His monobrow rises and he clasps his hands before laughing maniacally. Tears stream down his face as though seeing me is the funniest thing that's ever happened to him. I don't share his levity 'cause he once left me in the lurch and sicced the dogs on me while he was at it.

'Ropa Moyo, as I live and breathe,' he says, holding out his arms for a hug.

I let him hang.

'Lord Samarasinghe,' I say, and give him a nod in lieu of a bow. I may not like him, but my feelings don't matter much. He is still English magic's most powerful practitioner and I've got to treat him with the same respect one would any other dangerous man. Even now I sense his power pounding away like giant boots marching on parade. It feels inevitable, the force of an empire, looting, pillaging and genociding as it circles the globe.

He points at me with his right hand and exclaims, 'That's why I picked you. Plucky, resourceful and, most importantly, lucky. I heard the news that you were dead, honourably, in combat.' He waves both fists like a gleeful child shadow boxing. 'That's what I call going out in style. I wept for you and lit a candle in the ruins of the Abbey. Honest.'

'I doubt that.'

'Yet here you are. And you came back to me because you know deep in your heart that I've been more than fair with you in our dealings. I am curious, how did you get back from the other side?'

'Curiosity killed the cat,' I reply, walking to the centre of the room, directly under a crystal chandelier. There, right beneath it, I place my stick on the ground and let go. It remains upright and I register the slightest widening of Lord Samarasinghe's eyes. He did something similar to me at Dunvegan Castle. I don't make a meal of it, though, and instead walk over to the left side of the room to inspect the books on display.

'They named this library for King James I. He authored a tract you may have heard of: *Daemonologie*? The royals have always taken a keen interest in our field.' Lord S fills the silence.

'It's James VI in Scotland,' I correct him.

'My mistake,' he says.

I don't bother responding. I'd rather let him stew for a bit. This is the first time I've seen him off balance. Usually he's the one toying with people.

'I know you're enamoured with Scottish magic, but Dr John Dee revolutionized English magic, kind of like what Rasputin did for the Russians. John Dee was the court astronomer for Queen Elizabeth I and his work was well recognized. But when she was succeeded by your James VI, let's just say the Scottish king had some difficulty with the concept of having a sorcerer at the court. Dee was kicked out and died in penury. A pity really. But I think James, who considered himself a scholar of magic, may have been a bit jealous. There's a story that he asked John Dee if he'd read *Daemonologie* and what he thought of it, when they first met. Dee replied rather scatologically, "That book works magic in the privy and I have much improved the pages, as my chamber pot will attest."'

The Sorcerer Royal laughs heartily as if using books for toilet paper could ever be funny. I recall what a wild ride it was to be around him and his mercurial temperament. Hot one minute, cold the next. I place the book back on the shelf without looking at it and move to a different wall.

I'm here out of necessity, but I have no wish to be back in his favour. This man promised to stand with Sir Ian Callander against Henry Dundas on Calton Hill, even going as far as turning up. But when the time came to keep his promise, he broke his word and walked away like an Englishman. I still remember how he stole the wind from underneath our sails. How many lives would have been saved if he'd sided with Callander? But Lord Samarasinghe doesn't have the interests of Scottish magic at heart. He's been a cancer festering away since he first arrived, seeking to undermine the Society at every turn. But I finally figured out why he did the things he did. There was something he wanted. I wish I'd seen it sooner.

'Hello, Melsie and whoever else you have in there,' Lord Samarasinghe says, pointing at my head. 'You know, I see them too, the ghosts. My skills in this area aren't as well developed as yours. This is the one area of magic which unfortunately depends on aptitude as opposed to concerted application. It's quite frustrating to have a sliver of talent, but not the genius.'

'*Hello, Lord Samarasinghe.*' Gran gets the words out of my mouth before I can shut her up. My voice sounds like an old woman's when she does.

I'll do the talking, I tell my choir. I'm the conductor here.

Don't get your knickers in a twist, Gran responds.

'I'm here because you've badly miscalculated, Lord Samarasinghe, and you've put your sovereign in danger,' I say.

There's a flash of anger, a dark cloud settling on his face, and I feel a minor change in entropy before he regains his cool. The Sorcerer Royal's a man whose moods change upon a whim like the weather on these isles. He doesn't like to be questioned, or told he is wrong. Underneath that is a sense of insecurity which he covers up by being bombastic. From what I've learnt during my time ballroom dancing with the folks in this world, life looks great for them from the outside. They live in mansions or castles, eat good food and wear fine clothes while the masses starve to death, but all those things mask the central problem they grapple with from day to day. The positions they hold are precarious; there's always another who wants to take that spot and have those perks. I saw this with Sir Ian Callander, who was challenged first by his own friend and then by a ghoul.

'So out of the goodness of your heart you've come to save me,' he sneers.

'From yourself. You can thank me later.' Clearly Lord S finds it hard to believe.

'I'd be careful with my tone if I were you.' He's trying to regain the upper hand.

'I don't like you, I don't have to, but it seems our interests are aligned for the moment, Lord Samarasinghe. I've travelled from Iona to Aberdeen and taken the motorway to Glasgow. And then I came here by rail and wagon. Across the country I noticed something very odd.' I let him reel himself in.

'And that is?'

'All the banners and posters of the old king and queen. They're absolutely everywhere. It got me thinking why this was the case,' I say.

'Why should I care? The Scots can try to make amends all they like, but it doesn't change what they did to their *rightful* king and queen. It's only by the mercy of this sovereign that the slight is not avenged. Were it up to me I'd have taken every Scottish firstborn and put them to the sword.'

Ignore the bluster, Ropa.

'It seemed odd to me that after years of seeing the image of the king plastered everywhere, we're getting his parents instead.'

'Thanks for telling me, I'll be sure to pass on the sentiment. Now if that's all, I have a bit of work to do before the king arrives. This has been an amusing diversion.'

There's a sharpness in Lord Samarasinghe's tone and he falls silent, brooding. Clearly I've struck a nerve and so I keep on digging, 'cause I like seeing him squirm a wee bit. I walk over to a two-seater sofa in the corner and sit down on it. This makes him frown. I'm treading a fine line here, but as Carl von Clausewitz once asked, 'In what field of human activity is boldness more at home than in war?' There's too much at stake, including my own sister.

'A lot didn't make sense to me. Like, you're the Sorcerer Royal and should be more concerned about Henry Dundas and his cult, since it goes against the interests of the realm,' I say. '*Rule Britannia*. No, there had to be more to it.'

His monobrow rises a fraction, cunning in his eyes, he tries to read me. The corners of his mouth twitch, an almost smirk that doesn't come. But he seems uneasy, and I'm sussing that his footing in this scheme might not be as firm as he'd intended. I hold the silence. It's uncomfortable . . .

'Go on,' he says. There, he's blinked first.

'You know, I thought you were just being malicious when you betrayed Sir Ian Callander. Or maybe you'd been bribed.' Samarasinghe scoffs but remains silent. 'But of course not, money isn't what drives you. I figured Dundas and his cult must have something you desire. Why would the Sorcerer Royal embroil himself in this Scottish madness? What is it you want?'

'Stop fishing – this sea is too deep for your little hook, Ropa. You are beginning to annoy me.' The hanging light fixture sways as though shaken by his mood.

'The answer is nothing for yourself. Funny how you went off on a tangent about Dr John Dee, a sorcerer who once did well but was cast out of court. It made me realize that you're still just a lad from Edgbaston. Your life is devoted to winning the king's favour and he's an exacting man. He's been through a lot, hasn't he?'

Lord Samarasinghe steps backwards, retreating from me until he bumps into his desk. He sits on it, both hands gripping the edge. His face softens, morphing with a certain tenderness, the look of a man in love. It's a strange kind of love, one peculiar to the subjects of the old Empire. Patriotism spiced with zealotry. Lord S reeks of it. It used to send men to kill and die across all four corners of the world, waving a little flag for king and country.

'More than you could ever imagine. Our sovereign spends all his days doing things in the interest of the realm. His thanks? Subjects who hate him, especially the Scotch,' he says bitterly, as though it were a personal affront.

'It must be tough for him being an orphan and every day knowing his parents were murdered and he wasn't even allowed to cry over it. Without processing grief, we can become monsters. His brother and his wife fled to New Zealand, leaving him to clear up the mess. Maybe there are nights when that crown weighs down on him and he yearns for the simple days when his family was intact. The rift with his only brother is final, but maybe Dundas will reset things. The king can have anything he wants in the world, can force people to bend to his will, but that's not what he truly desires. Who wouldn't give the world just to hear their mother's voice again? I know that feeling all too well. The gifts of the gods are a two-edged sword.'

If Richard III was willing to trade his kingdom for a horse, what would this king trade for his mother? Lord Samarasinghe swallows hard and purses his lips. He's the king's confidant and so my speculations must be hitting home. Otherwise he'd not come across as so agitated.

'I struck a deal to help the king see his mother again, if that's what you're driving at. I don't see anything wrong with that.'

'Bring the mother back because she won't want to take the crown from your head, but leave your father to rot in hell? It's very Oedipal. His brother's in New Zealand and never coming back unless it's to wage war and reclaim his birthright, so the only person the king can have in his life is his mother. He's coming to Scotland because he wants to hear his mother speak out of my little sister Izwi's lips. They want to channel her through my sister. That's why my father and Dundas kept talking about how Izwi would speak like the queen.'

'And the king will reward his loyal subjects for their gift.'

I see how the stars aligned between Makomborero Moyo and the cult, how they might have had a beneficiary waiting for the results of my father's experiments. Me and Izwi are merely proof of concept. But the project was so secret one hand didn't know what the other was doing. Makomborero Moyo would have seemed like a dangerous man to Gran and Sir Ian Callander. They'd not have understood that his work for Dundas would have the king hooked because all he wants is his mum back. He's like the rest of us, yearning for love. But the king couldn't afford for it to leak that all he's been doing is waiting for his long-dead mother to return to him. In this he is very like my own father. A single-minded man. There's a desperation that comes from grief and loss. I know, I've experienced it every day of my waking life. I dealt with it too when I was a ghostalker. But, I tell Lord S, this plan will blow up in his face.

The Sorcerer Royal's grinding his teeth and his irritation is evident. For the first time since I've known him, the man who oozes self-confidence looks unsettled and unsure.

'Did you know they used to call Henry Dundas "King Harry"?

Maybe he's thinking of installing himself as the god-king. It's been tried before.' I keep turning that screw. 'And when it all comes crumbling down, who do you think will get blamed for it? You, of course.'

Cockburn said she heard Montgomery Wedderburn talking about wiping the chessboard. Pretty vague, but the most important piece is the king. You take the king, you've won, and Lord Samarasinghe's backhand deal's leading the king to them. Before Dundas murdered Frances Cockburn, he said something about the 'head that wears the crown'. It sounds to me like that's what he's after. There's this confluence of players all wanting different things from this disaster they've set up. It makes it harder to clearly spot who's winning or losing. My father wants to be made the lord of the underworld to have his pick of souls to play with in his horrific experiments. Henry Dundas wants dominion over this realm. He's a product of empire, the President of the Board of Control for the East India Company. His designs won't stop there, but he's come back to a different world in which his little island's no longer the centre of the universe. Everyone else's caught up.

I don't think Lord Samarasinghe's peers in England'll be that forgiving if something happened to the king. They have their share of republicans down south, and the chaos that would ensue if the king was murdered would bring so many genies out of every bottle.

'Your acquiescence has brought us to the brink. This hell that's settled over Edinburgh could just as easily consume London,' I argue.

And then I stop. You don't ever want to over-labour the

point. I think he gets it. Dundas will be a threat to everything Lord Samarasinghe wants to protect.

'I think you should leave now, Ropa Moyo. Consider it a professional courtesy that I haven't killed you today,' Lord Samarasinghe says, making Cruickshank stir from his resting place around my neck. The sorcerer smiles noticing this – it's in his nature to only respect strength. 'Things are in motion that can't be turned around.'

'On your head be it,' I say, standing up from the sofa. I reach out my hand and the walking stick floats over to me. Lord Samarasinghe sneers and turns away.

I've said my piece and if he wants to go forth, on his head be it. We could have used the might of English magic on our side, but if he truly believes that this thing can't be turned around then I won't waste my breath anymore. I've given it a shot. Lord S hates it when people ask him for stuff. More often than not he'll choose to stiff you. But today, if Dundas gets his way, Samarasinghe will be collateral damage just like all the rest.

I have to go, I have a meeting with some kickass witches in a cemetery – my idea of a great girls' night out.

XXIV

Briggs, Lord Samarasinghe's coach driver, is outside feeding apples to his horses, waiting with the sorcerer's carriage. He regards me coolly as I step out into the open.

'I see we've made some changes to the way we look,' he says in that broad Yorkshire accent of his.

'And you're still ugly,' I reply, making him laugh.

'My mum thinks so too. Then again, you should see her beard,' he jests. 'You've been up to see the gaffer?'

'Waste of my time,' I reply.

'Lord Samarasinghe's wise as he is powerful. He sees things none of us are able to. Remember, he's been playing these games since before you were in your father's balls.'

I wave and walk away. Briggs knows which side his bread's buttered on, so he's pretty useless to me. I go over and ask the armed policeman to open the gate. He frowns, baffled at seeing me, and looks to Briggs first, who nods, and then opens the gate. I've had enough of castles and palaces. Nothing good ever comes from these places.

I wait a moment for River to emerge from the shadows.

'Don't ask. We wasted our time,' I tell her.

It seems the palace stands alone now. The Parliament was

ruined by shells from a Challenger tank back in the day, and half the Canongate was levelled when Calton Hill collapsed. I go towards the rubble, tracing the old section of the Royal Mile from down here.

The right side of the street's covered in brick and stone and broken beams. Glass everywhere. I step over a hand basin and carry on up the road. There's an overwhelming reek of decaying flesh pouring out from underneath the collapsed buildings. I spot some bones, probably from the disturbed earth of the cemetery by Canongate Kirkyard. The old ghosts who used to wander this site trudge through the wreck in confusion.

There're scavengers at work amidst the ruins. Men and women scour the collapsed buildings hoping to score a bit of loot.

'There's one here,' a man shouts in the distance where the Old Tolbooth Wynd would have been. 'Bloody hell, she's alive!'

Other scavengers rush to where he is, digging with their bare hands. They pull a skinny figure from the hole below. I don't see her properly with all the people that have gathered round. I guess that's the good thing about what the scavengers are doing. It's not like I see any fire engines or rescuers helping out.

The voices in my head start arguing, the ones who died during the colonial era complaining that Europe isn't the paradise they'd heard about. I push on, annoyed they won't let me do my thing in peace. After all this is done, I'm doing an exorcism.

Don't you dare, you ungrateful child.

Watch me, I might send you all to the Other Place just for kicks.

She's joking, isn't she? I think she is?

Ropa!

I ignore them. There was a time I thought the ancestors were like serious, grown-up people, but they seem as confused as we are. Each generation's a bunch of nursery school kids blundering cluelessly from one mess to the next.

I already said there were no schools in my time.

Go back to pounding millet. This'll drive me nuts; they just don't know when to stop.

After Canongate, the city gets a bit more normal. There's a few folks trudging along and a load of cops. One of them standing by the corner leading onto North Bridge clocks me. Unlike the lads guarding the palace who only care for its security, the beat cops are on the lookout for criminals. He tenses up, nudges his colleagues and gets on his radio. This is the same corner where the separatists waylaid the old king and queen, and dragged them out of their carriage when they were coming from watching a play. I get why they might have pigs guarding it. They've drawn a massive red rose on the intersection.

'River, Cruickshank, let's change direction,' I say, hurrying along before the others get a proper look at me.

Rather cold and grey, isn't it?

'That too,' I reply in my head.

Good thing I know this city like the back of my hand and in no time I'm in the New Town. There's a torn text on the street. Half of it's missing and the rest is in a state. I pick it up and see it's a copy of William Cullen's *A Treatise on Chemical Transformations*. It must have flown from the Library when that got blown up. I throw it back on the ground where it belongs.

The Library is now a collapsed catacomb of grimoires, texts and books that will remain hidden for as long as the place goes unexcavated. Maybe a scavenger here and there will come across some rare magical treatise and discard it, thinking it worthless. Or they'll sell it to the second-hand book store on Haddington Place. Until then the Library will rest.

'Hey, Ropa, stop,' a man says, running up from behind me. I turn and it's Cameron, who used to stay on Camelot.

'You're a sight for sore eyes,' I say.

'I doubt that, but thanks all the same. Listen, I've been looking for Rob everywhere. Went to see my nan in Prestonpans 'cause she's poorly, and when I got back on the hill there's no one there. I knew the pigs had come back, but Rob's disappeared.'

I stare down at my boots. How do I break it to him? Cameron's one of those who's been on the hill the longest. It was his community and he stuck with Rob all the way through. I guess Camelot will live on after all, in the memories of lads like him.

'I'm sorry, I have no idea,' I reply.

'That's alright, I'm sure he'll pop up somewhere. You know the Rooster. Anyways, nice bumping into you. Be careful out here, the pigs are in a temper.'

'Take care of yourself, Cameron.'

He'll have hope for a couple of days and then, as the weeks stretch on, he'll realize Rob's not coming back and maybe then he'll find a new racket. Life goes on. It always does, no matter who we lose, and it's the same for those who lose us.

I cross the disused tram tracks, heading down Queen Street. They seem to have parked one on York Place. Maybe it's for show since the king's coming. The shops are already shuttered up. It's just me and River. My girl stays next to me as we go down the incline.

I'm just worried about our numbers. All I have on my side are a bunch of witches. Tough as nails if the rescue mission taught me anything, but I fear they won't be enough against the ghoul that took down Callander. And we have the added complication that should we intervene, Lord Samarasinghe will side with Dundas. I guess we're going to have to roll the dice one last time.

The day's already dimming, invisible except for a bright patch of sky far away. Something cool flutters on my face and then again. I look up and see snow's falling.

'Look at that, River. Isn't that just lovely?' I say.

I cross the road, feeling the cool flakes hit my bald head and lashes. The Queen Street Gardens are open to the public for the first time in two hundred years after the rioters broke the locks and tore down sections of the fence. It might be a neat spot for a lassie and her fox to hang around if we didn't have some important place to be.

It's a mile or so walking through a city where the fear keeps most locked up in their tenements and townhouses, but I make it over the river and to Dean Cemetery at last.

Oh look, just the perfect place for us, says a voice in my head.

I prefer my warm resting place. Can you imagine freezing your bones out here?

Melsie, how are your bones resting?

Better than yours, which are ground to dust.

The Travelling Folk have parked their wagons on Dean Path. There's a couple of horses tied to the cemetery fence. Mrs Guthrie's donkey Benjamin is there too with his cart. Then there's a handful of electric vehicles also parked out on the street. I wonder what the residents nearby make of it all.

I enter the cemetery, which is well kept compared to the others I've been to in the city. I used to say ghostalkers have no business with the dead in ancient cemeteries. Boy, was I wrong, 'cause they have business with us. My hustle was mostly confined to the new ghosts who had living relatives they wanted to pass messages down to. I couldn't see it's the ancient ones that have the most urgent shit to spew. They're the ones who built this messy world we live in and we might have forgotten them, but they're not done with us.

I get a nod from Sister Elspeth and Sister Edina stood under a yew tree. They're both quietly turning rosary beads in their palms.

I'd love a statue.

You'll be lucky to get a drink off a minor medium.

'Shut up, guys. I'm working,' I say.

It won't help none. Yep, I'll deffo do an exorcism, if I don't get killed again tonight. Note to self: I'm never coming back as an ancestor. The future can sort itself out.

Rude.

These old gravestones are history books in their own right. They carry snippets of epics, much as a haiku can contain so much in so few words. They tell you something about who the people that lived in Edinburgh were. The ages they died at tell you something else about what was going on at the time. It could be a war or plague. There's always lessons you can learn from an old gravestone.

There are strange women sitting atop tombstones. A good few men too, Lethington among them. Some are perched like crows on the branches of trees, while others hang about in clusters. Priya spots me and comes over.

'I've just been to see Lord Samarasinghe,' I tell her. 'We'll be getting no help from the English on this.'

Priya closes her eyes, resigned. We have less than a hundred witches here, and they must have been counting on me to shore up that number. Is this all there are in Scotland? That's less than two witches for each county. The magicians under Henry Dundas number nearly three times that, and that's without the involvement of Glasgow.

'Has Calista Featherstone managed to get us help from the north?' I ask.

'The magicians there are scared and most will wait it out,' she replies. It reminds me of when shitty stuff happened at Dunvegan Castle and very few magicians stood up to fight. These are businesspeople, not warriors.

What would Carl von Clausewitz do in this kind of scenario?

You are obsessed, Ropa.

'If any of you have answers, I sure as hell would like to hear them, not this sniping.'

'What?' asks Priya. 'You're mumbling to yourself. You've been doing that a lot lately. You're not losing it, are you? It takes years to train to be a medium and even then, I've never seen one host so many at once.'

Oh shit, there I was thinking I was having these conversations in my head. I must occasionally slip and vocalize stuff. It's hard to remember I'm talking to dead people living rent free in my noggin. Shrug it off. I'm good and there's a massive tuna we ought to be frying right now.

'I thought this was supposed to be a meeting but you're all milling about like you want to go trick-or-treating,' I say.

'I forgot that you've never been to a coven. We do things differently,' Priya replies. 'Mum and Theodosia would like to speak with you before the vote.'

Some of the witches seem to be deep in thought while others chat in hushed tones. By now they should have come up with a course of action. We need to do something. Say what you will but the meetings of the Society of Sceptical Enquirers are much more organized than anything this ragtag bunch has going on right now.

This one is very hasty.

Shut up.

Melsie wasn't so different at that age.

I swear if I had a gun I'd shoot myself in the head.

I recognize a lady who used to sell flowers on Nicolson Street – she's wearing a romantic-era bonnet with a dried sunflower tied by a ribbon to her red hair and she's sat on a grave, holding a bunch of pansies. Flower power's not going to win the night for us.

Ranjeeta Kapoor and Theodosia Lovell are sat on dining chairs on either side of the tomb that I suspect belongs to Louisa Stephenson. Standing beside Ranjeeta is Calista Featherstone in her distinctive red suit. I walk over to them and notice some of the witches sizing me up. A handful I've met via the Society but most appear to be working women like the flower seller.

'Is this all the Daughters of Scotia?' I ask.

'Many didn't heed the call. We were hoping you'd bring good news,' Ranjeeta says sadly.

'I'm afraid we're on our own,' I say.

'There goes that then,' Mrs Guthrie says, taking a swig from a bottle of cider. The woman next to her holds out her hand and Mrs Guthrie reluctantly passes the bottle along.

The flower seller stands tall and defiant. 'The Botanic Gardens used to have a rare corpse flower when I was growing up. I remember my father, a member of this coven, taking me there one year because it had bloomed. He told me the flower only emerged every two years and when it did, people would queue up to see it. Cicadas lie dormant for seventeen years and then they emerge. We should do what's kept us safe for centuries, go underground and wait out the storm.'

'That's sensible, Milligan,' someone behind me replies.

'Even if yer dinnae come, I'll avenge Frances myself,' Theodosia Lovell says with a cold calmness that raises the hairs on the back of my neck. She's staring off into the distance as though she's reading the falling snow. A solitary tear is frozen on her cheek.

The witches are uneasy and I realize that having stayed

hidden for so long, the last thing they want is to make their presence known to the Society. It seems to me there's been a steady truce. The witches ceded magic to the Society's practitioners and retreated to the shadows. And so long as they stayed there, the Witchcraft Act of 1563 would remain dormant. If they fought Dundas and lost, it might well be open season again.

'Sisters, we're all guided by our conscience and no one can ask for more than that,' Ranjeeta says solemnly. There's nerves in the air and very little backbone. 'Let's put this to a vote. "Aye" to avenge one of our own and settle old scores with the magicians, "nae" to slink home to our beds, craven.'

'We're sorry, Ranjeeta, but asking us to commit suicide is not what the Daughters were set up for. Secrecy has kept us alive. If even the Doric magicians won't stand then who are we to take part in their civil war?' a short, stout lady with a pug nose asks, moving to the left.

'Does that mean you vote nae, then?'

'It means we should go back to our homes and our families, store as much food as we can, and survive. I'm sorry for what happened to Frances, but embedding her in that place was a step too far. Please forgive me, but I cannot join in this suicide mission,' a young woman in white dungarees splattered with paint says. She too moves to the left.

'Who else votes nae, then?' Ranjeeta asks, her face a mask, betraying no emotion.

One by one the witches drift to the left side. When the woman next to Mrs Guthrie joins them too, the groundskeeper for the Edinburgh School snatches her booze back from her and spits on the ground. More than half the witches signal they do not want to participate in the battle against Dundas. So few ayes remain on the right.

'What a place we've chosen to shine our cowardice,' Mrs Guthrie says. 'Louisa Stevenson ought to be turning in her grave. She fought for women's education and suffrage, and I imagine if we'd been born in her age, you'd have shirked your duty then too. Pathetic, all of yous.'

'That'll be the Dutch courage speaking,' the pug-nosed woman says, which makes the others laugh. Nervous laughter.

'Better that than being a wuss,' Mrs Guthrie retorts. 'I'll go, Theodosia. The two of us are worth five of them.'

Priya steps up. 'I'll go too.'

Ranjeeta gives her a sharp look. But if Priya thought throwing herself in the ring would rally the refuseniks then it doesn't work. One after the other, the women give similar excuses. They won't put their lives on the line for a city that's caused them four hundred years of pain and suffering. There are a couple that side with Theodosia, but they're too few to sway their cautious colleagues.

A bell tolls in the distance.

The refuseniks on the left are starting to leave, heads bowed, shamed faces. Damn it, we need everyone we can get. I clamber onto the low wall behind Louisa Stephenson's grave and steady myself, left elbow on her tombstone.

'You can't leave now.' I wave my stick at the witches. 'I'm not one of you, but I've been in the trenches. My grandmother was Melsie Mhondoro who some of you knew well. It's okay that you're scared for your lives. I couldn't trust any of you if you weren't,' I say, stepping forward and planting my feet on the soft grass near the grave. A witch on her way out stops. And then another. A lady grabs hold of her companion's arm to prevent her from leaving. Theodosia Lovell gives me a subtle nod as the reluctant witches return to the coven. 'I once heard of a Japanese soldier called Hiroo Onoda who after the war in the Pacific finished, stayed in the jungle in the Philippines fighting. It took nearly thirty years before they brought him back to Japan. He kept on fighting. It seems to me you've been in hiding for so long that some of you have lost the will to fight. I know you're afeart. Frances Cockburn was too, but she held her nerve. I was there when Henry Dundas tested her against flame and found she was steel through and through. He may have destroyed her body, but her spirit was above him. Frances didn't flinch even as they stoked the fires under her feet. She stood tall and she was defiant to the end. Her last words were those spoken by Agnes Finnie and she promised Henry Dundas he would die at the hands of witches. With her blood, she swore you all, her sisters, to this task. Don't you dare turn away now.'

XXV

I've done it now, haven't I? Pushed us all to the brink even though we've got a bad hand. Still got to play the game anyway, I think that's how the saying goes. The history of this city is made up of women who've done the same, refused to be seen and not heard. Sarah Siddons Mair, Maude Edwards, Eliza Wigham, James Barry, Mary of Guise, Sophia Jex-Blake, Elizabeth Murray, Dora Noyce. It's not just those named and remembered, but many more whose graves are unmarked, their stories untold, forgotten or suppressed.

It is all being decided in a graveyard; there are some of the coven who'll see these ancient headstones and decide it's worth slinking off to live another day. Others, I hope, will realize we have one end in common in this great drama. Each of us can choose to play their part. I hope enough of us rally as though Wallace himself was calling to them.

Even Priya seems nervous, tapping her hand against the armrests on her wheelchair.

'I guess today's as good a day as any other to die,' Milligan says, throwing her hands up, resigned. She stares at me, then shakes her head. 'Goddamn it, there's a floral arch I was hoping to finish this week. I'll be needing some of that alcohol now.'

Mrs Guthrie hands Milligan the booze and the witches burst out laughing. It's a nervous laugh.

'The Doric School will stand with you,' Calista Featherstone declares. 'It's time to remind this arrogant city that us folks from up north are made of hardier stuff.'

'I couldn't trust any magician,' Milligan says.

'Aye, but my Frances was one of them,' Theodosia Lovell replies.

That shuts Milligan up. She shrugs as though to show that it was a last-ditch attempt to get out of this. I scan around, trying to get a better gauge of who might leave, but I'm relieved to see the stoic look on the witches' faces. There are doubters, but most of them seem set for the moment as we stand near Louisa Stevenson's grave.

The snow falls still, swirling in the sky, growing ever heavier. It's beginning to settle, a thin layer, not yet the magnificent white blanket of bleak midwinter, but the stage before when things could go either way. This is how things become set. Disparate wills bind into one and work towards a single goal. Maybe it's fate. It could be chance. Stuff that was fluffy like snowflakes hardens and becomes ice.

'Step forward then and make your oaths upon this tomb, Daughters of Scotia,' Ranjeeta says, a flinty seriousness in her voice. 'Take out your knives and let your blood fall upon this stone.'

I don't have my dagger anymore, but I step forward first and hold out my hand.

'This was yer granny's,' Theodosia Lovell says, a topstitch needle appearing out of thin air in my open palm.

I take the point and drive it into the heel of my left palm. It cuts the flesh keen enough and when I pull it out a few red drops of my own blood fall upon the new snow on Louisa Stevenson's grave.

I get a subtle nod from Ranjeeta. She seems proud of me and I feel Gran within beaming. She doesn't even need to say it, I know. I've joined my tribe at last. Feels like I was searching for something that was right in front of me all along. This right here is the First School of magic. Class is going to be rather interesting today.

Priya goes up next and soon all the other witches trickle forward under Ranjeeta's watchful eye. One by one they give a drop or two of blood. It feels like such an old way of doing things but there's power in it. We draw closer together in this ancient act. I feel the souls of the women within me stirring up, flashes of memories not my own – somewhere in the savannah, a cave and a full moon. A woman stands bare-chested in front of spear-wielding warriors, blessing them before they set off for war. Her name was Nehanda and she fought against the British as they sought to colonize her land. There've always been women like her holding firm against the flood. They can never be defeated; setbacks are only temporary 'cause time is on their side. I am seeing threads of a common story, but one woven so tight it becomes nearly impossible to disentangle all the elements within.

I watch the witches make their oaths. Ranjeeta gives hers last, retrieving a silver flick blade and pricking her right index finger before letting one final drop fall upon the headstone. When she is done, Theodosia closes off the ritual.

'Dinnae be afeart, sisters. Together we are strong. We offer oor gift tae the Egyptian princess who washed up on these shores and brought her magic here.'

She places her hands above the tombstone and makes an incantation which causes the blood to glow, rainbow colours shining through the prisms of ice and snow. I feel even more intensely tied to these women. I may not know them all, but we're clothed in one purpose now.

Calista Featherstone whispers something in Theodosia Lovell's ear before peeling away from the gathering and heading towards the cemetery entrance. The hem of her red dress swishes over the snow. She stops and looks over her shoulder to me.

'We'll get your sister back before the day is done,' she says. 'I promise.'

'You're right about that,' I reply.

Priya touches my hand and squeezes. I know she's usually the one pulling me out of tight spots, but if I had my way I'd let her sit this one out. I've already lost so much and I can't afford to lose her too. I rub her knuckles with my thumb. This is war and she's an adrenaline junkie so diving into the lion's den is precisely her sort of thing.

Up in the sky, the dead continue to shuffle. I look to watch them go.

'Am I hallucinating?' Priya asks, also looking up.

'You can see them too?' I'm shocked. It's not as if she's ever displayed that kind of gift before.

'We can all see them,' Milligan says, gazing upward.

'Is this what it's always looked like for you?' Priya prods.

It's certainly nothing like this. It's never been. The two realms are separate and travelling between them involves skill and risk. Never mind the cost. But now the everyThere's like knotweed and it's latched onto our realm without restriction. Whatever's left of the barrier between the two worlds is virtually gone. And if all the witches can see the dead wandering above the city, then others might also see it. A couple of the ladies have whipped out their phones and are taking videos. You can't normally photograph a ghost but it seems now you can. The rules have changed.

I wonder if this was a part of Dundas's plans, his return heralded by a group of dodgy dead folks. Or it could just be unintended consequences. Either way, the realm of the dead is perilously close and that's not so good for folks down here.

'Time's nae on our side now the lot's been cast,' Theodosia says. 'I'll take them head-on fae George Street.'

'Mrs Guthrie, you and your sisters will head them off from Princes Street. I'll be on Queen Street. Remember to choose your moment,' Ranjeeta says. 'Priyanka, be careful.'

'You too,' Priya replies, but she's holding back a flood of emotion. I understand why her mother didn't want her coming with me. I close my eyes and take a deep breath.

Back of the envelope plans are messy, but it's the best we've got. You can do all the planning you fancy, but as von Clausewitz said, 'War is nothing but a duel on an extensive scale. If we would conceive as a unit the countless number of duels which make up a War, we shall do so best by supposing to ourselves two wrestlers. Each strives by physical force to compel the other to submit to his will: each endeavours to throw his adversary, and thus render him incapable of further resistance.' That's all it is at the end of the day, a duel, our will against theirs.

Some of the sisters look skittish and I'd be worried if they weren't. It's those nerves that give you an edge, quicken your reflexes. I remember how it was for me when I first got dragged into the world of Scottish magic. The fear I felt trapped in Arthur Lodge. Being chased by the Midnight Milkman through the Cowgate. Gets the blood pumping right enough.

The pain in my left hand is still sharp from where I stuck a needle in it.

You can't stop the sands of time from flowing in this world. Theodosia Lovell beckons and I follow with Priya close to me. River's prancing along and we pick up a dozen witches, including Lethington. Our band's the vanguard of what will happen tonight. We make our way through the graveyard and out onto the street where Artchival's waiting patiently.

'This is witches' business noo, Artchival. Go hame tae the road and be free as the sparrows,' Theodosia says.

'You cannae shake me off that easily. I've got lead and steel and that's better than any spell them magicians can cast,' he replies, opening both sides of his coat to reveal a revolver tucked in the front of his trousers, and a machete dangling by his left leg.

'Foolish man,' Theodosia admonishes.

'The only sort you'll have around,' Artchival replies with a laugh. 'I cannae sit it oot while Frances's blood calls from beyond.'

We make our way across the Water of Leith and up towards the city centre. The residents in this part of town have shut themselves away from the chaos and the horrors outside. Lights burn through the windows of the townhouses and tenements, and there are plenty of folks staring outside. They hardly pay attention to us walking by. Wide-eyed in wonder, their heads are turned up to the dead roaming the skies above Edinburgh.

I push to help Priya's chair up the steady incline as we near Queen Street and then pull up to the Charlotte Square end of the western side of the city. The businesses are shut here too, with broken windows galore from the worst of the riots, and revolutionary slogans about an independent Scotland are sprayed onto the old walls. The road is wide and bare, save for a homeless man in a sleeping bag in the doorway of a shuttered pub. He has a dead glare in his eyes and pays no attention to us or the sky above.

The rough sleeper's a stark contrast to what the New Town of Edinburgh was supposed to be. The old part of the city, south of the new loch where Princes Street Gardens used to be, was always dirty and smelly and crime-riddled. Wealthy folks wanted to get away from all that and build something new and grand for themselves. A place of sophistication, the gifts of civilization. Straight lines, grand designs. The street grids the product of logic, planning and reason instead of the haphazard lanes that grew organically in the old part of the city.

We head east, falling into rhythm as though Theodosia Lovell's footsteps were our metronome. This is what it is to become one, to be a team, a collective, an army. There's an air of disdain about her: for a free woman, the grand architecture of this city holds little appeal. I wouldn't see her swapping her caravan for a flat. And I'm no different either, I decide. The things that I used to strive for back when I was seeking a foothold in Scottish magic seem like bollocks to me.

On Hanover Street we walk past the statue of George IV. A dead king. So many of them littered through time.

We are now close to St Andrew Square and the hairs on my flesh prick up. There it is, at the far end, through the snow, the headquarters of the Royal Bank of Scotland. The home of the Society of Sceptical Enquirers. I can't deny that it is a beautiful building, those neat lines, the neoclassical features, the detailing in the pediments, art etched in stone. This is the key entity that built the New Town, Scotland and the modern world. It's fallen from its great heights of the nineteenth and twentieth centuries, but it's still here like a stump you can't get rid of.

These are the roots of everything good and ill in this city. The Bank. Dundas House. It stands arrogantly withdrawn from the frontage on the street which its neighbours are erected on, with a front garden where the neighbouring buildings have their doors right next to the pavement.

When Scotland joined the Union in 1707 and became a partner in the Empire the riches really started to flow in. What was once Western Europe's poorest nation grew wealthy. Slaves and gold from Africa. Tobacco and sugar from the Americas. Silk and cotton from India. Wool and whales from Australia. The world was there for the taking. War. Plunder. Rape. Scots in the East India Company, Scots in plantations in the Caribbean, Scots in boats, Scots everywhere. A new age of abundance and flourishing. The remnants of those times are tied up in the stones of the New Town, financed by the Royal Bank of Scotland.

'The Athens of the North,' I mumble.

'You wouldn't think so now, would you?' Priya replies.

'It's still there.'

That's the thing, it's an indelible stain. No amount of statues and revisionism can ever get rid of the shame of all this. All these stones that have become buildings are bound together by the mortar wetted and mixed in with the blood and sweat and suffering of millions upon millions whose subjugation and dignity, their very humanity, was traded for fine material things. But isn't it just beautiful when you look past all that? Erase it all and be dazzled by the trinkets instead.

In the background the jagged peaks of the broken Library jut out ominously. The one pillar of Scottish magic brought down by Sir Ian Callander. Sharp rocks point to the sky above where the voykor circle ominously, waiting for their moment. I think of the people of the city hiding in their homes. Bricks and mortar'll be little protection if those creatures descend.

Theodosia Lovell leads us into the gardens on St Andrew Square. She stands in front of the Henry Dundas statue, looming a hundred and fifty feet in the air. The Tall Man. The One Above All. The Black Lord. He never lacked titles or offices: First Lord of the Admiralty, Member of Parliament, Lord Advocate, President of the Board of Control for Indian Affairs, British Secretary of State for War. The thing about titles is they mask a lot. They sound so impressive that you miss the dirty work they signify, much like the uniforms of armies dignify the business of murder. I guess it makes things a bit more palatable for those of us who have to swallow this shit.

Frances Cockburn's mother stands at the foot of the great

statue. She cuts a tiny figure in its shadow as she looks up at it and then down towards the building where her daughter used to work. We stand in a crescent shape, arced around Theodosia. The paths on the Square are still well maintained and the grass is somewhat overgrown, but not overly so. Swedish whitebeam, sycamore, weeping ash and Japanese cherry lining the wrought-iron fence that rings the square. Further back are the buildings, mostly old, but a few modern glass and steel structures on the side nearest Princes Street. And on the roof of the building to the right of Dundas House are six statues looking down at us like half the old Greek gods have come down to watch.

These are, after all, the gifts of the Scottish Enlightenment. The building nearer West Register Street was built when some plantation owner was given 'compensation' for loss of his human property. And in front of Dundas House is the statue of the Fourth Earl of Hopetoun, John Hope. He's the guy who helped put down a two-year slave rebellion in Grenada. Enlightened folk. *Fine men,* the lot of them.

'I'll give them a wee knock fer oor troubles,' Theodosia Lovell says, walking over to the base of the plinth. Grief is written all over her. The clothes she wears seem overly large on her tiny frame and her gait is uneven on the wet and slippery grass. Very gently she puts her hand upon the stone blocks as though reaching for someone far away. I can't make out what she whispers in Scottish Cant, but I fear Theodosia's confused the statue of the great man for the Bank in her grief.

'That's not the right door,' I want to say, but Priya touches my hand before the words can leave my mouth and I keep schtum.

Theodosia Lovell turns and shuffles back to her coven. I sense the anger in her roiling as the rustling of leaves in a dense wood. Her grief has turned into something terrifying to behold. Dark rings round red eyes.

She's one step away from us when a silent fracture appears on the base stonework she laid her hand on. It glows like the rays of the moon shining through a broken cloud. Soon there are five splits in the stone, one for each of her fingers spreading out. The rock may be breaking, but it remains silent as the base begins to rupture. They aren't like the usual sort of cracks one might see in stone. It's almost as though its very fabric was unravelling like a piece of cloth unstitched, continuing right down to the foundations of the statue, halting as it meets the soil.

But the statue stands proud and tall over the city, unmoved by what has happened below.

Theodosia Lovell turns and says, 'Nash avree fae here.'

In that instant a gentle breeze blows from the west, swirling the falling snowflakes, picking up her steaming breath in which those words were said. It's a solitary white cloud that drifts to the base of the plinth and then . . . *poof.* The long plinth rocks a fraction and wobbles back in place like a drunk man trying to regain his balance. I step back when it teeters over our way, but it recovers and centres itself again. The Tall Man will not fall so easily tonight. More than an object of stone, it's infused with the adoration of every single person who donated the subscriptions for it to be raised, magnificent in a grateful city.

There's a terrible silence.

I swallow hard.

Then, at last, the tall statue leans back, plinth and all, and starts falling through the snow. To my eyes it looks so slow, almost as though it might right itself any moment, but the statue continues in its arc. Delicate. A giant who's fallen asleep on parade. It continues, parting the snow as it does, leaving only a dark void in its wake, suddenly speeding up when it goes past forty-five degrees, accelerating, faster and faster, until the plinth smashes into the statue of the Earl of Hopetoun and then, with an earth-shattering bang, Dundas's statue slams into the western facade of the Royal Bank, right at the apex of the triangular roof. Thunder as it destroys the wall on that side of the building, throwing rocks and wood and glass high up into the air.

What a mighty knock Theodosia's given.

The debris flies out, smashing into the buildings on either side. The dust merging with the snow as it rises high into the sky. It takes a wee while to clear, and even then what we see shocks me. A ditch has been cut through grass and tar, a trail of damage from the base of the plinth all the way to the building. The fences between the square and Dundas House have been torn down and the entire front of the building's been ripped off. The gaps that remain on the roof are like broken teeth in a punched mouth.

Despite the damage to its western wall, 36 St Andrew Square still stands. Say what you will but they built things to last back in the day. I can't imagine the new steel and glass structures surviving that.

In the opening, figures protected in the bubble of a

325

Newtonian shield stand observing us. From this distance, they look like figurines in a doll's house. I spot Montgomery Wedderburn wielding a protective spell, joined by Lady Rethabile Lebusa on the other side of the room, the two of them holding the spell together. Henry Dundas is sat at the head of a long table where he must have been in the middle of a meeting or something. The most important magicians from Edinburgh and St Andrews are in one place, and I might not see my sister, but I know she's in there somewhere. They need her to channel the king's mother. Dundas doesn't seem too concerned by us or the destroyed western wall. He maintains his place while his underlings check us out from a distance.

I tap my stick on the ground thrice and finally the great ghoul turns to us. He bends down and scoops up the large cat that was lying at his feet before getting up from his seat. Wedderburn says something to him which we don't catch from way out here.

Theodosia Lovell's already on the move towards the building now we have their attention. I follow close, but the distance to Dundas House feels even further than the long walk we took from the cemetery to here. Each step I take is heavy and, maybe it's the effect of the everyThere or some trick in my mind, but we move as though through treacle. We go over the tram lines and across the street, onto the grounds of the old house. I stand with my right foot atop the Earl of Hopetoun's head.

Magicians who were in other parts of the building pour out through the ground floor. These are the underlings who weren't in the boardroom. Some of them seem confused that we are here at all.

Henry Dundas walks over the broken edge of the first floor, but he doesn't fall. Instead he descends as though coming down a set of invisible stairs. From this close up it's disconcerting to see how full he looks now: the picture of a middle-aged man in good health. There's a freshness to his flesh that wasn't there at Melville Castle. It's life flowing through him right enough, but I wonder whose essence has been stolen to animate him like this. His lieutenants Wedderburn and Hutchinson follow close behind. The heat exhaust of their protective spell makes the snow melt. We are outnumbered.

'Where's my sister?' I demand.

'Ropa Moyo, if I'd known you'd be this much of a nuisance I would have dealt with you a long time ago,' Wedderburn says. 'It's for the love of your father that I've spared you, but now even he would question the wisdom of that.' His words are always coated in honey. He has that posh way of sounding reasonable even when he's doing evil.

'Sir Ian Callander counted you as his friend and look where that got him. Don't waste my time, I want Izwi back,' I say, bristling. I don't have time for that posh bullshit, not now, not evermore.

'And what exactly do you hope to achieve with this rabble?' Wedderburn laughs. 'These pathetic women are who you're counting on? Your own grandmother didn't stand a chance and she once worked for the Bank. These cleaners and carers and Gypsies aren't going to help you.'

'I've decided I'm going to kill that one and eat his liver,' Milligan says, pointing at Wedderburn.

'I beg your pardon?' he stutters.

She licks her lips like some kind of carnivore. There's a disturbing sharpness to her teeth which escaped me before. Given her bravado now, I realize she's Theodosia's plant. Her protests at the cemetery were meant to encourage anyone who was afeart to speak out. You'd rather not go into the field with any such person, but the problem is that too often they are the last to state their reservations. Seeing her committed now really cements us together.

Henry Dundas bends to gently place his cat onto the ground. It seems tyrants have a fondness for certain animals. He strokes the cat's head and then stands up straight again. You can still tell he's not quite alive from this close up. His eyes are black sockets empty of warmth, without a trace of humanity.

The wickedness oozes out of that one.

Nothing we've not seen before.

It's not an ancestor like we are.

The ladies inside my head quibble but my attention's squarely on what's in front of me.

'What do you foolish women want?' Dundas asks.

'My world's whammel since yer put mine bairn tae the flame, but the good book commands an eye fer an eye and yer soul will suffice as recompense,' Theodosia Lovell says. Her voice is cold and void of emotion and it comes as a matter of fact. Even Dundas pricks up 'cause a leader recognizes command in another, more so in an adversary.

'You should have heard her scream,' he replies, a smile

forming. 'It was music to my ears. Scotland was born on sacrifice but it's gone soft. I bring back the old ways and we can be that great nation again. Had I more time, I would have explained this to you. Not that you would understand. But the king is coming and we have a gift to give him. I have no more time for these trivial games.' He looks up at the dead in the sky then commands his minions: 'Kill them all.'

The giant cat hisses and pounces, going straight for River. I swing my stick at it, but miss with a whoosh. It's too fast for me. River's already leapt back and bolted, which I guess is the better part of valour. I turn back and a purple fireball with a heron signature flies towards us in the flash of an eye, and before it reaches us a volley of solitons and thermospheres is lobbed our way. Priya's already incanting a heat sink to cover us from the flames while I prick a soliton with my stick causing it to burst out.

Dundas has turned away, taking a step to return to his headquarters.

'Dinnae turn your back on me,' Theodosia Lovell says, raising her hands. There's a tremor and moonlight pours from her hands, curly beams of it like plant vines reaching forward. I've been around a lot of magic but hers feels ancient and has an earthy texture to it combined with the scent that hits before a storm.

A golden strobe of light from Montgomery Wedderburn intercepts, but Lovell's magic slices through it as though it were butter. There are loud cracks as Zeusean lightning bolts are hurled at us and the smell of ozone becomes thick in the air.

'Chlanna nan con thigibh a' so 's gheibh sibh feòil!' Milligan shouts, leaping forward, bonnet flying one way, red hair flying everywhere as she bursts through a thermosphere and carries on as though the flames could do her no harm.

'Ginger don't burn,' Priya shouts, driving her chair forward, and I'm surprised to see a host of small bushes and hedges jumping into the fray. Topiary animals from the Edinburgh School grounds leap at the magicians, scratching at them with their thorns and beating them with their branches.

Hurrah. I imagine Mrs Guthrie incanting from Princes Street, doing her work at a distance.

I rush in too, realizing that while magicians are wont to lob spells at one another from a respectable distance, ten paces and all, the witches don't play by those rules. There's the report of a shot and Hutchinson clutches his chest, bleeding through his tailored suit, disbelief written all over his face. He gasps out a sharp Boreas anemoic spell, invoking the god of winter and ice, and an icicle whips through the air like a dart, shooting towards Artchival. The traveller reacts too slow, but a sliver of moonlight from Theodosia Lovell's vines darts away from Henry Dundas and captures the icicle inches away from his heart.

Artchival fires a second shot true and the principal of the St Andrews School's noggin explodes. There's an audible gasp on the side of the magicians as if this was cheating. Hutchinson was a wanker and got what was coming to him.

'Shoot the ghoul,' I yell.

Artchival empties the four remaining chambers of his gun into the Viscount Melville's back. That should do nicely. If he wants to be alive again then he can taste lead for his tea tonight.

But the bullets don't seem to hurt him, except for the holes they've made in the back of his jacket. I speed up, reach the magicians and swing at Lady Rethabile with my stick thumping her on the shoulder.

She shrieks and casts a soliton that knocks me back harder than a horse's kick in the chebs. I lie stunned for a fraction of a second. The noise is awful. Smoke thickens in the air and an acrid chemical scent is infused through the atmosphere. Waves of heat waft incredible entropic shifts all around me. Magic is doing work. I roll when a pink thermosphere comes my way and it explodes on the ground next to me. The shadows of the magicians and witches dance on the walls of the buildings on either side of us like puppets moving to someone else's tune.

I get up, and though I want to go for Dundas, Lady Rethabile's waiting for me.

She incants a Zeusean lightning bolt and it flies the short distance to me, but I sense its essence ripped from the charge in the air. *Mheni ndiyo yedu manje*, the voice in my head says, and I hear an ancestor weave a spell as the bolt explodes mid-flight, sparks flying off in every direction. Lady Rethabile raises her eyebrows, surprised.

'That's not a standard spe—'

I whack her on the mug before she's done speaking and a couple of teeth fly out. She covers her mouth and Cruickshank unfurls and punches her clean on the temple so she drops like a sack of tatties. Ninja scarf, yay. I'm about to finish the job when a blue soliton strikes me in the stomach and throws me backwards again.

The magicians are more numerous than we are. You hit one, another hits you. It's a melee but the numbers are on their side and we are being driven back. Priya's wheel rides over my shoe as she is forced back by two magicians lobbing spells at her. Theodosia attempts once again to strike her vines at Henry Dundas, but she's hit with a thunderbolt that burns her dress. It reminds me of Sir Ian Callander's arm burnt by Dundas, but the discharge doesn't seem to harm her.

'Cast and replace, magicians. We must work together – pairs in a line, the Edinburgh School way,' Wedderburn rallies, pointing furiously to show the magicians where to stand in formation.

They fall in like well-drilled redcoats, and I'm like, oh shit, do they teach this in magic school? The magicians in front lob their spells and the ones behind form a heat sink or shield, making good use of their numerical advantage. We, on the other hand, are only ready to fight woman to man or woman or whoever. The magicians gradually build a wall of magic that will singe any who try to break through.

The thermospheres become even hotter and the solitons more explosive. Since magic results from will, combining efforts magnifies the powers one might otherwise achieve on their own. The wall of heat is intense and I'm sure my eyebrows are burnt off. Henry Dundas is swallowed behind those who step forward to fight in his name.

'Fall back,' Milligan shouts.

Artchival's busy reloading his revolver when he's struck by a golden thermosphere and his clothes burst into flames. Priya mutters a Poseidon spell and a wall of water splashes him, saving him from the worst.

'Get to the back,' she yells.

I'm not paying attention because Rethabile's back up again with a lump on her noggin and looking really annoyed. There's a cry and Artchival falls to the ground. He's been hit again. This time he stays still and silent. Amidst the cracks of thunder we can all hear his last breath wheezing out.

A hiss and yelp from somewhere behind me, vulpine and feline. It's all kicking off now.

'There's too many of them,' Priya says, driven back by the blue and red flames. The smoke is so thick we're choking on it.

Inch by inch, step by step, Wedderburn and his magicians drive us back across the street and into St Andrew Square. I'm relieved when I see Ranjeeta and her gang come up to flank us from Queen Street, but the other side of the pincer, Mrs Guthrie's, doesn't emerge. Instead, there's a battle on Princes Street and I realize they've been discovered. But we're already under pressure and we can't support them, nor can they make it up to our side.

No plan survives contact with reality, that much is true, but it still sucks. With the ease of a general, Wedderburn splits his magicians, Lebusa directed towards Ranjeeta, while his cohort comes for us. There's more space out here and instead of fighting them in the confined grounds of Dundas House, now the magicians are able to spread out and thin our ranks in the process.

A burning bush runs out in front of us. One of Mrs Guthrie's topiary companions has caught light and instead of dipping into the new loch it's running in the wrong direction. It leaps into the window of an old department store near the bus station.

The voykor swoop from above, but they can't yet break into our world.

'Did you honestly think you could beat four hundred years of scientific magic with your parlour tricks? We control life and death now,' Wedderburn taunts, arrogant. I wish it was his brains that Artchival had blown. Instead I see Milligan struck by a jet spray that opens up the artery on her neck, spilling blood upon the snow. It happens so quickly and she falls down, clutching at her throat. She needs a healer, but Priya's too busy creating a heat sink to protect us from the endless thermospheres coming our way.

It's a magic I have no access to, yet I feel its clumsiness, the way it hammers fundamental forces instead of plucking at them and creates so much waste in the process. The heat and smoke belching. Even at the hands of a skilled practitioner like Wedderburn, the magic is wasteful because it doesn't incite the vibrating strings. The words of the incantations invoking another people's gods. It is magic born of imitation and rote rather than improvisation.

The exhaust fumes from all this spellery form a thick black smog that stings my eyes.

'For Frances!' one of the witches on Ranjeeta's side shouts out as they are driven backwards by Rethabile Lebusa and her magicians. More of them seem to pour out of Dundas House just as they take a quarter of St Andrew Square, and I'm losing heart when I spot hesitation on Wedderburn's face. I hear the roar of a motorbike and turn briefly in time to see Dalziel MacDonald and Calista Featherstone at the head of a small group of magicians.

The Doric School is here at last.

'I see you've come to your senses and decided to join our victory,' Wedderburn calls out across the fray.

'You attacked my school and took my student, Montgomery,' Featherstone shouts back. 'The Highlands is still a place of honour and you will pay the price tonight.'

'You still don't get it, do you?' says Wedderburn, sweeping his arm as though to show off the city. 'There's nothing you or anyone can do to stop the progress we've made. Though we may seem excessive, I hope you understand you can't make an omelette without breaking a few eggs.'

That's what we are to them. Disposable. I don't want none of their omelette and I would shove a thermosphere up him if I could. Benjamin the donkey comes bolting up the road, empty cart behind him. He barrels through the crowds, knocking a magician or two down on his way towards the north. Can't be going well for Mrs Guthrie if her trusted companion's on his own.

River's now over the fence, chasing after the massive cat. It seems the tables have turned in their scuffle. Bedlam out here. At least we have the Doric School with us now. Ms Featherstone appears in our ranks as she moves fast with her mastery of the Hermes spell.

'We'll repay your trust in us,' she says to Theodosia Lovell.

The old woman's vines reach out from her outstretched arms. They've grown thorns gathered from the snow around them as they fly over the magicians, reaching only for Henry Dundas. The magicians have a go at chopping them down with their countermeasures, but she doesn't let up. She incants something in her native tongue and the vines break out in moonlight flames, slamming down upon the first and second row of magicians. The vines crack like a whip when they touch flesh and the impact fells four on Wedderburn's side.

This helps, but Lovell is desperate to get to the Viscount who, standing by Hutchinson's body, is watching patiently as his lieutenants press us with every harmful spell they can muster. In battle, you can't afford to be hasty, lest you over-commit to the wrong course of action. If we get the ghoul then the cult has lost its master and with that its purpose.

I duck a grey thermosphere that was almost invisible in the smoke-filled atmosphere. It crashes into the sycamore tree behind me, setting trunk and leaf alight.

My boots squelch as I move. With the Doric magicians in the fray, the temperature rises high enough to melt the snow. Monstrous entropic shifts form all around me. The whispered words of incantations and formulae, scientific magic doing its thing. Priya's forced to retreat by a soliton, riding the strong gust of air backwards, three-sixtying in her wheelchair and launching it back to our enemies.

'We need to get to Dundas,' I shout.

'Through this horde?' she replies, ducking a thermosphere.

'It's the only way,' I reply.

'We need everyone here,' Sister Elspeth shouts. Her habit's flying all over the place, buffeted by the entropic shifts. Holy mother of God, her and Sister Edina are working up incredible magic, tinging their incantations with the names of Catholic saints. No time to admire their handiwork. I have to get to the ghoul, so I retreat back through the witches, remove my backpack and take out my mbira. Dump the bag on the ground. I won't be needing my gear for now. The main thing's to keep my head on my shoulders.

I feel the vibrations thrumming through my mbira.

Dalziel MacDonald brushes past me and launches a volley of water that's turned grey and hard, not exactly ice, but something resembling steel. He's in his Highland dress, kilt and all, and he shouts out his clan's rallying cry as he goes. There's a few more like him who've come down from the Highlands and Islands, and I'm surprised to see a good few MacLeods among them.

I retreat through our last line to the west end of the park nearer George Street where the bulk of the Doric magicians are. A stray soliton smashes into a window on the building opposite. There's so many people yelling and screaming at once. Burns and slashings can do that to you. Our side's barely holding on. It's not gone according to plan. We've failed to get our pincer in and Wedderburn's spreading out his magicians. I spot the danger. Soon it will be Theodosia's crew that's surrounded in St Andrew Square. Ranjeeta's team are fighting hard against opponents who have the high ground and they're being driven back towards Queen Street.

If our side breaks, we're going to be easy pickings for this bunch of cults.

I need to get around the fray and attack Dundas from the back. It's our only chance, I think, exiting the square. There's still fighting on Princes Street and fireballs explode off the Scott Monument that stands out on the waters of the loch. My plan's to take the lane that will lead me to West Register Street.

From there I can loop back round through the side of Dundas House.

I'm about to head left, ducking stray spells, when I notice Professor Fergus Cattermole, head of the Lord Kelvin Institute, and Mr Laidlaw coming up George Street with a massive column of Glaswegian magicians. Shit. There's too many. And they've brought Dr Maige with them. He walks with his head bowed and it seems they've broken his spirit at last.

'Watch your backs, Calista,' I call out, making some of the Doric magicians turn back. It's us who've been caught in a trap. We need to bail. There's still a chance. Two exits on North and South St David Street. We can use . . . Fuck, more magicians come out of Thistle Street and Rose Street which run parallel to George Street, blocking off our option to escape.

Against two schools we had a sliver of a chance, but not against three.

I guess they didn't make Dundas secretary for war for nothing. Cattermole's been brought on board at last. I scan the square, desperate for a way out, as a woman screams out in pain. There must be something I can do. There's a crack of lightning from the sky that splits a tree on the square.

'You are surrounded, witches,' Cattermole says, as he stands by James Clerk Maxwell's statue at the intersection of George Street and the Square. There's a smugness to his tone. I have the same disgust I felt in my gut as when he turned on Esfandiar. This man with his tweed elbow-patch jacket is screwing us. An explosion of gold and moonlight as Wedderburn tests his lightning against Theodosia Lovell's vines.

The mbira thrums from underneath my fingers.

The voykor circle, hungry for prey as they see into our world.

I take my instrument and stand by the narrow gate in front of Cattermole.

'You have a knack for being on the losing side,' he says.

'Seems that way, doesn't it?' I reply.

'Your riff-raff, even with Calista's thick-headed aid, can't ever hope to stand up to the magicians of Scotland's finest schools, Ropa. You were given every opportunity to join the Society. Think of it, you could have been something. That chance is gone. The same way these witches you're consorting with are a relic of the past. They were swept away hundreds of years ago.'

'They were not destroyed,' I reply.

'A good gardener knows you need to mow the lawn from time to time,' he says, lecturing as if I was one of his students. 'I won't ask you to surrender, though. Witches don't get given second chances.'

There's a sonic boom that nearly pops my eardrums, as Professor Cattermole in that instant hurls brilliant, sparkling, violet lightning my way. It's intricately sigilled in an elaborate K. I sense the seismic entropic shift as the web nears me. Without thinking, I play a note on my mbira, the harmonics interweaving with the vibrations of his spell, stopping it in front of my face. Mr Laidlaw fires off an emerald thermosphere, which also halts midair.

One note.

I feel the power in my fingers and decide to pluck the strings of this universe. I smile, ready to retaliate, when behind me comes the sound of hooves cantering on the tarmac. Men in British Army ceremonial uniforms and followed by a fair few wearing camouflage and carrying automatic weapons pour in from Princes Street. I check and see the fighting on Mrs Guthrie's side of the line has ceased.

The leading soldier, on a pale white horse, shouts coarsely, 'God save the king!'

XXVI

'On your knees you Scotch maggots.'

Crivvens, everyone's looking around all confused, but the lightning and thunder's stopped on St Andrew Square. This part of town had originally been envisaged with the streets in the shape of the Union Jack, and now the crown is here at last.

The king's army keeps its weapons trained on us and I recall Hutchinson's skull exploding. One by one we take the knee on tar and grass. Even the ghoul who would be a god complies and goes down on one knee. The king doesn't muck about, I think, seeing more English people pouring through. But these aren't soldiers. They are men and women in top hats and tails, a couple wearing capes of the kind Lord Samarasinghe likes. Some carry canes and a fair few hold out wands, the accoutrements favoured by the schools down south.

English magic sweeps through like a locust plague and we are humiliated on our knees. Our clothes are torn and bloody from fighting amongst ourselves. This is what Sir Ian Callander always feared, the very thing he so desperately sought to prevent from happening. The English interfering in the affairs of Scottish magic. They have the numbers and wealth, and on this snowy night I've come to learn just how small and insignificant we are in the face of this. We've always been the junior partner in the union. Given how divided we are, what chance would we stand against London?

No, I mustn't think like that. I'm no part of Scottish magic. I left the Society ages ago.

A classic Daimler from the 1940s drives up the road, flanked by military vehicles. It makes its way over the tram lines and parks in front of 36 St Andrew Square. Two soldiers open the doors and Lord Sashvindu Samarasinghe steps out from our end while the king emerges in combat fatigues on the other side.

His Majesty is here in Edinburgh.

He calmly surveys the carnage through the remnants of smoke, injured magicians and witches writhing on the ground. There's a dispassionate air to him as though he was strolling through his gardens at Windsor. I heard the story of how as a young man he'd served in the Middle East and had shrapnel in his body from an improvised explosive device. In his fatigues, you can't really tell he's the commander-in-chief. He looks like one of the troops, maybe an ageing sergeant, but nothing grand. Not how you'd imagine kings from the history books to look. There's tufts of prematurely greying hair poking out from under his soft cap. Two English magicians immediately stand either side of him. You can sense their power, even from afar, something like the roar of a steam engine, pistons, the might of the industrial revolution.

What confidence is this that makes them bring their monarch into the middle of a conflict? It seems like it's true then, that when the country was falling apart in the days of the

Catastrophe, the king had rallied his officers and gone onto the streets personally to deal with the renegades that threatened the state. All this while his elder brother had fled to New Zealand. Beside him were England's most promising young magicians, and one of them rose to become the Sorcerer Royal.

The king looks up and he too sees the dead wandering the skies above. Does he know how close we are to the everyThere consuming this city? If he does, then he'd not be looking at it with equanimity. He'd be bricking it like the rest of us.

'This pathetic display. Is this how Scottish magic welcomes her sovereign?' Lord Samarasinghe asks, furious, sweeping his cane to point out the carnage.

'God save our gracious king,' the soldier on the white horse shouts out again.

'Long live our noble king, long live our noble king, long live our noble king,' we call out in response under the watchful eye of the English magicians. You'd be mad to do otherwise.

'Who is responsible for this outrage?' Lord Samarasinghe enquires theatrically. It's as if he knows nothing about the politics of Scottish magic and has suddenly arrived to discover everything in chaos. I'm confused but not surprised by his behaviour. They switch on you so very quickly these powerful men, bending reality and facts as they go along.

'My Lord Sorcerer, we were attacked by these cowardly witches,' Montgomery Wedderburn answers, rising up, but keeping his head bowed.

'Are you the Secretary of the Society of Sceptical Enquirers, sir?' Samarasinghe asks, as though he does not already know the facts on the ground.

'I, I—'

'I am the Secretary,' Viscount Melville says, rising to his full height. 'And this city, despite appearances, welcomes Your Highness as it did your ancestor King George IV, whose statue stands yonder in the distance. I served George III and I am ready to serve you.'

The ghoul bows and I notice some disgust among the English magicians. I wonder if Lord Samarasinghe included them in his secret schemes. But the crafty Sorcerer Royal's done enough to distance himself from events. If the king is angry at the reception, he doesn't at all show it, taking his time to survey the damage to the Society headquarters and the buildings in the square.

'Your Majesty, Scotland has long had a problem with witchcraft, and immoral women who are dangerous to the crown, such as the witches who attempted to sink King James VI as he sailed from Scandinavia having married Anne of Denmark,' Dundas says.

'As you can see, such women have risen up again and threaten your rule,' Wedderburn adds, weaving his web of lies to buttress his master.

The same James VI of the *Daemonologie* book witnessed some wild shit out in Denmark where he'd gone to pick up his bride – as monarchs did in those days. Sow your wild oats in Scotland but choose your bride from some place more civilized. This was all round the time some German monk had written a book called *The Hammer of Witches* which spread like wildfire in Europe 'cause it was a manual for dealing with the 'servants of Satan'. James VI picked up some really nasty shit from there and lo, when his ship hit bad weather, it could only have been witches that done it. Of course, he arranged trials in North Berwick as soon as he landed to test out these new, *civilized* methods from Europe – torture, pulling nails out, pricking, the strappado, all that kind of thing – until a couple of old ladies confessed and were promptly garrotted for their evil deeds. The old monarch was convinced Auld Nick was out to get him so he set up a formal commission to seek them out, and that's how we got the Witchfinder General who later became Secretary of the Society of Sceptical Enquirers.

History's never dead in Edinburgh, it oozes out through the pores, through every cracked pavement and broken mirror. No question's ever truly settled. This city's the world's longest running soap opera and they don't even bother with the credits anymore.

'I'm aff the fang listening tae these conyeeched cocks haver in their sleekit tongues,' Theodosia Lovell says.

She's the only person who's not knelt, but being so short I'd not noticed she was on her feet before the king. The sovereign turns his gaze to her, but she doesn't wilt under it as anyone else might. How could she? She's a queen in her own right, moving through the land free without paying tolls and taxes. Theodosia Lovell gives me the courage to stand up too.

'On your knees, old woman,' the soldier on the white horse commands.

'My arthritis disnae allow, lad.'

'Your Highness, I pray you remember me,' Ranjeeta says, standing up and curtseying. 'I'm Shashi Kapoor's wife, the economist whom you commanded down to London to restore the shilling once the pound had collapsed, work for which you honoured him with an OBE. Shashi remains your loyal servant even though he's returned to Glasgow to teach. We fight tonight because these men murdered Theodosia Lovell's daughter Frances Cockburn in cold blood and we demand *your* justice.'

It's a smart move on her part. The king's reputation's built on him being a stickler for his law, a modern William the Conqueror. Not long ago I witnessed Lord Samarasinghe savagely slaughter some bandits on the road to Gorebridge 'cause they'd breached the king's peace.

There's a slight smirk on the Sorcerer Royal's lips, cunning in his eyes. That man is always calculating things to his advantage.

'The king has always allowed you Scotch to manage your affairs. He's left your courts intact and you may seek justice there. Isn't that right, Lord Advocate?' he asks Dundas and the ghoul nods. 'Why would you disturb him about matters that are beneath him?'

'They burnt a woman at the stake and that's beneath our king?' Ranjeeta asks angrily.

'You have your police and your judges for that. But it appears to me you've taken matters into your own hands and in so doing you have breached the king's peace.'

If the king has an opinion, he keeps it to himself. A thin wisp of white air comes out when he breathes; otherwise he is impassive, above it all. We appeal to him and he remains quiet. Dare I say he looks rather bored. It's as though he's enduring our squabble until he can get back to his business.

One gesture, a nod, a thumb drawn across the neck, and he could have all of us executed.

'I appeal to your mercy, Your Highness. My name is Calista Featherstone, head of the Aberdeen School of Magic and Esoterica, and I can vouch for these women, your servants. These men have kidnapped a little girl from my school and I humbly beseech you to have her returned safely to us,' Ms Featherstone says, standing up too.

There's the inkling of a frown, a slight twitch of the king's eyebrows.

'Can this all be true?' Lord Samarasinghe asks, reading that very small gesture. 'Are the magicians of Scotland truly breaking the king's law? Say it's not so, sirs.'

'It is a lie. You can't believe anything that comes from their mouths,' Montgomery Wedderburn says, adding with contempt, 'They are travellers, slum dwellers, thieves, the lowest of the low. It pains me that my esteemed colleague Calista Featherstone has taken to associating with such filth.'

And just like that, the king looks bored again. We almost had his attention. But bickering won't be enough. He said, she said, all that jazz doesn't appeal to a man who probably has to deal with a lot of that at his own court. We have to give him something solid. There's a wretched screech from the rooftop of the building next to Dundas House and a large object falls to the ground, startling the guards and some of the English magicians who point their guns and wands at it. But it's only the body of the secretary's cat that's fallen three floors down and dead, a few feet from the king.

River walks up to the edge of the roof, snout bloody, and looks down at her vanquished quarry. She barks, startling the English below. Her magnificent coat has been violently scratched but she's emerged victorious.

'Fucking A. That's my girl,' I cheer.

'A fox and a cat atop the roof. Isn't this city strange?' the king muses, his voice cut-glass clear in the winter air. But he's not addressing anyone, it's just a thought said out loud.

That's it, that's my in. He must be entertained and made to feel there's something real at stake. The king doesn't care for Frances Cockburn or Izwi Moyo, but he has his own interests that occupy his mind. Here goes.

'I challenge Henry Dundas, Lord Melville, to a duel for the position of Secretary of the Society of Sceptical Enquirers,' I say, loud enough for the king's ears.

Our sovereign turns to me and almost seems baffled.

'That's preposterous, the girl's not even a real magician. All of these women should be locked away until we can dispose of them,' blusters Montgomery Wedderburn.

The king raises his index finger, silencing Wedderburn without bothering to turn in his direction. That one finger carries so much authority that it silences everyone as they wait for the king to decide. Everything on these islands starts and ends with him. His power is absolute and I've only ever known it from afar, but witnessing it here in front of these wealthy, posh wankers, I realize they are fleas compared to him. The king turns from me, his eyes falling upon 'King Harry', a look which forces Dundas to bend his head.

Without saying a word the king's compelled the dead man

to his will. That's the thing about this world. For all the rules and customs, norms and laws that they hide behind, if you push through the glass ceiling, you'll soon come to see that it's all smoke and mirrors. The powerful make up the rules as they go along and then present them to the rest of us as if they were stone tablets from a mountain.

'Choose your seconds, the duel will begin soon,' Lord Samarasinghe announces with an exasperated sigh. 'The rest of you, clear the square.'

He's in sync with the king, like an obedient rottweiler. I am now certain the Sorcerer Royal holds no true opinions of his own, rather everything about him is an attempt to translate his monarch's will into action. It's a radical devotion, a deep kind of love, and you can see it in the way he steals reverent glances at the king, evidently grateful to bask in his presence.

'You've done it now, lassie. God help you against the likes of that,' one of the witches says to me.

'A desperate move, Ropa Moyo, but I admire your tenacity,' Professor Cattermole says begrudgingly. 'Perhaps you'd be so kind as to tell me before you die how you managed to hold a Zeusean thunderbolt in situ. It would make for excellent literature once you're gone.'

They're giving you all the credit?

No country for ancestors, this!

A bit of libation poured on our graves would be nice.

And some drumming too, girl.

I ignore them and turn to find Priya by my side. She's looking mighty worried. I decide to help her by pointing out that she'll be my second and her eyes widen.

'Ropa, I'll second you for anything and everything,' Priya says.

'Stay out of this, Priyanka. You young ladies have done enough, but this goes beyond your abilities. If Ian Callander couldn't withstand Dundas's might then you are no match for him either,' Ranjeeta says, stepping forward.

'I'll be the one tae end his reign o' wickedness an' avenge my bairn,' says Theodosia, joining us.

'That's the job for a qualified magician, and since, technically, none of you can even be Secretary, I think this mission should fall to me,' Calista Featherstone says. She's firm and determined.

'I've been dead twice already,' I reply to them all. 'Can anyone else here say that?'

'Ropa!'

'I made the challenge and have the king's permission,' I say. 'Priya, go and parley with Melville's second. Tell them to dispense with the ritual malarkey around reconciling and let them know that if they don't have my sister ready I won't stop at Dundas when I'm done.'

That's what von Clausewitz meant when he said, 'The best strategy is always to be very strong; first in general, and then at the decisive point.' We've reached that moment and my mind's made up. Magic is nothing but a battle of wills. Doesn't the Somerville equation pin this down perfectly? There are many elements in it corresponding to time, agitative threshold, but it's clear to me now that it's the question of will that charges the entire equation. You can't have magic happen without someone willing the impossible to become manifest. I've been dragged out of my grave twice now and there was a reason for that. This body I'm wearing as my own was taken from some poor soul and given to me. It would be all in vain if I didn't honour her by standing up.

For the first time in a long while, I feel at peace. I'm no longer running. I ain't that scared little rat in a maze, hurtling from disappointment to disaster. My mind's clear. This must be what it was like for the warriors before Culloden. When you're in the eye of the storm, embrace the turmoil that's to come.

Priya returns from the parley but now with Lord Samarasinghe in tow. He's rather on edge and trying badly to hide it, eyes darting around, so much so I can't be sure what outcome he wishes from all of this.

'You do know how to stir up the pot, Ropa Moyo. I should have sent you away to England when I had the chance,' the Sorcerer Royal says. 'Still, the king likes a bit of sport and you've put on quite the show for him. If there's a trait he admires, it's courage.'

'I'm not doing it for him. Your life might revolve around serving his every whim, but mine doesn't.'

'I guess that's me told then,' Lord S replies. He smiles awkwardly. 'For what it's worth, I'll be rooting for you.'

'Sod off.'

The Sorcerer Royal laughs and withdraws to the eastern side of St Andrew Square where the king is patiently watching and waiting. It's not his neck on the chopping block. This is just a play to these aristocrats. The king stands tall with his hands behind his back and Lord S has moved to the spot next to him. The Sorcerer Royal cups his hand and whispers something in the king's ear and the monarch nods. I recall how from the moment he arrived at Dunvegan Castle in his flying horse and carriage, Lord Samarasinghe sought to sow division and discontent amongst the ranks of the Scottish magicians. I can't help but feel that I've been dragged into another such machination. Whatever happens tonight, the result won't be the Scottish magic my old gaffer Callander battled so hard to keep alive.

'Gentleman and lady, please step forward,' an Englishwoman says. She is one of the magicians judging by her top hat and tails. She stands on the grass close to the ruined base of the pillar that Theodosia Lovell demolished. I check out the magicians and witches and soldiers as I go to take my spot on the grass opposite.

Priya's right beside me as I walk by Dr Maige. Nothing beats that good friend who'll come with you to the very edge of the world. Still, I have to say something to Jomo's dad, so I look back over my shoulder.

'Where's that rulebook you were so fond of now?' I ask.

He looks down at his feet, ashamed, and I wonder if he's recalling the first time I visited the Library of the Dead and he tried to have me hung by the neck until I expired. He was a stickler for the rules and believed that everything should follow patterns established by precedent. In a perfect world that might have been the case, but now it's a dog-eat-dog world and a code's as likely to get you slain as anything.

'Focus,' Priya says. 'I sure hope you know what you're doing, Ropa.'

'This one's for Callander, and Gran, and Sneddon, and everyone this cult has ever laid hands on,' I reply.

Henry Dundas approaches, hovering past the rubble of the statue that until recently bore his likeness, reminding everyone of his achievements in the service of the Empire. His dead eyes seem to see right through me. I refuse to be intimidated by the dead.

Wedderburn is beside the ghoul, looking at Dundas with devotion.

'Our paths keep crossing time and time again. You and I are like Bedouins in the desert, beings of strong will, but I've grown weary of your impudence. I offer you one final token of my generosity,' Dundas says.

My father's ghost appears beside him. Where Dundas has taken on a body of flesh and has become solid, Makomborero Moyo's an ephemeral wisp; unlike the healthier ghosts from the everyThere, his journey back from the Other Place has cost him dearly. My father makes his way towards me.

'There's no shame if you end this now. The matters you've been dragged into are none of your concern. These women must be proud of what they've accomplished with you. Don't you see that they are using you against your own father?' he says. His voice is raspy and faint. 'You've more than proven your worth, but it's time for you to join my cause like a good daughter should. I love you, Ropa, and I want us to be together as a family. Isn't this what you've always wanted?'

I shake my head. Though this path may have been laid for me, I choose to walk it of my own free will.

'In my day such wilful women were beaten into submission. We'll return the world as it was, a place where everyone knows their place,' Dundas says from across the road. 'The night falls so quickly in winter. I want you to know that your soul will not be coming back to life again after I'm done with you.'

Their words make me more certain they are on the wrong side of history. I don't want my father back – he's hurt a lot of people pursuing his ambitions. I'm happy with my little sister alone. The two of us against the whole wide world.

We take our place on St Andrew Square. The witches occupy the west side of the square, while the Society's magicians stand to the east. The south of the square is where the king, Lord S and the English magicians have moved to, and we are all surrounded by the armed soldiers whose fingers twitch uneasy on their triggers.

'Seconds, withdraw at least ten feet from the circle of fire. Combatants, you may begin,' the Englishwoman says.

I keep hold of my mbira in one hand, the wooden keyboard against my right thigh. My thumb sits on one of the keys. It's not thrumming, it's primed and ready. Cruickshank makes a full circuit around my neck before settling once again. My heart is pounding against my ribcage. I can't control it. Dundas seems to be waiting for me to make the first move, but I hold my position. He can't seem to truly believe he's been ordered to fight against someone of the opposite sex.

'We haven't got all night,' the Englishwoman goads us to get a move on. 'The king's not had his tea yet.'

I sense a radical entropic shift that assails all my senses, from the heat by-product of magic doing work to the harsh chemical smell.

Be careful, Ropa. We're here to get you through this, Gran says inside of my head. *Use your mbira.*

I wanted to beat these magicians using their own magic. To prove a point.

Foolish girl.

It's all those books they fed her.

Alright, alright. Mbira time.

Henry Dundas is gathering his might, weaving a spell. From fifteen paces away I sense the magic take on its contours. This knowledge feels like it's been at the tips of my fingers all this time, but I haven't been able to reach it 'cause I've been chasing cheddar down the hill. I sense the craft Henry Dundas puts into this thermosphere as it's launched towards me. I take half a step to the left and watch as it flies past my torso.

I've yet to reset my stance when Dundas calls down a lightning bolt from the heavens and I hear it crack as it comes down towards me. I press on a key, not to make music or even play a note, but rather to flex it so that this red lightning is halted in the heavens – and it breaks apart, showering shades of red light like a sparkler going off. I wince in pain 'cause some of them have hit me, leaving scorch marks on the back of my hands and wrists.

'Those old women inside your head have taught you a few new tricks,' Dundas says. 'But that won't be enough.'

'*We'll see about that,*' Gran says through my lips.

Use your gifts, You can't beat them like this.

She's a stubborn one.

She'll be joining us soon at this rate. Your mbira, Ropa!

No, I can do this. Dundas steps forward, graceful like a fencer, and I retreat, stepping off his line. He casts a soliton my way and I duck left, but as soon as I stand I'm hit by another hard gust of air on the chest. It throws me up but I land on my feet, barely. He's done a double and I fell for the decoy then got clobbered. Sneaky. I reach for a low bass note and latch onto the wind, retaliating with a wall of air like the Nyamavhuvhu. No more Greek deities for me. The air rushes forward, carrying the swirling snow and forming something hard, but at the last moment, Henry Dundas makes a slicing motion with his hand and steps into the breach.

He turns my spell backwards, almost as though time were rewinding and the air that had rushed past him speeds back towards me. I leap out of the way, but it explodes and the heat singes my hand on the mbira. The pain's incredible and I grit my teeth.

Priya gasps.

'Steady on, hen,' Theodosia shouts. 'He cannae triumph over Melsie Mhondoro's ain.'

I want to respond, but my fingers have been burnt and it hurts to reach for a key.

'There it is,' Dundas says. 'The look of terror and recognition that you've bitten off more than you can chew. I've seen it so many times in my past life, enemies vanquished, rivals put in their place, adversaries bested.'

'Eat my vag, Dundas. You won't beat me again,' I reply.

'The insolence!'

The ghoul's infuriated and there's a monumental entropic shift, almost cosmic, as if the material universe was being rearranged by his sheer will. The sound of it is like what I imagine the roar of a blast furnace must be, the noise of the industrial age of coal and iron. And then a bang as Dundas casts a thunderbolt my way, glowing red. Desperate, I press the keys of my mbira, hoping to halt it as I did the last one, but though it moves slow, Dundas's spell still comes for me. I feel its heat cutting through the cold air.

I counter, conjuring my own electromagnetic response, calling upon mheni, the lightning strikes of my grandmother's village. Static sings in the air, a brilliant flash of white, and I cast my own bolt to meet his. The two highly charged forces meet a few feet from me with an incredible crack but the white lightning frays like rope repulsed by a superior force.

This is going to hurt.

I'm hit by red lightning full-on and thrown backwards. Every nerve in my body's on fire. Everything in my vision is streaks of red and white. Cool snow falls on me yet still I burn.

'Get up, Ropa,' Ranjeeta shouts.

My body's spasming. There's my mbira. All these faces watching. The trees. The snow. The grass beneath me. The scent of my burnt flesh.

I'm dazed.

Okay, this ain't the grassroots league.

Roll over onto my side.

Focus, Ropa, focus.

I reach for my mbira.

Stop.

Why is it so heavy?

Playing.

The ground's spinning.

Spark of Prometheus . . . How does that basic fire spell go

again? If I can just get some sparks to blind him. Pro– Pro–
Prometheus.

Here we go again, she enamoured their magic.

Doesn't trust our gifts, does she?

You really picked a thick one, Melsie.

I shake my head trying to gain clarity.

Listen to our voices.

They're right, I've got to lean hard into my grandmother's
magic. Scientific magic's not my gig anymore.

'Throw in the towel now, Priya,' Ranjeeta says. 'The poor
lassie's done.'

'No more,' Priya cries out, waving her arms. 'Mercy.'

'Do you accept the surrender, Lord Melville?' the Englishwoman asks.

'Fuck that,' I moan.

'It pains me, but we have to set an example tonight,' Henry
Dundas declares, coming at me, his boots squelching through
the slush as he does. I'm reaching for a spell but I can't find
one from all the learning I did in the Library of the Dead. I
get to my knees, but the ghoul tips me over with his foot so I
fall on my back.

He hovers over me, a satisfied smile upon his face.

I look past him into the sky filled with the souls of the dead.
They are watching. The everyThere's closer than it's ever been.
The voykor are circling and I feel their hunger inside my gut.
Henry Dundas holds up his left hand and conjures a brilliant
bright thermosphere the size of the midday sun.

'Good god,' someone in the crowd says.

I press on my mbira, feeling the tether I have with the

guardians of the next realm, and I open the doorway, calling them to me. There's a burst of white light, a tear in the last fragile thread between our worlds, a monstrous squawk up in the sky, and then the voykor descend, large leathery wings beating noisily like dragons. The sound of it is awful. Henry Dundas looks up. The crowd begins to panic.

'Protect the king!' a man shouts.

There's shouting, the sound of the Daimler doors slamming shut. Gunfire. Gargantuan entropic shifts as the English magicians fire spells at the voykor who shoot across the sky like meteors.

'You did this,' Dundas says, frowning, prepared to strike me. But before his arm falls, Cruickshank sweeps his legs out from under him, and as he tumbles, a voykor, jaws wide open, snaps him up, thermosphere and all. The bite goes all the way to his shoulder. The ghoul cries out in agony, but two voykor who've burst through swoop down – one biting his torso, the other his right thigh. Up into the air they carry him. Squawking and squabbling. The voykor are hungry and they rip Henry Dundas apart. A chunk of him, maybe his head, is falling towards the ground, but before it lands, another of the terrifying monsters swoops and gobbles it up.

There's a stampede around me. Witches and magicians fighting in the chaos, soldiers blasting the everyThere with automatic weapons. Pure fucking bedlam. I lie back on the wet grass and watch the voykor fly away back to their own realm.

XXVII

There's a connection between me and the voykor, the creatures of the gloaming, those spaces in between realms. I was wrong when I thought they intended to munch on normal folks down here. Their instinct is to maintain the boundary between the worlds of the living and those of the dead. Letting them in was a Hail Mary, but I'm no longer trying to be a scientific magician – I've embraced who I am, a ghostalker.

Montgomery Wedderburn's distraught at the defeat of his new god. This has been his work for decades. His face is contorted in anguish as he steps through the pandemonium. Lady Rethabile Lebusa's taken off with a good chunk of the cult, and Glasgow's abandoned them too. Ranjeeta's shouting orders, telling the Daughters of Scotia to round up the remaining magicians.

I get up off my arse, still feeling a wee bit shoogly, when I spot Wedderburn coming at me. I ready my mbira. He has murder written all over his face and he begins to incant a spell aimed at me.

There's a blur of darkness and Wedderburn's chest explodes outwards. The darkness forms, taking the shape of Lord Samarasinghe, his clothes bloody as Wedderburn's body falls

360

to the ground. There's malice in his demeanour, but also a sense of psychotic enjoyment oozes out of him.

'I hate loose ends,' he says with a savage smile. 'You're welcome.'

'I didn't thank you.'

'That's what I like about you, Ropa Moyo.'

A blur and he vanishes again. I'm guessing he's not done me any favours. Lord Samarasinghe must not want whatever bargain he struck with Henry Dundas and his cult coming out. There's English magicians in the fray, systematically targeting the remaining Scottish magicians at the scene. They have the perfect excuse to do what they like to the Society and there's nothing anyone can do about it. In fact, the witches are helping them out.

River nudges me and I lay my hand on her bloodied coat. She's come down from the rooftop and seems satisfied with her hunt for the day. I give her a wee rub and am happy she's okay.

'Come on, girl. Let's go get Izwi,' I say, heading for Dundas House where I'm pretty sure they've stashed her. The Viscount Melville will have wanted credit for my sister's services, rather than letting the Sorcerer Royal claim it from a grateful monarch. I reckon that's how he aimed to get close enough *to play the king.*

I leave the square and cross the tram tracks, back into the grounds of the old building. Let the rest of them fight if they fancy. As far as I'm concerned, I'm handing over my invoice, including VAT. That's me done with this madness. There's debris all across the front of the building, and I step over

Hutchinson's cold body. There's snow settling in his bullet hole. It's kind of gory, but he wanted worse for me and mine.

I'm at the threshold of Dundas House, which now seems blurry like I'm looking at a picture taken with a glitchy camera. The building is confusing to look into because it was spliced in two to make room for the Society in the same geography as the Bank.

Do I go through the normal way or try to access the hidden dimension? I'm puzzling this over when Priya comes out of the building with Izwi sat on her lap. My sister! I run across the rubble and give them both a massive hug. My sisters.

I pull back and cup Izwi's cheeks, checking her over. She lights up. Normally I get surly Izwi, but I swear today she's beaming like I've dropped down the chimney wearing a red suit.

'Are you okay? Did they hurt you? I'm so sorry I wasn't there,' I croak, my voice breaking. My sister is back with me at last and it makes my heart flutter. I feel Gran's joy inside of me and that of all the ancestors. We've done it; we've got Izwi back.

'Their hot chocolate was awful but the marshmallows were nice,' she replies, making Priya laugh. 'You smell funny.'

'I know, it's been a long day, but I came out to find you,' I say, tears welling up in my eyes.

'Gran, what are you doing inside of Ropa's head?' Izwi asks. 'Who're those other women? You're weird.'

'*I'm so proud of you, Izwi. You are such a brave girl,*' Gran says through my voice.

'I made the sky crack,' Izwi replies, smiling. 'It was cool

and you could see ghosts floating about. The bad ghost was angry with me. He said I was only supposed to bring one person back from beyond.'

'You—'

I guess the dope skills in handling the afterlife run in the family. Dundas and his cult wanted to use Izwi to channel the king's dead mother, but it doesn't seem to have gone too well. That's what comes of relying on a precocious kid who doesn't like being told what to do. I wish I'd been there to see them bollocks it up. Izwi explains that hanging out with the cult was a lot more interesting than being at school in Aberdeen, except she didn't like it when they wouldn't give her steamed pudding which she's well fond of. She doesn't seem rattled by the experience at all and seems to have forgotten that they kidnapped her from the school.

'Oh hey, River,' Izwi says beaming, happy to see our fox.

'Let's get out of here,' I say.

'You'll be wanting some bulbine and honey for those burns,' Priya says.

'I don't feel a thing,' I lie. They hurt like a bastard, but that's the price you pay for playing with matches.

Priya checks under her seat and brings out her medkit. She pulls out an ointment and tells me to bend down. 'Even your eyebrows are singed,' she says, dabbing cream on my burns.

'You should see the other guy,' I quip and she laughs.

The ointment she's applying feels like jelly on my head and hands. It cools the burns down quite a bit and takes the sting out. Then she applies bandages which I suspect make me look like the Mummy's waddling about again. I guess I am a kind of zombie, aren't I? Would be better if I was a vampire, though. They have all the fun. When I'm all patched up, I stand up and check out the remaining magicians being routed from St Andrew Square.

Me and Izwi, Priya and River make our way out the narrow lane beside Dundas House. We get away from the smoke and the noise, the violence of the New Town.

I think we'll let the grown-ups take it from here.

I give Priya my mbira and let Izwi hop on my back for a wee piggyback ride. We escape onto North Bridge which looks stunning in the thickening snow. River pops up ahead, sniffing at stuff. Priya's chair leaves tracks in the snow and I'm following behind, trying to stop my mind ticking. Yep, I don't have anything to do with the Society anymore. I've got my little sister back, my best friend with me too and that's all I need.

'Am I the only one who's starving?' Priya asks.

'I don't think we'll find any place open at this time of the night,' I say.

'That's where you're wrong. There's an ace dessert place near my end in Morningside that never closes. Not for Christmas, Hogmanay, the riots, Catastrophe, not for nothing. I'll take you guys there and you can tell me how you like it.'

Priya wasn't lying when she said Decadent Delights was a belter. It's right on the corner opposite Colinton Road, along the long chain of stores, and it's near the church Gran's funeral service was held in. She was buried in Morningside Cemetery down the road.

You'll do anything to remind me I'm dead, won't you? Gran complains.

Trust me, you won't like it when they stop remembering you.

I can't blame Henry Dundas for wanting to come back.

Let's have another advent—

'Will you guys shut up for a bit?'

'We haven't said anything,' Priya replies, giving me a weirded-out look.

'I think she's talking to the old women inside her head,' Izwi explains.

There, now these ancestors have embarrassed me. Not that they seem to mind; one of them starts rambling on about respecting one's elders. I'm going to have to learn to tune them out otherwise I'll go crazy . . . if I'm not already.

We're sat in a booth near the window. The place is completely pink and has this retro American feel to it. Pictures of Johnny Cash, John Wayne, Marilyn Monroe, Jim Morrison, and some other celebrities I don't recognize. Probably local guys whose fame didn't spread much further than their own postcode. There's a pink rotary telephone on the wall near the door and a jukebox is there too.

The booth has room for four. Gets me missing Jomo and what we had . . . Nah, fuck him. I'm checking out the buffet Priya's laid out in front of us. She must have maxed out her entire salary in one go. We have gelato, Nutella waffles, churros with a white chocolate dip, New York-style cheesecake ordered by Izwi, cookie dough ice cream – Allahu Akbar – and milk-shakes. Mine's a super-duper fizzbomb with Creme Egg and Ferrero Rocher. Diabetes here I come.

This is far too sweet for my liking.

Who cares what you like; let the girl have a treat in peace.

She should be having mazhanje and tsubvu instead of this rubbish.

Watch me, bitches.

We're digging in and feasting like the world isn't half starving, and I'm not about to feel guilty about it, when Theodosia Lovell's face pops up at the window and Ranjeeta's right there with her. Calista Featherstone too.

'I'm sorry, I had to tell Mum where we were,' Priya says pre-emptively.

I gulp down my atomic fizzbomb, not fancying sharing our bounty. Spoils of war . . . well, not technically.

'You left for ice cream before the job was done, bitiya rani,' Ranjeeta says in mock disappointment, but she can barely mask her pleasure.

Theodosia Lovell plonks herself down bedside me and I'm forced to scoot over. Clearly not far enough because Ms Featherstone joins us and I'm virtually squished into the window now. Three of us in a seat made for two. Ranjeeta joins Priya and Izwi opposite me, and she takes her daughter's spoon and helps herself to some gelato.

'We've reached an understanding with the Sorcerer Royal tonight. The remaining practitioners who were a part of this folly will face justice. That much he's promised,' Ranjeeta says. 'There's some mopping up to do and the English magicians are willing to help. And you may be glad to hear you won't be getting any more bother from the police, Ropa. That's all getting taken care of.'

'Lord Samarasinghe also says the king bears no prejudice against witches. In the English tradition Merlin was a wizard, with similar roots, and they built their tradition around his legacy. They stopped harassing witches there a long time ago,' Calista Featherstone says.

'Glad the Auld Enemy's proving so useful,' I reply.

Theodosia Lovell takes a waffle with her bare hands, Nutella dripping everywhere. She sniffs it and takes a massive bite.

'Oor Frances loved this junk,' Theodosia says, mouth full.

'To Frances,' I reply, raising my milkshake.

'Aye, blood fer blood. 'Tis even now, the debt's been paid in full, but ah miss my bairn still,' she replies.

'*It's not the end. She's out there in the Land of the Tall Grass waiting for you. No one's ever truly lost to us forever. Now all you need to do is remember to keep her warm in your heart and spill a dram for her onto the ground now and again,*' Gran says through my voice.

''Tis good tae see yer again, sister o' mine.' Theodosia sighs wearily, weighed down as she is by grief. 'Oor sacrifice, heavy as it was, hasnae been in vain.'

'Frances asked me to tell you that she loves you very much.' At last I deliver my message to her mother as a ghostalker should.

A solitary tear drops from Theodosia Lovell's eye and Gran lifts my hand and I place it round her shoulder. Then I rest my head on on it. The grief is bittersweet. Used to be I would miss my parents and then Gran would comfort me just like this. It still sucks. But family's never gone forever, it just changes and new people come into our lives. We're like ships sailing through the night all alone, but if you reach out into the darkness, someone who's lost what you have might reach out too and take your hand. I can't replace Frances Cockburn, but who knows, if I pop in from time to time, maybe Theodosia Lovell might like that. And I could use another cool old lady in my life, not just the ones knocking about in my brain.

XXVIII

I wake up in a big pine bed that's all warm and cosy, me near the window looking out to a wee park where the snow's settled and there's already a couple of kids playing in the snow. Izwi's in the middle, snoring her wee snout off, and Priya's got an arm on the pillow beneath her neck. Priya's one-bed flat's snug, a wardrobe and chest of drawers near the door. No other furniture, I guess to leave room for her wheelchair. Last night Priya told me she likes to leave the curtains open so the light wakes her up.

I watch the two girls building a snowman, their mother hovering nearby. The sky's grey – that's Edinburgh whatever the time of year – but there's no dead people prancing about in it either. For the first time in ages I feel mondo-zen. I'm not on the edge anymore.

Could stay in bed all day if I wanted to.

A raven taps on the window.

'Nevermore, pal,' I say, then I shush myself. Don't need to wake these two up.

The raven taps the window again and cocks its head like it's pointing to the city centre.

'*Mile, mile, mile,*' it croaks.

'Fucksake,' I reply.

'*Mile*,' the raven insists, and then it takes off.

'The Sorcerer Royal's summoning you to the Royal Mile,' Priya says all drowsy.

'You talk to birds now?' I have to check.

'Get up.'

Knapf. I don't feel like it. My belly's full and this bed is so warm. I want a long lie-in. Reckon I deserve it after everything that's gone on.

Who do I contact about my early retirement? I've served my time.

These young ones think they've seen it all, don't they?

'Shut it.'

In our day . . .

I take the pillow from under my head and cover my face. Annoying.

Priya's already shifting about, getting up and into her wheel-chair. Last night she said I could stay for as long as I needed to. This is kind of what I always wanted, a wee home for me and mine. It'll happen one day, but for now I know there's a big bed waiting here if I need it.

I gently move the duvet, making sure Izwi stays covered, and swing my legs off the bed. The laminate floor's a bit cold under my feet. I yawn and have a good stretch and my back cracks. Oof, that's nice. The white covers are sooty from us lying in them. It must be all the smoke from the New Town . . . That and the grime of the last couple of days. Adventuring's not great for personal hygiene.

I squint, checking out a canvas on the wall at the foot of

the bed. It's the only one hanging in this bedroom. It's all yellowy like a desert with a little stream running in one corner and some brown. Rather weird that. It's not quite finished, I think.

'*Canal, Hill, Rail,*' Priya says, noticing my interest. 'It's by Carol Rhodes. Obviously not the original, but a print.'

'Hmm,' is all I can say about that. Definitely not the desert then.

I stand up and scratch my butt, stretching my legs by standing on my tippy-toes. When you get used to being busy and on the go, twiddling your thumbs feels like a job all on its own. I walk round the bed and go to the bathroom to take a wazz. Might as well have a shower now I'm up. It's a massive wet room in here with a drain in the corner. There's railings all around the walls and the handbasin's lower than usual, which I notice when I wash my hands. Then I take off my T-shirt and strip off my knickers and chuck them on the floor. Open the tap and – miracle – the water's actually warm. This is gonna be a mission, though. I nip out to the kitchen, grab two plastic bags and tie them round my hands before I get back.

Time for a long overdue shower. It's a pity I have to keep my bandaged head out of it, but I allow the water to run down my back . . . and this is the life.

Priya barges in and shifts herself onto the bog.

'Sorry, couldn't hold it,' she says.

'Way to kill my vibe,' I reply with a laugh.

When she's done, she joins me in the shower, making use of the purpose-built chair there. Priya helps me scrub my back and I'm embarrassed by all the grime that works its way down the drain. Yep, it's that bad. When I'm all done, I wash Priya's hair for her and massage her scalp, the plastic bags on my hands rustling away. That's what friends are for: you scratch my back, I do your scalp. Even von Clausewitz would agree that's how it's done. She inspects the hand-shaped mark Dundas left on my chest.

'It's healing rather nicely and will make for an impressive scar,' she observes.

It doesn't burn so much anymore. I guess this is my body now . . . or again. My father stole it, which is proper messed up, but I have to love it as much as my friends do. We carry in our bodies the wrongs done by those that came before us and all we can do is try to make the world a bit better. I will honour the girl whose life I was given with every breath I have left.

Doesn't take us very long to get ready. I have to borrow more of Priya's clothes and it's a good thing she's got decent taste. I go all black, T-shirt, jeans and socks, and have to borrow her lippie 'cause I left my backpack on St Andrew Square. Knowing this city, the odds are zero I'll ever be seeing it again. Ah well, we lose some, don't we. Priya's also lent me a penguin-themed beanie with a massive pom-pom. Not my style but it'll keep my noggin warm. I drape Cruickshank round my neck and give him a playful tug. His fringe floats up and he pokes my nose, making me laugh. Me and my ninja scarf have been through the trenches together and I love him to bits.

Takes a bit longer for Izwi to get ready and it's late morning by the time we leave. I wave at the fuzz on horseback patrol. They glare at me, but nothing exciting happens. Well, so far, so good. We have to pause in the Meadows cause Izwi wants to make a snow angel. Kids. I go down beside her and do one as well. River's not bothered by all this and she maintains a dignified air hanging out with Priya.

'God save the king,' an elderly man says, walking his beagle across the park.

'Actually, we saved him,' I reply, sitting up.

The man's sufficiently alarmed by my response to briskly walk away. I guess he doesn't believe me. Priya gives me a hand up and then we have to pretty much coax Izwi to get a move on. I'd rather be in the cosy flat if it could be helped. Hot chocolate. Nah, my stomach won't stand for more after the treats we binged on last night.

It's a beautiful winter's morning. The clouds and the heavy atmosphere of the everyThere has lifted and with it the scent of death and decay. A crisp blue sky is overhead. We make our way from the Meadows and through Bristo Square, all the university buildings around us. A couple of wary youths are hanging around, where usually there'd be more people about.

'I heard the king's in town and he's taking petitions,' one of them says.

'What would you ask him for?' his friend with the mullet replies.

'A job after I graduate.'

'Now what would the king do with your Scandinavian Studies qualification?'

The students burst out laughing and I'm not getting why it's so funny. But it's got me wondering what I would ask the king for if he offered. It's like that genie in a bottle problem, isn't it? You have to be careful what you ask for. It can't be too big or too small. Definitely wouldn't ask His Maj for a job, no way. Maybe a knighthood. They'd call me Sir Ropa Moyo, which would be cool. Dame's too damsel, which is distressing.

There's a few more folks about when we make our way down Nicolson Street. It might be just me, but the city feels lighter. Some shops are open despite bare shelves. That hasn't changed. The snow sanitizes the city and masks all its flaws. It's almost like how the old masters used to paint over their earlier works so you might find multiple paintings under a known work if you used an X-ray. Edinburgh gets written over again and again with each new generation. Yeah, an old ghoul pokes out every so often . . . a lot, to be fair, but the city keeps changing regardless.

This is where we meet my father's ghost, barely a wisp now. Only a vague outline of his head remains, hovering five feet off the ground, and he's lost any semblance of once having had a body. He approaches cautiously, an air of desperation about him. Izwi sees him and scowls, but Priya's oblivious, only stopping when we do.

'There's something wrong with this ghost,' Izwi says.

'I need your help, my children,' he gasps, reaching out, but I hold out my hand to stop him coming near us. 'Everything's unravelled and I am stuck here.'

'I don't know this strange man,' Izwi says angrily. She's too young to remember him. Makomborero Moyo's crestfallen at her words. He flickers, like a candle about to die.

'What would you have me do after everything that's happened because of you?' I ask.

'Send me to the astral plane where I might recover. There's nothing left for me in this world when even my own daughters have forsaken me.' His visage contorts in anger. 'I gave you life and this is how you repay me!'

'No, you didn't. You murdered a little girl's soul and stole her body. For that and much worse, I condemn you to wander the streets of the Old Town, powerless, for eternity. What you yearned for will be so close, but forever out of reach, just like Tantalus from the Greek myths. You will get no mercy, no rest for all eternity.'

That is my judgement upon him.

You condemn him to wander amongst those who are not in the light.

It is the worst fate of all.

This child has become hardened and I feel sorry for any who may cross her now.

'How could you pick those old women in your head over your own father?' He seems crestfallen. 'I beg you – even now at this late stage, we can still rescue this situation. We can be a family again. Don't leave me like this, please.'

We abandon him to the city.

At the crossroads of the Royal Mile wreaths have been laid on the spot where the king's parents were murdered. There's piles of winter-flowering heather and a fair few roses. Daffodils and some thistles. I am a wee bit surprised at the shamrocks placed there, though. The Irish haven't sent us flowers since they reunified, but hey-ho, it's none of my business.

There's folks milling about the Royal Mile and a fair few

armed soldiers too. Flags hanging all the way down the road into the Canongate. Seems like there'll be some kind of procession and the good people of Edinburgh are expected to cheer their king. We make our way down the road.

Izwi slips, but I catch her in time, anchoring myself with my handy walking stick. Patch of black ice. It hits you when you least expect it. They've cleared the rubble from the collapsed buildings on the right side of the road. Just enough has been moved for one lane of vehicles to pass through. With the snow, the scale of the destruction's been hidden from the king's view.

'I have a feeling we're due a huge reward,' I say as we near the Parliament.

'For services to king and country,' Priya replies.

Opposite Parliament, right at the bottom of the Mile, the black gates of Holyroodhouse swing open and troops on horseback trot out, but instead of ceremonial gear, they wear camouflage and keep their automatic weapons ready. It's like you'd imagine if Genghis Khan's hordes were given machine guns. The horsemen are followed by the king's Daimler, and behind that is Lord Samarasinghe's carriage driven by Briggs.

We gawk at the procession going past, but it stops when the Sorcerer Royal's carriage reaches us. The curtain draws open and I see Lord Samarasinghe in there and, opposite him, on the seat I once sat on, the king. Samarasinghe lowers the window and I'm frozen, a wee bit unsure what to say to His Maj. There's something intense about his blue eyes. You get the sense he is looking right at your soul.

'Don't embarrass me, Ropa Moyo. Curtsey,' Lord Samarasinghe prompts.

I dip my knees like Bambi. It's not quite the curtsey you get in period dramas and I reckon I succeed in looking awkward. I wait for the king to say something, but he turns away, already bored perhaps.

'You've played a very dangerous game, young lady, and you've come out on top,' says Lord Samarasinghe. 'Well, you've also attracted His Majesty's attention. Say your goodbyes to your sister and your friends. You're going to England. You work for the king now.'

'Nah, I didn't sign up for that,' I say, my voice quivering. It's not fair.

'We are chosen to serve. With your help we have at last broken Scottish magic and settled old scores. The Society of Sceptical Enquirers will not recover for a generation. Thank you for your service,' Lord Samarasinghe says. 'In the meantime, we are going to do what Britain does best.'

'Which is?' Priya asks.

'Conquering the world, what else? Starting with taking Ireland back. We need our best and brightest to rebuild our empire. You're in His Majesty's service now, Ropa Moyo. And you too, Priyanka Kapoor.'

'What the fuck?'

'Someone will pick you up and take you to London when it's time. For now I advise you to say your goodbyes.'

The king, still looking away, raises his left hand, index finger pointed up.

'Apologies, sir, I nearly forgot. You will be expected to find His Majesty's mother's soul in the realms beyond. You've proven yourself an excellent necromancer.'

The Sorcerer Royal taps on the roof of the cab with his cane and shuts the window.

Priya's holding out her arms, jaw on the floor. I bang on Lord Samarasinghe's window and he opens up, looking furious.

'How dare you,' he protests.

'I owe you nothing, Sashvindu, and I will not be compelled against my will anymore,' I say, my voice even. 'Your Majesty, heed my advice. Let the dead rest – this world is better off without them.'

The king looks at me for a good while and leans forward. His expression is blank but I know that he is thinking. It can't be often that someone defies him like this. He blinks a couple of times and the tense muscles of his shoulders relax.

'So much wisdom in one so young,' he says. 'You shall be left in peace for what you have endured. Let no man say we are unjust to those who have served us where our own Sorcerer Royal's schemes might have brought ruin. Lord Samarasinghe seems to believe breaking the Society of Sceptical Enquirers was to our advantage and there may be truth in that. But it seems in our eyes that for what we gain, Scotland's witches get double. And we are left wondering how pliant those women will be in the future.'

Lord Samarasinghe's eyes widen in alarm. The law of un-intended consequences has a way of poking its nose into everyone's business.

'Your Majesty—' he says.

'Centuries of order unravelled last night. King James I expended a lot on keeping the Scottish witches down and formalizing magic in these parts. Sashvindu, your excesses were done in our name. We should replace you; alas, the only practitioner we know of who exceeds your talents has declined the honour of joining our service. We shall think of a suitable punishment for you later. Now let us proceed; we shan't endure Scotland any more than we must.'

The king has set me free from this foolishness, but I can't help but flip the bird to Lord Samarasinghe as the coach lurches off up the Royal Mile.

'You're going to give me a heart attack, Ropa. I thought he was going to chop off our heads,' Priya says, sighing with relief.

I'm still giddy from the wee win when in the distance, coming out of the palace gates, I spot Dr Maige in his old scarlet robes. He looks like a lost clergyman, his hands clasped in front of him. The librarian's less sure in his walk than I've ever seen him. He takes a look at the rubble on the right, the broken, jagged remains of Calton Hill where his library is buried under rocks. I imagine the Sorcerer Royal's got plans for him too. English magic will be wanting access to those books and texts next.

Dr Maige crosses the road and approaches us timidly.

'Tell Jomo my friendship with him is over,' I say, tapping my cane on the pavement for emphasis. 'But you should be more kind to him, he'll always be your son.'

Dr Maige cracks his knuckles and shakes his head. Even now he can't bring himself to show a bit of love. It's not my problem anymore. Then he nods his head slowly.

'I've only ever tried to do what's best . . . Thank you for sparing him,' he murmurs. 'I can't make sense of this life anymore. Can you imagine if suddenly one day you woke up and were told the sum of angles inside a triangle in Euclidean space was no longer one hundred and eighty degrees? It could be more or less, but not the solid truth you built your life on.'

'It happens to me as many as six times before breakfast.' I turn around and put my arm on Izwi's shoulder and nudge Priya. 'Come on, let's go.' River's prancing away already.

'No, wait. Please,' says Dr Maige behind us. 'You won the duel against Lord Melville. Will you be taking up the secretary-ship of the Society of Sceptical Enquirers?'

'I'm not a member, remember?'

'I know, but the rules can be changed to accommodate present realities. The king allowed you to duel and his word is the law. The Society needs someone fresh who sees things a bit differently. It needs to . . . evolve,' he says, gasping after-wards as though in shock at what he has just said. The strain on his face is evident. Being flexible is likely to snap him in two.

Priya's got a mad grin on her face, I can tell she'd love for us to get another one over on the Society. If I became secretary that would ruffle a few feathers – imagine the looks on those posh toffs' faces. Dr Maige raises his eyebrows, expectant.

The women in my head pay close attention as I look back over my shoulder and give him my answer.

'I ain't no magician, man – I'm a motherfucking witch.'

Acknowledgments

There and back again, my friends. Ropa Moyo's been through the wringer in our pentalogy and it is now time for her to take a well-earned rest—hopefully on your shelves. It's been so much fun and a wee bit brutal, to be honest. Thank you for sticking with her story up to its conclusion.

Though my name alone appears on the cover, the Edinburgh Nights series bears the thumbprints of many awesome folks who believed in the story, and it was an immense privilege to work with them all. Jamie Cowen, superstar agent, you rooted for Ropa since day one and have been a great champion. You totally rock!

Bella Pagan, my first editor, quirk master extraordinaire and now publisher at Tor UK. I cannot thank you enough for your passion and work on this series. It's been one hell of a rollercoaster. Claire Baldwin and Michael Beale, poking holes, nitpicking diamond polishers, bloody hell. You both are exceptional editors. The whole army at Team Tor UK, copyeditors, proofreaders, sales, marketing, publicity, cover design, you all deserve OBEs for the work you did polishing the manuscripts and making sure the finished books got in front of as many readers as possible. Will Hinton and the team at Tor US, thank you for everything.

Behind the scenes, my dear friends and peers Mohammed Naseehu Ali, Chikodili Emelumadu, Iain Maloney, Jeanne-Marie Jackson, Lena Mattheis, Jane Morris and Brian Jones, words cannot express my gratitude for your support over the years. Lisa Williams and Ruth Boreham, you took me down the rabbit hole and your knowledge of Edinburgh's lesser celebrated histories proved so useful in my work.

The booksellers, librarians, book bloggers/Booktokers/Bookstagrammers and reviewers who shouted out about this weird wee series, you are all so fantastic. And you, dear readers, who stayed with our plucky heroine all the way through her adventures. I have enjoyed meeting so many of you online and in real life. Thank you all so much. You warm an author's heart!

Edinburgh, the city dearest to my heart, cheers for the many wonderful stories you threw my way. One lifetime will not be long enough to unearth all your mysteries.

About the Author

T. L. HUCHU is a writer whose short fiction has appeared in publications such as *Lightspeed, Interzone, Analog Science Fiction and Fact*, and elsewhere. *The Library of the Dead* won Best Novel at the Nommo Awards, presented by the African Speculative Fiction Society. Huchu's work has also been short-listed for the Caine Prize and the Grand Prix de l'Imaginaire. Between projects, he translates fiction from Shona into English and the reverse. He is the author of the Edinburgh Nights series.

Twitter: @TendaiHuchu
Instagram: @tendaihuchu